LETHAL MIX

The 12th Bernie Fazakerley Mystery

by

JUDY FORD

Bernie Fazakerley Publications

LETHAL MIXTURE

Published by Bernie Fazakerley Publications

Copyright © 2019 Judy Ford.

ISBN13: 978-1-911083-57-3
ISBN10: 1-91-108357-0

DEDICATION

Dedicated to

The Wirral Deen Centre,
Mosque and Community Centre

"Serving the Community"

CONTENTS

GLOSSARY OF ARABIC WORDS AND PHRASES

Allahu Akbar – God is the greatest.

Alayhi al-Salaam – Peace be upon him. This phrase, or its abbreviation "a.s.", is often used by Muslims after the names of prophets as a sign of respect. The English abbreviation, pbuh, is also sometimes used.

Bismillah ar-Rahman ar-Rahim – In the name of God, the lord of mercy, the giver of mercy. A phrase used to inaugurate many tasks, especially prayer. It appears at the start of all but one of the chapters of the Qur'an.

Dua – supplication to God.

Hadith – a record of the acts and sayings of the prophet Muhammad. The literal meaning is "news?" or "story". The hadiths are used within the Muslim community as a source of guidance and provide the basis for much Islamic law.

Halal – lawful, permitted. This word is frequently used in the context of permissible food and drink.

Haram – forbidden, in contrast with *halal* (permitted).

Hijab – barrier or partition. In Islam, it is used to describe the principle of modesty. Hence, it has come to be used for the head covering worn by many Muslim women.

Hidayah – God-given guidance.

Insha'Allah – God willing

Jummah – Literally "congregation", *Jummah* is also used to denote Friday, the day of congregation.

Khutbah – sermon.

Maghrib – The *salah al-maghrib* is the sunset prayer, one of five daily prayers that are obligatory for practising Muslims.

Salla Allahu alayhi wa sallam – Peace be upon him.

Muslims often say this phrase (often abbreviated "saw" or "pbuh") after saying the name of a prophet of Islam.

Salah al-Jummah – Friday prayers, said by Muslims in congregation (the literal meaning of *Jummah*) in a mosque or other gathering place.

Shahada – the solemn declaration of faith in God. Converts to Islam make this declaration in front of witnesses in order to be received into the faith.

Subhana Rabbiyal Adhim – Glory be to my Lord, the exalted.

Subhanahu Wa Ta'ala – Glory to Him, the Exalted. This phrase is often used when speaking of God (Allah). It may be abbreviated as "Allah (SWT)".

Sunnah – "tradition" or "way". This word is used to describe the words and actions of the prophet Mohammed, which forms a model for the behaviour of his followers.

Taqwa – the state of being fully conscious of God. Sometimes rendered in English as "God-fearing" or 'righteousness".

Umma – the worldwide community of Muslims (literally "nation")

Wudu – ritual washing performed by Muslims before prayer

Yawm al-Jummah – Friday (literally "day of congregation")

Zakah – Charity. The obligation to give alms is one of the five pillars of Islam (the foundation of Muslim life).

MAP OF LIVERPOOL "KNOWLEDGE QUARTER"

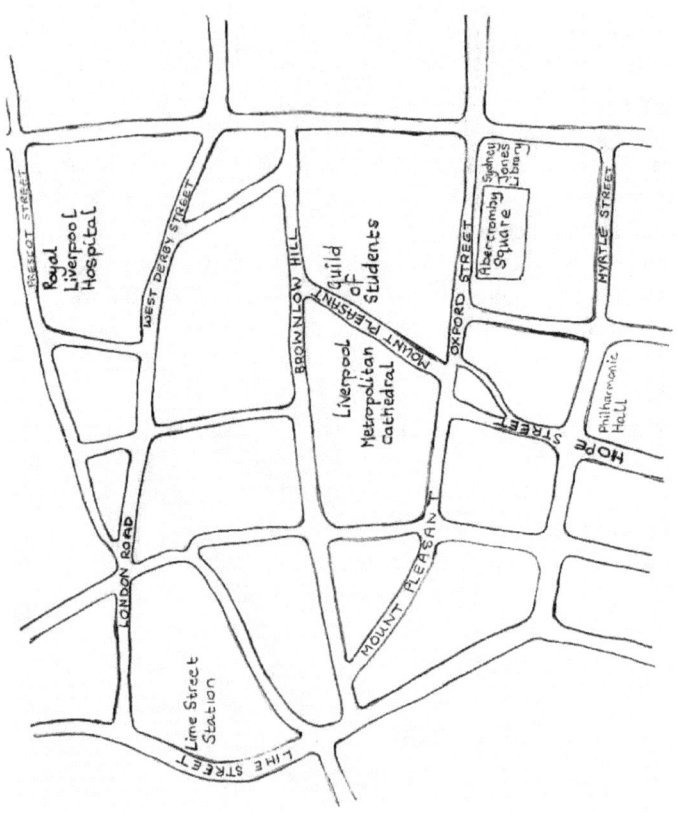

وَلَا تَسْتَوِي الْحَسَنَةُ وَلَا السَّيِّئَةُ ادْفَعْ بِالَّتِي هِيَ أَحْسَنُ فَإِذَا الَّذِي بَيْنَكَ وَبَيْنَهُ عَدَاوَةٌ كَأَنَّهُ وَلِيٌّ حَمِيمٌ

Good and evil cannot be equal. Repel evil with what is better and your enemy will become as close as an old and valued friend.

Qur'an 41:34

Translated by M.A.S. Abdel Haleem, 2004

1. EMERGENCY

Dominic looked up from the pile of exercise books on his lap and stared at the mobile phone lying on the coffee table. That was the third time in five minutes that it had started ringing; each time continuing until the voicemail message had cut in and the caller had rung off. Whoever it was must want to speak to Ibrahim very urgently. What should he do? His housemate was in his room, occupied with his Maghrib prayers. Dominic knew that they could not be interrupted, but what if the call were a matter of life and death?

He slid the books on to the sofa and leaned forward to look more closely at the phone. The display showed that the caller was Mariam, Ibrahim's younger sister, a student in her first year of a medical degree and another of the residents of their shared house. Dominic's heart started beating faster. Was she in some sort of trouble? He picked up the phone and swiped the screen to answer the call.

'Hello, Mariam?' he began. 'Ibrahim can't come to the phone right now, can I-'

He broke off as a woman's voice interrupted him, ignoring his words and speaking in a breathless, high-pitched voice – anxious, frightened almost. 'Hello? Ibrahim? It's Olivia – Olivia Akram – one of Mariam's friends – we met last term – I don't know if you remember – it was-'

'Hang on!' Dominic cut across her, keen to correct her mistake and even more keen to know what had happened to Mariam to explain her phone being in the hands of this other girl. 'It's not Ibrahim. I'm Dominic – his housemate. Ibrahim's busy praying. What's up? Is Mariam OK? Can you tell me, and I'll pass on the message?'

'I – I …,' Olivia hesitated as if unsure whether to trust

1

this young man, whom she only vaguely remembered from a visit to Mariam's house some two months previously.

'Or shall I get him to ring you back when he's finished?' Dominic asked, fighting down his instinct to demand to be told everything – and at once!

'I – I,' Olivia continued to stammer. Dominic heard her swallow hard before resuming in a slightly stronger voice. 'No. Mariam would want you to know. Please …'

Dominic, resisting the temptation to urge her to get on with it, listened as patiently as he could. After a few seconds that felt like years, she went on.

'I don't know if you remember me? I think we met last term when I came round for coffee with Mariam.'

'Yes. I expect so,' Dominic confirmed impatiently. 'But you were telling me about Mariam.'

'I'm sorry.' Olivia hesitated again. 'I – I … Please tell Ibrahim he needs to get down to the hospital right away. There's been-'

'Why? What's happened?' Dominic demanded, unable to maintain his fragile calm any longer. 'Is Mariam OK?'

'A man on a motorbike sprayed us with something,' Olivia explained, sounding a little more composed now that she had started relating her story. 'It mostly went on-'

'Acid, you mean?' Dominic interrupted again. 'Is she badly hurt?'

'Yes, I suppose that was what it must have been. Like I was saying, it mostly went on Salma, but some on Mariam and a bit on Emily. I called 999 and someone came and poured water on them to try to wash it off, and then the ambulance came and they used more water, and then they took them away to A and E. That's where I am now. Mariam gave me her phone and told me to ring Ibrahim.'

'Thanks,' Dominic muttered, his mind racing as he imagined Mariam's smooth brown skin being eaten away by some caustic substance. He had seen news pictures of acid attack victims and images of hideous disfigurement rose up involuntarily in his mind. 'I'll get Ibrahim and we'll be down there right away.'

'Good,' he heard Olivia say, almost inaudibly. 'See you soon then.'

'Yes. Right. See you.'

Dominic put down the phone and raced upstairs to Ibrahim's room. He could hear the rhythmic chanting of the Arabic prayers through the ill-fitting door, but he no longer cared about interrupting them. Taking hold of the handle, he flung the door wide open and strode in.

His friend was standing with his back to him. His bare feet were on the edge of a red and gold prayer mat and his short black hair was covered by a white skullcap made from intricate crochet work, something that Dominic had initially – when they all moved in together – found incongruous alongside Ibrahim's habitual jeans-and-tee-shirt dress code. At the sound of Dominic's entrance, his voice stumbled momentarily. Then, chanting quietly, 'Allahu Akbar,' he bent forward with his hands on his knees. 'Subhana Rabbiyal Adhim. Subha-'

'I'm sorry,' Dominic said more loudly than he intended. 'I know your prayers are important but this can't wait.'

Ibrahim's voice faltered again, but he continued to stare down at the floor in front of his feet. He drew breath to resume his prayer, but Dominic got in first.

'It's Mariam,' he continued, stepping forward and putting his hand on Ibrahim's shoulder. 'There's been an acid attack. She's in A and E. We've got to-'

Instantly Ibrahim spun round under his hand, his mouth open in shock and dismay.

'What happened? How is she? Why?'

'I don't know. I've told you everything. One of her friends rang your phone just now. That's all she said – except that you needed to get over there right away.'

Ibrahim sat down on his bed and started pulling on his socks.

'Do our parents know? Has anyone rung them?'

'I don't know. I don't think so. She just said that Mariam

gave her her phone and told her to ring you.'

'Mariam *gave* her her phone?' Ibrahim repeated. 'So she must have been conscious. I suppose that's something … but acid! Did she say anything about how bad it was?'

'She …,' Dominic struggled to remember Olivia's words. 'She said that most of it went on another girl – Salma, I think she said.'

'Salma Rahman, I expect,' Ibrahim nodded, reaching for his shoes. 'She's another one of their little group. Who was it rang?'

'She said her name was Olivia. She said she'd been here last term – to the house, I mean – she said she remembered me and she'd met you.'

'Olivia Akram? Yes, I remember her.' Ibrahim finished tying his shoelaces and stood up. 'Right, I'd better go.'

'I'm coming too,' Dominic insisted firmly, leading the way downstairs. 'I want to know how Mariam is, and … and,' he racked his brains to think of some other reason to justify accompanying his friend to the hospital, 'and you may have a long wait. It'll be better if there are two of us.'

Making no attempt to argue, Ibrahim opened the front door and stepped outside. In his haste, he slipped on the steep steps and almost fell, managing to right himself just in time to avoid an undignified slide to the flagstones below. He finished the descent and turned to the right, walking rapidly down the road in the direction of the bus stop. Dominic pulled the door closed behind them and hurried after him.

***

As the bus crawled along through traffic, which seemed far heavier than normal for a Wednesday evening, Dominic remembered his first meeting with Mariam and her brother. It was January, a bright but cold day with a biting wind. He was waiting outside the Medical School for Lucy to emerge from her first day of interviews for a place to study there. His mother had insisted that their young cousin should stay with them overnight, rather than accepting the university accommodation that she had been offered, and Dominic had volunteered to meet her and take her out to dinner before escorting her to their home in the Toxteth area of the city.

As he looked down at his watch and stamped his feet to keep warm, he noticed another young man, also waiting. Judging by his brown skin, shiny black hair and dark brown eyes, his family must have originated on the Indian subcontinent. He was clean-shaven, which was becoming increasingly unusual in young Asian men these days. He was wearing jeans beneath a fur-lined parka jacket. He stood with his hands in his pockets watching the doors, clearly waiting for someone to come out.

There was a flurry of activity as a group of teenagers emerged from the building. For a few seconds, they stood huddled together looking round and murmuring to one another. Then one took the lead and they moved off together giving Dominic a clear view of the doors once more, just in time to see Lucy coming out followed closely by a young woman of South Asian appearance. Dominic was immediately struck by her glossy black hair and smooth brown skin – a complete contrast to Lucy's golden curls and pale blue eyes. Both women had rucksacks on their backs and plastic wallets bearing the University of Liverpool crest in their hands.

'Hi Dom!' Lucy greeted her cousin, smiling as she caught his eye.

'Hi Lucy,' Dominic responded, stepping forward with his arms wide, anticipating an embrace. However, in this he was disappointed, because Lucy immediately turned to speak to the stranger who had been waiting with him.

'Ibrahim!' she called out warmly. 'It's good to see you. Let me introduce my second cousin, Dominic Fazakerley.' She turned back to face Dominic. 'Dom – this is Ibrahim Ali. We met him in Portugal. I think I told you about how he and his friends helped us after Jonah's wheelchair got smashed up on the plane[1]. And this is Mariam,' she added, waving a hand towards the young woman who was now standing beside her. 'She's Ibrahim's sister. She's applying to do Medicine too.'

'Hello,' Dominic responded, shaking the hands, which Ibrahim and Mariam held out towards him and trying to hide his disappointment at not having Lucy to himself. 'It's very nice to meet you.'

'I'm staying the night at Dom's,' Lucy told Ibrahim. 'I mean with his Mum and Dad,' she added quickly, seeing a look of surprise beginning on Ibrahim's face. 'Dom and his brother still live at home.' Then, for the sake of her cousin's self-esteem, she added, 'Setting up on your own is so expensive and Dom's a teacher, so he isn't earning big bucks.'

'Tell me about it!' Ibrahim agreed with feeling. 'The lease is ending on my flat in a few weeks and the landlord says he's planning to sell up. I can't find anywhere decent that doesn't cost an arm and a leg.'

'And my parents are expecting him to find somewhere with two bedrooms so that I can share with him,' Mariam put in, speaking for the first time. Dominic noted that her voice was soft, but firm and that, like her brother, she had a strong East Lancashire accent.

'Dom's mum is hoping I'll live with them if I get into Liverpool,' Lucy chimed in, 'but they don't really have room, so I'm trying to think of excuses not to.'

'She has agreed to let me take you out to dinner, instead of cooking,' Dom interjected, trying to steer the conversation round to a point where he and Lucy could go off on their own.

'Why don't we all go for a meal together?' Lucy suggested, smiling round at them all. 'I'd like to catch up on Ibrahim's news, and Mariam and I had a few things we'd like to put our heads together on before the interviews

---

[1] See *Death on the Algarve* © 2016 ISBN 978-1-911083-16-0

tomorrow morning.'

'OK.' Dominic tried to sound enthusiastic, realising that there was no point attempting to oppose Lucy's plan. She was a very determined young woman and used to getting her own way. 'Where shall we go?'

'There's a vegetarian restaurant that's quite good, not far from here,' Ibrahim suggested.

'Sounds good to me – if the girls are happy with that?' Dominic looked round at Lucy and Mariam, mentally noting that Ibrahim's choice of eatery would avoid any difficult questions about the presence of pork or whether the slaughter methods employed for any meat content in the meal were strictly halal. His training as a Religious Studies teacher made him conscious of the problems associated with sharing meals between people from different faiths. He wondered whether Ibrahim knew that he was adopting the same approach as the prophet Daniel when in exile in Babylon.

'Fine by me,' Lucy nodded.

'Lead me to it,' Mariam agreed. 'I'm starving!'

***

'How exactly are you two related?' Ibrahim asked, looking across the table at Dominic and Lucy a short while later. 'I know you're second cousins, but what does that actually mean?'

'My mam and Dom's dad are cousins,' Lucy answered promptly.

'My grandfather – my dad's dad – and Lucy's grandfather – her mum's dad – were brothers,' Dominic expanded.

'The way you work it out,' Lucy went on, 'is, you go up the family tree until you get to a common ancestor – in this case our great grandparents – and you count the generations and then subtract one.'

'I see.' Ibrahim said thoughtfully. 'But what if it's further up to the common ancestor on one side than the other? My mum's sister has a baby grandson, for example. What relation is he to me and Mariam?'

'That's where *removals* come in,' Lucy explained, clearly enjoying the opportunity of showing off her knowledge. 'You and the baby are first cousins once removed – like Dom and my mam or me and Dom's dad.'

'You two are lucky your family isn't Pakistani,' Mariam observed in the silence that followed, while Ibrahim counted generations in his head. 'If you were, you'd be prime targets for an arranged marriage!'

'Is that what's going to happen to you?' Dominic asked, so shocked by the deadpan voice in which Mariam delivered this bombshell that he spoke without thinking. 'I mean … how do you feel about that?'

'It's not for me to have an opinion is it?' Mariam replied, still speaking in a serious voice and keeping her eyes lowered. 'We Muslim women are all brought up to be submissive, aren't we?'

'But that's awf- … I mean …,' Dominic struggled to think of a way of expressing his consternation without the risk of causing offence or appearing to criticise Mariam's family. 'Presumably you have some sort of say in it? After all, you're training to be a doctor. It's not like-'

'Don't worry,' Ibrahim broke in, seeing the look of alarm on Dominic's face. 'She's pulling your leg. Nobody would ever attempt to dictate to any of the women in our family!'

'Oh Dom! You should've seen your face!' Lucy joined in, laughing out loud.

Mariam looked up at last and smiled across the table at Dominic. Their eyes met and he smiled back.

'I'm sorry,' he mumbled, going red. 'It's being a teacher that does it. Forced marriages is one of the things we're trained to be on the lookout for.'

'Alongside Muslim terrorists, I suppose,' Mariam replied coldly, her smile vanishing. '*Prevent*[2], and all that?'

---

[2] The Prevent programme is part of the UK government's counter terrorism strategy. It places a statutory responsibility on

'Well, yes,' Dominic admitted. 'We've all been briefed on ways of spotting if any of our students may be becoming radicalised.'

'And have you had any that were?' Lucy asked, also sounding somewhat hostile. 'I read that there were lots of quite young kids being reported for completely spurious reasons.'

'We've only had one,' her cousin answered, sounding more confident now. 'We found him pinning up National Action posters on notice boards all round the school.'

'National Action?' Lucy sounded puzzled. 'What's that?'

'It's a neo-Nazi group,' Dominic explained, feeling that he was on safer ground at last. 'It was an off-shoot of the National Front. It's been illegal since 2016, after they publicly supported the guy who murdered Jo Cox[3]. Before that, one of the things they tried to do was to organise a march in Liverpool, but there was so much opposition from local people who didn't want it that they had to give up. They ended up hiding in the left luggage depot at Lime Street.'

'Liverpool has always been very tolerant of minorities,' Ibrahim commented in an attempt to support Dominic whom he felt was coming under unfair criticism from the women of their group. 'I haven't had any trouble since I moved here.'

'Would you expect trouble?' Lucy asked, looking at him wide-eyed. 'What sort of trouble?'

'Nothing much,' Ibrahim shrugged. 'Just the usual: telling me to go back where I came from; calling me a Paki; that sort of thing.'

'That's racial harassment! Lucy declared. 'Did you report it to the police?'

---

schools and other public services to act to prevent individuals becoming radicalised.

[3] Jo Cox MP was a Labour MP. She was murdered in June 2016 by Thomas Mair, a far-right activist.

'No.' Ibrahim shrugged again. 'What's the point? They couldn't do anything and it'd only mark me out as a troublemaker. Besides, it used to happen too often; you get used to it.'

'You shouldn't have to get used to it,' Lucy insisted dogmatically. 'And the police will never be able to do anything to stop it if you don't report these things when they happen.'

'Honestly, Lucy,' Mariam intervened. 'It isn't worth it. There are some battles it's just not worth fighting. I'm not going to let a few morons with limited vocabulary upset me by calling me names.' She paused, and then continued in a lower voice, smiling round at the others enigmatically. 'I'd rather keep my powder dry for more important things.'

***

Ibrahim stood up and rang the bell to stop the bus. Dominic followed him to the door as the vehicle slowed to a standstill outside the Royal Liverpool Hospital. Was it really only sixteen months since that evening when they had hatched their plan to rent a house together? Whose idea had it been? He could not now remember. The arrangement suited everyone. He escaped from living at home, sharing a room with his older brother and under constant parental scrutiny; Ibrahim got greater security of tenure and better accommodation than he could afford on his own; Mariam's parents could sleep easy, in the knowledge that she was not alone in a strange city; and Lucy could turn down his mother's offer of hospitality without appearing to be shunning her family.

How different everything would have been if they had never come up with their "cunning plan"! He felt as if he had known Mariam and her brother all his life. The thought that someone had deliberately attempted to injure her shook him to the core.

The two young men hurried along the pavement, past the rank of taxis waiting in the street, and into the forecourt of the hospital. They skirted round an ambulance to reach the entrance of the Accident and Emergency department. As they approached the doors, Ibrahim put up his hand and snatched the prayer cap off his head. He must have caught sight of his reflection in the glass and realised that he still had it on. He stuffed it into his pocket, striding purposefully on into the reception area. Dominic followed him.

As usual, in the evening, the place was bustling with people. Ibrahim stopped suddenly and stood staring round as if uncertain what to do next. Dominic also hesitated, looking towards the uniformed woman at the reception desk, who was currently attempting to take down details from a young couple with a baby in their arms.

'Ibrahim?' A young woman got up from a row of seating at the side of the room and came towards them. Her hair, shoulders and neck were covered by a royal blue hijab, pinned together on the right-hand side of her head by what looked to Dominic like a hatpin. She was wearing a blue and white dress over leggings in a colour to match her headscarf. Her deep brown eyes looked up at them anxiously.

'Olivia?' Ibrahim responded, turning at the sound of his name. 'Where's Mariam? Can we see her?'

'They're all being treated for acid burns.' Another woman, coming up behind Olivia, spoke more confidently. 'The first thing they have to do is to make sure they've washed it all off. Then they'll start assessing the injuries. I'm Tahira,' she added, holding out her hand towards Ibrahim. 'I don't think we've met before.'

'And I'm Mariam's brother, Ibrahim. And this is Dominic Fazakerley, who lives with us.'

Tahira turned her attention towards Dominic, who smiled nervously back, taking her hand when she offered it to him. She was shorter than Olivia, but had a good deal more presence. He felt that she would dominate any conversation and be noticed in any company. Her shiny black hair was cut short enough for him to see that she was wearing small diamond stud earrings. Her clothes were typical student garb: jeans, hooded sweatshirt and training shoes. Her hoody was emblazoned with the female symbol ♀ and some lettering, which Dominic's background in Religious Studies told him was Arabic. However, he had no idea what it said – a quotation from the Qur'an, perhaps?

'Have you met Hibaaq?' Tahira half turned, gesturing towards a third woman, who had joined them and was now standing next to Olivia. Dominic's eyes widened and he tried not to stare at this stunning apparition. She was tall – Dominic had a sensation of having to look upwards to meet her eye – and slender, but not skinny. Her deep brown eyes shone out from a dark brown face with high, prominent cheekbones. Her hair was hidden beneath a brightly patterned scarf, which hung down over her shoulders to her waist. 'We were both inside the Guild building when it happened, but we were in time to see the attacker riding away. I didn't get his number though,' Tahira added regretfully.

Hibaaq smiled, first at Ibrahim and then at Dominic, but she did not speak. Dominic got the feeling that she was studying him: trying to assess who he was and why he was there. He dropped his eyes and looked towards Ibrahim. His friend was staring silently up at this African beauty, apparently transfixed.

'Have you told your mum and dad about Mariam?' Olivia asked, addressing Ibrahim. 'I wasn't sure whether I ought to ring them too, but ...'

'No,' Ibrahim pulled his eyes away from the statuesque Hibaaq to look at Olivia again. 'I thought of it, but then I decided it'd be better to wait until I know more about how she is. How long do you think it'll be before we can see her? Or is there anyone I can ask?' He looked round vaguely as if hoping that one of the uniformed staff would pause in bustling about their business and approach him with news.

'The nurse said to wait here and they'd come and get us,' Olivia answered uncertainly, looking towards Tahira for confirmation.

'That's right,' her friend agreed. 'She said that they'd be assessed by a doctor as soon as they were sure all the acid had been washed off, and then someone would come and tell us whether they were being admitted or if they could go home.'

'So we just wait?' Ibrahim asked in an incredulous tone. 'Isn't there anyone who can tell us more than that?'

'I'm just telling you what they-,' Tahira began, but she was cut short by the sound of Dominic's phone ringing. She broke off and looked towards him. Smiling apologetically, he fished it out of his pocket and looked down at the screen. It was Lucy.

'Hi Dom!' Her cheerful greeting sounded out of place somehow. 'Where are you all? I got home and the place was deserted. Mariam and I were supposed to be doing revision together. I tried ringing her, but her phone's switched off. Do you …?' Her voice trailed off and became more serious. Something about the silence with which Dominic had responded to her call was starting to make her feel anxious. 'Has something happened?' she continued in a subdued tone. 'Where are you?'

'I – I … Ibrahim and I are at A and E,' her cousin answered at last. 'Mariam's … there's been an acid attack. Mariam was involved. We don't think she's badly injured,' he added hastily, hearing Lucy's sudden intake of breath at the mention of acid, 'but we won't know for sure how she is until she's been assessed by a doctor. We're waiting to hear. I'll-'

'I'll be right there,' Lucy interrupted. 'Give me a ring if there's any news.' She ended the call and Dominic was left staring down at a blank screen.

'That was Lucy,' he explained to the three women. 'Mariam's probably told you she lives in our house.'

'She and Dom are cousins,' Ibrahim added.

'I know Lucy,' Hibaaq said, speaking for the first time. Her voice was low and melodious and her accent that of somewhere in southern England. 'She's doing medicine too, isn't she? I'm in the second year. Mariam introduced us.'

They found five seats together and sat down to wait. Ibrahim looked round nervously, his eyes darting between a display screen on the wall (which showed a sequence of information videos interspersed with occasional messages for waiting patients and their families), the double doors through which staff appeared and disappeared at intervals, and the entrance where Lucy would eventually arrive.

Dominic, trying to stay calm, thought back to the day in September when the two girls had moved into their house in the Kensington area of Liverpool. Mariam had arrived first, her parents bringing her across Lancashire from Blackburn in their car. Lucy, with the longer journey from Oxford to make, did not arrive until the afternoon, giving Dominic three hours in which to get to know his new housemate before his cousin arrived and took her away to discuss pre-course reading lists and lecture timetables.

***

'They're here!' Ibrahim called out.

Dominic heard the sound of the door of the next room slamming shut, followed by noisy footsteps as his friend descended the stairs. He saved the lesson plan that he was preparing on his desktop computer and got up to meet his new housemate and her parents.

Arriving in the hall, he saw that the front door was already open and Ibrahim was standing outside on the step. Dominic came up behind him and looked out. A smart four-wheel-drive car was pulled up at the kerb outside the small front garden. Through the open front passenger door, he could see a woman in a black trouser suit. Her hair, fastened in a bun at the nape of her neck, was just starting to turn from black to grey. That must be Ibrahim's mother.

Another door opened and he recognised Mariam emerging from the back row of seats. She looked up and waved towards the two young men.

'We made it!' she called out. 'Dad insisted on going

down the A666, because it's seven miles shorter than the M6, but there were sheep on the road coming over the top there, and then the traffic was horrendous when we hit the M60 round Manchester, and then-'

'Anyway, we're here now,' her mother cut in, hurrying past Mariam to embrace her son.

After a quick hug, she turned her attention to Dominic, looking him in the eye and smiling approvingly.

'And you must be Lucy's cousin Dominic,' she said warmly. 'We've heard a lot about you – all good,' she added hastily, seeing his look of consternation at these words. 'Lucy tells me you teach Comparative Religion in a high school.'

'Well, it's called Religious Studies,' Dominic replied, rather taken aback. 'We try to give students a flavour of a wide range of religions, but it's only the few who choose to do the A' Level that really cover them in any depth.'

'Sorry!' Tahmina Ali smiled kindly at him. 'I didn't mean to put you on the spot. It's just that educating people about the differences – and similarities – between religions is a bit of a passion of mine. So much of the conflict and prejudice in society is down to ignorance.'

'Well, I do my best,' Dominic smiled back nervously. 'We don't get a lot of trouble, here on Merseyside. In fact, there's been a real upsurge of interest in Islam since Mo Salah[4] started scoring goals for Liverpool,' he added with sudden inspiration.

'Where do you want these books?'

Dominic looked up to see a man in his late fifties carrying a cardboard box. He looked like an older version of Ibrahim – or was that just his own inability to notice

---

[4] Mohamed Salah Hamed Mahrous Ghaly is a professional footballer from Egypt. He joined Liverpool in 2017, soon becoming their most prolific goal-scorer. He is a devout Muslim and is known for his habit of prostrating himself in praise of Allah after scoring a goal.

differences between individuals from another ethnic group?

'Oh Dad!' Mariam protested. 'You didn't need to! I could've carried them.' She looked towards Dominic with an expression that said, 'Parents! They simply won't listen to reason!'

'Let's all help,' he suggested, coming down the steps and heading for the open car boot. 'If we all carry something, it'll be done in no time.'

Ibrahim followed his lead and, not to be seen to be giving way to male superiority in the business of carrying luggage, Mariam turned back and pulled out two large trolley cases, which she proceeded to trundle to the bottom of the steps. She carried one into the hall and turned back to retrieve the second, but her mother had been too quick for her and was already up the steps with the case in her hand.

'I'm still waiting to be told where to take these,' Abdul Ali complained, holding up the box of books.

'Lucy and I are on the second floor,' his daughter told him. 'Just keep going on up the stairs to the top and then my room's the one at the front of the house.'

Carrying their various burdens, they all made their way upstairs, past the first floor landing where Dominic's and Ibrahim's rooms were, and on up into the attic.

'We thought Dom would keep banging his head on the ceiling if we put the lads up there,' Mariam called out to her father, who was leading the way. 'Mind how you go when you get in my room. The roof comes down quite low on one side.'

As Dominic had predicted, it took only a few minutes to unload the car. Then, feeling that he ought to play the host, he volunteered to make coffee while Mariam and Ibrahim showed their parents found the house. He was relieved that they appeared to like the accommodation and location and to approve of the living arrangements.

His qualms lest they suspect him of having designs on their daughter evaporated as they sat drinking coffee together in the small living room. Abdul talked about how pleased he was that Mariam would be staying with trusted friends, rather than being thrown in among strangers in a university hall of residence. Tahmina praised the homemade cinnamon cakes that Dominic's mother had insisted on leaving with him to welcome the new arrivals, and asked for the recipe.

When coffee was over, Ibrahim suggested that his parents might like to stay for lunch. Mariam, however, eager to begin her new life of freedom as soon as possible, failed to make any encouraging noises and her mother quickly took the hint.

'We'd better be getting back,' she said, getting to her feet. 'I'm on an early shift tomorrow and I've got a million and one things to do around the house before we can get to bed.'

'Your mum's right,' Abdul agreed. 'We'll leave you to settle in. Give our regards to Lucy and her mum when they get here.'

'I will!' Mariam got up and went ahead to open the door for her parents. 'Thanks for bringing me.'

***

Despite the seriousness of the present situation, Dominic could not keep himself from smiling as he remembered that day. Mariam had been so much in charge – and so determined not to allow anyone to treat her differently because of her sex – and yet she did it so quietly and unobtrusively, quite unlike the loud protestations that Lucy was in a habit of making whenever she saw something that she considered to be an injustice. They were so similar in many ways … and yet, so different.

Lucy would be vehement in her condemnation of this atrocity, demanding that the perpetrators be found and brought to justice. Mariam? She would want to know why. Why had she and her friends been targeted? What had been going through the perpetrator's mind when he – or could it be she? – made the decision to drench three young women in a lethal fluid? And yes, she would want them to be found and held to account, but she would make her demands quietly and thoughtfully without banging her fist on the table or attempting to bang heads together.

Accident and Emergency Department, Royal Liverpool University Hospital

2. SISTERHOOD

Lucy stood impatiently at the bus stop staring up the road, willing a bus to come. Would she have done better to walk all the way? It was only twenty minutes or perhaps a bit longer, but usually buses came past so frequently that it saved time to use them. She drummed her feet on the ground as she thought about what Dominic had told her.

Why would anyone want to attack Mariam? It must have been racist – or, perhaps more likely anti-Muslim. There had been an upsurge in anti-Muslim abuse ever since that incident back in October, when a disaffected young Libyan refugee had driven a van into a crowd of people, but nothing like this. And Mariam wasn't overtly Muslim in any case. She didn't wear a headscarf, for instance, like some of her friends from the mosque.

A bus approached and Lucy held out her hand to stop it, still pondering on the question that seemed to have no rational answer. Could it have been precisely *because* Mariam did not conform to Islamic stereotypes that she had been targeted? Not an Islamophobic attack but some sort of punishment from a radical Islamist who thought that she was betraying her religion by flaunting herself before the world?

She climbed aboard, swiping her walrus[5] card while looking around to locate a seat. There was plenty of space. She chose a position close to the door, thinking to get away as quickly as possible when they arrived.

---

[5] Merseytravel's walrus card is a smartcard used by regular travellers to pay for public transport (bus, train and ferry) across the Merseyside region.

What was that group called that Mariam belonged to? The Sisterhood, or something like that? And feminism came into it. The *Feminist Sisterhood of Islam*! That was it. Perhaps some very conservative Muslims might take offence at that. But surely they wouldn't go so far as to throw acid over one of them?

No, it was much more likely that it was right-wing extremists attacking her because she was a Muslim – or because she was non-white. Like the firework that someone had stuffed through their letterbox a few weeks after Guy Fawkes Night. Dominic thought it was just kids messing about, not understanding the danger; but Ibrahim had said that it was because someone didn't like having Muslims living in their street. Mariam had just got on quietly with cleaning off the smoke marks from the walls and replacing the burnt doormat.

Lucy had insisted on reporting the incident to the Police, although the others did not want to make a fuss. She'd held her ground and made the call, but there was nothing much the authorities could do. There were no witnesses and no forensic evidence to help identify the culprit. The crime was logged and would eventually go into the hate crime statistics, but nothing would change.

The bus came to a halt to allow more people to get on. Lucy moved up to make room for one of the newcomers to sit down next to her. Then another thought struck her. In their search for witnesses, police officers had interviewed local residents. What if that had increased their antipathy towards their Muslim neighbours? Were the others right in saying that they should have just let the firework incident go?

As they lurched off again, Lucy's mind turned back to the *Feminist Sisterhood of Islam*. She had met some of the members when they had come round to their house a few weeks before Christmas to celebrate Mariam's birthday. There had been two of them: a tall African with laughing eyes and a soft voice – when she spoke at all, which was seldom – wearing a brightly patterned headscarf and some sort of ethnic dress; and a serious-faced Asian with cropped hair and large dangling earrings looking very glamorous in a long sparkly dress.

Lucy liked Hibaaq very much. Like Lucy and Mariam, she was studying medicine and she was free with help and advice on making the most out of their course. She told them that her parents were also doctors. They had fled the fighting in Somalia thirty years earlier and were now naturalised British citizens. Hibaaq's ambition, once she was qualified, was to join the Médecins Sans Frontières relief effort in the country of her ancestors.

The other student had intimidated Lucy – an unusual thing for this self-confident young woman – by expounding feminist theory at some length, peppering her lectures with quotations from writers whose names Lucy did not recognise. If the attacker were an Islamist extremist who objected to their feminist agenda, she would have been a much more likely victim than mild-mannered Mariam.

What was her name? Lucy felt shame that she could not remember. She kept getting confused when Ibrahim and Mariam talked about their friends and family – so many unfamiliar names, some of which sounded similar to Lucy's untrained ear. This one was a bit like Mariam's mother's name – Tahmina – but it wasn't the same. No! It was no good, she couldn't remember. It did begin with a T, she was sure, but she could not remember anything more. She did remember some of her conversation, however. She had told Lucy that Islam was really the first truly feminist religion, but that it had lost its way in respect of women's rights since the death of the Prophet (peace be upon him). Lucy had felt compelled to acknowledge the underlying patriarchy in western society and, in particular, in the church, while secretly wishing for an opportunity to argue the case from the other side. There were, after all, far more female priests than imams and no churches where the sexes were segregated during worship!

Mariam was much less combative – but perhaps that was because she had never had to fight for her rights. Both her parents had been born in Britain and were very western in outlook – or was that just Lucy's own prejudice in assuming that first generation immigrants would have behaved differently? For all she knew, their Pakistani parents had also been liberal about dress and enthusiastic about women's education and equal rights!

As the bus continued its slow journey down Prescot Street, she remembered the previous Christmas, when Mariam had come to stay at her home in Oxford. She had told them that she wanted to experience a traditional English family Christmas and to find out what it was all about. Lucy's mother, Bernie, had snorted with laughter at this suggestion and retorted that, she'd come to the wrong place in that case, because they were such an eccentric lot!

There was some truth in that, Lucy smiled to herself. What other family attended Midnight Mass on Christmas Eve and then followed it up with a Methodist service in the morning? And, while the turkey and Christmas pudding might have been traditional, the Jamaican patties and curried goat were definitely not!

***

'This is St Cyprian's,' Lucy told her friend as they turned in at the gate of her local Roman Catholic Church. 'It's where we'll be going to Mass on Christmas Eve. I'll show you round and introduce you to Father Damien. He's very nice. You'll like him.'

She led the way inside. Mariam closed the door softly behind them and they both stood near the back looking around.

'There are a lot of pictures,' Mariam said at last. 'I like that window,' she added, looking up at a large stained glass representation of the story of Noah in the wall to their left. The Ark lay rather precariously perched on top of a mountain peak while animals streamed out of a door in its side. A bright rainbow arched above, its ends disappearing behind green hills in the background.

'That's Noah's Ark,' Lucy told her. 'You have Noah in Islam too, don't you?'

'Yes,' Mariam concurred, still looking up at the colourful array of animals, her eyes drawn to a black-and-white rabbit in the bottom right-hand corner. 'Only we call him Nuh.'

Lucy set off down the right-hand aisle heading towards the front of the church and the altar, which was covered with the purple hangings associated with Advent. Mariam followed, gazing upward at a row of smaller windows, each with a saint depicted in it. Then, looking higher, she caught sight of the ceiling.

'Wow!' she breathed in amazement. 'I've never seen anything like that before!'

'Neither have I,' Lucy grinned back. 'I think it may be unique. According to Father Damien, they had an artist in the congregation, who designed it and then the youth group did the painting. It was ages ago. I don't know any more than that.'

For a few seconds they remained still, staring up silently at the arched ceiling. It was blue, with puffy white clouds dotted around it, seemingly at random. The blue grew gradually paler towards either side of the church, merging into the white of the walls. At the front of the church, over the sanctuary, the blue became paler and turned to purple, pink and then finally yellow as the ceiling curved down over the main altar.

'I like the look of those angels,' Mariam commented, pointing upwards at two golden faces smiling out from behind one of the clouds. 'They look much more friendly than ours. I remember being quite frightened when I was little and someone told me that there were two invisible angels on my shoulders – one writing down all the good things I did and one making a note of all the bad ones!'

'A lot of Catholics believe in a recording angel too,' Lucy smiled back, 'but I think that's just one who keeps account of everyone's good and bad deeds. And lots of them believe that we each have a guardian angel that looks after us.'

'You talk as if you don't believe in them.'

'I'm not sure if I do or not,' Lucy confessed. 'I'm only sort of half Catholic – maybe not as much as that. My mam says it's just picture language to explain how God communicates with people. Jonah says it's all a load of nonsense and God doesn't delegate to saints and angels and "all that superstitious rubbish". Now, let me show you the organ. We had a water leak last winter and it broke down and had to be fixed … and you'll never guess what they found underneath it when they took it all apart!'

'Oh yes I will! Your friend Jonah told me about it last night while you were helping your dad with the washing up after dinner. And he showed me the newspaper reports of how he found out who the corpse was and who'd killed him[6].'

'I bet he did!' Lucy smiled. DCI, Jonah Porter had made a name for himself as the only police officer on the force who continued to solve crimes while confined to a wheelchair following a devastating injury to his spinal cord. Now retired, he revelled in recounting his past exploits to anyone willing to listen. 'And I don't suppose he bothered to mention that Peter and Mam worked just as hard as he did on that case!'

'Well, maybe he wouldn't have, except that your mum was there too, so she kept adding bits about your dad really being the brains of the outfit.' She giggled. 'I think she thinks Jonah's too big for his boots! It reminded me of the way my mum teases my uncle Yusef.'

'Hello!'

They turned to see a man in a dog collar emerging from a door on the other side of the church. His short brown hair was tousled and his brown eyes twinkled as he hastened over to greet them.

---

[6] See *Organ Failure* © 2018 ISBN: 978-1-911083-38-2

'I'm Father Damien Rowland – and you must be Mariam. Lucy said you might drop by.'

'Hello,' Mariam replied, looking up at him a little nervously. 'Lucy's been showing me round. It all looks very … magnificent,' she finished eventually, having toyed with "pretty" and "nice" before selecting an adjective that she hoped conveyed more than simply an appreciation of the artwork for its own sake.

'Mariam is the same as Mary – am I right?' Father Damien asked, also conscious of the need to pick his words carefully.

'Yes,' Mariam nodded. 'I think my parents were being a bit over-ambitious when they named me after her. The Qur'an says that she's better than all other women in the world!'

'Lucy's stepdad would like that idea, wouldn't he, Lucy?' Damien smiled at Mariam and then gave Lucy a wink. 'Has Lucy shown you our statue of Mary? It's rather special for Peter.'

They crossed the church and approached a statue of the Madonna and Child, which stood in front of a pillar separating the main church from a side chapel. It was almost life size and standing on a substantial stone plinth, so that Mariam had to tip her head back to look up at the Virgin's face. She was dark-skinned – a similar shade to Mariam's own – with deep brown eyes focussed anxiously on the child, which she held in her arms. Her hair was hidden beneath a pale blue headscarf and her body was covered by a long blue gown.

'Peter says that the Christ-child is the spitting image of his son, Eddie, when he was a baby,' Lucy explained.

Mariam studied the infant, noting the dark skin, brown eyes and curly black hair. 'He looks a bit like the pictures we've got of Ibrahim when he was a toddler,' she said. 'Only his hair wasn't so frizzy.'

'Jesus is one of your prophets too, isn't he?' Damien asked. 'You call him Isa, is that right?'

'Yes, that's right,' Mariam confirmed. 'Have you studied Islam?'

'I did a bit of boning up after Lucy said you were coming,' Damien confessed with a nervous laugh, 'but I'm sure I've got a lot more to learn.'

Mariam smiled back politely. For a few moments, there was an awkward silence with nobody knowing what to say next.

'There's another picture of Mary you might be interested to see,' Damien said at last, leading the way into the side chapel. 'This chapel is dedicated to Our Lady – that's Mary – and so we've got a painting of her over the altar.' He gestured towards a large rectangular picture featuring a young woman squatting on the floor, hard at work grinding flour with two millstones. She was looking up, with an expression of fear and amazement, towards a bright light that was coming in through an open door at the left of the picture. Just visible outside the doorway was the suggestion of a human arm, reaching out towards the woman, and a wing covered in golden feathers shielding from sight the face of whatever being was out there.

'It's the Annunciation,' Lucy told her, 'when the Angel Gabriel told her she was going to have a baby.'

'That's Jibril, in Arabic,' Damien added. 'The angel who revealed the Qur'an to the Prophet Muhammad.'

'Do you believe that?' Mariam asked in surprise.

'Well, I try to keep an open mind. Of course, I do have to assume that some things got a bit muddled in the telling – Jesus categorically denying his deity, for example, and the idea that he didn't die on the cross.'

***

The bus came to a standstill. It was not a bus stop. There was a holdup caused by crowds of people on the pavement spilling out on to the street. Lucy wished that she had got off at the previous stop. She could see the hospital from here, but tantalisingly could not reach it because the bus was surrounded by traffic and the doors were firmly shut.

***

Christmas Day. Mariam's introduction to the variety of Christian approaches to worship was continuing apace. The solemn pageantry of Midnight Mass had been followed by an informal service at a Methodist Church in East Oxford, which included children showing off their new presents, a talk during which the minister took out a sequence of unlikely objects from an enormous Christmas stocking, and a selection of Christmas Carols, sung with gusto.

As they stepped out on to the steps that led down to the road, they were greeted by one of Lucy's friends – Stella Gilbert, a third generation immigrant from the West Indies.

'Hi Lucy! Happy Christmas,' she said cheerfully, and then, shyly, turning to face Lucy's friend, 'Happy Christmas Mariam – or shouldn't I say that to you?' she added hastily, gabbling on in her embarrassment, 'I mean, Lucy said you're a Muslim, so you don't believe in Christmas, do you?'

'Don't worry!' Mariam reassured her with a smile. 'Actually we do have decorations up at home and send cards and give presents, just the same as you do. That's got nothing to do with religion. We don't believe that Jesus was born on December the 25th.'

'But then neither do we,' cut in Lucy. 'Everyone knows that was just a convenient date chosen because it was when the pagans used to celebrate the winter solstice.'

'So do you believe in Jesus?' Stella asked in a puzzled tone. 'I thought ...'

'He's one of our greatest prophets,' Mariam smiled back. 'Second only to Muhammad (peace be upon him).'

'Oh.' Stella fell silent, apparently deep in thought. After a few moments, she plucked up courage to ask, 'Do you mind? I was wondering ...?'

'Go ahead,' Mariam said encouragingly. 'What is it?'

'I was wondering why you haven't got a hijab on. I thought Muslim women had to cover their heads.'

'No. That's just a cultural thing. The Qur'an says that everyone – men *and* women – should dress modestly. Scholars waste a lot of time disputing exactly what that means, and of course, since most of them are men, they sometimes come up with some pretty silly ideas, but … no, I've never worn a hijab, and neither has my mum.' She laughed suddenly and turned to Lucy. 'You know, I was going to ask you. What was it that girl was wearing last night – the one who read about the shepherds and the angels? I thought it looked just like a hijab.'

'That was a chapel veil,' Lucy told her. 'Niamh always was a bit of a show-off. Then, she went off to uni and got this boyfriend who was into reviving old Catholic traditions and …'

'Not so very old,' Bernie cut in, coming up behind them and joining in the conversation. 'Wearing a hat in church was still compulsory when I was your age – or so all my aunts used to tell me! People have short memories.'

'Come to think of it,' Stella admitted thoughtfully, 'my gran never goes anywhere without a hat on – I just never thought of it as the same thing.'

***

Seeing that the bus was pulling up outside the hospital, Lucy scrambled to her feet. As she stepped down to the street, her mind turned back to wondering why her friend had been attacked. Could it be revenge for that incident back in October? She remembered her stepfather, Peter, shaking his head and muttering about repercussions for Muslim students after it came out that the accused man had attended Liverpool University. There had been calls in the popular press for the Islamic Society to be closed down – just in case it could have been instrumental in his radicalisation.

Entering the waiting area in the Emergency Department, she looked around for Dominic and Ibrahim. Eventually she spotted them, standing in a corner, in conversation with a white couple who looked to be of her parents' generation.

They appeared agitated – the woman in tears and the man raising his voice in anger. Who could they be?

Ibrahim looked across in her direction and waved to her. She started across the room, still wondering who the older couple could be. She recognised Hibaaq's elegant figure, standing straight and tall above the others – and that smaller woman was Tahira (she remembered her name now) – and wasn't that Olivia, sitting down next to them?

'Lucy!' Ibrahim put has arm round her shoulder and held her in a brief embrace. 'You needn't have come – but I'm glad you did!' He lowered his voice, as he escorted her back to join their little group. 'Maybe you'll be able to help us with Emily's parents. They're upset, as you'd expect, but …,' he dropped his voice still further, 'it's difficult when they talk as if it was our fault, what happened.'

Her mind racing as she tried to think what she might say to calm the angry man, Lucy walked with Ibrahim to join the cluster in the corner. As she approached, the weeping woman slumped down into the seat next to Olivia, who tentatively put her arm around her and leaned close to speak to her. Her husband continued his tirade against Muslims in general and the group there in front of him in particular.

'She was a marked woman!' he snarled. 'Ever since you lot got your claws into her and made her wear that ridiculous costume! Something like this was bound to happen. It was just a matter of time.'

'Mr Armstrong,' Tahira said, stepping forward and looking him squarely in the eye, 'I realise that you're upset, but that is no reason for twisting the facts.'

Her voice was quiet and calm, but Lucy recognised a controlled anger in it that was more dangerous than a more heated outburst would have been. The dam was holding fast, but it might burst at any minute, with potentially disastrous consequences.

'No one has forced Emily to change how she dresses,' Tahira continued. 'It was completely her own decision to start covering her head and wearing a niqab. In fact, I for one told her that I disagreed with it! But she has a right to choose for herself and no man – not even her father – has a right to dictate to her about it.'

'You – you - !' spluttered Steven Armstrong, his outrage palpable.

'Please!' Lucy interrupted, hoping to de-fuse the situation by creating a diversion. 'Can someone tell me what happened?'

Reilly Building, Liverpool University.

3. POLICE OPERATION

'I'm sorry, love. I know I said I'd be back by nine, but something serious has cropped up.' DCI Sandra Latham of Merseyside Police had been due to go off duty half an hour ago, but she had been called to the incident at the university and was now ringing her teenage daughters to let them know that she would be late home. 'Can't Sophie help you with your homework? ... Well, I'll have a look at it before you go to school in the morning then. ... No, you can't ... Look, we'll talk about it tomorrow, OK? Now I've got to go. Bye Pippa! Love you!'

She pocketed her phone and turned to speak to the uniformed officer who had greeted her and her assistant, DS Charlotte Simpson, on their arrival at the hospital.

'OK! You'd better take me to speak to the witnesses.'

'The principle witness is Olivia Akram,' PC Robert Thomas told her as he led the way across the crowded waiting room. 'She was one of the students in the group that was attacked, but none of the hazardous substance went on her. She's sitting down over there with a couple of her friends who came out of the Guild of Students building just as it happened. One of them saw the assailant riding away and got part of the bike's number. The tall black girl's name is ...,' he consulted his notes, 'Hib ... Hibaaq Galaal. And the other one's called Tara ... no, Tahira Siddiqui.'

'And who are all the others?' asked Charlotte, gazing across the room at the little group of people clustered in the corner, some tearful, some pacing impatiently, some in conversation.

'There's the parents of one of the victims,' PC Thomas told her, consulting his notes again. 'A Mr and Mrs

Armstrong. And the Asian lad is Ibrahim Ali. His sister's another of the victims. And the other two are with him – apparently they all share a house together. Their names are … Dominic Fazakerley and-'

'Lucy!' Sandra exclaimed, catching sight of her as Ibrahim moved to one side, giving her a better view.

'Sandra!' hearing her name, Lucy looked round and recognised her as the Senior Investigating Officer (SIO) in a murder case[7] that she and her mother had been caught up in a few years earlier. 'Ibrahim, this is Inspector Latham. She caught the people who killed a Catholic Priest on board one of the ferries – and nearly killed my Mam too! I must have told you about it.'

Sandra advanced towards them holding up her identification.

'Good evening,' she said, looking round at the members of the little group. 'My name is Detective Chief Inspector Sandra Latham. And this is Detective Sergeant Charlotte Simpson. We need to ask you all some questions about what happened.'

'Olivia was the only person who actually witnessed the assault,' Tahira said at once, pushing her friend forwards. 'And Hibaaq and I saw the attacker getting away. He was dressed in black and riding a motorbike – but we told all this to the police who came when we rang 999.'

'That's right,' Sandra replied, as soon as she could speak without interrupting. 'We have your initial statements. Now we need to ask some more questions to try to piece together exactly what happened and, more importantly, who did it and why.'

'I'd've thought it was bloody obvious why!' Steven Armstrong elbowed Tahira out of the way and stood face-to-face with Sandra staring down at her belligerently. 'These stupid girls go round dressed up in these bloody burkas, like a load of terrorists, and then they wonder why people don't

---

[7] See *Mystery over the Mersey* © 2016 ISBN 978-1-911083-19-1

like it!'

'And your name is?' Sandra asked coldly, staring back at him.

'Armstrong – Steven Armstrong – and this is my wife, Fiona. Our daughter Emily's one of the girls who got sprayed with this acid, or whatever it was. She's been brainwashed by these bloody Muslims, and now she's – she's – well we don't know what, do we?' His voice grew louder and more aggressive. 'Why will nobody tell us anything in this bloody place? When are they going to let us see her? What are they keeping from us? That's what I'd like to know!'

'Please, Mr Armstrong,' Sandra said calmly, taking him by the arm and gently pushing him towards a row of seats that was fixed along the wall behind him. 'I understand how stressful this is for you, but please try to stay calm. Your daughter is receiving treatment and I'm sure someone will be here soon to tell you how it's going. Meanwhile, if you could just sit down and wait while I interview Miss Akram … You'll have a chance to tell us all about what you know in a few minutes.'

Steven Armstrong opened his mouth to argue, then sighed as he closed it again and flopped down into the seat next to his wife. She put out her hand and slipped it through his arm, smiling tearfully towards him and then flashing a look of relief towards Sandra.

'Miss Akram?' Sandra turned her attention to Olivia, relieved at having managed to quieten the aggressive Armstrong so easily. 'If you would just come with me, there's a private room just over there, where we can talk.'

Olivia followed Sandra into a small room furnished with easy chairs, upholstered in green plastic, grouped around a low coffee table. Charlotte closed the door behind them.

'Please – sit down,' Sandra said, gesturing towards the chairs.

Olivia did as she was told, perching on the edge of her seat and looking earnestly towards her inquisitors, who settled down opposite her.

'Now, Olivia,' Sandra began. 'Is it alright if I call you Olivia?'

'Yes,' Olivia answered inaudibly. She cleared her throat and tried again. 'Yes. That's fine.'

'Would you like me to fetch you something to drink?' Charlotte asked. 'Some tea? Or a glass of water?'

'No. I'm OK.' Olivia shook her head.

'Alright then – if you're sure.' Sandra looked across the table at this young woman, so similar and yet so different from her own two daughters. That brightly patterned dress and blue leggings were just the sort of things that Sophie might choose to wear for a night out with her friends. But she would never dream of concealing her long blond hair beneath that austere headscarf! Olivia's wide-eyed look of anxiety reminded her of Pippa's face when she had witnessed the family dog running out into the road and being hit by a car. But this girl's eyes were brown, not blue, and they were set in a face several shades darker than Pippa's. 'Perhaps you could start by telling us, in your own words, exactly what happened.'

'We'd been having a meeting in the bar at the Guild of Students,' Olivia began.

'Let me stop you there a moment.' Sandra put up her hand to indicate that she had a further question. 'Who exactly is "we"?'

'Me and the other girls – Tahira and Hibaaq that you saw outside, and Salma, Mariam and Emily who …'

'Yes, I've got it now,' Sandra smiled at her reassuringly. 'I'm sorry to have interrupted – please go on.'

'Tahira and Hibaaq were checking over the notes of the meeting, so they didn't come out right away.'

'Notes?' queried Charlotte. 'This was some sort of formal meeting then? Not just friends having a few drinks together?'

'Well, yes – sort of. We're a sort of society – the Feminist Sisters of Islam. It's just the six of us at the moment. There were some more, but they were in the third year last year so they've left uni now.'

'I see.' Sandra hesitated, wondering whether to press Olivia for more details in case this society had any bearing on the case. She decided to leave that line of enquiry for the time being. 'Go on. What happened after your meeting ended?'

'The four of us – me, Emily, Salma and Mariam – came out and walked together up to the road. We stopped just beyond the bus stop – where the pavement widens out, outside Starbucks. Salma was planning to get the bus from there. We were talking, so we waited with her. She was the closest to the road. Then Mariam was next to her and then Emily. All of a sudden, a motorbike came round the corner from Brownlow Hill. The others had their backs to it, but I saw it turn in. I remember seeing Salma turning to look to see what the noise was. He stopped right next to them. He was dressed all in black with one of those garden sprayers that you use for killing greenfly strapped to his back.'

'Go on,' Sandra said gently, as Olivia hesitated. 'What happened then?'

'I remember seeing him standing there with his legs still astride the bike. He shouted out something, but I didn't really take it in – something about "murderers", I think. Then he sprayed them all with whatever it was he'd got in the bottle on his back and they started screaming. I heard someone shouting out from over by the coffee shop. I don't know if that frightened him or what, but he rode off after that.'

'Did you see his face at all?' Sandra asked.

'No.' Olivia shook her head vigorously. 'He had one of those black visors on his helmet.'

'Are you sure it was a man?' queried Charlotte. 'Or could it have been a woman?'

'The voice sounded like a man – at least I think it did. Why? Do you think you know who it was?'

'No,' Sandra took the reins again, 'the sergeant was just

wanting to cover all possibilities – so we don't jump to conclusions. Now, you were the one who called 999 – did you do that right away?'

'Yes. I could see the girls needed medical attention, so I rang for an ambulance. A man came over and poured water on Salma's head from a bottle he was carrying and he shouted for people to bring more water from the coffee shop. He somehow got them lying down on the pavement and kept pouring water over them. Salma looked awful! She turned round, you see, and got it in her face. I've never heard anyone scream the way she did. And she was scratching at her face with her hands and … It was just *awful!*'

Without warning, Olivia collapsed into sobs. Sandra fumbled in her pocket and pulled out a small packet of tissues. She took one out and pressed it into Olivia's hand.

'Just take your time,' she murmured. 'You're doing great.'

There was a knock at the door. Charlotte got up to answer it. A young man in nurse's uniform was standing outside.

'You asked us to tell you when the victims were ready for you to talk to them,' he said. 'Mariam Ali is on the ward now. We've just taken her family up to see her. Do you want to come now? The doctor says she'd rather you didn't leave it too long, because it would be better for her to settle down for the night and get some sleep.'

'OK. I'll come right away.' Sandra turned to Olivia. 'Thank you, Olivia, I think we'll leave it at that for now. Do you want to come with me to see your friend?'

'Yes please!' Olivia hastily composed herself and smiled a watery smile of gratitude.

'You'd better interview the Armstrongs,' Sandra said to Charlotte. 'I don't want to keep them waiting any longer. You can use this room while I go up to the ward to see Miss Ali.'

As they were on their way up to the ward, the nurse

explained to Sandra that Mariam's acid burns were serious, but not extensive.

'They're mostly confined to one side of her head,' he told her. 'It was very lucky that a passer-by had the sense to dowse them all with water right away. I don't know how much she'll be able to tell you – she'll be quite sleepy because she was given a sedative while we examined her. The burns are very painful – but in a strange way that's good, because it means that the nerves haven't been destroyed. The consultant will see her in the morning and she'll most likely be transferred to the burns unit at Whiston[8].'

He opened a door and stepped back to allow Sandra to step into a single room on one of the wards. The patient was lying on her back with her head turned so that the left-hand side rested against the pillow. Most of her hair appeared to have been shaved off – or had the acid burned it away? Her right cheek and ear were hidden beneath a dressing, which also extended round the back of her head.

On either side of the bed sat the two young men whom Sandra had met in the waiting area, while Lucy stood with her back to the door, looking down at her friend. At the sound of the door opening, she looked round.

'Hello!' she greeted Sandra. 'Have you come to interview Mariam?'

'If she's up to it,' Sandra replied.

Ibrahim got up and stood next to Lucy, allowing Sandra to sit down on the chair to Mariam's left. Sandra looked down at Mariam, who looked silently back.

'I know this isn't a good time,' Sandra began, 'but I need you to tell me everything you can remember about what happened. Do you think you can do that?'

'I understand,' Mariam said slowly and painfully. Dominic leaned over her and helped her to water from a

---

[8] Whiston Hospital in Prescot houses the Mersey Regional Burns and Plastic Surgery Centre.

plastic beaker. She nodded and smiled towards him and then looked back at Sandra. 'It's all a bit of a blur,' she admitted, her voice a little stronger now. 'I heard this roar from behind me and then ... something wet on the back of my neck and my whole head seemed to be on fire. Salma was screaming – it was awful – and then I realised that I was screaming too. That was really scary, because I'm not like that.'

She paused. Dominic offered her more water, but she shook her head slightly and he sat back in his chair.

'You didn't see your attacker?' Sandra asked.

'No. Olivia may have done. She was facing the other way.'

'He had a motorbike helmet on,' Olivia told her. 'I didn't see his face at all.'

'Just one more question, and then I'll leave you in peace.' Sandra leaned a little closer and spoke to Mariam in a low voice. 'Can you think of anyone who might have wanted to hurt you or your friends? Anyone at all?'

'No.'

'No one with a grudge?' Sandra suggested. 'Nobody trolling you on social media?'

'No,' Mariam whispered. 'Nothing like that.'

'Only the usual racist attacks,' Dominic blurted out suddenly. 'Like the firework through our letter box and the spray paint on the wall of the mosque!'

'When were these incidents?' Sandra asked sharply. 'Were they reported to the police?'

'The firework was in November,' Lucy told her. 'I reported it, but they didn't find out who did it.'

'And the graffiti?' Sandra looked round at them all.

'We just borrowed a power hose and cleaned it off,' Olivia told her. It didn't seem worth reporting and ...'

'The language was so offensive that we wanted to remove it right away,' Ibrahim finished for her.

'And presumably you don't have any idea who was responsible?'

They all shrugged and shook their heads.

'Never mind.' Sandra got up to go. 'I'll probably need to talk to you all again later, but for now,' she looked towards Mariam, 'goodnight, and I hope you have a quick recovery. I promise you that we will be doing everything we can to find out who did this and to bring them to justice.'

'We'd better go too,' Ibrahim said. 'Try to get some sleep. I'll ring Mum and Dad and let them know what's happened and I expect they'll come to see you in the morning.'

'Don't worry,' Dominic added, putting out his hand and touching Mariam briefly on the shoulder. 'You're in good hands. Everything's going to be alright.'

'Insha'Allah,' Mariam murmured, flashing him a smile.

'How could anyone want to do such a – a – an appalling thing?' Dominic demanded angrily, once the door was shut safely behind them and they were on their way down the corridor. 'What could anyone have against Mariam and the others?'

'It's too early to say for sure,' Sandra answered, filling the awkward silence that followed this outburst, 'but it's probably safe to assume that it was an Islamophobic attack. Four girls in Muslim headdresses, standing on the corner of the street were an easy target for someone who was out looking for trouble.'

'But Mariam never even *wears* a hijab!' Dominic protested.

'The others do,' Ibrahim reminded him, 'and I don't suppose the attacker noticed who was wearing what.'

'Anyway, that sort of person probably doesn't care what religion she is,' Lucy added. 'Blaming Muslims for Islamist terrorism is just their excuse for racism.'

'We will be treating it as a potential terrorist incident,' Sandra told them firmly, 'while keeping an open mind in case it turns out to have been aimed at one or more of the victims personally.'

'She's talking like a press-release,' Ibrahim whispered to Lucy, grinning in spite of the grim situation.

'Well, she's got to be careful what she says to us, in case we quote her all over social media,' Lucy whispered back.

When they got back to the reception area, they saw that Tahira and Hibaaq had been joined by Salma's parents, Munir and Fahima Rahman. Charlotte was in conversation with them. Seeing Sandra returning she looked up.

'Mr and Mrs Armstrong are with their daughter now,' she told her. 'The doctors say she'll probably be able to go home tonight. They only live in St Helens, so they said they'd wait and take her with them when she's ready.'

Sandra and Charlotte took the Rahmans away to interview them in private. The others stood looking at one another for a few moments before Olivia expressed the intention of leaving for home. Tahira and Hibaaq insisted on escorting her back to her lodgings.

The mobile phone signal was poor inside the hospital building, so Lucy and Dominic stood waiting under the canopy outside the Emergency Department while Ibrahim telephoned his parents.

'They're going to come over right away,' he told them. 'I tried to persuade them to wait until tomorrow, but they want to speak to the staff who treated Mariam. That's medics for you!' he grinned. 'I expect Dad wants to grill them over whether they followed all the latest treatment guidelines! Anyway, that means I'd better stay here and wait for them.'

'We'll wait with you,' Lucy said at once. Then, after a moment's thought, 'or no – Dom, you stay with Ibrahim and I'll go back and make up the sofa bed for them, so they can stay overnight with us instead of going all the way back to Blackburn tonight.'

'You can't go back on your own,' Dominic protested. 'Not when there's a madman throwing acid around,' he added, conscious that Lucy would be affronted at the suggestion that she was incapable of looking after herself and needed a male escort in order to make a journey of little more than a mile.

'Dom's quite right,' Ibrahim agreed. 'I'll be fine here on my own. You two go home. Thanks for thinking of the sofa bed,' he added. 'That's a good idea of yours. I'll try and persuade Mum and Dad that it'll be better if they come straight home with me and leave off cross-examining everyone until tomorrow.'

'OK. If you're sure you wouldn't like someone to wait with you.' Lucy reached out and laid her hand on Ibrahim's shoulder. 'And don't worry. DCI Latham knows what she's doing. I'm sure she'll get to the bottom of all this.'

Guild of Students building

4. FAMILY TIES

In the large kitchen of their home in the Headington suburb of Oxford, Dr Bernadette Catherine Fazakerley ("Our Bernie" to her friends) and her "family" (comprising her husband, Peter Johns, and their great friend and live-in companion, Jonah Porter) were eating breakfast, preparatory to driving up to Liverpool to celebrate Lucy's birthday. As usual, the radio was on and they were all half-listening to the morning news broadcast.

'Merseyside Police are treating the acid attack on a group of Muslim students last night as a terrorist incident,' the newsreader said calmly.

At this, they all fell suddenly silent. Bernie froze with her hand outstretched, holding a piece of toast and marmalade towards Jonah, whose mouth dropped open as he listened intently.

'One of the victims – a Muslim convert from St Helens on Merseyside – has been discharged from hospital with minor injuries,' the voice continued. 'The other two young women are reported to be stable, with serious acid burns. Sally Cousins of Radio Merseyside has more details.'

Bernie's phone rang and she hurried to answer it. It was Lucy, hoping to break the news before her mother heard it through the media.

'There's been an acid attack,' she said at once. 'You may have heard about it on the news.'

'Ye-es,' Bernie agreed cautiously, her heart speeding up as the thought occurred to her that Lucy would not have rung merely to keep her abreast of local events. She switched the phone to loudspeaker, to avoid the necessity of relaying the content of a difficult conversation to the others later. Peter reached over and turned down the volume on the radio.

'Well, I thought you ought to know – before you come up, I mean – Mariam was one of the people involved.'

'She's one of the victims, you mean?' Bernie asked sharply.

'That's right. She's not as bad as one of the others,' Lucy added hastily, detecting the note of alarm in her mother's voice. 'But they've kept her in overnight, and they said she might have to go to the burns unit at Whiston.'

'That doesn't sound good,' Bernie said, trying to think of the best way of sounding sympathetic but not overly alarmed. 'And what about Ibrahim? Is he OK? Has he seen her since it happened?'

'Oh yes!' Lucy assured her. 'We all did – last night in the hospital. She's got a big dressing on her head, but her face is hardly affected at all. They'd sedated her because it's so painful – but the nurse said that pain is a good sign, in a way, because it means that the nerves are still OK.'

'And Mariam's parents?' Peter called across the table. 'Have they-?'

'They came over last night. We put them up on our sofa. They're going to see Mariam again this morning, but then they've got to get back, because Abdul can't cancel his clinic. Ibrahim thinks he'll be able to take the day off as compassionate leave, but he hasn't been able to ring work yet to make sure.'

'OK, love,' Bernie was about to end the conversation when Jonah interrupted.

'What do the police say about it?' he demanded. 'Do they have any idea who did it?'

'They are *treating it as a potential terrorist attack*,' Lucy said, repeating part of the initial press release word-for-word with a hint of amusement in her voice, 'but they are *keeping an open mind and not ruling anything out.* In other words, they haven't a clue at the moment! Actually, that's something else I was going to tell you – guess who the SIO is!'

'Not Sandra Latham?' came back Jonah immediately, naming the only senior officer in the Merseyside force with whom they were personally acquainted.

'That's right – and she's still got Charlie Simpson as her bag-carrier.'

'OK love,' Bernie repeated, giving Jonah a warning look. He took the hint and refrained from any further questions about the police investigation. 'We're nearly ready to set off. As soon as we've finished with breakfast, we'll be on the road, so we'll probably get to you round about lunchtime, unless there are any hold-ups. Give our love to Ibrahim and his parents – and to Mariam too, of course, if you see her again before we get there – and take care.'

She ended the call and looked round at the others. Peter started clearing the table. Jonah, abandoning what remained of his slice of toast, moved his electric wheelchair away from the table and headed off to his bedroom. Bernie could see that he wanted to complete the remaining preparations for the journey without delay. Smiling to herself at the invigorating effect on her friend of the prospect of helping with (or would DCI Latham see it as *interfering in*?) a police investigation, she followed him out.

'Stop moving your head around like that,' she grumbled at him a few minutes later, as she attempted to clean his teeth while Jonah searched through various news websites for details of the acid attack, using the handy computer screen attached to his wheelchair. A bullet in the back of his neck almost a decade earlier had left him paralysed from the shoulders down, apart from three fingers of his left hand; but he made full use of those three fingers (together with a range of technological gadgets) to maintain a surprising degree of independence. 'You'll have plenty of time for surfing while we're in the car. OK – now have a rinse and we'll be all set to go.'

Jonah obediently took a mouthful of water from the glass that she held up to his lips, swished it round and spat into a kidney bowl.

'OK. Off you go,' Bernie shooed him out like a recalcitrant schoolchild. 'Go and wait by the car and I'll come and strap you in as soon as I've put these away.'

Peter was already outside by now, busily packing their large, specially adapted car with all the paraphernalia needed to support a severely disabled man for a few days' stay in a hotel. He turned and smiled at Jonah, when he saw him descending the ramp from the front door.

'Just wait while I find somewhere safe for Lucy's cake,' he said, 'and then I'll let you in.'

A few minutes later, they were off. Peter was driving for the first half of the journey, while Bernie sat in the back of the car with Jonah, whose wheelchair (with him in it) was strapped securely into its space there. Looking across at him, she thought she detected a surprisingly smug expression on his face.

'What are you so pleased about?' she asked.

'While you two were busy just now, I rang Sandra Latham,' he told her. 'She said she'd be pleased to have some help with this acid attack case.'

'You mean, you told her that she'd be pleased to have your help and she was too polite to tell you to get lost!' Peter cut in, in a voice that mixed amusement with exasperation. 'You've got a bloody nerve – that's all I can say!'

'So I've arranged to meet her this afternoon at two thirty,' Jonah went on, ignoring Peter's intervention. 'You can take me, Peter, while Bernie has some quality mother-and-daughter time with Lucy.'

'We'll see about that,' Bernie replied. 'I want us all to go to the hotel first to check out that their *accessible room* really is as accessible as it claims. And then-'

'Can't you and Lucy do that?' asked Jonah impatiently.

'Not without you there as *Exhibit A*,' Bernie insisted. 'They won't believe me if I tell them your chair won't fit through the door, unless they can see it for themselves. Look – I'm not saying you can't have your case conference with Sandra,' she added, seeing the sulky look on Jonah's face. 'I'm just warning you that half past two may be rather optimistic timing, that's all.'

As it turned out, Bernie's schedule fell to pieces as soon as they arrived. Despite roadworks on the motorway, they managed to reach Liverpool in time to have lunch with Lucy, who told them that Ibrahim had gone into work after all. He had decided, on reflection, that it would be more useful to Mariam if he were to save his allowance of *special leave* for when she was discharged and might need him to help her at home or escort her to outpatient appointments.

'I think as much as anything, he wanted to keep himself busy,' Lucy added. 'It was getting on his nerves, us all sitting around speculating on what was going to happen to Mariam. I promised I'd try to get over to see her this afternoon. The number 10 bus goes past Whiston, so I can do that while you all get settled in at the hotel.'

'Or we could drive you,' Peter suggested. 'Then we can all visit Mariam.'

'Parking's supposed to be awful,' Lucy objected. 'And didn't Jonah say he's arranged to meet Sandra Latham this afternoon?'

'What time is visiting?' asked Bernie. 'Would there be time to check in at the hotel first?'

'It starts at two,' Lucy told her. 'I could do with going out for the bus in a few minutes.'

'Tell you what,' Peter suggested, still reluctant to allow Lucy to embark on what might be a traumatic expedition on her own. 'Why don't you and I go on the bus to visit Mariam, while Bernie and Jonah check in?'

'That's a good idea,' Jonah agreed promptly. 'We'll just drop the bags off at the hotel and then nip off down to meet Sandra.'

'Well, it may be a bit more than just dropping off the bags,' Bernie said cautiously, 'but I suppose that's as good a plan as any – unless you're willing to give up on this ridiculous idea that you're going to swan in and solve the case in a matter of minutes!'

'I never said anything of the sort!' Jonah protested, pretending to be indignant, but in fact, as everyone around him knew full well, highly delighted at having got his own way so easily.

'I think that's an awesome idea!' Lucy said eagerly. 'I bet Sandra's pleased you're here. She knows what a good record you've got. And I don't know why you two are so negative about it,' she added, rounding on Bernie and Peter. 'Don't you want to help find out who did it?'

'Of course we do, love,' her mother sighed. 'It's just that we're all supposed to be retired now and it's not for us to be butting in on a police investigation.'

'Not to mention the conflict of interest involved,' Peter added. 'But, of course, his nibs here never listens to reason, so we might as well go with the flow and hope it doesn't all end in tears.'

Bernie looked at her watch.

'You'd better be going, hadn't you?' she asked, glancing towards Lucy. 'If you lend me your spare key, I'll lock up the house when we leave, and then we'll see you back here at whatever time I manage to prise Jonah away from his precious investigation.'

***

'The attack took place here,' Sandra said, pointing at a large map of Liverpool attached to a board on the wall of the open plan office that housed her team of CID officers. 'The victims were standing here, on the pavement outside the Starbucks by the Guild of Students[9] building. A motorbike came round the corner from Brownlow Hill and pulled up next to them. The rider was dressed all in black with a helmet that obscured his face. He sprayed them with what we believe to have been sulphuric acid – although we're waiting for confirmation on that – from a plastic bottle

---

[9] The Liverpool Guild of Students is the students' union for the University of Liverpool.

strapped to his back. He belted off down Mount Pleasant.'

She moved her finger along a road on the map.

'A couple of other students got a partial number off the back of the bike, which fits with the number on an abandoned bike that we found this morning in the cycle parking outside the Sydney Jones Library in Abercromby Square.'

'So it looks as if he must've turned left into Oxford Street,' Bernie murmured, stepping up beside Sandra and tracing her finger along the map. 'He left the bike, presumably because someone might have got the number and alerted the police, and went off on foot, I suppose.'

'He'd have been a bit conspicuous dressed in motorbike leathers and a helmet,' Jonah observed. 'In his place, I'd have been looking to ditch them as soon as possible.'

'We've got officers out searching the area around the Sydney Jones,' Sandra told him, 'and we've taken the bike away for forensic examination. I've told them I want the works doing – DNA, fingerprints, traces of the chemical used in the attack, analysis of any mud on the tyres – the lot.'

'The most noticeable thing would've been the plastic spray bottle on his back,' Bernie commented. 'He surely can't have gone far with that.'

'We've put out a call on local radio and in newspapers asking anyone who saw the rider, either before or after the incident, to get in touch,' Sandra assured them. 'You're right. It's that bottle that will make him stand out from any other biker. No response yet – or at least nothing reliable. We've had reports of sightings of men with black crash helmets riding bikes all over Merseyside at all times of day and night, but they all look like just people wanting to feel important, and maybe to get a bit of the limelight.'

'The bike will have been stolen, I assume,' Jonah said, looking towards Sandra for confirmation.

'No – or at least it hasn't been reported. It's registered in the name of *Darren Galgate*, at an address in Skelmersdale.

We're doing background checks on him, but so far he looks squeaky clean – not so much as a speeding fine or a parking ticket! Anyway, surely nobody would commit a crime while riding their own motorbike and then dump it for us to find.'

'You said in your press-release that you're treating this as anti-Muslim terrorism. Is that just an assumption based on who the victims were, or do you have more to go on than that?' Bernie asked.

'It's basically just an assumption,' Sandra confirmed. 'We had a bit of an upsurge of anti-Muslim incidents after the Shaladi van attack back in October, and then again last month when he was convicted. They put off sentencing while they waited for a psychological assessment. I'm assuming that this could have been triggered by reports of his court appearance earlier this week. He made a bit of a scene shouting out at the judge.'

'I remember seeing the TV pictures of him being escorted to the prison van,' Jonah nodded. 'Still shouting defiance as if he expected a thunderbolt to strike down the wicked infidels. I could imagine his victims being angry at his lack of remorse.'

'And there was speculation in the press that he may have been radicalised while he was a student at the university,' Sandra added. 'When that came out in the papers, back in January, there was a sudden spate of anti-Muslim graffiti appeared round the campus ... which brings me neatly on to our other main suspect.'

She turned and pointed to a photograph pinned to a board in the centre of the room.

'Mark Lansdale, age thirty-seven, lives in Old Swan. His wife, Kimberley, and daughter, Scarlet, were on their way home from a show when Shaladi's van careered on to the pavement and mowed them down. They both died of their injuries a day or two later. Lansdale was responsible for most, if not all, of the anti-Muslim messages that appeared on buildings around the university after the press reports linking it to Shaladi. His case was fast-tracked through the magistrates court and he agreed to be bound over[10], so the prosecution dropped the charges. I think they were trying to avoid the case getting into the media and influencing the Shaladi trial.'

'So you're suggesting that the publicity around the sentencing of Shaladi prompted him to go out looking for revenge on Muslim students?' Bernie asked.

''It's a bit of a leap from graffiti to a well-planned acid attack like this one,' Jonah observed. 'He couldn't have done it on the spur of the moment, the way you seem to be making out. Sulphuric acid isn't something you can just pick up in your local supermarket.'

'But Lansdale is a motorbike mechanic,' Charlotte Simpson chipped in triumphantly, coming up behind them. 'So, he'd have access to battery acid, wouldn't he? *And* using a motorbike to get away from the scene would be the obvious thing for him, wouldn't it?'

She turned to Sandra. 'I came to let you know that a plastic sprayer has been found, hidden in among the bushes in that little park place in the middle of Abercromby Square. It contains a small amount of some colourless liquid. I've had it sent off to the lab.'

'Good,' Sandra nodded her approval. 'If only they can come back with confirmation that the liquid is the same stuff that was sprayed on the girls, and a few fingerprints off the outside of the sprayer, we'll be close to catching our attacker.'

'He's been pretty meticulous so far,' Jonah observed drily. 'I'll be surprised if he's left any fingerprints. I don't really buy this Mark Lansdale theory either. In my experience, spraying graffiti around in anger emanates from a different sort of personality from this sort of carefully

---

[10] Under certain circumstances, a magistrate has the power to issue an order "binding over" a person to be of good behaviour. This is sometimes used as an alternative to prosecution. Failure to comply with the order is a contempt of court.

choreographed operation. Who else have you got?'

'Apart from Darren Galgate, the owner of the motorbike?' Sandra asked, playing for time. 'Well, of course, we're checking out everyone who's come on our radar as a right-wing extremist. There are a few of them, but none with a history of violence, as far as we can see – more just verbal abuse and online trolling.'

'And?' Jonah asked quietly, sensing that there was more. 'Anyone else?'

'There's PCSO Shelley Conway,' Sandra answered reluctantly. 'You may remember that a police officer was seriously injured in Shaladi's attack. He was just on a routine patrol, keeping an eye on late night punters at the bars and nightclubs. He wasn't in time to stop it, but he did manage to push a couple of youngsters out of the way of the van. Shelley is his wife. She's currently suspended from duty after using some very unprofessional language towards some Muslim students.'

'Is there any evidence that Shaladi really *was* radicalised while he was at the university?' Bernie asked, the reference to students reminding her that she had meant to ask this question earlier.

'No,' Sandra said promptly. 'None at all. It was all just press speculation based on nothing more than the fact that he was studying there. We tried to dampen it all down, but you know what journalists are like.'

'And if it *isn't* a backlash following the Shaladi incident?' Jonah asked.

'Well, obviously it *could* be a personal attack on one or more of the women,' Sandra acknowledged. 'Salma Rahman seems to have been the focus of the attack, so it could be that it was aimed specifically at her, and the others were just collateral damage so to speak. It's going to be some time before she's fit to be interviewed, but I've arranged to speak to her parents this evening. Maybe they'll be able to suggest someone who might have a grievance against her – an ex-boyfriend, for example.'

'Lucy tells me all the victims were members of a feminist group,' Bernie said thoughtfully. 'Could that have been why they were targeted?'

'Conservative Muslims objecting to them demanding equal rights, you mean?' asked Charlotte.

'Not necessarily Muslims,' Bernie replied carefully, wanting to avoid cultural stereotyping. 'It could just be men, who felt threatened by a group of strong women. There are plenty of them out there – as prominent women soon find out if they venture on social media!'

'We'd better try to find out if they've had any opposition to whatever it is they do,' Sandra agreed, 'and you're right about social media – we ought to have a look at their accounts and see if there have been any threats made on those. It could be that the attacker threatened them, but they didn't take it seriously.'

'Or he may be so pleased with himself that he'll post messages to them now in order to gloat,' Jonah suggested. 'He probably thinks he's got away with it, having successfully fled the scene.'

'I should have thought about that before,' Sandra said, reaching for the telephone that lay on her desk. 'I'll get someone to monitor all their Twitter and Facebook accounts – and any other sorts of social media that youngsters use these days. I must be getting old – I can't keep up with all the different things my girls are into. Personally I can't tell my Instagram from my Pinterest!'

Bernie looked at her watch. 'It's time we were getting back,' she told Jonah, while Sandra gave instructions to one of her colleagues. 'I'd like to be there when Lucy gets back. She may be upset after seeing her friends in the burns unit.'

'Peter's with her,' Jonah pointed out complacently. 'He'll look after her.'

'I know, but I'd still rather be there.' Bernie lowered her voice and bent down close to Jonah's ear. 'And you've had a long day already and are due for your physio.'

'OK,' Jonah sighed, realising that Bernie was not to be

swayed. 'You win.'

'That's that sorted.' Sandra finished her call and turned towards Jonah again. 'I don't think there's anything more to tell you at the moment. We've got people checking out all the known far-right activists across the whole of Merseyside, which may turn something up. Other than that, it's a matter of seeing what comes out of the search of the area where the bike was dumped and waiting for responses to the appeal for witnesses. I've got appointments with all the victims' parents later today. Did you want to be in on them?'

'No,' Bernie said quickly, before Jonah could respond. 'We've got other things on.'

'I'm afraid we have to go now,' Jonah replied. 'But I'd be interested to hear what you learn from the victims' families. Can we come over again tomorrow morning?'

'Oh no you don't!' Bernie intervened. 'It's Lucy's birthday tomorrow, remember? That's the only reason we're up here at all. You've given Sandra the benefit of your advice and now it's time we allowed her to get on with the investigation without any more distractions from retired cops who don't know how to keep their noses out of other people's business!'

'Of course you mustn't disappoint Lucy,' Sandra agreed, imagining her own daughters' reaction if she had cavalierly ignored their birthdays in favour of work. They had always been the only days in the year when nothing was allowed to prevent her being at home with them. 'It's been really useful talking things over with you – I've got it a lot clearer in my mind now,' she added, not wanting Jonah to think that she did not welcome his intervention.

She turned to Bernie. 'I may need to speak to Lucy and her housemates. According to the files, they've had one or two incidents at their home – anonymous notes and that sort of thing.'

'Such as a lit firework through the letterbox?' Bernie asked. 'Yes. They told me about that.'

'I wasn't involved personally,' Sandra told her, 'but it looks as if there was a thorough investigation of that incident. The trouble is there were no witnesses, so all we could do was to increase the frequency of patrols in that area to prevent it happening again.'

'It's alright,' Bernie assured her. 'You don't have to justify yourself to me. We know how difficult it is to get to the bottom of that sort of thing.'

'I'll bet the local officers have got a pretty good idea who was responsible, though,' Jonah added. 'It'd be well worth having a word with them. Just because there isn't the evidence for a prosecution, it doesn't mean they don't know who to watch.'

'You're right again,' Sandra smiled. 'I'll have a word with them. There's probably quite a lot they could tell me that they wouldn't put down in writing in the files.'

Liverpool university original "redbrick" building.

5. NEAREST AND DEAREST

Dominic was already at home when they arrived back at the house that he shared with Lucy, Ibrahim and Mariam. He held open the gate to allow Jonah's wheelchair in from the narrow lane that ran down behind the back yards of the Victorian terrace. The steps at the front were too steep, even for his sophisticated hi-tech chair, but there was a ramp at the back giving access to the kitchen door.

'Is there any news of Mariam?' Dominic asked anxiously.

'Lucy and Peter'll be able to tell you when they get back from seeing her,' Bernie told him. 'They should be here any moment.'

'So where have you two been?' Dominic asked, bolting the gate and hurrying past them to open the back door of the house. 'I thought you'd have wanted to-'

'Jonah here has been giving DCI Latham the benefit of his forty-odd years in the police service,' Bernie told him with a wry smile. 'Or, to put it another way, we've been gate-crashing her investigation.'

'And is there any news?' Dominic asked eagerly. 'Do they know who did it?'

'They are following up a number of leads,' Bernie said, using the well-worn phrase familiar from many police press conferences, 'or, to put it more succinctly – no.'

'They've found the motorbike,' Jonah added, gliding past Dominic, through the kitchen and on into the hall, 'and-'

'Yes, I heard that on the news at lunch time.' Dominic closed the door and followed Jonah and Bernie into the lounge.

'And the spray bottle that contained the acid,' Jonah

continued. 'They're being checked for fingerprints and DNA. That could lead them to the attacker.'

'But unlike in TV dramas, it all takes time,' Bernie added. 'It could well be a few days before the results come back, and even then, they're usually not nearly as clear-cut as you're led to believe.'

'Apart from anything else,' Jonah backed her up, 'you've got to remember that, unless you've committed a crime in the past, the police won't have your fingerprints or DNA on file, so mostly that evidence is only any use after we've found the perpetrator some other way.'

'Are you saying you don't think they'll catch him?' Dominic asked, sounding rather despondent.

'No, not at all,' Jonah hastened to reassure him. 'Just don't expect instant results, that's-'

He broke off at the sound of the front door opening. Peter and Lucy were back. Dominic immediately raced out into the hall to meet them.

'Did you see Mariam?' he demanded. 'How is she?'

'Give them a chance to come in and sit down first,' Bernie admonished him gently, coming up behind him. 'Go back in the lounge while I make us all a brew.'

She disappeared into the kitchen in search of kettle and teapot. Dominic smiled apologetically towards Peter, who shrugged his shoulders and grinned sympathetically.

'She's doing very well, considering what happened,' he said, following his wife's instructions and settling down on the sofa.

Lucy, unusually silent, sat down next to him. Dominic chose a chair at the other side of the room from which he could look them both in the eye.

'Her mum and dad got there just as we were leaving,' Peter continued, and they let us sit in while they talked to the doctor. 'He said that the burns aren't as deep as they thought at first. They can't be sure yet, but she may get away without needing any skin grafts.'

'And how long is she going to be in hospital?' Dominic

asked. 'Will she be able to continue her course? She's got exams coming up in a few weeks.'

'How long is a piece of string?' Peter answered patiently. 'They really don't know yet. The main thing is that none of the acid went on her face, so her eyes aren't affected at all. She's lost some hair, and they don't think it'll all grow back, and one ear is affected, but only on the outside, her hearing is still fine. And she's awake and able to talk to us – just in quite a lot of pain and, of course, very shocked.'

Bernie returned with mugs of tea on a tray. Dominic leapt up to hold the door for her.

'Would I be getting in the way if I go over to see her at evening visiting?' he asked Peter anxiously. 'I wouldn't want her mum and dad to think I was intruding.'

'I'm sure Ibrahim will want to go,' Bernie answered quickly. 'So you might as well both go together.'

'Yes,' Peter agreed. 'I expect he'll be glad of your company on the bus.'

'You can ask him now,' Bernie added, standing up and waving through the window. The others turned their heads to see Ibrahim coming in at the gate. Soon he was sitting with them in the lounge and Bernie was coming back from the kitchen with another mug of tea, which she set down in front of him. He looked expectantly towards Lucy and Peter.

'I was just telling Dominic that the doctors are very optimistic about Mariam,' Peter told him. 'Depending on how the healing process goes, she may be able to go home next week or the week after.'

'Will she be left with scars?' Ibrahim asked anxiously.

'Yes, I'm afraid she probably will,' Peter answered, trying to be honest (and knowing that Lucy would put Ibrahim right in any case if he attempted to conceal the worst from him) but not alarmist. 'The good thing is that none of the acid went on her face, so she ought to be able to keep them hidden if she wants to.'

'And what about Salma?' Ibrahim asked, after pausing to

digest this information. 'Did you see her too?'

'No.' Peter's voice changed slightly. He hesitated, as if wondering whether to say any more. 'Her parents were there – and her brother.'

'They wouldn't let us see her!' Lucy burst out, suddenly breaking her long silence. 'They said she was too drowsy with all the morphine to recognise visitors, but it was really because they didn't want us to see how she was.'

'What do you mean?' asked Dominic. 'Why would-?' He broke off, seeing that Ibrahim was signalling to him to be quiet. Both young men leaned forward, listening intently as Lucy continued.

'It's awful! She turned round to see what was happening, so the acid went all over her face. The doctors said they're hoping they may be able to save part of the sight in her left eye, but she's definitely lost the right one … and her lips are all burnt away, so they're feeding her through a tube … and … and …'

Peter put his arm round her shoulder and hugged her tight to him as the tears began to flow. Dominic sat with his mouth open in stunned silence. Ibrahim got up and started across the room towards Lucy; then he stopped and returned to his seat. Bernie took out a handkerchief from her pocket and put it into her daughter's hand. Then, without speaking, she gathered up the mugs and headed out to the kitchen to re-fill them with more tea.

Lucy's sobs gradually subsided. She raised her head from Peter's shoulder and opened the handkerchief. She wiped her eyes and blew her nose.

'I'm sorry,' she apologised, looking round at the others and trying to smile. 'I didn't mean to … It's just that it's all so awful! Why would anyone want to do that to Salma and Mariam – or to *anyone*? It just doesn't make sense!'

Still nobody spoke. Bernie returned with more tea. As she handed it round, everyone tried to make themselves very busy with their mug to avoid catching one another's eye. A car went past outside. A seagull called on the roof.

Someone's stomach rumbled.

'I know it's not the same,' Jonah ventured at last, breaking the long silence, 'but when I was shot, asking why never seemed that important really.'

All eyes turned to look at him.

'What *was* important?' Lucy asked in a tiny voice.

'That depends what you mean,' Jonah replied. 'If you mean, what made the most impact on me – what was the worst thing about it – then that was feeling that I was useless and a burden to the people I cared about.'

'But what was the most important for your recovery?' enquired Dominic. 'How did you get back on your fee- … I mean, what can we do to help Mariam and Salma?'

'Discovering that I wasn't completely useless after all – realising that there were people who still valued me, even if I couldn't do most of the things that I used to think were important – learning that having to rely on other people to do things for me didn't make me a failure. It took a long time, but I was fortunate enough to have a few friends who were willing to stick with me for the long haul.'

Lucy got to her feet and crossed the room to where Jonah sat. She went round behind his wheelchair and put her arms round his shoulders. He felt the wetness of her face against his cheek as she hugged him tight, murmuring, 'Oh Jonah!' softly in his ear.

***

Meanwhile, Sandra and Charlotte were at the Armstrong home in St Helens (an industrial – or post-industrial – town about ten miles to the East of Liverpool) attempting to interview Emily's parents. Steven and Fiona Armstrong were sitting together on their living room sofa, with Sandra and Charlotte in two armchairs, facing them across a low table strewn with women's magazines. Emily herself had been banished to her bedroom to rest, and Mrs Armstrong was insistent that she could not be disturbed for something as trivial as a police interview.

'She's already told you that she didn't see whoever it was,' she repeated dogmatically. 'I don't understand why you want to talk to her yet again.'

'We just wanted to ask her if she knows of anyone who might bear her or her friends a grudge,' Sandra explained patiently, determined not to allow herself to be riled by the implication that her request to supplement her single five-minute interview in the hospital by asking a few more questions constituted police harassment. 'As I said before, although we think that this may be racially-motivated, we can't be sure that it wasn't directed at one or more of the women personally.'

'Don't give me that!' Steven Armstrong broke in angrily. 'It was all because she was wearing that ridiculous thing over her face, and you know it! You just can't say so because it wouldn't be politically correct.'

'We've been worried about her ever since she converted,' his wife added, putting her hand on his thigh in a restraining gesture. 'We've never tried to tell her what to think, but this Islam stuff is something else. She's taking it all so seriously.'

'And making a right exhibition of herself!' Steven added. 'It was only a matter of time before something like this happened. Nothing justifies throwing acid in someone's face, but I'm not the least surprised about it. I feel nervous myself seeing someone in one of them – them – what-ya-call-em – you know! Where you can only see their eyes peering out at you.'

'I think you mean a niqab,' Charlotte prompted, having done some extensive online research overnight into the different forms of Muslim headcovering.

'Yeah. That's right. It stands to reason – if someone's keeping their face hidden, you start wondering if they're up to no good, don't you?'

'How long has your daughter been a Muslim?' Sandra asked.

'It must be about a year now,' Fiona answered.

'No – more than that,' her husband disagreed. 'It was February when she dumped Jack, remember? He'd got it all planned out that he was going to propose to her on Valentine's Day, and then when he asked her out, she told him she wasn't seeing him anymore because these new so-called friends of hers didn't like him.'

'She didn't start wearing them weird clothes until quite a bit later than that,' Fiona argued. 'So I don't know when you'd say she actually *converted*.' She looked towards Sandra. 'We hoped – we still hope – that it was just a phase she was going through – teenage rebellion and all that.'

'Maybe now she'll come to her senses and realise it's not just a dressing-up game,' Steven agreed. 'I *told* her she was drawing attention to herself and making herself a target, but would she listen?'

'Jack was her boyfriend, I gather,' Sandra said in the hope of diverting the conversation on to more fruitful ground. 'How long had they been going out together?'

'Three years, would it be?' Fiona answered, looking towards her husband for confirmation. 'From when they were both at school, at any rate. They both chose Liverpool Uni, so they'd be together – which is another reason why it was so hard on Jack when she told him it was over.'

'So he lives locally too?' Sandra asked.

'Just round the corner,' Fiona confirmed. 'He's a nice lad. His mum and I used to work together. They've known each other since they were tiny tots.'

'How did he take it when she converted?' Charlotte asked.

'How d'you think he took it?' Steven growled. 'How would any man take being given the push because his girl's taken up with some foreign terrorist religion?'

'Was he angry?' Charlotte persisted. 'Did he make any threats at all – in the heat of the moment, perhaps, without meaning to carry them out?'

'Course he was angry!' Steven retorted, 'but it's no good you trying to pin this on him –oh no! He'd never hurt a hair on Emily's head – no way!'

'He wasn't angry with *her*,' Fiona added. 'Or at least, only for a bit. He blamed those other girls – the ones that brainwashed her into becoming a Muslim.'

'Any of them in particular?' Charlotte asked eagerly. 'Did he mention any names?'

'He may have done,' Steven answered in a sulky voice, 'but you can't expect me to remember any of them. Why do they all have to have such stupid names? They all go round claiming to be British, but they don't do a thing to integrate – swanning around with their foreign names and foreign religion, putting all sorts of ideas into the heads of our kids!'

'So he didn't mention Salma Rahman, for example?' Sandra queried, 'or Mariam Ali?'

'I told you – I don't know, do I?' Steven snarled. 'Why d'you keep asking the same questions over and over, instead of getting out there and catching whoever did this to our Emily?'

'That is exactly what we are trying to do, Mr Armstrong,' Sandra told him coldly. 'We'll go now.' She got up, walked across the room and handed a business card to Fiona. 'If you think of anything that could help our enquiries, please ring that number.'

***

Their next interview – with Salma's parents – would have been much easier, had it not been for the presence of her brother, Waseem. He had come down from Preston, where he was studying at the University of Central Lancashire, to join them at the burns unit. He seemed intent on finding fault with everything, and questioning everyone's motives and goodwill. Sandra, telling herself that this aggressive attitude was his way of coping with his distress over his sister's injuries, tried to remain calm and to respond to his sneers and accusations in a conciliatory way.

'I'm sorry you feel like that,' she said for the fourth or fifth time. 'I can only reiterate that we are doing our best to find the person who did this, and that we have a large team of officers working on this case. Now, if we could just get back to where we were … Mrs Rahman, you were telling me that Salma is interested in sport?'

'That's right,' Fahima Rahman nodded. 'She plays hockey and tennis and she belongs to the university Hill-Walking Club.'

'So, as far as you could tell, she was well-integrated into university life and had plenty of friends?' Sandra asked. 'In her sports teams and the walking club and so on?'

'Yes,' Fahima's husband agreed. 'We gather she's very popular. She was made captain of her hockey team last term.'

'Here's a picture of her with them,' Fahima said, holding out her phone towards Sandra, who looked down at the screen politely and saw a group of young women in short-sleeved jerseys and sports skirts, each holding a hockey stick. 'That's Salma – there in the middle. We're very proud of her.'

Sandra looked up at Mr and Mrs Rahman. Fahima was dressed in a traditional shalwar kamiz with a headscarf fastened tight under her chin. Her husband was attired in a dark grey business suit and white shirt.

'You don't mind your daughter wearing this sort of … revealing sports kit?' she asked tentatively. 'It's not against your religion or anything?'

'Oh no!' Munir smiled at her indulgently. 'That's quite alright. It's all a matter of dressing for the occasion, isn't it? And it's an all-girls team, after all. It would be a different matter if she expected to wear her hockey kit when she's helping in the kitchen!' He laughed and then fell abruptly silent, remembering that his daughter was unlikely to be participating in either of those activities again for a very long time, if at all.

'But we're wasting your time with all these reminiscences,' he said soberly. 'Is there anything else we can tell you that might help you to find out who did this to her?'

'You don't really think they're bothered about finding them, do you?' Waseem mocked. 'You don't get it, do you? You're so busy trying to fit in and not offend anyone that you don't realise that none of them want us here, and they couldn't care less about what happened to Salma.'

'Be quiet, Waseem!' his father said sternly, glaring at him at him over the top of his spectacles. He turned back to address Sandra. 'You must forgive my son. He is very upset about his sister and it makes him say things he doesn't mean.'

'It's alright, we're used to it,' Sandra assured him, unconsciously echoing Ibrahim's words to Lucy about being on the receiving end of abuse. 'We understand how stressful it is for you all. Just one more question, and then we'll let you go. Did Salma have a boyfriend at all?'

'Oh no – nothing like that,' her father replied at once.

'She isn't like that,' her mother added. 'She's studying to become an Occupational Therapist. She wants to get her career settled first before thinking about marriage. We agreed tha-'

'The inspector wasn't talking about marriage,' Waseem cut in, sneeringly. 'She was asking about all those men Salma goes round with at uni. They're not interested in marriage! They're only thinking about one thi-'

'Quiet, Waseem!' his father exploded. 'I will not have you talking about your sister like that!' He turned back to Sandra. 'Salma is very popular with her classmates, including the boys, but I'm sure there's nothing of the sort of thing you're talking about going on. She is very sensible and modest and understands that there are boundaries that must not be crossed.'

***

Her encounter with Mariam's parents came as something of a relief to Sandra after the difficult interview with the Rahmans. Stroke Physician, Abdul Ali and his wife,

Tahmina, both remained calm and answered her questions without criticisms or complaints. Sandra learned that they had met and married in Manchester, while Abdul was a doctor in training and Tahmina was working as a nurse. They had settled in Blackburn in order to be near her ageing parents, who had come there from the Punjab in the nineteen sixties. Both of the Rahmans were British citizens, Abdul having arrived from Pakistan as a young child, while Tahmina was a native of East Lancashire.

'And you have just the two children?' Sandra asked. 'Mariam and Ibrahim?'

'That's right,' Tahmina answered. 'My mother's always saying we ought to have had more, but ...,' she shrugged. 'Well, you can understand her attitude when you think that she was one of ten and only three survived. It's different here.'

'Mariam and Ibrahim live in a shared house with two other young people,' Sandra commented. 'Do they all get on together, do you know?'

'Yes.' Abdul and Tahmina said together.

'We were very pleased when they came up with the idea,' Abdul added. 'I didn't dare say anything to her, but I have to admit I was a bit nervous of Mariam being all on her own in a strange town. I suppose all fathers tend to feel like that about their daughters.'

'Ibrahim met Lucy and her family when he was on holiday with some of his mates, a few years ago,' Tahmina told her. 'And then she came to visit us the summer before the girls applied to university. Lucy put down Liverpool because that's where her mum comes from and I think that influenced Mariam.'

'More than her brother having gone there,' Abdul agreed with a laugh. 'We tried not to make our hints that it might be convenient for her to share his flat too obvious, but ...'

'Anyway,' Tahmina resumed, 'the arrangement they came up with seems to be working very well. Lucy's cousin Dominic seems a nice lad and it's good for Mariam to have someone else who's doing her course to bounce ideas off. They all seem very happy together.'

'And do you know anything about this group of women that Mariam belongs to?' Sandra asked. 'The *Sisterhood of Islam*?'

'Just the usual thing,' Abdul said dismissively, 'just few students getting together, all very earnest, trying to set the world to rights.'

'We met some of them before Christmas when we went over for Mariam's birthday,' Tahmina added. 'I must say I found their leader a bit intimidating – very intense and didn't seem to have much of a sense of humour.'

'I think she's probably aiming to be the first Muslim woman Prime Minister,' Abdul said with a smile. 'And she might well make it too. She's got the drive and the tenacity, sure enough.'

'Are you aware of the group having attracted any adverse comments – from other students, for example?' Sandra asked, trying to sound casual, but watching her interviewees intently for any reaction to this suggestion.

'Not that we know of,' Abdul shrugged.

'To be honest,' his wife added, 'I don't think anyone really knew about them or took them very seriously.'

***

'Mariam's being tremendously brave,' Dominic said earnestly as he and Ibrahim boarded the bus for the journey home. 'I don't know how she manages to stay so positive after …'

'I don't know how she'll be when she finds out about Salma,' Ibrahim mumbled gloomily. 'It won't be long before we'll have to stop putting her off with, "the doctor's haven't finished assessing her yet" and all that stuff. What happens if she asks to see her?'

Like Lucy, Ibrahim had been unnerved by the news of Salma's injuries and dismal prognosis. The medical team were still only allowing close family to enter the room where she was being treated, giving his imagination full rein to create horrible pictures in his mind of features eaten away by acid and eyes bleached white and sightless.

They sat in silence.

'I just wish she'd keep a lower profile,' Ibrahim muttered suddenly. 'Why can't she just concentrate on getting her degree, instead of all this *Sisterhood of Islam* stuff? You can be a good Muslim without drawing attention to yourself the way those girls do.'

'Mariam doesn't do anything to make herself stand out,' Dominic protested. 'She doesn't even dress like a Muslim. The only reason she was targeted was that she was with her friends – and why shouldn't she be? I can't think of anyone less provocative than Mariam,' he added loyally. 'You can't blame her for what happened.'

'I'm not blaming her!' Ibrahim retorted indignantly. 'I just think ... I ... I don't know what I think, if I'm honest ... I just hope she'll be more careful after this.'

Houses in the Kensington area of Liverpool

6. BIRTHDAY

Lucy's birthday celebrations were disrupted by her determination not to miss the last few lectures of her course before the examination period began.

'I'm sorry,' she apologised, looking round at Bernie, Peter and Jonah as she let them in at the back door of the house shortly after breakfast, as agreed the previous day. 'Like I said before, when you announced you were planning to come up I arranged with Mariam that she'd go and take notes for me, but now ... well, I'd better make notes for *her* to have. She said last night that she wanted to take the exams, if the doctors will let her, so as not to get behind.'

'Aren't there any re-sits she could take in the Autumn?' Dominic asked.

'I suppose so,' Lucy admitted, 'but she says she'd rather do them with everyone else.'

'If she's up to it, I'd agree that's a better idea,' Bernie backed her up. 'For one thing, it's better at this stage not to dwell too much on how long her recovery may take in the end, and the other thing is that, if she can get the exams out of the way now, she'll be able to relax over the summer ready for next term.'

'Now, where do you want these presents?' Peter asked, holding up a gaily-coloured paper carrier bag. 'Are you going to open them now or wait until later?'

'Just bung them in the front room,' Lucy answered. 'I won't open them until Ibrahim and Dom get back from work. They'll have to go soon and it's more fun when we're all together. Or – could we take them over to Whiston and open them with Mariam?'

'I don't know, love,' Bernie answered, bending down to

retrieve more parcels from the storage space at the back of Jonah's chair. 'It might be a bit overwhelming for her if we all descend on her at once. Maybe it would be better just to give Ibrahim some cake to take over to her this evening.'

'I'll get my present and put it with the others,' Dominic said, disappearing upstairs.

'It looks like a big pile,' Lucy observed a few minutes later, as they all stood staring down at the collection of packages and envelopes lying on the floor in front of the television set in the lounge. 'Where did they all come from?'

'You're a popular young lady,' Peter began, but he broke off at a snort from Lucy, who punched him playfully in the chest.

'Less of the *Lady*!' she exclaimed. 'I'm never going to be a lady, so there!'

'Good for you, love,' Bernie agreed. 'No Fazakerley has ever been a lady, and I don't think we ought to start now.'

'Lucy isn't a Fazakerley,' Dom pointed out, 'and my mum *is*, and I think she'd like people to think she was a lady.'

'Your mum is only a Fazakerley by marriage,' Bernie argued. 'Lucy has it in her blood, whatever her name is. Think of Aunty Dot, for example.'

'When are we going to see her?' Jonah asked suddenly. He was very fond of Bernie's elderly aunt, whom he regarded as an accomplice in the fight against the forces that conspired to restrict the activities of people with disabilities. 'We can't go home without paying her a visit.'

'Don't worry,' Bernie assured him. 'I've got it all arranged. We're all going over there on Sunday afternoon – after lunch with Ruth and Joey.'

While this interchange was going on, Lucy was examining the labels on her presents, nodding and smiling as she remembered friends and family whom she had left behind in Oxford.

'This one says "With love from Jane"! Who on earth's that?' she exclaimed suddenly, picking up a small rectangular parcel, neatly wrapped in pink paper, and looking round with a puzzled expression. 'I don't know anyone called Jane.'

'It's my sister Jane,' Peter explained. 'You know – from Stockport. She didn't know your address, so she sent it to us to bring. She seems to want to develop a relationship with us all. I can't think why.'

'I thought you didn't have any family,' Ibrahim said, in a puzzled voice. 'Bernie said you were brought up in a children's home.'

'Her mother – or I suppose I should say, our mother – tracked me down,' Peter explained. 'She's dead now, but Jane persists in writing letters and inviting me to visit. She's only my half-sister, but she doesn't have any other family, so I suppose ...,' he tailed off into a shrug. 'Anyway, that's who it is.'

'How exciting!' Ibrahim commented. 'It must have been quite a surprise suddenly discovering you had a mother and sister after all those years of thinking you were all on your own – like those reunions you sometimes see on the telly.'

'Yes,' Peter agreed flatly. 'It did come as a bit of a shock.'

Ibrahim stared at Peter in puzzlement. He could not quite make out what was going on here and felt that he had not been told the whole story. He opened his mouth to ask another question, then thought better of it and looked down at his watch instead.

'I'm afraid I'm going to have to run,' he announced, heading for the door. 'See you later!'

'Don't be late!' Lucy called after him. 'We can't start my birthday tea without you.'

Dominic reached for a bulging briefcase that lay on the floor beside the sofa.

'I'd better be making tracks too,' he told them. 'I mustn't be late for registration.'

'And I'd better go as well,' Lucy added, scrambling to her feet. 'I've got lectures till twelve. Then, after that, shall we go for lunch somewhere?'

'Let's all meet at the Catholic Cathedral café at quarter

past,' suggested Bernie.

'OK, Mam. See you later!'

Lucy swung her rucksack onto her back and headed out of the front door. Bernie and Peter stood looking at one another for a few moments, while Jonah pressed buttons on a keypad on the arm of his chair.

'Hi Jonah!' Sandra's voice came through on the loudspeaker. 'How's the birthday girl?'

'Gone off and left us,' Jonah replied cheerily. 'So I was wondering if you'd like any help with tracking down your acid wielding terrorist.'

'I wouldn't mind having you around this morning,' Sandra confessed. 'I've got some of those Muslim girls coming in – the three who weren't hurt, so they had time to see the biker riding away after the incident. I want to see if they remember any more about that and I'd also like to find out more about that society they all belong to, but I'm not sure how to go about asking them about it. That little Indian one in the black glasses is rather aggressive, and I'm afraid I'll say the wrong thing. Maybe you've got more experience, coming from Oxford?'

'And people don't tend to feel threatened by a cop in a wheelchair,' Jonah suggested, voicing, as Sandra had not dared to do, her real reason for wanting him at the interview with Tahira. 'That's great. We'll be over right away.'

'We will, will we?' asked Bernie, pretending to be annoyed.

'Do you have any better ideas for whiling away the time until Lucy's free?' Jonah smiled back complacently.

***

'Come in!' Sandra called out, looking up from the printout that she had been studying. It contained an analysis of the liquid in the garden sprayer that had been found in Abercromby Square. The door of her private office opened and Bernie entered. Sandra smiled. 'It's good to see you both again – and Peter! They've dragged you along too this time, I see.'

Bernie nodded towards Sandra while holding the door wide to allow Jonah's wheelchair to pass through. Peter, bringing up the rear, advanced towards Sandra with his hand held out. Bernie closed the door behind them before hurrying across the room and moving a chair to one side to make room in front of Sandra's desk for Jonah's wheelchair. She took off her jacket and hung it on the back of the chair before sitting down in it.

'Hello, Sandra.' Peter shook hands across the desk, before taking a seat on the other side of Jonah. 'How are you? And how're the girls?'

Sandra pulled a face at the mention of her two daughters.

'Still fed up with having to share a room – and still blaming me for not staying with Gary! He's had to sell the big house – my fault too, of course! – and he and Mel and the baby have moved into a tiny flat in Bootle. So the girls can't go and stay with them anymore and it's cut off their last links with their friends in Southport. All a bit of a mess really. I just hope things will improve now we've got a place of our own. I finally managed to get a mortgage on a house in Dovecot – not as big as we'd like, but at least they'll have their own rooms. We're moving in tomorrow – I hope!'

'It sounds as if you could've done without a high-profile case like this one at the moment,' Peter observed sympathetically. 'Unfortunately journalists never seem to need time off to spend with their families!'

'So the bottle did have sulphuric acid in it,' Jonah commented, craning his neck to read the report, which was still lying on Sandra's desk. 'Any fingerprints?'

'No.' Sandra shook her head. 'This is just the analysis of the liquid inside. I rang the fingerprint people this morning for an update and they said the initial visual check hadn't found anything. There are some smears of an oily substance round the screw top, which suggests that the person who tightened it up was wearing oily gloves. They're trying to get a sample to find out what it is, but I doubt it'll tell us anything. I bet every biker's gloves have oil on them.'

'Anything else new?' Jonah asked, impatient to move on from this unproductive line of enquiry.

'I talked with the families of the victims. None of them had any suggestions as to who could have done it or any motives other than the obvious one. So not a lot of progress there. That's why I've asked those other three students to come in this morning. I want to find out more about this society that they belong to, in case that's what made them stand out as potential targets.'

'It sounds harmless enough to me,' Peter told her. 'From what Lucy tells me, it's just a group of friends getting together.'

'That's right,' Bernie agreed. 'As far as I can see, they're just like any other student group – hanging about together, talking and drinking. The only difference is that it's coffee rather than lager!'

'You might like to see this,' Peter added, handing Sandra a small piece of thin card. 'Mariam left it lying around in their house. It lists the aims of the *Feminist Sisterhood of Islam*.'

Sandra looked down at the card. It was covered with strange symbols printed in white on a blue background.

'That side's in Arabic,' Bernie told her. 'I think it's a quotation from the Qur'an.'

Sandra turned it over and read out, 'Our Aims. Together we will promote a feminist interpretation of Islam through Qur'anic study, salah and zakah.' She looked round at them all. 'What does that mean, exactly?'

'Salah means the prayers that Muslims say five times a day,' Jonah told her, 'and zakah means giving to charity.'

'You seem to know a lot about Islam,' Sandra commented.

'Well, we're doing our best to learn,' Peter smiled, 'but we don't know much yet.'

'It sounds just like the Christian Union to me,' Bernie added. 'Bible study, prayer meetings and helping the needy. They're just a group of earnest young women wanting to live out their faith. It's no more sinister than the MethSoc or SCM!'

'MethSoc? SCM?' Sandra queried.

'Methodist Society and Student Christian Movement,' Bernie explained. 'Most universities have them – or they used to. There'll be a Catholic Society too. They're all harmless enough – just like-minded students getting together.'

'Except that people don't always like the idea of like-minded Muslims getting together,' Sandra murmured thoughtfully. 'I wonder how many people knew about this little group.'

There was a knock at the door and Charlotte's head appeared round it.

'Tahira Siddiqui, Olivia Akram and Hibaaq Galaal are here,' she announced, speaking slowly and carefully and consulting a piece of paper in her hand to make sure that she got the names correct. 'I've put them in Interview Room One and given them a cup of tea and a biscuit. Do you want to see them now?'

'Yes, but not in an interview room. They've already given their formal witness statements. This is just a friendly chat to get a better feeling for what life is like for the victims and their friends.'

'So, what do you want me to do with them?' Charlotte asked, coming further into the room.

'We'll all go down to the canteen and get some coffee – no! Hang about. Let's all go out for a coffee. There's a decent place just round the corner. It'll only take a couple of minutes to walk and it'll be much more comfortable than anywhere in this place. Can you go and get them and bring them down to reception, and we'll meet you there?'

'OK.' Charlotte looked down at the card that was lying on the desk in front of Sandra. 'The Feminist Sisterhood of Islam,' she read aloud. 'That sounds like a contradiction in terms if ever there was one!'

***

'My girls both like these double-choc chocolate chip cookies,' Sandra said, putting down a plate in the centre of the table. 'Go on – help yourselves!'

The three students hesitated, so Bernie reached out and took one of the biscuits. She dunked it in her coffee and then nibbled the softened end. Olivia stared at her for a moment and then took one herself. Soon there was only one cookie left on the plate.

'I'll save mine for later,' Jonah said, not wanting the embarrassment of being fed in public by Bernie or Peter. 'I'm more interested in hearing about this society of yours.' He looked towards Tahira. 'Lucy tells me you are one of the founding members.'

'That's right. It all started about two years ago,' Tahira told him. 'There were four or five of us in my year who got fed up with the way some of the male Muslim students were behaving – acting like they ruled the world and what we thought didn't count. And then we found this mosque in Stanley that lets men and women pray together – well, more or less together, in the same room anyway.'

'You mean most mosques don't?' asked Sandra. 'Why's that?'

'Some don't allow women in at all,' Tahira told her, 'but not so many as there used to be.'

'Things are changing,' Olivia added, 'but it's hard for some of the older people – especially those who grew up in countries where it was just normal for women to be confined to the home.'

'Which is why, in this country, younger Muslims are starting to set up their own mosques,' Tahira continued. 'The mosque in Stanley was started by young professional people – graduates – who wanted to get away from all the old divisions that their parents and grandparents had.'

'Between Shia and Sunni, you mean?' asked Jonah.

'And between Muslims from different backgrounds,' Olivia nodded. 'As far as we're concerned, it doesn't make any difference whether your family came from Bangladesh, like my mum's parents, or from Somalia, like Hibaaq's mum and dad. We're all part of the Umma, wherever we come from.'

'And getting back to the *Feminist Sisterhood*?' Jonah prompted.

'Like I said,' Tahira resumed, 'some of us started going to this mosque in Stanley. The Imam is from Leeds – not like in a lot of places where they bring in someone from abroad who knows a lot about the Qur'an and classical Arabic, but doesn't speak much English. He's very keen on the social aspect of our deen – making a positive contribution to the community, and –'

'Hang on a moment,' Jonah interrupted gently. 'Deen? What does that mean?'

'It's Arabic for "religion",' Olivia explained.

'Well, more precisely, it means actions that bring us closer to God,' Tahira added. 'It means our whole way of life as Muslims, not just what you might think of as religion – ritual prayers and that sort of thing. Anyway, after a bit we decided that we wanted to do more to promote the role of Muslim women in society. We wanted to counteract the stereotypes of submissive women who can't think for themselves being forced into early marriages. We wanted to show the world that Islam is really the first – maybe the only – religion to treat women equally with men.'

'But what about Saudi Arabia?' Charlotte blurted out without thinking. 'Women not being allowed to drive or to go outside the house without a male guardian?'

'What about Hillsborough[11]?' Tahira countered at once.

---

[11] In 1989, 96 Liverpool Football Club supporters died in a crush at the FA Cup semi-final at Hillsborough Stadium in Sheffield. After many years of campaigning by Liverpool fans, South Yorkshire Police were found to have contributed to the disaster through poor crowd control and to have attempted to evade responsibility and to shift the blame on to the fans. The trial of the officer in charge of policing the match, on a charge of gross negligence manslaughter, began on 15th January 2019.

'Would you like me to judge all police officers on the ones who spread lies about Liverpool fans and refused to accept responsibility for people getting crushed to death?'

'I don't quite see …,' Charlotte began, taken aback by this onslaught.

'What I'm saying is that Saudi Arabia isn't representative of Islam any more than Hillsborough is representative of the police,' Tahira continued. 'Most societies have a problem with patriarchy – and a lot of them use religion as a way of maintaining the status quo, but that doesn't mean that their arguments are legitimate.'

'It's understandable,' Hibaaq added in her low, melodious voice. 'If you remember that it's not so long ago that women necessarily spent most of their time and energy on child-bearing and child-rearing. It's only now that we have effective contraception – and less of a need to have large families in order to work the land – that women have been able to take on leadership roles. And naturally some of the men don't like it.'

'And has there been any opposition to this *Sisterhood* of yours?' Sandra asked. 'Do any of the men here feel threatened by it, for example?'

'Well, there was Emily's ex,' Olivia said cautiously. 'He gate-crashed the mosque when she made her Shahada for the first time, and shouted out all sorts of stuff about us brainwashing her.'

'Her sha-? I'm sorry, what was that you said?' Sandra looked round in some confusion, feeling that she was getting out of her depth with so many new words to learn.

'Her shahada. Ashadu an laa ilaha illa llah, wa ashadu anna muhammadun rasulu llah,' Tahira rattled off. 'It means, "I testify that there is no God but Allah, and Muhammad is his messenger." To become a Muslim, you have to believe that and declare it wholeheartedly. It's a very solemn occasion and that stupid boy spoiled it.'

'Two of the brothers managed to get him outside,' Olivia added, 'and they locked the door. He kept hammering on it and shouting, but eventually he got fed up and went away. Poor Emily was ever so upset.'

'When exactly was this?' asked Charlotte. 'Were the police called?'

'Almost exactly a year ago, I suppose,' answered Olivia. 'It was a couple of weeks before Ramadan started. Emily wanted to be "proper Muslim" in time to take part.'

'And no, we didn't call the police,' Tahira added coldly. 'We didn't want to make things any worse for Emily. We just stayed inside the mosque until he stopped shouting and went away.'

'Just to get this straight,' Sandra said, flicking through her notes,' this is Jack Hampton we're talking about? The boyfriend that Emily had from when she was at school?'

'That's right,' confirmed Olivia. The other women nodded in agreement.

'He was angry with her for converting to Islam?' Charlotte asked.

'And angry that she'd dumped him,' Tahira nodded. 'It hurt his pride that she'd found something more important in her life than him.'

'Angry enough to throw acid over her head?' suggested Charlotte.

'Perhaps,' Tahira shrugged. 'Some men find the idea of a woman thinking for herself very hard to accept.'

'I'm not so sure,' Olivia said quickly, darting an anxious look in Tahira's direction. 'I don't think he's really vicious like that. And – and it's a long time ago now.'

'You said it was the anniversary of her – her – shara- – her conversion to Islam,' Charlotte pointed out. 'That could have been the trigger.'

There was a long silence, while everyone thought about this.

'Actually, I think he was genuinely in love with her,' Hibaaq said at last. 'I don't think he would have done anything to hurt Emily herself, whatever he thought about the rest of us.'

'It was Salma who seems to have been the main target,' Charlotte persisted, reluctant to abandon the idea that that they might have identified the attacker. 'Could he have blamed her in particular for Emily's conversion?'

'I suppose he *could* have done,' Olivia said slowly. 'All three of them were members of the Hill-Walking club. I suppose Salma will have been the first Muslim he ever met.'

'And Emily had her face covered, didn't she?' Charlotte continued, delighted at the thought that she could have uncovered the perpetrator of the crime. 'So, he might not even have realised that she was the other girl in the group. Does he ride a motorbike at all, do you know?'

'I don't remember seeing him on one,' Olivia answered. Charlotte looked at the others. They shook their heads.

'OK. It looks as if we'd better look into Jack Hampton,' Sandra said in a voice that made it clear that she did not want any further discussion on this topic. 'Have you had any problems with anyone else? Nobody suggesting that any of your ideas are un-Islamic, for instance,' she added cautiously.

'They're not in the least un-Islamic,' Tahira protested immediately. 'As I said before, Islam is the first religion that recognised the equality of women!'

'I thought the Qur'an said that you needed two women to testify in a court of law to be equal to one man,' Charlotte said unguardedly. 'That's not exactly equal.'

'You have to look at it in context,' Tahira came back at once. Jonah got the impression that her answer was well rehearsed. 'You have to remember that this verse was addressed to a very patriarchal society, where women were very unlikely to be educated or to take part in the sort of legal transactions that this is about. You could say that it is actually *affirming* the status of women by saying that a woman's testimony is valid, when the norm was probably to discount it altogether. And when it says that another woman should be there in case she forgets, that's simply a recognition that women would be illiterate and therefore more likely not to remember all the details of some complicated documents. Asma Barlas argues powerfully that the Qur'an is *anti*-patriarchal. For example, it explicitly condemns the practice of killing girl babies, which was something that went on among the polytheists in the Arabian Peninsula at the time of the prophet (Salla Allahu alayhi wa sallam).'

'And who is this As – As …? Sandra struggled to remember the unfamiliar name. She wondered if this was another member of the group, whom they had forgotten mention.

'She's a great scholar,' Tahira told her enthusiastically. 'She comes from Pakistan, but she's a professor at a university in America. She's written a book that completely re-interprets the Qur'an from a female perspective. As soon as you realise how misogynistic society was *before* it was revealed to the prophet (Salla Allahu alayhi wa sallam) you can see how revolutionary it was and how empowering of women! That's where so many male scholars have gone wrong. They confuse sex with gender, and difference with inequality, because they forget that the Qur'an was originally addressing a society in which women were subservient to men. Ultimately, those patriarchal readings distort our ideas of God as well as promoting an out-dated model of society.'

'Not that everyone agrees with what she says,' Olivia observed quietly when Tahira paused for breath. 'Salma's brother, Waseem, for instance.'

'He needs to grow up,' Tahira pronounced dismissively. 'He's just a silly little boy who doesn't want his sister to have fun playing sports and mixing with whoever she likes. He thinks she ought to stay at home with her mum until they find a nice boy with good prospects to marry her off to. He doesn't know anything! Salma said he was always skiving off his Arabic classes and it really shows. Salma's way ahead of him, even though she only started learning after she came to uni, because their parents didn't think it was important for a girl to learn to read the Qur'an for herself.'

'We've met him,' Sandra told them. 'He didn't seem very friendly towards your *Sisterhood*.'

'*He* didn't spray Salma with acid, if that's what you're suggesting,' Tahira responded quickly. 'He's stupid and ignorant, but he isn't vicious like that.'

'No,' agreed Olivia. 'I'm sure he wouldn't do anything like that.'

'He's insecure,' Hibaaq added quietly. 'He was born here, but people treat him as an immigrant. Trying to integrate and behave just like white people hasn't worked for his parents, so he's asserting his difference and rejecting the way western society does things.'

'That's exactly it!' Olivia agreed. 'It's his way of rebelling – like my mum giving me an English name, because she was bullied at school for hers. When I started taking my religion seriously, I thought of changing it to something more Islamic, but then I thought it'd be a bit of a betrayal of Mum. She used to hate the way nobody could ever remember her name, or if they did, they pronounced it wrong.'

'You wear a hijab,' Charlotte pointed out. 'Is that to please your parents too?'

'You must be joking!' Olivia laughed out loud. 'I just told you – my mum wanted us to fit in and not be noticed. She dresses just the same as you – except when she goes round to visit my nan. 'I cover my head as a sign of respect to Allah, not to please *anyone* else.'

'And you don't?' Charlotte turned to Tahira. 'Why's that?'

'Because, as far as I'm concerned, that's all just cultural,' Tahira replied. 'I've never covered my head and neither has my mother. She says that Muslim women ought to stop doing it, because it perpetuates the stereotype of them as submissive. I happen to think she's wrong about that. I don't think it's necessary to wear a headscarf or a niqab, but it should be up to each woman to decide for herself.'

'That's all very interesting,' Sandra said, draining her cup and glancing up at a clock on the wall. 'Now, if you don't have any other ideas who might have-'

'If you'd like to know more about Islam, and meet a few of our friends, why don't you come to Friday prayers this afternoon?' Tahira suggested suddenly.

'That's very …,' Sandra hesitated. This could be a good opportunity to talk to some of the other members of the Muslim community, and perhaps to find out whether there was more opposition to the aims of the *Feminist Sisterhood of Islam* than its members liked to admit. However, she was nervous of blundering into a place of worship where she might inadvertently do the wrong thing and cause offence. 'Thank you,' she said at last. 'What time is it? And where do we come?'

***

'Tahira certainly knows her own mind,' Peter observed as they made their way back to Sandra's office. 'I see what you mean about her being intimidating.'

'Yes,' Bernie agreed with a grin. 'I bet Salma's brother felt intimidated alright!'

'I still don't get how they can claim that Islam is a feminist religion,' Charlotte muttered. 'After all, everybody knows that the men expect their wives to be submissive and stay at home and look after the house and the kids.'

'There were plenty of people who criticised my wife for going out to work when our kids were young,' Peter cut in. 'People have short memories. Back in the seventies, we were still arguing about whether children growing up in homes where both parents worked would become juvenile delinquents.'

'Middle-class people, that was,' Bernie added. 'People who didn't realise that for some women it wasn't a choice to go out to work, they simply needed the money to put food on the table.'

'I'm sure it never occurred to my mother to take a job after she married my father,' Jonah backed them up. 'She saw being a pastor's wife as a job in itself. Times change and you can't expect everyone to change at the same pace.'

'Mariam told me that the prophet Muhammad's first wife was a wealthy widow who ran her own business and employed him to work for her,' Bernie told Charlotte mischievously. 'He was so good at his job, that she proposed marriage to him to keep it in the family! Apparently she bankrolled the whole enterprise at the start of it all – not a lot of submission there!'

'You're kidding!' Charlotte looked round in surprise, wondering if Bernie was teasing her.

'No – straight up!' Bernie smiled back. 'I checked it out. It's not just some strange idea dreamed up by those feminist writers that Tahira keeps quoting – it's mainstream.'

'As Peter said,' Jonah went on, 'people have short memories. My grandmother was a suffragette. We should be careful about lecturing other people about equality when we only discovered it ourselves so recently!'

'And Islam isn't the only religion that has problems with women,' Bernie pointed out. 'Think of the Catholic Church – the services may be full of women, but there's always a man at the front!'

***

As they entered the large room where Sandra's team of officers and staff were working, DC Oliver Ransom came over to speak to her.

'I've interviewed Darren Galgate,' he told her. 'You know – the guy who owns the bike that was left outside the Sydney Jones. Only it turns out it wasn't his bike after all.'

'Oh?' Jonah looked up at him with interest.

'Go on,' Sandra told him. 'Tell us more.'

'His bike is still safe in his garage in Skelmersdale,' Ransom explained. 'He showed it to me. He says it's never been out of his possession. What *did* go missing was the number plate! It was stolen back in February. He rode it into Liverpool and left it while he went into the museum. He's a teacher and he was prospecting for a school trip. Anyway, when he came out the number plate was gone. He didn't bother to report it to the police. He just got a new number made and fitted. He showed me the receipt for the work, and the garage that did it confirms his story.'

'So the bike had its number plate switched?' asked Charlotte. 'Do we know what its real number is?'

'I rang forensics, who are still going over it, and they gave me the Vehicle Identification Number,' Ransom replied, clearly enjoying himself. 'I checked that against the DVLA[12] database and got the registration number. Then I cross-referenced with the police national computer and guess what?'

'It's been reported stolen,' Jonah answered promptly.

'That's right.' Ransom sounded a little disappointed that his punchline had been anticipated. 'It was taken from a house in Knotty Ash on Tuesday – in other words, the day before the acid attack!'

'Have you got the details of the theft?' Sandra asked. 'Who attended the scene?'

'PC Robert Thomas. I've got his notes here. It occurred during the day while the residents were out at work. The thieves gained access to the back garden by putting their hand over the gate and unbolting it. Then they forced a window and got inside the house. The only things that were taken from the house were the keys to the bike and to the shed where it was kept. So it looks like the burglary was only done in order to get the bike.'

'Where were the keys kept?' asked Jonah.

I'm not sure … let me see if it says …,' Ransom flicked through a folder of papers. 'It doesn't seem to … Oh yes! Here it is! They were hanging up on a hook inside the cupboard under the stairs. Why do you ask?'

'I was wondering how easy it would have been for the intruder to find them,' Jonah answered. 'Was there any sign

---

[12] The Driver and Vehicle Licensing Agency is responsible for maintaining records of drivers and vehicles registered in the UK.

of a search for them? Drawers open, stuff taken out and thrown down, that sort of thing?'

'It doesn't mention anything,' Ransom shook his head. 'I could ask Rob Thomas if he remembers.'

'Yes. I think you'd better do that,' Sandra said. Then she turned to Jonah. 'Are you suggesting that the burglar was familiar with the house and knew where to look for the keys?'

Jonah inclined his head slightly. 'What do *you* think?'

'I certainly think that the bike was most likely stolen to order,' Sandra answered. 'And, assuming that they did go straight for the cupboard with the keys in it, it looks as if they must have known that was where they would be.'

'We had a case in Oxford last year where a car's owner reported it stolen in order to avoid a conviction for dangerous driving,' Jonah said impassively.

'You mean – the attacker could actually be the owner of this motorbike?' asked Charlotte.

'That would explain the rather minimalist burglary and the switched number plates,' Sandra murmured. 'Yes. You're right. We ought to check out the owner of the stolen bike.'

'His name's Alexander Knowsley,' Ransom added helpfully. 'He's thirty-four and married. He works as a plasterer and his wife's a medical secretary.'

'It should be easy enough,' Sandra continued. 'I'll just get someone to go over and talk to them about the burglary. They'll probably be delighted! The chances are no one's had time to give them any news on how the investigation's going … and I suppose we'd better find that out ourselves first.'

'I already have,' Ransom told her. 'As you sort of implied, nobody's has time to do much about it. There was an alert put out for the stolen bike, but of course, the number was wrong, so nothing came of it. It looks as if there's been no progress at all.'

'In that case, Mr and Mrs Knowsley certainly deserve a visit,' Sandra smiled.

Looking into Liverpool University School of Health Sciences building

7. YAWM AL-JUMMAH

'Aren't we supposed to take our shoes off or something?' Charlotte whispered to Sandra as they pushed open the door to the Stanley Mosque and Islamic Centre. The building did not look at all as she had imagined it would. It was a converted shop, in a small row of shops, none of which appeared to be flourishing.

'I'm sure someone will tell us what we have to do,' Sandra whispered back, looking around nervously.

They were in a wide room. To the right and the left were tables of the sort often seen in church halls and community centres, with plastic chairs grouped around them. Straight ahead, beyond several small groups of people standing around chatting, she could see an archway in the back wall. Through that, three shallow steps led up to an empty area that seemed to be strewn with discarded shoes of all descriptions: sandals, trainers, smart black business shoes and flip-flops.

Sandra continued to stare round, unsure what to do next. Tahira had assured them that she would be there to meet them, but none of the faces looked familiar. At last, she spotted Hibaaq, standing tall among a small cluster of young people, principally men of South Asian appearance. Ah good! She had seen them and was making her way across the room to greet them.

'Come in!' she called, all smiles. 'I'm so glad you made it. Let me introduce you to our imam.'

She turned towards a short wiry man dressed in a long black robe, which reminded Sandra of the cassock worn by Father Brown in the television series of that name. He seemed very young to be in such a position of authority.

'Welcome!' he said heartily, holding out his hand. 'My name's Imran – Imran the imam!' he added with a little laugh. 'I'm very pleased to welcome you to our mosque. As you can see, people are just arriving. Please, come and sit down and have some tea while you're waiting.'

He led the way over to a small table set against the wall. He put teabags into two mugs and poured hot water over them. Sandra and Charlotte stirred their tea, removed the teabags with a spoon and added milk from a jug that stood next to the kettle. Imran guided them across the room to one of the tables and they sat down. Hibaaq joined them.

'Tahira and Olivia won't be long,' she told them. 'They're just preparing themselves for the prayers.'

'You can come and join us and listen to the sermon if you like,' Imran told them. 'You'll see that the believers sit on mats on the floor, but we have a few chairs at the back for visitors. The only thing we ask is that you take off your shoes before you go into the prayer room.'

'And you must sit in the right-hand half of the room,' Hibaaq added. 'That's the side for women.' She smiled mischievously and added in an undertone, 'although Tahira often tries to sit just beyond the middle so that she can feel that she's invading the space reserved for male privilege!'

The imam smiled. 'You'll find that we're mostly very tolerant and open here,' he told them, 'but old habits die hard and we don't want to exclude those men who still find mixed prayers uncomfortable.'

'Lots of women feel more comfortable not being exposed to the male gaze all the time too,' Hibaaq added.

'We all have lunch together afterwards,' Imran told Sandra. 'I hope you'll stay and join us. Would you like to say a few words to everyone? It might help to reassure them that the police are taking this atrocity seriously.'

'Yes, please,' Sandra answered. 'That would be great. And then, over lunch, it would be good if we could talk to people who were friends with the girls who were attacked. They may have some ideas about who could have wanted to harm them – or why.'

'OK.' Imran got up. 'I'll have to go now, but I'll do my best to encourage people to talk to you. See you later.'

***

'And the Prophet (Salla Allahu alayhi wa sallam) came upon Fudhala yet again. And still he was muttering and mumbling to himself his plans for attacking Muhammad (Salla Allahu alayhi wa sallam) and killing him. The Prophet (Salla Allahu alayhi wa sallam) could see into his heart and knew what it was that he was planning, but again, he did not challenge him. He did not express anger towards him. He did not call upon his followers to arrest him. Instead, he smiled at him and asked him again, 'what are you conversing to yourself about, Fudhala?'

'Not surprisingly, Fudhala was a bit annoyed at being asked this for the third time, but he didn't want to give away his intentions, so he replied, "Nothing, nothing. I was just making my dua. I am remembering Allah (Subhanahu Wa Ta'ala)."

'Then the Prophet (Salla Allahu alayhi wa sallam) smiled again and he said, "I seek forgiveness from Allah for you." And he put out his hand and held it there on Fudhala's chest and made dua for him.

'And from that moment Fudhala's heart was changed. Up until then he had hated the Prophet (Salla Allahu alayhi wa sallam) and he had wanted to kill him; but after that moment, his heart was changed and he loved the Prophet (Salla Allahu alayhi wa sallam). He said to people, "There is no name on earth that is more beloved to me than Muhammad (Salla Allahu alayhi wa sallam)."

'Now Muhammad (Salla Allahu alayhi wa sallam) could have arranged for Fudhala to be captured or killed. He could have punished him for scheming to assassinate him. But he chose to be merciful. He chose to show him love. And that, my dear respected brothers and sisters, is how we are called to act towards people who try to harm us.'

Imran looked round at the rows of faces looking up at him from the brightly coloured mats on the floor of the prayer room. Then he raised his eyes to take in the two police officers sitting in silence on chairs at the back of the women's area. Sandra stared back, trying to look attentive and wondering how much longer the sermon was going to last.

'Two days ago, as I'm sure you all know by now,' Imran resumed, 'three of our sisters were attacked in the street. Someone came up on a motorbike and sprayed them with acid. Two of them are still being treated in the burns unit at Whiston hospital.'

He paused and looked slowly round the room again.

'Not surprisingly, I've heard some of you expressing anger about this. That's understandable. I feel angry too. I would like that man to pay for what he has done to our beloved sisters. But I would urge you all, brothers and sisters, to follow the example of the Prophet (Salla Allahu alayhi wa sallam) and put aside your anger. Do not talk of revenge. That is not our religion. That is not our deen. Our deen is to submit to the will of Allah (Subhanahu Wa Ta'ala), and we will all be answerable to him for our actions. We will *all* be answerable – you, me, *and* the man who attacked our sisters; we will *all* be answerable to Allah (Subhanahu Wa Ta'ala).'

He paused for several seconds allowing this declaration to sink in.

'We have two visitors today,' the imam said, speaking in a much less dramatic voice now. 'They are officers from Merseyside Police CID. They are investigating the attack on our sisters.' He glanced towards Sandra and Charlotte, who smiled nervously back as they became conscious that heads had turned and all eyes were on them. 'If you want the person responsible to be punished for what they did, the best way you can help is by talking to them and answering their questions. They are going to be here for lunch, and I hope that everyone will make them very welcome.'

He paused briefly, looking up and down the rows of faces staring up at him, before concluding, 'and I ask you all to make dua for the man who attacked our sisters. Make dua for him that Allah (Subhanahu Wa Ta'ala) will forgive him and that he will eventually come to a proper understanding of our deen and submit himself to Allah (Subhanahu Wa Ta'ala), as did Fudhala bin'Umair bin Mulawwah Laithi when the Prophet (Salla Allahu alayhi wa sallam) showed him kindness and made dua for him to Allah (Subhanahu Wa Ta'ala).

There was the briefest of pauses, or so it seemed to Sandra, before he switched abruptly back into Arabic. Everyone turned back to face the front. After a few seconds, which seemed much longer to Sandra and Charlotte, Imran sat down in his seat behind the wooden lectern. There was a low rustling sound as people adjusted their sitting positions.

Then Imran was on his feet again, chanting words that Sandra and Charlotte could not understand. They exchanged silent glances, as the unfamiliar sounds seemed to go on and on forever. Looking along the lines of people on the floor in front of her, Sandra noticed two young boys sitting with their father. They were both gazing up at the imam in rapt attention. She could not imagine her girls at that age being prepared to stay still and silent for so long!

At last, the call to prayer – if that was what it was – was over. Imran stepped down from the low pulpit and moved into the side of the room where the men were sitting. At the same time, everyone stood up. Sandra noticed the father of the two boys taking one of them by the hand and positioning him in the centre of one of the prayer mats that covered the floor. Further away from her, a teenager was helping an elderly man to clamber to his feet.

'Straighten up your lines, please,' Imran called out in a low, but authoritative tone. 'And can you move forward over there, to make room for the people behind you?'

Feet shuffled as the congregation followed his

instructions. Imran looked silently along the lines of people ranged in front of him. Apparently satisfied, he turned to face the wall at the far side of the room. There were a few more moments of silence; then he began chanting again.

As the incomprehensible prayers continued, Sandra was glad that she and Charlotte were seated behind everyone else. At least nobody could see their faces and realise how bored they were waiting for this seemingly interminable ritual to end. What did those strange guttural sounds mean? Were she and Charlotte the only ones in the room who did not understand them? How did the people know when to bend forward with their hands on their knees and when to prostrate themselves, touching the floor with their foreheads? Or were they all just following what the imam did?

At last, the chanting ceased and everyone seemed to relax. Imran made his way down the aisle created by the separation of men and women to the back of the room and on through the archway to the outer area, where Sandra and Charlotte had sat drinking their tea earlier. Sandra noted with a smile that his black robe brushed against Tahira's arm as he passed her, standing, as Hibaaq had predicted, at the very edge of the women's section.

'Come and get some lunch, and then I'll introduce you to a few people.'

Sandra looked up to see Olivia smiling down at her. Hibaaq was close behind her, also smiling. She looked across at Tahira and waved to her to join them. Soon they were sitting together at one of the tables with paper plates piled with dahl and yellow rice in front of them. Tahira handed them each a fork and a paper napkin, but before they could start eating, they were interrupted by Imran clapping his hands together and calling for silence. Everyone stopped their conversation and turned to look at him.

Sandra saw that he was standing on the lowest of the steps that led up to the prayer room. There was a microphone set up in front of him. He beckoned to her to come and stand beside him.

'Please give a very warm welcome to Detective Chief Inspector Sandra Latham,' Imran said as she came forward. A woman sitting at the table closest to the front started clapping and the rest of the room followed suit. Somehow, to Sandra, the applause sounded dutiful, rather than warm or spontaneous. She reached the front and stood on the step, smiling round nervously.

'DCI Latham is leading the investigation into the acid attack,' Imran continued, when the applause died down. 'I've asked her to say a few words to you all, and then after that, she would like to meet you and have a chat about what happened and anything you may know about it.'

He stepped to one side, allowing Sandra to take the microphone. She looked round at the expectant faces gazing up at her from the dozen or so tables spaced around the room, trying to gather her thoughts into some sort of coherent message.

'First of all,' she began, after what seemed to her an embarrassingly long pause, 'I would like, on behalf of Merseyside Police, to say how sorry we are that this horrific incident has taken place, and to extend our sympathy to the victims and their families and everyone else who has been impacted by it. I – I've spoken to the hospital today, and I'm pleased to be able to tell you that Mariam Ali is likely to be discharged in a few days' time. As you may know, Emily Armstrong is already recovering at home.'

She took a deep breath before continuing, 'I'm afraid that Salma Rahman is still being treated in Intensive Care. Her condition is grave, but not life threatening, and there has been some improvement over the last twenty-four hours.'

She hesitated again, struggling to think how to go on.

'We have a substantial team of officers dedicated to this enquiry,' she resumed at last, 'and we are treating it as our highest priority. We are following up a number of leads and we have some useful forensic evidence. In particular, we now know that the motorbike was stolen the day before the incident and we have stepped up our efforts to discover who took it. What I need from all of you is background information to help us narrow down the field of potential suspects.'

She scanned the room again, noting with relief that Hibaaq and Olivia were smiling back encouragingly at her.

'My colleague, Sergeant Charlotte Simpson, and I will be here for as long as you are happy for us to stay. If you know anything that could help us – anything at all – please speak to us about it. It could be someone using threatening behaviour, or trolling on social media, or any number of things. We'd particularly like to speak to anyone who was a friend of any of the victims. You may remember things that they have forgotten or that they didn't think were important enough to tell us about – and we haven't yet been able to speak to Miss Rahman, so we'd particularly like to hear about her activities over the last few weeks.'

She looked round the room again. Several dozen faces looked back impassively at her. Nobody moved or spoke or looked as if they were eager to talk to her.

'I'll let you get on with your meal now,' she finished, stepping away from the microphone. 'Thank you for listening to me.'

Imran thanked her and reiterated his call for co-operation with the police enquiry. Then they both returned to their seats.

A young mother, sitting opposite Sandra, paused from helping a small girl with her food to lean across the table and speak to her.

'Has anyone told you about Emily's boyfriend, who came here ranting and raving about us brainwashing her?' she asked.

'When she became a Muslim?' Sandra queried. 'Or did he do it more than once?'

'No. It was just that once that he came here, but Emily

told me that he's been following her around since – stalking her. I advised her to tell the police, but she said she didn't like to. She didn't want to get him into trouble. I think she felt guilty about dumping him. They'd been friends for years.'

The woman made eye contact briefly with Sandra before turning her attention back to feeding her daughter.

'I see. That's very helpful. Thank you.' Sandra paused, trying to think of a way of prolonging the conversation. This looked to be someone who knew at least one of the victims well. 'And did Emily ever talk about anyone else objecting to her conversion? Other old friends, for example?'

'Well, her parents weren't exactly chuffed about her reverting,' the woman answered without looking up. 'Her dad in particular.'

'And Jack Hampton – the boyfriend – did he make any actual threats at all?'

'Not that I know of,' the woman shook her head. Then she looked up and smiled. 'He was never coherent enough for that. He just ranted on about brainwashing and Islamic terrorists. I don't think he had much between his ears, to be honest. Emily was much brighter than him. Their relationship would never have worked, even without her reverting to Islam.'

She bent down and took out a packet of baby-wipes from a bag hung over the back of her chair. Then she pushed away the paper plate that lay on the table in front of her daughter and started wiping the child's hands and face. She looked across at Sandra again as she did so.

'I'm sorry! I should have introduced myself. I'm Khadija. I'm Imran's wife. We live over the shop.' She gave a little laugh and raised her eyes towards the ceiling. 'So I saw quite a bit of Emily while she was coming here to learn about Islam.'

'So you must know her quite well,' Sandra said eagerly. 'What's she like? I mean …,' she trailed off, not sure how to finish her sentence.

'I must introduce you to my mother-in-law,' Khadija announced, getting up and picking up her daughter. 'She won't want to have missed speaking to you.'

She led the way forward to the table closest to the steps and put her hand on the shoulder of the woman who had led the applause when Sandra came up to address the assembly. She turned round, and Sandra saw that she was older than most of those present – in her fifties or sixties, perhaps? It was difficult to estimate age in someone from an unfamiliar ethnic group.

'Inspector, this is Imran's mother, Nadia.'

'Good afternoon.' Sandra held out her hand.

'Thank you for coming,' Nadia smiled back, getting to her feet and taking Sandra's hand in a firm grip. 'It means a lot that you bothered to come, even though I doubt that we'll be able to help you much. It's all so-,' she broke off and stood rigid staring towards the door.

Sandra turned and followed her gaze. A young white man stood there, looking round nervously. He had evidently just come in and was unsure what to do next. Within seconds, the hubbub of conversation died down as more people noticed the intruder. Imran hurried over to greet him, squeezing between the tables as he made his way across the crowded room.

'Hello!' he called softly as he approached. 'Welcome to our mosque. Would you like some food?'

'Er – no – no, thank you,' the young man stammered. 'I – I just wanted to ask ... I was wondering if anyone here knew how Salma is?'

Sandra noticed that the green tee-shirt that he was wearing had the words, "University of Liverpool Hill-Walking Club" printed across the front. Presumably, this was one of Salma's friends from that society. She got up and made her away across the room to speak to him.

'As it happens, we have the officer in charge of the police investigation with us now,' Imran told him. 'Would you like to speak to her? She has the latest information from the hospital.'

'Yes – yes please!' The young man looked suddenly relieved that his mission was turning out to be so easy. 'I'm Luke, by the way. I know Salma through the Hill-Walking Club. I couldn't believe it when I heard her name on the news!'

'I'm Imran. I'm the imam here. I know Salma very well. You'll find lots of people here who are shocked like you at what happened.' Imran turned slightly as Sandra came up beside him. 'And now, here's Inspector Latham. She can tell you what you need to know. Why don't you sit down and have some food while you have a chat?'

'Thanks – but no thanks. I won't stop. I just wanted to know ...,' Luke turned abruptly to address Sandra. 'How is she? The Echo[13] said, "Serious but stable". What does that mean?'

'I'm sorry.' Sandra looked into the young man's face wondering how best to explain to him the severity of Salma's injuries. 'I'm sorry,' she repeated, playing for time.

'Yes?' Luke prompted impatiently. 'Go on! Tell me – I want to know!'

'I'm afraid it's not good news,' Sandra said gravely, speaking in an undertone so as not to be overheard. She was grateful that the rest of the room seemed to have resumed its conversations and that Imran had drifted away to speak to someone else. 'The acid went all over her face and caused severe burns. She's in Intensive Care at the moment, and the doctors say that she's going to need extensive surgery to reconstruct her face. I – I'm really sorry. Were you – I mean, are you close?'

'No, not really ... at least ... I don't know ...,' the young man shifted his feet uncomfortably. 'We just ... we just do a lot of things together, that's all,' he finished after a long pause. 'Do you – do you think they'd let me visit her?'

---

[13] The Liverpool Echo is a regional daily paper based in Liverpool.

'They're only allowing family in at the moment,' Sandra told him, 'but maybe if you spoke to *them* …?'

'I wouldn't dare,' Luke said miserably. 'I'm sure they wouldn't … I mean … Her brother doesn't like the idea of her mixing with anyone who isn't a Muslim.'

'You've met him then?'

'Sort of. I walked her home after we got back from a day in the Lake District and he was there outside her room, waiting for her. He'd come over to see her for some reason – spying on her, it seemed like – and he told her she shouldn't have been alone with me, and she was bringing shame on her family by mixing with men the way she did – as if he knew anything about it at all!' His voice rose in indignation and then suddenly dropped as he remembered where he was.

'I completely respect her religion,' he continued in an undertone, 'and I'd never do anything she wasn't comfortable with. But he didn't seem capable of getting that.'

'I think Salma's parents might be a bit more understanding,' Sandra said, also keeping her voice low. 'It might be worth talking to them.'

'I wouldn't dare,' Luke repeated, shaking his head. 'I don't know how they'd react. I don't want them jumping to conclusions and … I'm afraid they might take it out on Salma, if they think … I mean, you do hear awful stories, don't you?'

For a moment or two, Sandra was at a loss. Then she recalled a television documentary, from some years previously, about so-called "honour killings" in which women had been murdered by members of their own family, because they were deemed to have brought disgrace on them. She could not imagine Munir and Fahima Rahman acting in such a way, but of course, Luke had not met them and might expect them to think in the same way as their son.

'I see.' Sandra took out a notebook and a pencil and handed them to Luke. 'Write down your name and phone number, and I'll let you know when she's allowed to have more visitors.'

People were starting to leave now. Sandra took back her notebook and turned to look for Charlotte. Ah! There she was, among a small group of women at the side of the room standing around a sink unit, washing and drying mugs and cutlery. Catching Sandra's eye, she put down the tea towel that she was holding, said a few words to her new friends and came across to join her boss.

'Everyone seems to have a story of low-level harassment,' she reported, 'but nothing that could have been expected to escalate to what happened on Wednesday.

***

They all went in the car to the hospital that evening to visit Mariam. Lucy had a slice of her birthday cake for her; Ibrahim, of course, had to go to see how his sister was progressing; and Dominic made it clear that he also was anxious about her condition. Jonah was careful not to say anything, but Bernie and Peter were well aware that he had hopes of speaking to her about the incident, confident that he might somehow discover a nugget of information that the official police interview had failed to unearth.

'We can't all go in at once,' Peter said firmly, as they approached the burns unit. 'I think Lucy and Ibrahim ought to go first, to give her the cake.' He sat down on one of the seats built into the wall of the corridor near the door of the unit. 'The rest of us can wait here.'

'OK.' Dominic tried to hide his disappointment at not being one of the first. 'We've got two hours, so that's half an hour each if we do it in pairs – that's if Abdul and Tahmina come too. Does anyone know if they're planning to be here?'

'No.' Ibrahim turned back briefly to answer Dominic's question. 'They said they wouldn't be able to get over this evening, but they're going to spend the whole day with us tomorrow. I hope that's OK with everyone?'

'Of course! It'll be nice to get to know them better,' Dominic replied heartily.

'We might as well pop round and see Joey and Ruth,' Bernie put in, thinking that perhaps Ibrahim and his parents might like a little time to themselves. 'We haven't seen them for ages and we may not get long on Sunday before we go on to Aunty Dot's.'

'No, there's no point going tomorrow,' Dominic said quickly. 'Dad's working – he's promised Mum a new gas cooker and they need the extra cash. It'll be much better if we all stay at home – or at least, I'll stay. You could go and do some sight-seeing. There must be lots of places that Peter hasn't seen yet. Why don't you …?'

Lucy allowed the door to swing closed behind them, cutting off her cousin's speech. She followed Ibrahim down the corridor to Mariam's room. She was pleased to see that her friend was now sitting up in bed looking much more alert than she had on their previous visits.

'I brought you some of my birthday cake,' Lucy told her. 'It's good – Peter made it.'

She crossed the room and put the small parcel of cake down on the standard-issue table-on-wheels that stood at the side of the bed. She unfolded the paper serviette, in which it was wrapped, to reveal a slice of gooey chocolate sponge cake layered with chocolate butter cream and with a topping of chocolate fudge icing. She turned the table, positioning it over the bed, and adjusted the height so that Mariam could reach the cake easily.

'It looks delicious!' Mariam smiled back at her.

'Go on!' Ibrahim urged her. 'Try it!'

'I don't know,' Mariam hesitated. 'I think it'd be better to keep it for later – when I don't have visitors around. It'd feel funny stuffing myself when you aren't eating too.'

'You'd better try it,' Lucy told her earnestly. 'Peter's outside. He'll be disappointed if he thinks you don't like it!'

'Oh alright!' Mariam grinned round at them both. 'You've twisted my arm. I'll give it a go.'

While Mariam demolished the cake, Lucy recounted the lectures that she had attended that morning. Ibrahim watched with satisfaction, pleased that his sister seemed to be enjoying the chocolatey treat. Then she turned to reach for a tissue to wipe her hands and he was brought back to reality with a jolt as he saw the extent of the injury to the back of her head and neck.

'That was lovely,' Mariam told Lucy, pushing the tray table away. Then her face became suddenly serious and she looked round at both her visitors, fixing them each with her eye in turn. 'Now, you *must* tell me about Salma. I'm fed up with being palmed off with "We haven't been allowed to see her yet", "The doctors will only talk to members of her family", and all that stuff. I *know* she got sprayed more than the rest of us. So it's no good you trying to pretend she wasn't badly hurt.'

Lucy and Ibrahim looked at one another, struggling to think what to say.

'Come on!' Mariam pleaded. 'I'm not a child. I'll have to know sooner or later —and if you don't tell me, I'll just go on imagining how bad it must have to be to make you so desperate to keep it from me!'

'She looked round when she heard the motorbike coming up behind her,' Lucy explained slowly. 'So when he sprayed you all, she got it right in her face. And then, her wet headscarf flopped down over her eyes, which made it worse still.'

'So, her eyes?' Mariam asked in a small voice, shocked in spite of having been sure that things could not be worse than she had already guessed. 'She's going to be blind?'

'They said she might still have some sight in her left eye,' Lucy told her, 'but ...,' she trailed off unable to finish the sentence.

'She's had surgery to remove the dead tissue,' Ibrahim added, 'but there was some reason why they couldn't do a skin graft right away, so she's just got a temporary covering on the wounds. At least, I think that's what they said. I'm not really sure. It was all a bit complicated.'

They sat in silence. Nobody liked to start talking about ordinary things. It felt disrespectful to Salma somehow. At last, the door opened and Dominic's head appeared.

'The nurse said it was fine for us all to come in together,' he announced quietly. 'She said, so long as you don't mind, it's daft the rest of us waiting outside,' he added, looking towards Salma. 'Is it OK for us to come in?'

'Yes, of course,' Salma's face lit up as she smiled back. 'Be my guest!'

Dominic held the door open wide to allow Jonah to enter in his wheelchair, followed closely by Bernie and Peter. Then he closed it again and hurried round the bed to take up a position next to Lucy. He looked down on Mariam.

'You look great,' he said earnestly. 'How do you feel?'

'The pain is a bit worse than yesterday,' she admitted with a wry smile, 'but I think I prefer that to feeling so drugged up to the eyebrows that I can't think straight. I thought earlier that they were going to let me out today – to cut down the number of patients in over the weekend – but then the doctor decided she wasn't quite satisfied I was ready. A different doctor's going to review me on Monday, so I expect I'll manage to make my escape then.'

'You must stay until you're really ready,' Dominic told her seriously. 'There's no point trying to rush things and making yourself worse.'

'But I'm perfectly fine in myself,' Mariam argued. 'And they've more or less decided that I don't need surgery – or at least not right away. They said they'd review it after two weeks. That's why I think I might as well be at home. All they're doing here is giving me painkillers and checking the dressing every so often.'

'And monitoring your temperature and blood pressure,' Bernie added, picking up the chart that hung at the end of the bed. 'Presumably they want to make sure you haven't picked up a wound infection or anything.'

'That's far more likely to happen in here than anywhere else,' Mariam argued. 'Hospitals are full of bugs.'

'Well we all washed our hands like good children before coming on to the ward,' Peter said equably, 'so we're doing our best to help you get out soon.'

'I don't suppose you've remembered anything more about what happened?' Jonah asked hopefully in the silence that followed. 'Or thought of anyone who might have wanted to hurt any of you?'

'No,' Mariam shook her head. 'All I remember is a noise behind me – but that wasn't surprising because it's sometimes quite busy there – and then Olivia looked up and opened her mouth to say something … and then the world just exploded. I'm sorry I'm such a useless witness.'

'Don't you mind him,' Bernie cut in. 'He's completely incapable of behaving like an ordinary human being instead of a police officer. Just ignore him.'

'But I have been thinking about who might have wanted to do it,' Mariam continued, 'and I did just wonder about Emily's ex-boyfriend. Do the police know about him? He was very upset when she told him she couldn't go out with anyone who wasn't a Muslim. And …,' she hesitated.

'Go on,' urged Jonah, 'and?'

'And he did seem to blame Salma in particular – because she was the one who invited Emily to learn about Islam. They were all in the Hill-Walking club together – did you know that?'

'You don't happen to know if he ever rode a motor bike at all?' Jonah asked casually.

'No. Emily never said anything about it.' Mariam shook her head. Then she smiled and added, 'but then that's a phase that a lot of lads go through isn't it? I mean, even Ibrahim had one when he was a teenager.'

'It was only a moped,' Ibrahim protested. 'And I gave it up as soon as I was old enough to drive a car.'

'Not just lads.' It was Jonah's turn to smile. 'And they don't always grow out of it as soon as Ibrahim did. 'My wife was still obstinately in the saddle up to a couple of months before she died.'

'Oh! I'm sorry,' Mariam sounded flustered. 'I didn't realise you'd been … I sort of assumed … I suppose that's how you came to be living with Lucy's family.'

'That's more or less it,' Jonah agreed. 'Bernie was my personal assistant for a while before that, and then they took me on full-time when Margaret went into the hospice, but you were telling us about Jack Hampton …'

Abdullah Quilliam Mosque and Islamic Centre, Liverpool: the first mosque to be opened in England.

8. FAMILY WEEKEND

'I still don't see why I can't have the room Sophie's got,' Philippa Latham complained as she looked round her new bedroom. 'I'm never going to fit all my things in here. It's so-o-o not fair!'

'Look, Pippa,' Sandra sighed. 'We've been through all this. You can't both have the biggest room – unless you want to share again – so we agreed that Sophie would have the big room, but she's got to have the cupboard for the spare sheets and towels and stuff in it. Once you take that into account, her room's hardly any bigger than yours.'

'But in the big house, we both had bigger rooms than this,' Pippa persisted. 'If you'd stayed with Dad and-'

'And he'd been better at running his business,' Sandra cut in sharply, 'and if he'd kept his hands off the staff!'

'If you'd been there to help, maybe the garden centre wouldn't have gone down the tubes,' Sophie observed through the half-open door. 'And maybe he wouldn't have needed to turn to Mel for a bit of TLC.'

'You keep out of this!' Sandra snapped back. She often found it difficult to keep her temper when her daughters appeared to blame her for the breakdown of her marriage. After all, it was Gary who had fathered a child with one of the workers at the garden centre that he had inherited from his parents, and Gary who had been forced to sell the family home to pay off his debts. She had merely worked all the hours God sent earning money that he then squandered propping up his failing business.

She drew a deep breath and told herself that the situation would only escalate if she allowed her anger to surface.

'Look girls,' she said as calmly as she could, 'I know this

105

house isn't ideal, but it's the best we can afford, and at least you *have* got your own rooms now. We've just got to make the best of things. We can't expect Gran and Grandad to put up with having us living there with them forever – which reminds me, Grandad will be over in a few minutes to put up some shelves for your things. Just put away as much as you can now, and I'm sure we'll fit the rest in once he's done that.'

As if on cue, there was the sound of the back door opening and footsteps in the hall.

'Anyone at home?' came a cheerful voice calling up the stairs.

'We're up here, Dad!' Sandra called back, 'just unpacking the girls' things.'

While her father discussed the positioning of shelves in her daughters' bedrooms, Sandra retreated to her own room. It was the smallest bedroom in the house, which she had taken in an attempt to placate Sophie and Pippa. She sat down on the bed and pulled out her phone.

'Hi Ollie!' she greeted DC Ransom when he answered her call. 'How're things going with the acid attack case?'

'Well, I've found out a few interesting things about Mr Alexander Knowsley,' Ransom replied with an air of satisfaction.

'Is that the guy who owns the motorbike?'

'Yes – that's the one. After you suggested he might have been lying about it being stolen, I did a few background checks. He's got a very interesting history.'

'Oh?'

'Sorry to barge in, love.' Before Ransom could finish, the bedroom door opened and Sandra's mother came in. 'Could you just tell me where you want the rabbit hutch? One of them's gnawed a hole in her carrying case and I'm afraid she'll get out if we don't get them into it soon.'

'Sorry, Ol. I'll have to go. I'll ring again later.' Sandra ended the call and turned round to face her mother. 'OK. I'll come and show you.'

'The garden's absolutely minute!' Pippa declared as she followed her mother and grandmother outside. 'The rabbit run's going to take up practically the whole lawn. We used to have a trampoline at the old house – and there was room for us to play swing ball and badminton!'

'There's a park not five minutes away,' her grandmother told her sharply. 'And we're only just down the road. You can come round and play badminton in our garden as often as you like. It'll be much easier for your mum only having a small garden, seeing as she's working full time.'

'I expect we'll be able to fit the swing ball in as well as the rabbit run,' Sandra added, giving her mother a grateful smile. 'The first thing is to get Flopsy and Mopsy settled into their hutch. Why don't you take the water bottle into the kitchen and fill it up for them?'

An hour and a half later, the adults sat drinking tea in the lounge while Pippa and Sophie were engaged upstairs arranging their books, ornaments and other precious possessions on the newly erected shelves. Sandra drained her cup as quickly as she could and then took out her mobile phone again.

'I'd just better ring work,' she told her parents apologetically, getting to her feet and heading for the door. 'It's a big case and Charlie and I are both off duty this weekend.'

She went into the kitchen and closed the door, just as Oliver Ransom answered her call.

'You were saying you'd found out something interesting about Alexander Knowsley,' she prompted him.

'Yes,' he replied, sounding rather smug. 'It turns out he's a known right-wing activist. He started out in the BNP[14]

---

[14] The British National Party is a far-right political party, associated in the public mind with racism, anti-semitism and Islamophobia. Founded in 1982 it was at its height in the 2000s when it gained seats in local government and the European Parliament. It has been in decline since 2011.

before switching to the *English Defence League* and then *Britain First*. He's been associated with several other neo-Nazi groups. Most recently, he seems to have gone with a splinter group called "Britain for the British", which split off from *Britain First* a few months ago. I reckon it's a fair bet he's-'

The door crashed open and Sophie stormed in. Hastily cutting short the call, Sandra put away her phone and looked enquiringly towards her daughter.

'Someone's taken my headphones,' she declared accusingly. 'I put them in the box with my computer and now they're gone.'

'Alright,' Sandra sighed. 'I'll come and have a look. I'm sure no one's taken them really. I expect they've just dropped out somewhere.'

***

'Your Daughter is very good with your disabled friend,' Tahmina Ali commented to Bernie as the two of them washed the dishes in the small kitchen of the shared house. They had all lunched together on Tahmina's "special dahl", which she had brought with her from Blackburn. 'Comfort food,' she had announced, when Ibrahim opened the door to them that morning, 'to cheer us all up.'

There was no visiting allowed at the hospital during the morning but, anxious not to leave Ibrahim alone on a day when he would not have his work to distract him from thinking about his sister and her potentially life-changing injuries, they had arrived shortly after Lucy and her friends finished breakfast and spent the morning chatting with Lucy's family.

'Yes,' Bernie agreed, feeling a little uncomfortable at hearing Jonah described as "your disabled friend". It conveyed the impression that he was wholly defined by his disability. 'But then, it's been a long time now. It'll be ten years next month since it happened.'

'He's not always been like this then?'

'Oh no! I assumed you knew. He was shot in the neck by someone who wanted revenge for him putting away a fraudster. He was a DCI with Thames Valley Police. In fact, he only retired last summer – very reluctantly, I might add!'

'It must have been difficult, being a police officer in a wheelchair,' Tahmina suggested. 'But I suppose there must be plenty of desk jobs for senior officers.'

'That would never have suited Jonah,' Bernie laughed. 'No. He expected to go out to every crime scene and to visit every witness. That's where I came in. I was his personal assistant for five years. With me and his trusty wheelchair, there isn't much he can't do.'

'And Lucy helps a lot too.' Tahmina came back to her original observation. 'I'm sure she'll make an excellent doctor. She's so patient and she seems to know what he wants without him having to ask. Watching her feeding him at lunchtime, I wished my student nurses were as understanding and intuitive.'

'As I said, she's had plenty of time to learn,' Bernie smiled. 'When you're only nine and one of your greatest friends suddenly has a devastating injury its … Well, it was sort of therapeutic for her having things she could do to help. And it was easier for Jonah too. I think he found it … less demeaning being fed by a nine-year-old than by an adult nurse. He's come to terms with it now, but it was a slow process. It's hard when you've always been energetic and independent, having to slow down and rely on other people for everything.'

'I was talking to Salma's parents at the hospital the other day.' Tahmina said in a sombre voice. 'It sounds as if she's going to have a lot to come to terms with too.'

'Yes,' agreed Bernie. 'It's hard to imagine, isn't it? And it's shaken the others up too – Lucy and Ibrahim and Dom, I mean.'

'And Mariam? Does she know?' Tahmina asked anxiously.

'Yes. She insisted on being told.' Bernie turned from

putting away the bowls that they had used for the dahl and smiled at Tahmina. 'She's very determined in her own quiet way, isn't she?'

***

'Should we bring Knowsley in for questioning?' Oliver Ransom asked.

Sandra had slipped away to her room after lunch, leaving her parents supervising Pippa and Sophie, who were very reluctantly washing the dishes. She hoped that they would all remain occupied for long enough for her to complete her much-interrupted telephone conversation.

'No,' she said decisively. 'We don't want to show our hand too soon. Let him carry on thinking that we believe his story about the burglary and that's what we're talking to him about. He's much more likely to open up if he thinks we're treating him as the victim of a crime than if he cottons on to the idea that he might be a suspect. Now, did you get the details of the burglary from PC Thomas?'

'Yes,' Oliver answered promptly. 'He confirmed that the house was pretty much completely undisturbed. As far as he could see, nothing had been touched. The intruder – if there was one – went straight to the cupboard under the stairs, took the keys and scarpered.'

'Good.' Sandra thought for a moment. 'Now, what I'd like you to do is to go round there and ask to have a look in the shed where the motorbike was kept. Take ... is Bryony Foster on duty this weekend?'

'Yes. She's been doing some more digging into Knowsley's fascist past,' Oliver confirmed.

'Well, take her with you. Then one of you can distract Knowsley while the other has a good look round the shed. If he *is* our attacker, that's the most likely place for him to have stored the acid. So keep a lookout for suitable containers, spare car batteries or anything of that sort.'

'Right you are. Anything else?'

'No. I think that's all. Give me a ring if you find anything interesting.'

***

The family attended the early morning Mass at the cathedral the next day. It was an intimate affair in the Blessed Sacrament Chapel. The priest who officiated greeted Dominic and Lucy warmly, evidently recognising them as regular attenders.

'This way, I can truthfully tell Mum that I've been,' he confided to Bernie by way of explanation for not returning to his home church in Toxteth on Sundays, 'without her expecting me to spend the whole day with them and having Father Nat roping me in to help with the youth club and stuff.'

Bernie nodded and smiled her understanding. At twenty-three, it was reasonable that the young man should be trying to escape from constant parental oversight.

Bernie, Peter and Jonah waited outside after the service, while Lucy and Dominic lit candles for Mariam, Salma and Emily. Lucy had checked carefully with Ibrahim the evening before that this would be acceptable to them. He had shrugged his shoulders and mumbled that he couldn't see why anyone could object, seeing as they were all praying to the same God however they did it.

'We ought to decide what we're doing tomorrow,' Bernie declared emphatically. 'This trip has got rather overtaken by events. The whole point of us coming up this weekend was to encourage Lucy to take a bit of time out from studying before her exams, but so far that hasn't happened at all.'

'She's coming with us to lunch with Joey and Ruth, Peter pointed out,' and then we're going on to Aunty Dot's.'

'Which is why I said we needed to think about tomorrow,' Bernie repeated. 'How about taking her to Chester Zoo for the day?'

'Won't it be very busy, with it being a Bank Holiday?' Jonah objected, visualising long queues for a limited number of accessible toilets.

'Southport then,' Bernie suggested, 'or West Kirby.'

'I think we ought to give your Aunty Dot a day out,' Jonah said decidedly. 'She must get bored, shut up in that Care Home all day.'

'And if we dress it up as a day out for Aunty Dot, Lucy won't be so likely to try to tell us she needs to revise or something daft like that,' Peter added.

'Yes, that's a good idea,' Bernie agreed. 'We can ask Aunty Dot where she'd like to go this afternoon.'

'She'll be bound to want to know all about the acid attack,' Jonah said brightly. 'Why don't we take her to view the scene of crime?'

'Because the only reason you want to do that is that you want to see it for yourself,' Peter answered promptly.

'And you've already been past there anyway,' Bernie told him. 'We drove down Mount Pleasant just now to get here.'

'Why didn't you point it out to me?' Jonah demanded in an aggrieved tone.

'Because I didn't want us to have to stop for you to get out and have a look round,' Bernie said patiently. 'I know you – you always think you'll manage to spot something that everyone else missed.'

'Personally, I'll be glad when we get home and you're forced to accept that it's all in the hands of Sandra Latham and her team,' Peter sighed. 'Your inability to recognise that other people are just as capable as you at investigating crimes can be extremely wearing at times!'

'Ah! I was just thinking about that,' Jonah said, shifting his gaze to avoid catching Peter's eye. 'There's no particular reason why we *have* to all go home on Tuesday, is there? I mean, we haven't got anything on this week, have we?'

'*I've* got the kids from Wednesday,' Peter objected, reminding his friend that he was childminder for two of his grandchildren. 'So I'm committed to going back on Tuesday whatever you and Bernie do.'

'And who's to say the hotel will have a room for us?' Bernie added. 'Besides, Lucy won't want us-'

'What won't I want?' Lucy interrupted, coming up behind her mother.

'Jonah here is angling to stay in Liverpool for a bit longer so he can carry on interfering in DCI Latham's investigation,' Peter told her.

'And I was just saying that you'd rather we went home so you can get on with preparing for your exams without feeling you've got to entertain us,' Bernie answered quickly, sensing Peter's irritation and trying to deflect attention away from his argument with Jonah.

'Sandra Latham probably oughtn't to have involved him in the first place,' Peter continued oblivious of her intention. 'Seeing as he's just an ordinary civilian these days. The sooner we're all out of her hair the better.'

'But not until Tuesday,' Bernie cut in at once. 'We were just discussing what we might do tomorrow. We thought we might take Aunty Dot out somewhere for the day. What do you think?'

'I think that's a great idea!' Lucy agreed enthusiastically. 'Don't you Dom?'

'I'm sure she'd love it,' he acknowledged. 'Did Lucy tell you? We managed to get her a second-hand electric wheelchair. It's not as swish as Jonah's, but it gives her a bit more independence now that her arthritis is so bad. And she's been moved into a ground floor room too.'

'That'll be better for us this afternoon,' Bernie said approvingly. 'Now we won't have to worry about getting Jonah into the stair lift.'

They started walking back to where they had parked the car.

'As far as the hotel is concerned,' Jonah said nonchalantly. 'I checked with them this morning. 'Our room is free for the rest of the week, so there's no problem about us staying on.'

'Except, as I said-,' Peter began.

'I think it's a great idea,' Lucy broke in at the same moment. 'Then you can keep us all up to date with the investigation.'

'Not really,' Peter argued. 'Even if DCI Latham wants him – and there's no reason to assume she does – Jonah wouldn't be supposed to tell you any more than the press releases let out.'

'The police are supposed to keep the victims informed of progress,' Jonah pointed out. 'That's all I'd be doing. You don't need to lecture me on procedure,' he added in an aggrieved tone. 'I'm not your DC anymore.'

Peter and Jonah had once been rivals, Jonah having joined Thames Valley CID shortly after Peter had been promoted to the rank of sergeant. Although Peter claimed never to have had any ambition to attain great heights within the force, his friend still suspected that he resented having been overtaken so soon, as Jonah rapidly rose to Sergeant, Inspector and finally Chief Inspector.

'Boys, boys, play nicely!' Bernie teased, trying to ease the tension. 'Tell you what – let's just wait and see if Sandra Latham *wants* any more help, shall we? For all we know, her team will have got the case all wrapped up by tomorrow.' She turned and looked sternly at Jonah. 'And whatever happens, we are not staying any longer than to the end of the week, d'you understand? Apart from anything else, it won't do you any good to have your physiotherapy regime disrupted for any longer – not to mention that we'll most likely run out of supplies for keeping you clean and dry, and I'll have to check how much of your medication we've got with us too.'

'Yes Miss,' Jonah mumbled, pretending to be contrite but secretly delighted at the outcome of the conversation.

'I don't believe it!' Peter sighed, raising his eyes heavenward. 'I simply do not believe it! How does he do it?'

'Never mind, Peter,' Lucy murmured, slipping her hand through his arm and resting her head against it. 'Look on the bright side. You'll have a whole five days without Jonah around to mither you!'

***

'What kept you so long, young Bernadette?' Miss Dorothy Fazakerley demanded to know, as one of the Care Assistants showed them into her new room on the ground floor of Park View Care Home in the Wavertree area of the city. 'I wouldn't have thought it ought to take three days for you to get round to calling in on your favourite aunt – in fact, your only remaining aunt!'

'I'm sorry, Aunty,' Bernie apologised, hastening across the room to kiss Dot on the cheek. 'We've had rather a lot of other things to keep us occupied, what with Lucy's birthday and her friends being attacked in the street and everything.'

'Ah yes!' Dot smiled mischievously, 'I was coming to that. I gather young Jonah here has been "helping the police with their enquiries" as they say.'

'What do you mean?' Bernie asked, wondering how her aunt could have become aware of their activities.

'See here!' Dot reached out a bony hand and picked up an iPad from the table that stood next to her high-backed chair. She turned it on and started flicking through screens. Then she handed it over to Bernie, who looked down and saw a page from the website of the Liverpool Echo, the region's foremost daily paper.

'We have it on good authority that the team investigating the attack has been joined by DCI Jonah Porter, the famous *Wheelchair Cop*,' she read aloud. 'Where on earth did they get this from?'

'Perhaps someone in Sandra's team has been gossiping to journalists,' Peter suggested.

'Or it could easily have been one of the students that Jonah helped to interview,' Lucy added. 'Either way, it's not that surprising when you think about it. Jonah's a celebrity and people can't help noticing him.'

'So, are you going to give me the low-down?' Dot demanded. 'Do they have any suspects? Is an arrest imminent?'

'Yes, they do have some suspects,' Jonah smiled back at

her. 'But, it'll be a while before they've got sufficient evidence to make an arrest. It's always a mistake to jump too quickly. That's the way you end up with guilty people getting acquitted.'

'So, do they know why he did it?' Dot persisted. 'Was it just racism or was there more to it than that?'

'We can't be certain yet,' Jonah replied, delighted at the opportunity to talk about the case to such a willing listener. 'There are three main possible motives. It could be just a general anti-Muslim attack, or it could be a personal one aimed at one or more of the women as individuals, or it could be a reaction to an incident outside a lap-dancing club back in October.'

'When Mohammed Shaladi drove a van into a group of people on the pavement?' Dot asked excitedly. 'I was wondering about that myself. I did some research about it. He killed two people and injured a police officer, didn't he? And he was sentenced only last week. Could that be what sparked it off?'

'It's impossible to tell at the moment – that's the sort of thing I meant when I said there were several suspects, but no immediate likelihood of an arrest.' Jonah was pleased, but not surprised, to find that Dot shared his enthusiasm for the case. 'There are a number of people who might want to get revenge for the Shaladi incident, but as far as we know, there's no direct link between Shaladi and any of the victims of this more recent attack. On the other hand, there are plenty of people out there who equate *all* Muslims with terrorism, and they might attack Muslims at random, incited by fury about what he did.'

'And then there are people who abuse Muslim women just because they're visibly different,' Lucy added. 'Mariam told me that her friends often get people yelling at them to take off their hijabs.'

'That's something I've never been able to understand,' Dot said, shaking her head. 'We all used to wear headscarves during the war. I remember making them from old curtains and worn out dresses. We didn't want to waste clothing coupons on hats, and there was no question of a woman being seen out with her head bare. Now – what about this boy, Shaladi?'

'He's not exactly a boy,' Bernie protested.

'It says in the papers he's twenty-one,' Dot argued. 'That's not much more than a boy. 'But what I was wanting to ask was: do we know why he did it?'

'I hadn't really thought about it,' Jonah confessed.

'It can't be relevant to this other incident,' Bernie added. 'I mean – if the two are related, surely it must be just that someone is blaming Muslims in general for what Shaladi did. Why does it matter what his motives were?'

'The report of his trial says that he told the court that he was protesting against Western depravity,' Dot told them. 'That was why he did it outside a lap dancing club. He saw it as a symbol of all that was wrong with society. I was just wondering whether there might be people who felt particularly threatened by that stance.'

'Like the owner of the club, do you mean?' queried Lucy.

'Or anyone else who has a vested interest in the clubbing industry,' Jonah agreed. 'Are you suggesting that it might not be so much revenge as trying to warn people off attacking those sorts of targets?'

'Maybe not so much *warning off* as just lashing out at a group that seemed to pose a threat,' Dot replied. 'I was remembering the anti-Irish rhetoric that got bandied about during the IRA bombing campaign. People were frightened and wanted someone to blame. And, getting back to the Shaladi boy,' she went on after a brief pause, 'I was thinking back to the nineteen sixties, when the Abortion Act came in. I remember some youngsters from our church protesting outside an abortion clinic when it first opened. You cousin, Mary Agnes, was one of them, Bernadette.'

'Sorry – I don't see the connection,' Jonah said, bemused.

'I was thinking it was the same sort of thing – young

people protesting about something they thought was wrong with society. Come to think of it, I don't suppose any of them would have had much truck with lap dancing clubs either, but that's beside the point. What I was thinking was: the police moved them on because they said they were a danger to the women who were trying to get into the clinic, and poor Father O'Malley got hate mail from people who blamed the church and accused him of brainwashing them.'

'So what are you saying?' asked Peter, who was becoming interested in spite of his disapproval of Jonah's involvement in the case. He felt that he had lost the thread of this argument. 'That the attack was some sort of counter-protest in favour of lap dancing clubs?'

'I'm not sure,' Dot said slowly, sounding less certain of herself. 'Put like that it sounds a bit far-fetched, I suppose.'

'We were thinking it might be nice for us all to go out somewhere tomorrow,' Bernie said brightly, taking the opportunity to change the subject. 'Where would you like us to take you, Aunty?'

'What sort of thing did you have in mind?'

'Anything you like!' her niece replied. 'You name it. I wondered about Southport – or maybe somewhere across the water. What do you think? Let's get out in the open air and put your new wheelchair through its paces!'

'Anything?' Dot repeated with a wicked gleam in her eye. 'Anything at all?'

'Within reason,' Bernie answered quickly, sensing danger in her aunt's tone. 'What had you in mind?'

'Well, what I'd really like would be to meet those students – the ones who saw the man spraying the acid – and I'd like to have a look at the place where it happened.'

'Oh Aunty! You are incorrigible!' Bernie exclaimed. 'You're as bad as Jonah!'

'I expect I could arrange for you to meet Hibaaq,' Lucy volunteered. 'I don't really know any of the others.'

'Would you?' Dot's eyes shone and her wrinkled face lit up as if she were a small child who had just been promised a treat.

'Yes – but only if you stop treating it like a game,' Lucy said seriously. 'People have had their lives ruined! It's not just a puzzle for you to solve.'

Dot leaned forward and took hold of Lucy's hand.

'I know that, love,' she said gravely. Then, after a short pause, she grinned cheekily and added, 'Don't worry! I'll behave myself.'

Interior of Liverpool Metropolitan Cathedral.

9. HOLIDAY

Lucy had arranged for them to meet with Hibaaq the following afternoon, in the café at the Metropolitan Cathedral. Meanwhile, they spent the morning exploring Sefton Park, one of Bernie's childhood haunts, with Aunty Dot. While Bernie strode ahead with Peter, and Jonah entertained Aunty Dot with stories of his exploits as a serving police officer, Lucy fell in with Ibrahim at the back of the little procession. They had tried to persuade Dominic to come as well, but he had been adamant that the pile of marking that lay untouched in his room could wait no longer.

'Do you really think Mariam will be able to do the exams?' Ibrahim asked Lucy, as they strolled along the wide path at the side of the lake. 'Don't you think it might be better for her to take a year out? Go back and live with Mum and Dad until she's completely better.'

'I don't think she ought to let this muck up her life,' Lucy said defiantly. 'I think she ought to show whoever did it that it isn't going to stop her getting her degree and becoming a doctor. And I know *I'd* be driven absolutely bananas stuck at home with nothing to do except wait for my next hospital appointment.'

'I was just thinking, it's going to be difficult for her having to keep walking past the place where it happened,' Ibrahim argued. 'I'm worried she isn't taking into account the psychological effect that it must have had. I'm afraid she'll push herself too hard.'

'Then we'll just have to rein her in a bit,' Lucy said, putting her arm through his. 'She'll be much better off living with us than hanging around at home, with your parents both working full-time. She'll have three watchdogs keeping an eye on her and making sure she doesn't overdo it.'

'I suppose you may be right,' Ibrahim conceded reluctantly. 'It just seems … What if she has to have lots of operations – skin grafts and stuff? And … whoever did it is still out there. What if he tries again?'

'If he does attack again – which is highly unlikely – there's no reason to think Mariam would be a target,' Lucy argued resolutely. 'Anyway,' she giggled, giving Ibrahim's arm a gently squeeze, 'we've got ex-DCI Jonah Porter on the case! The offender won't be on the loose for long now with Superdetective on his trail!'

Ibrahim joined in her laughter. 'Well, I hope you're right. It isn't very pleasant knowing that there's someone out there who thinks Muslims are fair game for awful attacks like that one. That firework was bad enough, but this … it's just horrible!'

'What are you two doing, skulking at the back like that?' Dot demanded suddenly, spinning her wheelchair round with alarming speed to confront the young people. 'Stop your canoodling with my grandniece young man and come and tell me all about yourself!'

'Wh – what did you want to know, Miss Fazakerley?' Ibrahim stammered, taken aback by this sudden injunction.

'Lucy tells me you're a mechanical engineer. Where do you work?'

'Wavertree Technology Park. It's a small company that nobody's ever heard of. We specialise in lifting gear of different kinds – mainly in the construction industry, but in manufacturing too, and even hoists for lifting patients in hospitals.'

'I see.' Dot turned her chair and set off along the path again. 'And where do you come from? You sound like a woolly back to me.'

'I'm afraid I am,' Ibrahim admitted, falling in beside her, while Lucy and Jonah dropped back behind them. 'I was born in Chorley, but I've lived most of my life in Blackburn – or Darwen to be more precise.'

'I thought so,' Dot said in a satisfied voice. 'I thought I recognised your accent. I'm glad you saw the light and moved to Liverpool. You won't regret it.'

'So Lucy's mum keeps telling me,' Ibrahim laughed.

***

Sandra did not have the luxury of a long weekend. Police work does not stop just because forty years previously a prime minister tried to win public approval by giving workers an additional day off each year. Still, at least she had not had to go through the daily routine of shouting and cajoling to persuade Sophie and Pippa out of bed and into their school uniform on time. She had left them in their rooms, with instructions not to go out without locking up the house, and a plea to empty the washing machine when it finished its cycle and hang the clothes out to dry in the garden.

Now she was standing in front of a dozen or so officers summarising what they knew of the case so far.

'Our number one suspect is Alexander Knowsley,' she said, clicking a button to display a photograph on a large screen attached to the wall behind her. Everyone stared at the face of a nondescript white man in his thirties or early forties with mousey brown hair and eyes that might be blue, grey or possibly hazel. 'He is the legal owner of the motorbike that was used in the attack. He claims that it was stolen, but the theft took place as part of a burglary that made surprisingly little mess and in which nothing else was taken. If he's telling the truth about that, it must have been done by someone who knew the house very well. DC Ransom interviewed him. Tell us what you found out, Ollie.'

She sat down and Oliver Ransom came forward and took her place at the front of the room.

'According to Knowsley, the burglary took place on Tuesday 30th April,' he began. 'That's the day before the acid attack. He says that he was out working all day and discovered the break-in when he got home. I asked him for more details, and it turned out that the job was on an extension to a house only a few minutes' walk away from his home.'

'Knowsley's a plasterer,' Sandra added by way of explanation. 'He works freelance with a mate of his called Shaun Marsden.'

'That's right,' Oliver confirmed. 'They were at school together. They both grew up in Dovecot, although Knowsley's moved to Knotty Ash now, and they're *both* members of *Britain for the British*.'

'Did you ask him where he was on the Wednesday evening?' asked Sandra.

'Yes. He wasn't very coherent. He said he was working late on a job, but his wife insisted that was Thursday not Wednesday. She was round at her parents' house on the Wednesday evening, but she says they had tea together first before she went.'

'So Knowsley doesn't have any alibi for the attack?' Sandra asked.

'Not as far as we know,' Oliver agreed, 'but he didn't really say what he was doing that evening. He started being rather abusive at that point – wanting to know why we were going on about Wednesday evening, when his bike had been taken during the day on Tuesday, and accusing the police of not taking his burglary seriously. I didn't press the point because you said you didn't want him to know that he was a suspect.'

'That's right,' Sandra assured him. 'You did the right thing. There'll be plenty of time to press him on that point after we've accumulated enough evidence to charge him. Now, did you get a look in the shed where he kept the bike?'

'*I* didn't. I kept the Knowsleys talking in the house while DC Foster checked that out.'

'Bryony?' Sandra looked round the room in search of the young detective constable.

'Yes.' Foster got to her feet. 'I had a good look round, like you said to, for any signs of acid, but I didn't find anything.'

'After we got back, we did some research online into Alex Knowsley and Shaun Marsden,' Oliver continued. 'We also checked out their police records. According to the Counter Terrorism Unit, there's a little group of them that they've been keeping an eye on for a while – all from Knowsley's class at school, and all members of *Britain for the British*.'

'Oh?' Sandra prompted.

'The others are Liam O'Neill and Craig Williams,' Oliver told her. 'Liam's a taxi driver and Craig writes computer games. They both live in Dovecot. The unit doesn't have anything very definite on them – mainly just a few reports of them mouthing off about immigrants, and they've been seen on one or two *Britain for the British* demonstrations at various places across the country.'

'There's something else about them that may be significant,' Bryony put in eagerly. 'A passer-by videoed the motorbike on his phone as it left the crime scene. I had a look at it. A taxi followed the bike down Mount Pleasant – and guess what? It belongs to Liam O'Neill. Of course, it could be just coincidence, but …'

'Yes!' Charlotte said excitedly. 'It would fit perfectly. Alex rides his bike – with the stolen number plate on it so he won't be recognised – and sprays the girls with acid. His mate follows behind in the car. They get far enough away that nobody chasing them on foot will be able to catch up with them, and then he ditches the bike and gets away in the taxi.'

'Mmm,' Sandra agreed, 'but if he had a car to get away in, why did he dump the bottle containing the remains of the acid instead of taking it with him?'

'To avoid getting traces of acid in the taxi?' Oliver

suggested.

'But they couldn't be sure there wasn't any of it on his motorbike leathers, and he seems to have kept them on,' Sandra argued. 'I'm not saying you're wrong,' she added, seeing Bryony's rather crestfallen expression. 'I'm just playing devil's advocate to make sure we don't miss anything. If it is those two working together, what's their motive?'

'They just hate Muslims?' Oliver ventured. 'It was their Islamophobia that drew the attention of the Counter Terrorism Unit.'

'Williams especially was very active in the campaign to free Tommy Robinson[15],' added Bryony.

'But there's no reason to think *he* was involved in this,' Sandra argued. 'So that doesn't prove anything.'

'We don't know for sure that it *was* Alex Knowsley riding his bike,' Charlotte pointed out. 'One of his friends could've borrowed it.'

'Or it could even have been a genuine burglary,' Bryony agreed. 'Williams or O'Neill would probably have known where Knowsley kept his keys. They could have broken in and taken the bike while Knowsley was out at work, the way he said he was.'

'Hmm!' Sandra thought for a few moments. 'I suppose you're right. We'd better keep all four of them on the suspect list. Now, let's see who else we've got.'

She clicked a button and brought up a new photograph on the screen. It was a standard police mugshot of a red-headed man with a rather blotchy complexion and what might either be designer stubble or a couple of days' growth

---

[15] Stephen Christopher Yaxley-Lennon, known as Tommy Robinson, is a far-right activist. In May 2018, he was sentenced to 13 months' imprisonment for contempt of court, after publishing a video of defendants entering a law court, contrary to a court order prohibiting reporting of the trial while procedures were ongoing.

of beard.

'This is Mark Lansdale,' she announced. 'He's thirty-seven and lives in Old Swan. His wife, Kimberley, and daughter, Scarlet, were killed when a Muslim student called Mohammed Shaladi drove a van into a group of pedestrians outside a nightclub last October. He was arrested in February for painting anti-Muslim graffiti on buildings across the university. He was bound over and hasn't been in any trouble since.'

'But Shaladi's trial and conviction may have set him off again,' Oliver suggested. 'The burglary was the same day that Shaladi was sentenced.'

'Yes,' agreed Sandra. 'He certainly has a strong motive for the attack, and he's a motorbike mechanic, which could be how he knew that Knowsley had a bike that he could steal, but how did he know where to look for the keys? You'd better do some digging and see if you can find any connection between the two of them.'

'OK,' Oliver nodded. 'I'll get on to that.'

'Another suspect that unfortunately we can't rule out, is Shelley Conway,' Sandra continued, bringing up a new photograph on the screen. 'Some of you may know her. She's a community support officer in Kirkby and married to PC Robert Conway, the officer who was severely injured in the Shaladi van attack She's currently suspended from duty following an incident in which she verbally abused a group of Muslim women.'

'Tom went round to see Shelley yesterday,' Charlotte intervened. 'He was Rob's sergeant for a while, so I asked him to pay her a friendly visit – just checking how they were doing kind of thing. I was hoping he'd be able to establish an alibi for her, but she more or less slammed the door in his face. Do you think we ought to bring her in and question her formally – to eliminate her from the suspect list?'

'No. Let's leave Shelley on the back burner for now,' Sandra decided. 'We don't have any evidence to link her with this attack, so it's better not to make her think we suspect her. It's unlikely that she *is* our attacker – all the witnesses seem to think it was a man, for a start – so there's no point putting her through any more hassle. And if she *is* guilty,' she added, 'she's more likely to relax and give something away if she doesn't realise we're on to her.'

She turned to look round the room at her colleagues. Most looked back attentively; a few, whispering together on the back row, fell suddenly silent as they felt her eye resting on them; one or two hastily looked up from smartphones.

'The other possibility is that the attack was more personal,' she told them, once she was sure that she had their full attention. 'Emily Armstrong's family are not at all happy about her converting to Islam, and her ex-boyfriend has been openly hostile and made threats against her friends.'

'And there's Salma Rahman's brother too,' Charlotte chipped in. 'Remember what her boyfriend said about him spying on her? He seemed genuinely worried that he might consider that she'd somehow brought disgrace on the family.'

'You mean that lad Luke that we met at the mosque?' asked Sandra. 'We don't actually know that he's Salma's boyfriend, do we?'

'I dunno,' Charlotte shrugged. 'It seemed pretty obvious to me. At least – I reckon that's how *he* sees it. I don't know about *her*.'

'And that's not really relevant, is it?' suggested Oliver. 'If this brother of hers is convinced that she's about to go off with a non-Muslim, he might believe that he's got to defend the family honour by doing something to stop her.'

'Throwing acid in her face is a bit drastic, though,' protested Bryony.

'I dunno about that!' a voice called out from the back. 'I know we're not supposed to say it, but them people don't think the same as us. He *might* think that being disfigured for life was better than having it off with a white guy, 'cos after that none of them'd agree to marry her. There's probably some cousin waiting out there in Pakistan or

Bangladesh or wherever, that she's been promised to since she was a baby. And he'll be so desperate to get a visa to come to Britain that he won't be too fussy what she looks like.'

'Have you quite finished?' asked Sandra coldly, walking the length of the room and standing over DC John Fisher, a middle-aged officer who had transferred to CID late in his career, having decided that detective work would be less physically demanding than patrolling the streets. 'As you yourself pointed out, it's important not to stereotype ethnic minorities. While we have to include the possibility that the attack was a personal one and that it could have been perpetrated by a family member of one of the victims, you have no justification for making allegations about forced marriage or anything of that sort.'

She turned and walked slowly back to the front, looking round at each of the officers in turn as she passed them. Then she turned again and addressed the room.

'Right! It's time we all got to work. Charlie! I want you to take charge of investigating that burglary. Organise a house-to-house across the area and put out an appeal for witnesses. Make sure Alex Knowsley thinks we've bought his story. Take Fisher with you. He and Knowsley will get on like a house on fire, I should think.'

She turned to address Oliver and Bryony. 'You've done some good work over the weekend. I'd like you to carry on with looking into the background of Knowsley, O'Neill and the others. In particular, see what you can find out about their online activity. These sorts of people often give themselves away by boasting to their cronies on social media.' She looked round the room again. 'OK, that's it. Get back to work all of you.'

***

'I hope you don't mind,' Hibaaq said, advancing to meet them as Lucy and Bernie entered the café. 'I invited Tahira and Olivia to join us.'

'All the better!' Aunty Dot called out from behind before Bernie could answer. 'I want to hear all the gen about this despicable acid-throwing business.'

'This is Aunty Dot,' Lucy told Hibaaq with a grin. 'As I told you, she fancies herself as a Miss Marple. Aunty – this is Hibaaq. She's a year above me and Mariam, doing medicine.'

'I'm very pleased to meet you,' Dot smiled up at Hibaaq. 'I used to be a nurse, you know, at the old Royal Infirmary – before they built the new hospital; and now there's a new hospital to replace that one – if they ever get it finished!'

Lucy and Hibaaq moved chairs out of the way to allow Jonah to manoeuvre his wheelchair over to the table where Olivia and Tahira were sitting. To Bernie's relief, Dot opted to park her chair in a corner near the entrance and to walk across the room to join them. The arthritis in her hands, coupled with a reluctance to slow down when approaching obstacles, made Dot a somewhat erratic driver, and her niece had visions of her leaving a trail of destruction behind her if she had attempted to follow Jonah's lead.

Bernie helped her aunt out of her chair and took her arm as she shuffled painfully across the room to where Peter was waiting to help her into a chair. She sat down, propping her stick against the table, and looked round. 'How lovely to see so many young faces! Now, tell me your names and where you come from and what you're studying. I don't get out much, so I want to make the most of it when I do.'

While Peter and Bernie went to the counter to order coffee, the students did their best to satisfy Dot's curiosity. Olivia described seeing the motorbike coming towards them, and Hibaaq told her about watching it disappear down the street and straining to see the number on the back.

'But it's so frustrating not to have been able to recognise him or to give the police a description,' Tahira finished. She looked towards Jonah. 'Do you honestly think they will ever find out who it was?'

'I'd say there's a very good chance,' he assured her.

'They've got the bike and they know who owns it.'

'But the news reports said it'd been stolen,' Tahira argued.

'Yes.' Peter came back with five cups of coffee on a tray. 'And the number plate was also stolen. So they have two separate crimes to investigate, each of which could lead to the attacker. These things take time, but they won't give up.'

He handed round the coffee to Lucy, Bernie and Dot. Then he put Jonah's cup on a special tray attachment that was fixed on to the arm of his wheelchair. Lucy pushed a straw into a hole in the lid and positioned it carefully so that he could reach it with his mouth.

'Aren't you girls having anything?' asked Dot, looking round at Hibaaq and her friends.

'We're fasting,' Tahira explained. 'Ramadan started yesterday. 'We don't eat or drink anything between sunrise and sunset.'

'Of course!' Dot nodded. 'I should have thought of that.' She thought for a few moments and then added, 'but what about the girls who were injured? They'll need to keep up their fluid intake while they're recovering. Will they-?'

'Oh! They don't have to fast,' Tahira broke in quickly. 'Anyone who's ill is exempt. It's not about doing anything that will put people at risk. It's a religious exercise to help us to reflect more deeply on God during his holy month.'

'Yes. I understand. Catholics believe in fasting too,' Dot told her, 'but we aren't quite as ambitious as you. We give up eating meat on Fridays and during Lent, but only a few Religious go in for real fasting from all food. It's a good discipline; we probably ought not to have abandoned it.'

Tahira stared back at Dot, unsure how to react to this. She had been expecting Lucy's elderly aunt to be ignorant of Islamic practices and most likely hostile, or at best dismissive, towards them. Bernie watched her face, carefully hiding her own amusement at her aunt's ability to wrong-foot this hitherto supremely confident young woman.

'It said in the Echo that this acid attack could have been

retaliation for that Libyan lad driving his van into the night club,' Dot said casually. 'He was a student too, wasn't he? Did any of you know him?'

'Er, well …,' Olivia and Tahira exchanged glances.

'Yes?' Jonah prompted, his eyes lighting up at the prospect of gaining some insight into why an intelligent young man had suddenly decided to attack a group of innocent bystanders.

'He was nice,' Olivia said at last. 'At least what I saw of him.'

'He was a bit conservative,' Tahira conceded. 'He didn't like our mosque because he thought the khutbah ought to be in Arabic, not English.'

'But then, English wasn't his first language,' Olivia pointed out. 'So I suppose …'

'And he didn't approve of me, because I don't cover my head,' Tahira went on. 'But that's nothing unusual. I get a lot of stick for that from ignorant Muslim men who think that anything different from the way their mothers and grandmothers behaved is haram for women.'

'Back in my first year, some girls started jeering at me when I was on a bus,' Olivia recounted. 'It wasn't really late, but it was winter so it was dark. They called me names and shouted at me to take off my hijab. Mo Shaladi was somewhere behind me. He got up and came and sat next to me and he told them to stop.'

'Do you know who the girls were?' Peter asked. 'Did you report them to the police?'

'They were only young,' Olivia shook her head. 'They were in uniform, I don't know which school. I thought they were just being silly – showing off to each other. But when I got off, they got off too, and then they started trying to physically pull my hijab off my head. There must've been three or four of them, I think. I was really scared then. All the time I was on the bus, I kept telling myself that they couldn't do anything, because I could always call the bus driver and he'd turn them off, but once we were all in the street …'

'What happened?' asked Lucy, wide-eyed.

'Mo must have followed us off the bus. He grabbed two of the girls and pushed them back against the side of the bus shelter. Then he shouted at me to run, so I did. I don't know exactly what he did after that, but it wasn't long before he caught up with me, and then he walked me home, lecturing me all the way about being out alone without a man to protect me. I invited him into my room for a coffee, but he said it wouldn't be appropriate for him to go into a woman's bedroom, so he left.'

'I tried to explain to him that the answer to gender-based violence was to make our streets safe for women, rather than requiring them to go everywhere accompanied by a male protector,' Tahira told them. 'But he wouldn't listen.'

'My personal take on that would be that we need to do both,' Peter said quietly. 'Obviously we ought to be making sure that *everyone* is safe, but it's also sensible to take precautions. I'm not suggesting for a moment that Olivia shouldn't have been on that bus on her own, but sometimes people do take unnecessary risks. There are some places in Oxford that I wouldn't want Lucy wandering around on her own late at night, for example – or my son, Eddie, either for that matter,' he added hastily, seeing Tahira opening her mouth with a look of indignation on her face.

'Getting back to Mohammed Shaladi,' Jonah said quickly. 'I take it you were surprised to hear that he'd been arrested for driving a van into people on the pavement?'

'Completely flabbergasted,' Olivia nodded. 'I hadn't seen him for ages, but I never thought he'd do a thing like that. At first I thought it must have been some sort of accident – though I couldn't think how he came to be driving a van at all!'

'He was very quiet and gentle,' Hibaaq agreed, 'and very close to his family. He used to go back to Stockport to see them almost every weekend.'

'Tell me about this society that you all belong to,' urged

Dot. 'According to our Lucy, it's some sort of feminist movement – is that right?'

'I don't think I'd call it a *movement* exactly,' Tahira answered with a smile. 'It's more just a group of friends getting together. We're trying to show that it's possible to be a good Muslim *and* a feminist. There are far too many people – both Muslims and non-Muslims – who think that Islam requires women to submit to male authority, but it's not like that at all.'

'And how do the men feel about that?' asked Dot innocently. 'I don't know about Muslim men, but I'm old enough to remember men complaining that women were stealing their jobs, and it wasn't right allowing them to take work away from men with wives and families to support. When men are used to being in charge, they don't always take kindly to women expecting to be treated equally.'

'You're dead right there!' Tahira agreed vehemently. 'You should have heard the fuss there was when I said I wanted to become an Imam! Even men who'd been on the side of letting men and women mingle together during Friday prayers started telling me I was being ridiculous. Some of them told me it would be counter-productive because no one would ever allow me to lead men in prayer, so it would end up with men and women praying in separate rooms again. And there were others who just said it was forbidden and started going on about men and women being equal but different and that it was like pretending that men could have babies or breast feed! Talk about tunnel vision! Sometimes I feel like I'm banging my head against a brick wall, I really do!'

'I know how you feel,' Dot smiled ruefully. 'After the Second Vatican Council, I thought it was only a matter of time before we had women priests, but sixty years on, we don't seem to have advanced an inch!'

'That's the patriarchy,' Tahira said dogmatically. 'It's ingrained in practically every society. That's why it's so infuriating when people talk as if women are uniquely disadvantaged within Muslim communities.'

'Well, I certainly hope that you succeed in your ambition,' Dot said gravely. She raised her coffee cup as if proposing a toast. 'And let's hope you youngsters all live to see the first woman become Pope!'

Liverpool Metropolitan Cathedral

10. MODESTY

While Peter headed home to Oxford on the train, Bernie and Jonah accompanied Sandra to Emily Armstrong's family home in St Helens. Once again, Sandra was hoping that Jonah's presence – whether as a police hero or a man in a wheelchair, she was not sure – would reduce the likelihood of tempers flaring. The aim was to interview Emily, but Sandra knew that first she would have to convince her parents that this was a necessary part of the investigation, rather than police harassment of a vulnerable young woman who was recovering from a traumatic injury.

'Don't you have any Muslim officers that you could call on to help you with this case?' Jonah asked Sandra, as they passed the entrance to Knowsley Safari Park and sped on along the dual carriageway that took through traffic round to the north of Prescot town centre. 'I can't help thinking that it would be useful to have someone who could talk to members of the university Islamic Society and the mosque – or should I say mosques? – that students attend, on their own terms.'

'Someone they would trust, you mean?' asked Sandra. 'I'd been thinking that myself, but we don't have a lot of officers from any of the ethnic minorities, I'm afraid. I've already spoken to the uniformed officers who liaise regularly with the mosque leaders over security. They seem to have a good relationship with the Muslims, but they're all white – like ninety-six percent of the force.'

'But then the population must be about ninety percent white, isn't it?' put in Bernie.

'Ninety-four,' agreed Sandra, 'so we're not doing so badly from that point of view, but it does mean that it's hard to find officers that particular groups can identify with. I'll have a go, though. You're right – we do need someone who can get alongside the other Muslim students and find out what they really thought of the feminist sisters. On the other hand,' she added, as Bernie turned the car off the main road into a residential area, 'with any luck, we'll manage to nail Alex Knowsley and his cronies soon and then it won't matter.'

'Is this the right road?' Bernie asked, slowing down as they approached a turning on the left.

'Yes,' Sandra confirmed. 'The house is just a few doors down on the left … That's it! Pull in here.'

Bernie parked the car and got out to help Jonah down from the back. Sandra brushed down her jacket and ran a comb through her hair as she waited for them. Bernie locked the car and stood clutching the portable ramp that would enable Jonah to take his wheelchair up and over the Armstrongs' front doorstep.

'Come on then!' he urged impatiently. 'Let's get a move on.'

Sandra walked ahead and rang the bell, before stepping aside to allow Bernie to set up the ramp. She was still bending down checking that it was secure when the door opened and Fiona Armstrong looked out.

'Good morning, Mrs Armstrong,' Sandra said politely. 'Do you remember me? DCI Sandra Latham. I rang earlier. Could I speak to Emily, please? It's important for helping us find out who attacked her.'

'That's OK,' Fiona replied, sounding much more friendly towards the police than she had on the previous occasions when they had met. 'Steve's gone back to work.' Perhaps that was the reason for her improved mood. 'But I'm staying off for a bit longer to see she's alright. Come in and sit down and I'll fetch her for you.'

'Thank you.' Sandra half-turned and waved her hand towards Jonah. 'I've brought DCI Porter with me. He's an extremely experienced detective. He's helping us with this case on a consultative basis, because it's so important that we get to the bottom of this as soon as we possibly can.'

Jonah smiled up at Fiona, tilting his head a little to one side in a gesture of greeting. She stared back for a moment and then exclaimed, 'the wheelchair cop! I remember you – you caught that nurse who was doing in all her patients at that Care Home in Wavertree, didn't you? Munchausen Syndrome wasn't it they said? Are you going to find out who did this to our Emily?'

'We're going to have a very good try,' Jonah assured her, gliding up the ramp and into the narrow hall, forbearing to correct her inaccurate recollection of the successful investigation[16] that he had taken part in two years previously. 'Inspector Latham and her team already have several good leads that they're following up.'

Sandra held the door open for Jonah to enter the lounge, while Mrs Armstrong disappeared upstairs to get her daughter.

'I'm glad Mr Armstrong isn't here,' Sandra confided in a low voice. 'I think that's going to make things a lot easier.'

She and Bernie sat down in the two armchairs while Jonah positioned his wheelchair between them. That left the settee free for Emily and her mother to sit side-by-side. Soon there was the sound of footsteps descending the stairs followed by voices in the hall. The door opened and Emily came in – or at least, Sandra could only assume that it was Emily. What she actually saw was a slim woman, a little taller than Fiona Armstrong, dressed in a knee-length blue dress over navy blue trousers. Her head and shoulders were covered by a lighter blue scarf fastened tight under her chin; and her face was obscured by a veil of black material, which covered her nose and mouth leaving only her pale blue eyes visible.

Sandra got to her feet and advanced towards Emily with her hand extended. 'Hello Emily. I'm DCI Sandra Latham.

---

[16] See *In my Liverpool Home* © 2017, ISBN: 978-1911083351

I'm leading the investigation into who attacked you and your friends.'

Emily shook hands nervously, looking round at Jonah and Bernie and avoiding making eye contact.

'And this is DCI Jonah Porter and his personal assistant, Dr Bernie Fazakerley,' Sandra continued. 'Shall we all sit down?'

Emily nodded and then sat down on the settee. Her mother closed the door before joining her. They sat expectantly, looking across the room at the police contingent. Sandra looked back, unsure how to start the interview.

'I'm sorry to have to ask you this,' she began at last, 'but we do need to know from you exactly what happened. I realise it must be something you don't want to think about, but it will really help us if you can try to remember. Is that OK?'

Emily nodded. 'What do you want to know?'

'Just tell us, in your own words, what happened on Wednesday evening,' Jonah said gently. 'Start from when you and your friends came out of the Guild of Students.'

'We came out,' Emily recounted obediently. 'That's me and Olivia and Mariam and Salma. The others stayed behind for a bit to write up the minutes. I wanted to ask Tahira something, and Salma was going to get a bus from the stop just outside Starbucks, so we all hung around there for a bit. I was watching the door for Tahira to come out.'

'So that means you had your back to the road – is that right?' asked Jonah.

'Yes. I was like in the middle of the pavement, and Salma was on my right – no! Mariam was on my right and Salma was to the right of her … at least, I think so.'

'That's OK,' Jonah said gently. 'Take your time.'

'That's what Olivia told us too,' Sandra added reassuringly. 'And it fits in with the way Salma got most of the acid on her and you got the least.'

'I'm sorry, I don't really remember much.' Emily's eyes

suddenly filled with tears and she wiped her hand across her face to brush them away. Sandra caught a glimpse of pale skin and narrow pink lips as the veil slipped briefly to one side.

Bernie reached out a small packet of tissues from the storage space at the back of Jonah's chair and held it out to Emily. She stared at it for a few seconds before taking it, nodding her thanks and blinking furiously. Fiona reached across and tried to undo the veil. Emily immediately jumped up and backed away from her mother.

'Don't do that!' she shouted. 'Leave me alone!'

'I only thought it would be easier for you to …,' Fiona began in an irritated tone. 'I mean, you can't blow your nose or anything with that thing on, can you?'

'Shut up! You don't know anything about it!' Emily pulled out a tissue, threw the rest of the packet down on the coffee table and stormed out of the room.

'I'm so sorry,' Fiona apologised. 'I'll go and fetch her back for you.'

'Let me have a go,' Bernie got up and stood between Fiona and the door. 'I've got a daughter her age. She may be more likely to respond to someone outside her family.'

Fiona shrugged her shoulders and sat back down on the settee. 'Be my guest. Ever since she took up with this Muslim nonsense, she hasn't listened to a word Steve or I say. He says they've brainwashed her. I'm beginning to think he's right.'

Bernie left the room, closing the door firmly behind her. The others waited in silence. There was a murmur of voices outside, but they could not tell what was being said. After a few minutes, the door opened again and Emily came back in followed by Bernie.

'I'm sorry,' she said, looking first at Sandra and then at Jonah. Sandra noted that her eyes were bloodshot and the lids were red and swollen. Most likely, these recent tears had merely added to earlier ones. 'I'm ready to answer your questions now.'

Bernie sat down next to Fiona, leaving the chair next to Jonah free for Emily. He smiled at her as she took her seat.

'If you don't mind,' he said gently, 'I'd like to ask you about how you came to convert to Islam and what it means to you. Is that OK?'

'What do you want to know?' Emily asked suspiciously.

'Well, I don't really know a lot about Islam and I've never considered converting to another religion myself, so I'm interested to know what attracted you to it,' Jonah explained. 'It must mean a lot to you to change your whole way of life like that.'

'Well, for a start, you shouldn't call it *converting*,' Emily told him dogmatically. Sandra suspected that she was repeating words that someone else – probably Tahira – had given to her. 'Islam means submission to Allah (glory be to him). It's the natural state that everyone has before they rebel against him. When I became a Muslim, I *re*verted to Islam, because I returned to that primeval state and restored the correct relationship between Allah (glory be to him) and myself.'

'I see,' Jonah said encouragingly. 'That's very interesting. And what was it that made you realise that you needed to revert?'

'I met Salma. We both belong to the Hill-Walking Club. Jack does too. You know about Jack, I suppose?'

'Your ex-boyfriend? Yes, your friends told us about him,' Jonah confirmed. 'But go on – you met Salma and ...?'

'She just seemed so full of life, so – so – I can't really explain. It was like she enjoyed everything *more* than anyone else did. She was always laughing and joking, but not in the nasty way that some people have – not laughing at other people, just – just full of – of – like *joy*, I suppose you might call it.'

'And you thought you'd like to have a share in that ... joy?' suggested Jonah quietly.

'That's right,' Emily nodded. 'Then one day, we were out walking with the club. Jack couldn't come – I don't remember why – so I got talking to Salma. She told me all about how liberating it was submitting to Allah and not having to worry about anything else. And I thought how great it would be not to have to bother about what other people think of me, because Allah was the only one who mattered.'

'That's interesting,' Jonah commented. 'Did you worry a lot about what other people thought of you – before you reverted, I mean?'

'Oh yes!' Emily's eyes sparkled and Sandra felt sure that she was smiling beneath her veil. 'I was awful like that! I always imagined people were talking about me behind my back – like, criticising me or laughing at me.'

'Why didn't you tell us about that?' Fiona asked, sounding both anxious and annoyed. 'If people were bullying you, we could've-,' she broke off as Bernie placed a restraining hand on her arm.

'I understand what you mean,' Jonah told her gently before Fiona could recover. 'I can see why it would be attractive to be able to get away from all that. Go on – what happened next?'

'Salma introduced me to the others – Tahira and Hibaaq and some others who've left uni now – and they explained more about what it means to be a Muslim.' Emily turned to look Jonah directly in the eyes, her own eyes shining with passion. 'And everything just sort of fell into place, and it was such a relief!'

'Yes,' Jonah said softly, 'I can understand that, but some of your old friends found it harder to comprehend, I gather?'

'Well, I didn't have that many friends, so that wasn't really an issue,' Emily told him, her eyes smiling a little sadly now. 'Almost all my friends are people I've met through the mosque. Salma-,' she stopped short suddenly and turned to look at Sandra. 'Is Salma going to be alright?' she asked in a fearful whisper.

'The doctors are all doing their very best for her,' Sandra

answered evasively, 'but ...'

'Is she going to die?' Emily's voice trembled as she looked from Sandra to Bernie and finally to Jonah.

'No,' he answered kindly. 'They don't think she's going to die, but she is very seriously hurt. She's going to need all her friends to help her adjust to a very different sort of life in the future, when she comes out of hospital.'

'Oh!' Emily bent her head and seemed to be thinking. For several minutes nobody spoke. Sandra became aware of the ticking of an old-fashioned clock on the mantelpiece over the fireplace.

'And, in the meantime,' Jonah went on eventually, 'you can help her by helping us to find out who did this to her.'

'How?' Emily sounded like a frightened child. 'How can I help?'

'By answering our questions. We were wondering if you could think of anyone who might have wanted to hurt Salma – or Mariam or any of you. Has there been anyone making threats or anything like that?'

'Well, only Jack – but I'm sure he wouldn't ... I mean ...,' Emily looked towards her mother.

'Of course he wouldn't,' Fiona snapped back at once. 'How could you even suggest it? You could never find a nicer lad than Jack.'

'Only he *has* been stalking me,' Emily said almost inaudibly. 'And he hates Salma. He told me he did.'

'Stalking you? How exactly?' asked Sandra.

'Waiting for me outside lectures; following me around; texting me all the time,' Emily shrugged. 'It got so bad I had to get a different phone. He just can't accept that it's all over between us – and he blames it all on ... He keeps saying I've been brainwashed. He just doesn't understand.'

'A good friend of mine became a Catholic not long ago,' Jonah said confidingly. 'I found it hard to understand why he would want to sign up to a religion that seemed to me to be out of date and, in many ways, just plain absurd. Don't you think that might have been how your Jack was feeling when you reverted to Islam?'

'But he didn't have to make fun of it, the way he did!' Emily protested. 'He used to try to pull my niqab off. He said I was stupid wearing it and it just showed how I'd let "those Muslim cretins" brainwash me.'

'But none of the other girls wears a niqab,' Jonah pointed out gently. 'What made you choose to do that?'

'It's so liberating not having to worry about people judging my appearance all the time!' Emily answered fervently. 'The girls at school were always criticising me – telling me how to do my makeup, giving me advice on how to get rid of my blackheads, laughing at the way my face always goes red in the sun. Now, I don't have to think about that. I can make myself up to please myself – or not bother, if I don't want to.'

'But that's-,' Fiona began, but she stopped short, seeing Sandra raise her hand in a warning gesture.

'So it hasn't got anything to do with you being a Muslim?' queried Jonah.

'No, it's not that. Of course, it's because I'm a Muslim. I'm just saying that, now that I've decided to cover myself out of respect for Allah (glory be to him), I also feel so much more comfortable in my own skin, because I don't have everyone else looking at my face and my figure and judging me.'

'But people sometimes judge you for wearing what you do,' Sandra suggested cautiously. 'Doesn't that bother you?'

'That's different!' Emily declared forcefully. 'I don't mind what happens to me if it's because I'm being true to Allah. I'm not ashamed of being a Muslim. If other people don't like it that's their problem. *I'm* not going to change.'

She looked defiantly across the room at her mother as she made this last statement. Fiona seemed about to respond but then thought better of it and looked back in silence. Sandra lifted her briefcase on to her lap and took out a cardboard folder.

'I've got some photographs here,' she told Emily. 'I'd

like you to have a look at them and tell me if you remember seeing any of these people before. I'm not just talking about last Wednesday – I mean any time since you started uni.'

Emily took the sheaf of pictures that Sandra held out to her and looked at them one by one, putting them down on her lap after she had scrutinised each. Jonah recognised them as Alexander Knowsley, Shaun Marsden, Craig Williams and Liam O'Neill – the band of four school friends who had grown up to become far-right activists.

'No.' Emily shook her head. 'I don't recognise any of them. Who are they? Why do you think I might have seen them?'

'They're just some guys with a history of racist behaviour,' Sandra told her, being deliberately vague. 'We were wondering if they'd been hanging around the university at all. OK,' she added, getting a business card out of her jacket pocket and handing it to Emily. 'I think we'll call it a day. If you think of anything else that might help us find out who did this awful thing, give me a ring on this number.'

Fiona was on her feet at once, ready to show them out of the house. As soon as they were all in the hall, she closed the door to the lounge firmly behind them and said in a low voice, 'You see what she's like. She simply won't listen to reason. I was hoping that this might have given her a fright and made her see sense, but if anything it's just made her all the more … Oh! I don't know. I just wish she'd stop making a show of herself with this ridiculous costume of hers. It's … it's as if she doesn't realise she's only turning herself into a target for this sort of thing!'

'Try not to worry, Mrs Armstrong,' Sandra said in her offering-vague-reassurances-to-members-of-the-public voice. 'These incidents really are very rare, and we're working hard to make sure your daughter is safe whatever she chooses to wear.'

The "statue exceedingly bare" outside Lewis's department store, made famous in the song "In my Liverpool Home" by Peter McGovern.

11. SOLIDARITY

At Lucy's insistence, Bernie and Jonah had their evening meal (which Jonah called "dinner" and Bernie insisted on referring to as "tea") with her that evening. When they arrived at the shared house in Kensington, they found Tahmina and Abdul Ali in the hall, saying goodbye to their daughter, whom they had brought home after she had been discharged that morning. Mariam looked tired, but cheerful. Like all patients, she was relieved to be out of hospital. Her injuries were hidden beneath a colourful headscarf.

'Tahmina brought over lots of these,' Lucy told them, after Mariam's parents had departed in their car. 'After the dressings come off, the new skin will need protecting from the sun for a long time – maybe forever. I think these are a dead cool way of doing it, don't you?'

'Dead cool,' Jonah agreed solemnly. Then he turned to Mariam. 'It's good to see you looking a bit more yourself again. What have the doctor's said? Are they going to let you take your exams?'

'They said to take it easy and see how things go,' Mariam answered. 'The exams don't start until next week, so I've got a few days to get back into things again before that.'

'There aren't any lectures or anything this week,' Lucy told them, 'so Mariam and I are going to revise quietly together here.'

'That's a good idea, love,' Bernie agreed. 'And let me know if there's anything we can do to help,' she added, turning to Mariam. 'Running you to outpatients to have your dressing changed, for instance. You might as well make use of us while we're here.'

'Thank you,' Mariam smiled shyly back, 'but a nurse is

going to come here to do that. I think they like to have an excuse for checking up on patients at home, in case they're living in squalor or ... well, I gather a lot of burns are related to domestic violence.'

'Go on in and sit down,' Lucy urged impatiently. 'We won't be long. I just want to go up and choose one of Mariam's new hijabs to put on before the boys get back.'

The two girls were still upstairs when Dominic arrived home, but they came clattering down to greet him when they heard the front door opening. He stared in amazement as Lucy descended the stairs dressed in a lime green hijab. He opened his mouth as if to pass comment on her attire, but then closed it again when he saw Mariam following behind.

'Mariam! You're out!' he gasped as she reached the bottom step. 'How are you? When did you get back?'

'I'm fine,' she assured him. 'They discharged me this morning. Mum and Dad brought me home.'

'Where are they? I didn't see the car outside.'

'They've gone back to Blackburn. They're on duty again tomorrow.'

'It's wonderful to see you here,' Dominic declared fervently, 'but are you sure it's a good idea? I mean – wouldn't you be better at home with your mum and dad?'

'No,' Mariam said firmly, but with a twinkle of amusement in her eyes. 'I told you – I'm fine, just a bit tired after all the excitement of coming home, that's all. Lucy's looking after me. I'm going to be just fine.'

'So you're going to do the exams and everything?' Dominic asked. 'Are you sure that's wise?'

'Yes, I am. And yes I'm sure,' Mariam smiled up at him. He was taller than she was, even when she was a step higher on the stairs. 'Don't worry. Lucy's promised my dad that she won't let me overdo it.'

She put her arms round his chest and Dominic found himself lifting her in his arms. She felt strangely small and light. He held her close for a moment before setting her down in the hall.

'Well, just mind you listen to her, if she tells you to slow down, that's all,' he said, trying to sound stern. 'I know you think you're tough as old boots, but you can't expect to get over something like this all in five minutes.'

'I know,' Mariam continued to smile. 'I'll be sensible – scout's honour!'

Lucy and Mariam talked with Jonah in the lounge, while Bernie and Dominic prepared the evening meal. Bernie noted an air of suppressed excitement in Dominic's demeanour as he stirred a large pan of scouse (made, as he explained to her, from ingredients that Ibrahim had checked and passed as halal) and chatted about his day at school.

'How do you think Mariam is, really?' he asked, returning to the subject that was most on his mind. 'She looks tired to me. Don't you think she ought to go home and leave the exams for next time?'

'She's bound to be tired after the excitement of getting out of hospital,' Bernie told him patiently. 'But I'd say she's looking remarkably well, considering. And I still think that getting the exams out of the way is the better option, providing she's up to it.'

'It was a good idea of her mum's to bring over those headscarves,' Dominic commented, in an effort to be more positive. 'They hide the burns completely, and I think it sort of suits her. I don't get why Lucy's wearing one too, though.'

Ibrahim, arriving home a few minutes later, was equally perplexed by Lucy's new headgear.

'What's that you've got on your head?' he demanded as she emerged from the lounge to greet him in the hall and to let him know that his sister was home.

'Your mum brought it over,' Lucy told him. 'She got about a dozen different ones for Mariam to cover up the acid burns. We're going to share them. What do you think of this one? I like the embroidery round the edge. Mariam's been showing me how to fasten it on properly.'

'But why do *you* want to wear one?' Ibrahim asked, still

staring at her with an expression of shock and amazement on his face. He hardly recognised his friend in this new costume, which completely hid the mass of golden curls that usually stood out round her head. '*You* haven't had your head burnt.'

'I'm wearing it out of solidarity with all the Muslim women who do. So long as wearing a hijab makes women identifiable as Muslims, they're going to be targets for nutters like that idiot on the motorbike. If everyone started wearing them, they wouldn't be able to tell, would they?'

'And you'd all become targets,' Ibrahim argued. 'This is ridiculous! You don't think for a moment that the whole of womankind is going to spontaneously start covering their heads, do you? And so long as there are any that don't, the ones who do will be seen as traitors by the sort of people who attacked Mariam and her friends.'

'If there are enough of us, they won't be able to attack us all,' Lucy insisted obstinately. 'So I'm helping to spread the risk. Anyway, that's not the point. It's symbolic – standing by our Muslim sisters to show the fascists that we're not afraid of them.'

'But – but you don't realise … These people are dangerous,' Ibrahim protested. 'I don't want you putting yourself at risk like this.'

'Why not?' Lucy flashed back. 'Why should I be safe, when Mariam and Hibaaq aren't? And they'd be targets whatever they wear, because they can't change the colour of their skin, can they? What right have I to be treated differently, just because I'm white? I want to know what it's like to have people look sideways at you on the bus, wondering if you're a terrorist. I want-'

'Stop treating it as if it's some sort of game!' Ibrahim cut in sharply. 'These people are dangerous. Look what they've done to Mariam and Salma.'

'I *am* looking! That's why I want to do something to-'

'Hello Ibrahim!' Bernie had heard the raised voices and come out of the kitchen to see what was up. 'Presumably

Lucy's told you that Mariam's home. We're just about to have tea. I know you can't eat until later, but do you want to sit with us so that we can give you the latest on the investigation?'

'Yes please.' Ibrahim smiled at Bernie, trying to forget his annoyance with Lucy. Why did she always feel the need to turn every injustice that she saw into a personal campaign? 'Is there anything I can do to help?'

'No thanks,' Bernie smiled back. 'Dominic's got everything under control. Perhaps you could just stick your head round the door of the lounge and ask the others to come through to the dining room.'

The dining room was rather dark, because its small window, facing on to the back yard, was in the shadow of the kitchen, which was a single-storey outrigger leading off it.

Lucy showed Jonah to a space for his wheelchair at the end of the table and then sat down on his right. Mariam took the place on the other side of Lucy. Ibrahim hesitated for a moment before choosing the chair on the other side of Jonah. This put him immediately opposite Lucy, who smiled across at him defiantly, almost as if she were daring him to resume their argument.

Bernie entered carrying a pile of plates, which she set down on the table before sitting down next to Ibrahim. Dominic followed with the pan of scouse, which he ladled out and handed round. Soon everyone, apart from Ibrahim, was tucking in to the lamb stew accompanied by doorstep slices of bread from a large oval plate in the centre of the table.

'You were going to tell us how the police investigation's going,' Ibrahim prompted, turning to look towards Bernie.

'There's nothing definite yet,' Jonah responded at once, 'but it's looking increasingly likely that it could be the work of a small group of right-wing extremists. DCI Latham has applied for a warrant to search two of their houses. One's the owner of the motorbike and the other was seen driving his taxi down Mount Pleasant immediately after it left the crime scene.'

'And she's got two officers looking into their online activity and past history,' Bernie added, 'as well as stepping up the investigation into the theft of the bike – if such a theft actually happened at all – and of the false number plate that they used to avoid it being identified.'

I've got photographs of all four of the group on my computer,' Jonah went on, turning his head away from a spoonful of scouse that Lucy was attempting to put into his mouth, in order to concentrate on manipulating the computer screen attached to his wheelchair. 'Have a look at them for me. Have you ever seen any of them before?'

Ibrahim got up and walked round behind Jonah to look more closely. He studied the pictures one by one.

'No,' he said at last, shaking his head. 'None of them look familiar.'

'Mariam?' Jonah rotated the screen to face her. She leaned across the table to see the photographs.

'No.' She too shook her head. 'Why did you think we might have seen them?'

'If they'd been hanging around the university campus or the mosque looking for likely targets for their hate,' Jonah answered. 'This was a well-planned attack. The logistics would have needed to have been worked out in advance.'

'You said the police are searching their houses,' Dominic said, putting his knife and fork together on his plate and looking round to see if anyone else had finished eating. 'What exactly are they looking for?'

'Anything to connect them with the incident,' Lucy told him.

'That's right,' Jonah agreed. 'Most importantly, evidence of possession of concentrated sulphuric acid. It's not something you can just walk into a chemist's and buy over the counter.'

'And the motorbike leathers and crash helmet may well still have traces of it on them,' Bernie added. 'I know when

I use one of those garden sprayers to kill greenfly, it always blows back on me. The chances are the same will have happened to the attacker.'

'Another good reason for him dressing up in biking leathers and a crash helmet,' Ibrahim observed thoughtfully. 'I see what you mean about meticulous planning.'

'Do you think they could be part of a bigger group?' Dominic asked suddenly. 'If you catch these four, will there still be others out there, scheming to attack innocent people like Mariam and her friends?'

The room fell silent.

'Impossible to say for sure,' Jonah said after what felt like a long pause. 'But I don't think it's likely. There may be a depressingly large number of people routinely abusing Muslims on social media or even verbally in the street, but very few would go as far as serious physical attacks.'

'That's right,' Bernie agreed. 'It was the same with Irish nationalism back in the sixties and seventies when I was growing up. Your dad will tell you the same, Dom. There were lots of Irish families in our church who believed in a united Ireland, and maybe a handful of hotheads – mainly young men – who sympathised with the IRA and argued in favour of the armed struggle, but none of them would have dreamed of planting a bomb themselves.'

'The people at the top of these right-wing organisations don't want their members to do this sort of thing,' Jonah added. 'They want to gain political power by portraying ethnic minorities as a threat to civilised society. If there is violence, they want to dress it up as the fault of the other side, for example by holding a rally that deliberately provokes a response, which they can then portray as the enemies of democracy attempting to prevent their peaceful protest. Attacking innocent women doesn't advance their cause at all.'

'I hope you're right.' Dominic got to his feet and started collecting the empty plates. 'There's plenty of scouse for you to have later, Ibrahim. I'll leave it in the kitchen. Now, what about afters? There's ice cream in the freezer. Is that OK for everyone?'

Ibrahim helped his friend to carry out the plates and then went to sit in the living room while the others finished their meal. He got out his phone and selected the Qur'an app. He had promised himself that, as part of the self-discipline appropriate to the holy month of Ramadan, he would study a few verses every day. However, at the moment, he found it very hard to concentrate on anything apart from his sister's injuries and hoped-for recovery, and the hunt for the man who had attacked her.

Was it really wise of her to insist on going straight back to her studies, instead of taking a long break and starting back when she was no longer in pain from the burns and had a better idea how much surgery might be needed? Bernie seemed to think that getting back in the saddle as soon as possible was the best way of speeding her recovery, and she did have years of experience of dealing with students from her days as a tutor at one of the Oxford colleges, but did she really know?

And then there was Lucy! What had induced her to make herself into a target for those neo-Nazis by dressing up as a traditional Muslim. It was bad enough to think that Mariam had broken her resolve and donned a hijab, but that was at least in order to hide the dressing on her head and to protect her healing skin. With Lucy, it was just a gesture, and a potentially dangerous one.

He scrolled the words up the screen, reading, but conscious that he was not taking in their meaning. Then he stopped, scrolled back and started reading again.

God will defend the believers ... Where was God last Wednesday night? ... If God did not repel some people by means of others, many monasteries, churches, synagogues and mosques, where God's name is much invoked, would have been destroyed. God is sure to help those who help His cause. ... How? How was God helping Mariam and Salma and Emily? Or was this saying that God's help would come through other people? The police, perhaps? Or Lucy and her strange, misguided ideas of solidarity?

Footsteps and voices in the hall, told him that the others had finished their meal and were on their way to the lounge. Ibrahim hastily closed the app and pocketed his phone. The door opened and Bernie came in.

'We'd better go now,' she announced. 'We've got things to do before bedtime.'

'Thank you for coming round,' Ibrahim said, getting to his feet. 'And thanks for the update.'

'Talking of bedtime,' Dominic put in, glad of the opportunity to raise the issue, 'wouldn't it be a good idea for you to get an early night, Mariam?'

'Go to bed before eight?' Mariam protested. 'I'm not a kid any more – and I'm not an invalid either.'

'I know how you feel, love,' Bernie said, smiling to herself at Mariam's indignation. 'I'd be exactly the same, but unpalatable as it is, Dom's probably right. You've had an exciting day, what with being discharged and everything – not to mention having to entertain difficult guests like us! If you're serious about being ready for your exams next week, you'll do better getting plenty of rest between now and then.'

'Mam's absolutely right,' Lucy backed her up. 'Come on up. I'll help you with your pyjamas to make sure you don't dislodge the dressings by mistake.'

'But-,' Mariam began, but Jonah got in first.

'You might as well give in gracefully,' he told her. 'Take it from me, once this lot get fixed on the idea of making you do something for your own good, there's not the slightest point trying to fight it. If it's any consolation, what Bernie means by *things to do* is the lengthy routine that we have to go through to get me to bed. You don't want to know the details, believe me.'

'OK,' Mariam, smiled back at him. Then she turned to Lucy. 'Go on then. I'll come quietly.'

The Sydney Jones Library

12. ARREST

When Bernie and Jonah arrived at Sandra's office the next day, they discovered that a lot had been happening since the previous morning.

'We've arrested Knowsley and O'Neill,' she told them, smiling grimly. 'We don't have enough evidence to charge them, but we're going to have to caution them if we're going to question them any further. They knew we were on to them the moment they saw those warrants, so they've been brought here while our officers search both houses. Would you like to sit in on the interviews?'

'Need you ask?' Jonah smiled back. 'Is there anything else I need to know before we start?'

'Not really. I've got a file full of examples of Islamophobic tweets and Facebook posts. No doubt, we'll have more to add to that after the IT boffins have had a look at the tablet computer and mobile phones that we've taken away from them. Disappointingly, Alex Knowsley's crash helmet is red; so if he *is* our attacker, he must have worn a different one.'

'But, if he had any sense, that's exactly what he would have done,' Jonah pointed out. 'This doesn't look like an amateur affair. There was a lot of planning went into it. I'll bet you won't find the leathers in his house either. He'd be frightened you'd find traces of acid on them.'

'Forensics are going over both houses looking for acid,' Sandra went on, 'and they're also looking at O'Neill's taxi. They've collected a load of fingermarks from both inside and outside that, but of course, the chances are they'll all either be his or from perfectly innocent passengers.'

'So, apart from it being Knowsley's bike – which he

claims was stolen at the time – and O'Neill's taxi having been seen in the vicinity of the incident, there's nothing to link either of them with the crime.' Jonah summarised. 'If they exercise their right to silence, it's going to be pretty nigh impossible to nail them.'

'Unless we find something in the house searches,' Sandra admitted. 'But Alex Knowsley is a cocky so-and-so. I reckon there's a good chance he won't be able to resist showing off his cleverness, which may just enable us to trick him into slipping up.'

'OK then, which of them are we going to interview first?'

'We'll start with Knowsley. I don't want to have to admit to O'Neill that we aren't sure who was riding the motorbike. If we can get to the bottom of whether it was Knowsley or one of the others, then it'll be easier to get O'Neill to admit that he was following on behind to pick whoever it was up, after he dumped the bike.'

***

Alexander Knowsley, "Alex" to his friends, stared stonily back at them with his greeny-grey eyes, as Sandra finished recording the date, time and list of those present in the interview room. His solicitor – a plump young man in a suit, which appeared to be a size too small for him, and a union jack tie – watched her carefully, as if hoping to detect some irregularity in the interview procedure, which he might be able to turn to his client's advantage.

Sandra was seated opposite Knowsley, with Jonah on her left and Charlotte to her right. She fixed him with her eye for a second or two before asking her first question.

'Can you explain how it was that the burglar who broke into your house last week knew exactly where to look for the keys to your shed and motorbike?'

'Who says they did?' Knowsley retorted belligerently.

'If they didn't, they must have been remarkably tidy and considerate burglars,' Sandra observed calmly, 'not to have left any trace of a search behind them.'

'Maybe they just struck lucky,' Knowsley suggested.

'Or maybe you told them where to look,' countered Sandra. 'Did you arrange it all yourself, Mr Knowsley?'

'No! Why would I want to steal my own bike?' Knowsley snarled back.

'As it turned out, it was rather convenient for you that it had been stolen, seeing as it was involved in a serious crime the very next day,' Jonah said calmly. 'Are you quite sure you didn't lend the bike to one of your friends?'

'No,' Knowsley insisted. 'It was stolen, like I said.'

'Why didn't you report the break-in until the Thursday morning?' asked Charlotte sharply, holding up a sheaf of papers. 'I've got the documentation here. If you found out you'd been burgled on Tuesday afternoon, why wait so long to go to the police?'

'We didn't think nothing had been taken,' Knowsley muttered. 'My wife came home and found the window swinging open, so we know that's when it happened, but she had a look round and nothing was missing, so she thought whoever it was must've bottled out and run off. We thought it was probably kids, just messing about for the hell of it. It weren't 'til Thursday, when I went to get the mower out of the shed that I realised the bike was gone.'

'And where was the key at that point?' Jonah asked quietly. 'You say the burglar took it from the cupboard under the stairs and used it to open the shed. How did you get in to see that the bike was missing, if the key was gone?'

'It weren't locked, was it?' Knowsley answered, after a slight pause, which might be a sign that he was having to think on his feet in order to maintain a consistent lie, or might just be because he had not anticipated the question. 'The robber didn't bother locking up after him, did he?'

'And the key?' Jonah repeated.

'I – I'm not sure …,' Knowsley broke off and appeared to be deep in thought. 'It must've been still in the lock,' he concluded at last. 'Yeah, that's it. I remember now. It was in the lock. I thought one of the kids must've left it there. We keep their bikes and outdoor toys in there, you see. When I saw my bike was gone, I was going to give them what for; but then I remembered the break-in and I realised what'd happened.'

'When had you last been in the shed?' Jonah asked. 'Before that Thursday morning, when you found your bike had been stolen, I mean.'

'It must've been Sunday, I suppose. I was out with the bike club all day. I put my bike away in the shed and brought the key in and hung it up in the cupboard, and I never gave it another thought until I went in on Thursday and it was gone.'

'So the bike could have been taken any time between Sunday night and Thursday morning,' Jonah suggested.

'Except the key was hanging up in the cupboard under the stairs, weren't it?' Knowsley retorted scornfully.

'Unless one of your children *did* leave it in the lock at any point,' Jonah reminded him.

'But they didn't,' Knowsley blustered. 'That's why the thief had to break in, wasn't it? To get the key.'

'If there ever was a real break-in,' Charlotte observed sceptically. 'Why don't you admit that was just a story you made up after you realised that your bike had been used to commit a crime?'

'How?' Knowsley came back at once. 'Tell me that! How could I know it was my bike, when the number they gave on the news was nothing like mine? The first I knew about it was when you lot came hammering on my door asking questions.'

'Maybe you knew because it was you who was riding it,' Charlotte suggested menacingly.

'Well, it wasn't.' Knowsley was beginning to sound angry now. 'And it's no good you trying to frame me for it. My bike was stolen, just like I said.'

'Where were you on Wednesday the twentieth of February?' Sandra asked unexpectedly.

'How would I know? That's months ago!' Knowsley

protested, clearly baffled by this new line of enquiry.

'It was the school half-term,' Sandra told him. 'According to your wife, she was working that week, so you looked after your two children. Does that jog your memory at all?'

'Look – what's this got to do with anything?' Knowsley demanded, leaning forward across the table and staring into Sandra's face.

'I'm asking the questions,' she replied calmly.

'My client has every right to be told what bearing this has on the crime for which he has been arrested,' the lawyer intervened smoothly.

'The number plate that was on the motorbike when the crime was committed was stolen on that day,' Sandra explained, fixing the solicitor with her gaze for a few seconds before turning back to address Knowsley again. 'Now, Mr Knowsley, you've had time to think about it. Can you remember where you were on the Wednesday of half-term week?'

'I 'spect I was at home with the kids,' Knowsley shrugged. 'Like I said, it's too long ago to remember.'

'Let me refresh your memory,' Charlotte offered, smiling as she took out a page of computer printout from a folder that she had on the desk in front of her. 'I have here a document that shows that your credit card was used on that day to buy one adult and two children's tickets to the planetarium at the Museum, for the "We are Aliens" show, which showed at 2.55 p.m.'

'Oh yeah! That's right,' Knowsley agreed, seeming to relax a little. 'I did take the kids to the museum. Kyle's mad on dinosaurs and he wanted to see the skeletons they've got of them there. Then, when he saw the notice about the aliens show, he wanted to see that. If you say it was the Wednesday, I'll believe you. It must have been Tuesday or Wednesday, anyhow.'

'That's very interesting,' Sandra told him emphatically. 'Very interesting indeed, because the stolen number plate was taken from a motorbike that was parked in William Brown Street, just outside the museum that afternoon. According to the owner, it must have happened between one and four that afternoon.'

'That's quite a coincidence, isn't it?' Charlotte added, pressing their advantage.

Knowsley stared back without speaking.

'My client denies any involvement in this crime,' his lawyer stated. 'If you have nothing more substantive than a list of coincidences to justify holding him, I suggest that you allow him to return home immediately.'

'*Did* you remove the number plate from a motorcycle, parked in William Brown Street on Wednesday, February the twentieth?' Sandra asked.

'No! And you can't prove I did!' Knowsley shouted, half rising to his feet and then subsiding back into his chair as his solicitor put a restraining hand on his arm. 'How could I? I had the kids with me all the time, didn't I?'

'You could easily have slipped away for a moment,' Sandra suggested.

'Perhaps we ought to ask your children?' added Charlotte. 'Maybe they'll remember Daddy finding a number plate that nobody wanted or-'

'You keep my kids out of this!' Knowsley screamed.

''I can see no justification for harassing innocent children,' the lawyer added, 'when your accusations are all mere speculation.'

'If they were able to confirm that Mr Knowsley was with them for the entire afternoon, then that would support his claim that he had no opportunity to steal the number plates,' Sandra answered. She turned to Knowsley, speaking low in a tone of supreme reasonableness. 'Why not allow one of our female officers to speak to them – in your wife's presence, of course – so that we can clear this up?'

'Because I don't want you talking to them – any of you!' Knowsley shouted, clearly upset as well as angry now. 'I don't want you filling them up with ideas about me stealing number plates and throwing acid over women in the street. And – and what if they did tell you I couldn't've done it? You'd just say I put them up to it, wouldn't you? So what's the point? Heads you win; tails I lose. No thank you!'

'OK,' Sandra said equably. 'Let's put that to one side for now. Tell us where you were last Wednesday evening between six and ten.'

'I told that other guy – the one you sent round to talk about the break-in – I was working late that night.'

'Your wife says different,' Charlotte told him. She says you had tea with her at six, and then she went out and left you at home.'

'Yeah, well, if she says that, maybe I got the days mixed up,' Knowsley conceded. 'But it don't make no difference, does it? If I was at home all night, I couldn't've been doing whatever it is you're saying I *was* doing, could I?'

'You could've gone out after your wife left and got back before she came in again,' Charlotte pointed out.

'What? And leave the kids in the house on their own?' Knowsley exploded. 'What sort of dad d'you think I am?'

'We've got CC-TV footage of you buying a four-pack from the off-licence on the corner of your street at nine thirty-four that night,' Charlotte told him triumphantly. 'And your wife says she didn't get home until gone ten. So much for not leaving the kids in the house on their own!'

'That's different!' Knowsley argued. 'Popping out to the offy for five minutes after they're both in bed is different from leaving them alone all evening, isn't it?'

'Indeed, Mr Knowsley,' Sandra agreed, 'but it still casts doubt on your story that you were at home all night, doesn't it?'

Knowsley looked down at his hands, which were clasped together on the table in front of him. He seemed to be thinking. After a while, he raised his head again and looked towards Sandra.

'OK,' he said cautiously. 'Don't tell the wife, but I had Craig round that night. That's why I went for the beers.

Janice doesn't like him, so I didn't tell her he was coming. She thinks he's a bad influence on the kids.'

'Craig?' queried Jonah. 'He's a friend of yours, I take it?'

'Yeah. Him and me were at school together. He still lives with his Mum and Dad. I can give you their address if you like,' Knowsley seemed to brighten up at the thought that he had produced an alibi. 'He'll soon tell you I'm telling the truth.'

'Thank you,' Sandra said politely. 'We'll send someone round to ask him.' She looked towards Jonah. 'I think we'll stop there for now – unless you have any more questions?'

'Just one thing.' Jonah fixed Knowsley with his eye. 'If you really didn't have anything to do with this attack, you'd do far better to be completely honest with us about that burglary. Are you quite sure you didn't lend your bike to any of your mates? Or is there anyone you can think of who would have known where you kept those keys?'

'I told you,' Knowsley insisted sulkily. 'I came back Tuesday afternoon and found the window open, and then on Thursday morning my bike was gone. And that's *all* I know, OK?'

***

'Mr O'Neill,' Sandra began, looking across the table at the red face and shaved head of Knowsley's friend, 'please will you tell us why you were driving your taxi down Mount Pleasant at half past seven last Wednesday evening?'

'It's simple enough,' O'Neill told them, giving an exaggerated sigh. 'I dropped off a fare at the ozzy. I was heading back up Prescot Street when I got a call come through for a pick-up outside the Phil. So I turned right and then right again into Brownlow Hill and then down Mount Pleasant.'

'Why did you turn left at the bottom?' Charlotte challenged.

''Cos the traffic was bad and I couldn't turn right,' O'Neill replied patronisingly, as if explaining to someone of limited intellect. 'I turned left and came round by Myrtle Street.'

'Did you happen to notice a motorbike ahead of you?' Jonah asked casually.

'Yeah. When I came round the corner into Mount Pleasant it was stopped in the road. I was just about to overtake when it shot off like a bat out of hell; must've been doing fifty or sixty by the time it got to the bottom.'

'Did you see which way it turned after that?' asked Sandra.

'Well, it wasn't there when I got to the junction, so left I suppose.'

'But you didn't see it ahead of you, when you turned left yourself?' Sandra pressed him.

'Not that I remember.'

'You went past Abercromby Square and the Sydney Jones Library,' Sandra continued. 'Did you notice a motorbike left in the cycle parking there?'

'No. I had my eyes on the road, being a careful driver, like you lot are always telling us to,' O'Neill answered in a sneering voice. 'I didn't have time to go round counting how many motorbikes've been left lying around.'

'Tell us more about this fare you picked up outside the Philharmonic Hall,' Jonah coaxed. He had a map of Liverpool on the screen in front of him and had been studying the route that O'Neill had described. 'What were they like? Where did you take them? Did they pay with cash or credit card?'

'It was an old couple; wanted to go to Lime Street. He paid with cash.'

'It's a strange time of day to be leaving the Phil,' Charlotte observed. 'Whatever show was on could hardly have started.'

O'Neill shrugged. 'Not my business. They said they wanted to go to Lime Street, so I took them. They had bags with them – looked like they'd been shopping.'

'Not exactly an obvious part of town to be doing that,'

Charlotte said sceptically. 'Are you sure these people actually existed?'

'You accusing me of lying?'

'DS Simpson is just asking for more information about these people,' Sandra told him, before Charlotte could respond. 'In case we need to find them to confirm what you've said. Did they tell you their names? Or where they were going?'

'No. They just got in the back and said to take them to Lime Street. They didn't say who they were and I didn't ask – OK?'

'Did you pick up anyone outside the Sydney Jones Library in Abercromby Square, when you passed there?' demanded Charlotte, impatient to get to the crux of the interview.

'No. Like I said, I was on my way to pick up a fare outside the Phil.'

'But, if you saw a friend, while you were passing, you might give them a lift, mightn't you?' suggested Sandra, 'if you were going their way?'

'Maybe, but I didn't – OK!'

'So, you categorically deny seeing Alex Knowsley in Abercromby Square and giving him a lift in your cab?' Charlotte challenged.

'Yes,' O'Neill snapped, closing his mouth firmly and looking round with lips pressed tight together as if to indicate that he did not intend to answer any more questions.

'OK, let's have a break,' Sandra sighed, judging that they would achieve little by prolonging the interview. 'DS Simpson will take you back to the cells. We'll speak again later.'

***

'We're going to have to let them go,' Sandra sighed, leaning back in her chair and running her hands through her hair. 'It'll be days before we've got all the analysis back on the samples and fingerprints from O'Neill's taxi, and had a proper look through what's stored on their phones. If only they'd found evidence that either of them was storing acid on the premises – then we'd have had something concrete to go on.'

'You're right,' Jonah agreed. 'There's no point flogging a dead horse. You've got their fingerprints and DNA now. Let's just hope that links them to the acid bottle or the number plates or something, once the forensics people have done their stuff.'

'And we can interview Craig Williams,' Charlotte suggested, 'and see if he supports Knowsley's alibi.'

'Yes.' Sandra brightened up a little. 'Yes. You do that. Take Bryony with you.'

Charlotte got up to go and almost collided with Oliver Ransome, who was approaching with a piece of paper in his hand and a broad grin on his face.

'I think you might want to see this,' he said, holding out the paper towards Sandra. 'It's a receipt from Mark Lansdale for repairs to Alex Knowsley's bike. It's from December, so not directly relevant to our investigation, but it does prove they knew each other.'

'You're right,' Sandra agreed, taking the paper and glancing down at it. 'That certainly opens up several possibilities.'

'Yes,' Jonah nodded. 'It could be that Knowsley is telling the truth and it's Lansdale who's the attacker. He'd have easy access to battery acid and would know Knowsley's address. Knowsley could even have mentioned where he keeps his keys. Or, on the other hand, if they're mates, Knowsley might have been motivated to do it after hearing about Lansdale's wife and daughter being killed.'

'Or they may both be in it together,' Sandra added. She turned back to Oliver. 'OK. Let's go over and have a word with him, shall we?'

'And Bernie and I will pay a friendly call on PC Robert Conway – as one disabled police officer to another, so-to-speak,' Jonah declared. 'We mustn't forget that his family have the same motive for wanting revenge against Muslims as Lansdale does.'

Abercromby Square Garden

13. ALTERNATIVES

'Police?' Jennifer Williams queried nervously, as she stared down at the identification cards that Charlotte and Bryony were holding out towards her. 'Craig's not in any trouble, is he? I mean – he hardly goes out these days.'

She was a plump woman of around sixty, with straight hair dyed blond and a good deal of makeup on her face. She was wearing an old-fashioned floral-pattern overall on top of black trousers and a red blouse.

'No, Mrs Williams,' Charlotte replied coldly, 'He's not in any trouble – yet. We just want to ask him a few questions in relation to an ongoing enquiry. May we come in?'

'I suppose you'd better.' Mrs Williams opened the door wider and stepped back to allow the police officers to enter the house.

They stood in the narrow, rather dark hall, waiting while their host closed the door behind them.

'You'd better come up to his room,' she told them, starting up the stairs. 'He won't want to come down. He's working.'

Mrs Williams led the way upstairs and knocked on the door of one of the bedrooms. She waited with her ear to the door. Then she knocked again. Finally, she opened the door a crack and peered round it into the room. Charlotte heard her speaking to someone inside.

'Craig, love, there's some policewomen to see you.'

There was a mumbled response, which Charlotte could not make out. Then Mrs Williams spoke again, 'I think you ought to. They said they want to ask you some questions. It'll look bad if you don't.'

Craig's response was louder this time, 'OK. Let them in.'

Mrs Williams pushed the door further open and gestured to Charlotte and Bryony to go through. 'I'll be downstairs if you need me.'

Charlotte stood looking round the room. There was a single bed pushed up against the wall under the window, and a small wardrobe in a corner. The rest of the room appeared to be dedicated to technology. One corner seemed to be set up as a recording studio, with a microphone dangling from the ceiling and a pair of headphones lying on a table beneath it. Another table housed a top-of-the-range colour printer/scanner and a strange contraption, which Bryony informed her afterwards was a 3-D printer.

The walls were covered with posters. Some featured computer games – some of Craig's own creations, perhaps – but most were campaigning posters for *Britain for the British* or other right-wing causes. The duvet cover, pillowcase and curtains were all printed with a union jack design.

Craig Williams – a pale-faced man with straggly brown hair and a bald patch on top of his head – was sitting with his back to them, apparently engrossed in the display on two enormous computer screens on a desk that appeared larger than the bed. He did not look round when Bryony closed the door, deliberately banging it in order to attract his attention.

Charlotte advanced towards him and looked over his shoulder at the screen in front of him. He hastily closed the browser window, but not before she had seen the words of a vicious tweet that he had just posted threatening to rape a woman with whom he appeared to be having an online argument. The other screen displayed a part-finished poster being edited in some graphic design program. The headline read, "Save our girls – clamp down on Muslim grooming gangs!" Clearly, Craig's "work" was more wide-ranging than just his game-writing and web-design activities.

'Mr Williams?' she said with all the authority in her voice that she could muster. 'I am Detective Sergeant Simpson, and this is my colleague, Detective Constable Foster. We need to ask you some questions in relation to an acid attack that took place last Wednesday evening outside the Guild of Students building on Mount Pleasant.'

Craig minimised the graphic-design software window, revealing a background image of a group of men carrying union jacks in their left hands while raising their right arms in a Nazi-style salute. He slowly turned his computer chair round to face the two police officers.

'What's that got to do with me?'

'I'm asking the questions,' Charlotte told him coldly. 'Where were you between eight and ten last Wednesday night?'

'Here, in my room, working,' Craig answered promptly. 'Is that it? Can I get on now?'

He made to turn back, but Charlotte took hold of the back of his chair to prevent it from moving.

'That's not what your mate Alex says,' she informed him menacingly. 'According to him, you were round at his place. Is that true?'

'Maybe,' Craig shrugged, forcing his chair round and opening the design software on his screen again as if to resume working on it.

'Maybe?' Charlotte pressed him. 'Maybe? Or definitely? Answer me, Mr Williams! This is important. Your mate Alex's motorbike was involved in a serious incident that evening. He says it was stolen and someone else was riding it. He says it couldn't have been him because he was with you. Now, think hard, where were you last Wednesday evening between eight and ten?'

There was a long silence. Craig continued to stare at the screen in front of him. Eventually he turned back round to face Charlotte.

'I remember now,' he said confidently. 'I did go round to Alex's. His Janice was on a girls' night out and he was stuck in with the kids, so he gave me a buzz and I went round.'

'What time was that?'

'Half seven, quarter to eight,' Craig shrugged.

'And you stayed until, when?'

'Dunno. Half ten, maybe.'

'Did you see Mrs Knowsley while you were there – or the children?'

'No. I told you – she was out.'

'You might have got there before she left,' Bryony pointed out, 'or stayed until after she got back.'

'Well, I didn't.' Craig insisted sulkily. 'And the kids were in bed, so I didn't see them either, OK?'

'OK,' Charlotte answered as calmly as she could. She was feeling very frustrated with this witness's refusal to engage with her enquiries, and suspected that he was choosing his answers with less regard for the truth than for persuading her to give up and leave. 'Now tell me – did you both stay in all evening, or did either of you go out of the house at all?'

'We stayed in.'

'The whole time?' Charlotte pressed him. 'From quarter to eight until half past ten?'

'Yeah.' Craig hesitated, looking at her through half closed eyelids as if he suspected her of laying a trap for him. 'At least, apart from when Alex went to get some beers from the offy on the corner.'

'Ah!' Charlotte gave a satisfied nod. 'It's coming back to you now, is it? Alex popped out for some beers. About what time would that have been? And how long was he out for?'

'Dunno.' Craig shook his head. 'Not right away after I got there, but it must've been before ten.'

'And he got back … what time?' Bryony prompted.

'In time for us to drink the beers before Janice got back.'

'I thought you said you left before she got back,' cut in Charlotte sharply.

'Yeah, I did. I meant, we had time to drink the beers before Alex said I'd better go because she might be home soon – OK?'

'Yes, thank you. That's clear now,' Charlotte

acknowledged. 'Now tell us about this little group you've got – you, Alex, Liam and … is Shaun Marsden one of your gang too?'

'What d'you mean, "my gang"?' Craig snarled.

'You all belong to *Britain for the British*, don't you?' Charlotte clarified, 'and you get together to plan activities to support their aims – is that right?'

'We all want to stop our country being over-run with Muslims and blacks and scroungers from Europe, if that's what you mean.'

'I see,' Charlotte said coldly. 'Do you have any specific plans as to how to do that?'

'We're campaigning to change the law to get rid of all that human rights shit,' Craig said at once, becoming more animated as he related what appeared to be well-rehearsed arguments. 'Too many immigrants are getting away with crimes because the police are scared to arrest them in case they're accused of racism. And when they do get convicted, they just go to jail for a few months – or even get community service – and then they're back out robbing our houses and raping our girls. We want to send them all back where they came from – never mind if they *are* going to be tortured or executed there. They should've thought of that before they started breaking our laws. Take them Muslims in Rotherham[17] who raped all them white girls. Hanging's too good for them in my opinion!'

'I see,' Charlotte repeated, keeping her temper with some difficulty. 'And what about Muslims who were born here? You can't send them back, can you?'

'Why not? They've all got family back there somewhere, haven't they? That's why they never bother to integrate. They're not interested in being British; they just want to turn Britain into another Paki state, with sharia law and

---

[17] The Rotherham child sexual exploitation scandal was a high-profile case involving groups of mainly British-Pakistani men sexually abusing vulnerable children.

everything. They're all a bunch of terrorists. I say lock 'em up and then deport them.'

'One of the girls who was hurt in this recent incident is white British,' Bryony told him. 'She doesn't have any family in Pakistan or anywhere else except here.'

'That's exactly the sort of thing I'm talking about!' Craig crowed triumphantly. 'That's what them Muslims are like – tricking our kids into converting to their terrorist ideas. Telling them they'll all go to paradise if they blow themselves up for Allah.'

'These girls weren't planning to blow anyone up,' Charlotte said firmly. 'They were just standing waiting at a bus stop. One of them's training to be a doctor – like her father.'

'Well you won't catch me letting some Paki doctor get me on the operating table!' Craig declared. 'Send 'em all back and let 'em look after their own people. There's plenty of them over there in India, or wherever, who'd be only too glad to have a doctor to go to. I've heard people saying – university professors and that – that we're robbing them third world countries of doctors and nurses that they need back there. I'm not a racist. I just think it's better for them *and* us if they stay over there and we get to have our country back.'

'The health service wouldn't be able to function without doctors from overseas,' Bryony began.

'And why's that?' demanded Craig, 'I'll tell you why? It's because the government keeps pandering to all these fucking immigrants and favouring them instead of training our own people. My Auntie Patsy lives in Oldham. There isn't a white face left in her street now. She says she feels like a foreigner in her own country. Get rid of them all, I say, and give the jobs to British people who've never had a chance. President Trump had the right idea with his "America First" idea. We're campaigning for the politicians to start putting Britain first and making Britain great again.'

Charlotte reflected that she was glad that Craig Williams

was not one of those hypothetical Britons whom he thought ought to have been accepted to take a medical degree. She doubted that he would ever be capable of learning a good bedside manner, in contrast to the calm compassionate air of Mariam's physician father. She hesitated for a moment, pondering on whether to prolong the interview. However, it did not look as if Craig was likely to provide them with any more concrete evidence about the acid attack. She wondered if they could justify taking his computer equipment away for examination. She would have liked to find out more about his campaigning activities and whether they were within the law. She would ask Sandra about that when they got back to the incident room.

'Thank you, Mr Williams,' she said at last. 'That will be all for now. We'll see ourselves out.'

Craig immediately swung round in his seat and started working on his poster design again, paying no further heed to his visitors. Charlotte and Bryony descended the stairs and went in search of his mother. They found her in the kitchen, busily scrubbing the inside of the oven.

'We'll be going now, Mrs Williams,' Charlotte called to her from the doorway. 'But, just before we do, can you just answer one question for us?'

Mrs Williams straightened up and looked towards them enquiringly.

'Can you cast your mind back to Wednesday of last week? Was your Craig at home that night between eight and ten?'

'Yes,' Mrs Williams nodded. 'He doesn't go out much. His computers are his life. I sometimes think he lives in a world all of his own.'

'Are you quite sure, Mrs Williams?' Charlotte pressed her. 'One of his mates says he went over to his house – in Knotty Ash. Could that be right?'

'Wednesday?' Jennifer Williams appeared to be thinking. 'I dunno. I think he was here, but if you asked me to swear to it ... I don't take much notice of where he is to be honest.

He could've come down and gone out without me noticing. We'd've been in the back room watching the telly – that's me and my husband Len. We don't go out much either, to be fair.'

'Thank you Mrs Williams. That's fine,' Charlotte assured her. 'We'll see ourselves out.'

'Craig isn't in any trouble, is he?' Mrs Williams asked anxiously.

'No, not at all. These are just routine enquiries,' Charlotte insisted, hoping that she sounded more sincere than she felt. 'We're going now. Have a good day.'

***

'His wife's with him at the moment,' the receptionist told Jonah and Bernie when they asked after PC Robert Conway on their arrival at the Care Home where he lived. 'I'll ring for a member of staff to go and tell her you're here. Take a seat.'

Bernie looked round the entrance hall of the home and saw two plastic seats standing against the wall. She sat down in one and Jonah brought his wheelchair over to wait next to her. An elderly woman came past, creeping along slowly with the aid of a walking frame. A white-haired man followed close behind, watching her anxiously.

'No, Mum, let me,' they heard him say as she reached out to press the button that operated the automatic entrance doors. The woman put her hand back on the walking frame and stood wheezing, while her son pressed the button. The doors slid open and they made their way slowly out into the car park.

'It must be dreadful for a young man like PC Conway to be stuck in a place like this,' Bernie commented, once the doors had closed again, 'surrounded by people old enough to be his grandparents.'

'Yes,' Jonah agreed.

They waited in silence. A member of staff in uniform nodded to them as she came past to have a whispered conversation with the receptionist. She turned and went back the way she had come, nodding and smiling at them again as she passed, her eyes full of pity. Bernie suddenly realised that she had assumed that Jonah was a new inmate, or perhaps a prospective inmate come to view the facilities.

'I'm very lucky,' Jonah said quietly, watching her disappearing down a corridor to the right. 'I could so easily have ended up in somewhere like this, if you and Peter hadn't taken me in.'

Bernie leaned over and put her arms round his neck.

'Don't worry! I think we can manage to put up with you for a while longer yet.'

'Inspector Porter?' They looked up to see another woman in uniform approaching. She smiled warmly. 'I'm Pam. I'm one of the Care Assistants who looks after Mr Conway. His wife says you can see him now. If you'd just like to follow me, I'll show you to his room.'

She chatted as she led the way down a long corridor with doors on either side.

'It'll be nice for him to have a visit from another police officer,' she said cheerfully. 'You mustn't worry if he doesn't respond much. His brain injury has affected his speech badly, but we *think* he can understand some of what you say. He seems to enjoy having visitors, anyway.'

'Do you think he remembers what happened to him?' Jonah asked, trying to sound casual, as if he were simply making conversation.

'It's difficult to say. We don't encourage people to talk to him about it. It's probably better if he doesn't dwell on that, don't you think?'

'Yes. I'm sure you're right,' Jonah agreed insincerely.

'Now, here we are!' the Care Assistant declared in the bright, slightly patronising tone that healthcare workers so often adopt when speaking to patients and their visitors. She opened the door of a room on their left and looked into it. 'I've got Inspector Porter and his wife here,' they heard her say. 'Shall I show them in?'

There was a muffled response from inside the room, presumably in the affirmative, because Pam proceeded to push the door open wide, holding it to allow Jonah to steer his wheelchair through.

Bernie followed him into a large, light room furnished with a hospital-style bed, four high-backed easy chairs and a low table. Built-in cupboards covered one wall, while the wall opposite the door appeared to be almost all glass, through which the sun was shining so brightly that she was momentarily dazzled by it. Sitting in the two chairs closest to the windows were two dark figures. As her eyes adjusted to the brightness, Bernie saw that they were a woman, who looked to be about thirty with brown eyes and black tightly curling hair, and a man, whose age she could not determine because his face was distorted by a droop to his left eye and a sagging of his left cheek. There was a prominent scar on the left-hand side of his face zig-zagging down from beneath short black hair. He was wearing a dark blue dressing gown over grey pyjamas and had slippers on his feet.

'I'll leave you all to get to know one another,' Pam said. 'Give us a buzz on the intercom if you need anything.'

She went out, pulling the door closed behind her. The woman stood up and started towards them with her hand outstretched.

'Hi! I'm Shelley – Robbie's wife. Thank you for coming. He used to get lots of his old police mates, but … I suppose they're busy with other things and, well he's not exactly a bundle of laughs anymore.'

'I'm Bernie,' Bernie told her as they shook hands. 'I'm not Jonah's wife – just his PA.'

'When we heard about what had happened, we had to pay you a visit,' Jonah added, pointedly addressing Robert Conway, rather than his wife. 'Cops – and ex-cops – ought to stick together.'

'Inspector Porter was shot,' Shelley told her husband, speaking slowly and carefully. 'He's come to see how you are.' She turned back to speak to Bernie. 'Excuse him being still in his pyjamas. He's not been too good today and we've only just got him out of bed.'

The injured police constable looked towards Jonah and nodded. His mouth widened in an attempt at a smile and his eyes brightened. He looked as if he was attempting to speak, but only managed a few unintelligible grunts.

'The bullet damaged my spinal cord,' Jonah explained, still looking towards Robert, rather than Shelley Conway, and manoeuvring his wheelchair across the room to take up a place next to Robert's chair. 'It paralysed me from the shoulders down, apart from three fingers on my left hand – but it's surprising how much you can do with just three fingers and a lot of technology!'

'I don't know about three fingers,' Shelley burst out suddenly,' But I can think of a load of people I'd like to give two fingers to – starting with that Muslim scumbag who did this to Robbie and the fucking judge who didn't have the guts to give him a whole life order[18]. Thirty years! Thirty bloody years! What's that compared with what Robbie's going through? He's the one who's got a life sentence!'

'I suppose the judge must've been taking his age into account,' Bernie said tentatively. 'He was only twenty when he did it – or so I read.'

'Twenty! My dad had his own business by the time he was twenty. I'd been working for two years by that age. Don't go telling me a lad of twenty doesn't know what he's doing when he steals a van and drives it into innocent pedestrians!'

Bernie went over and sat down on the opposite side of Robert Conway from where Jonah had positioned himself. She turned to speak to him.

'We're up here visiting my daughter,' she told him. 'It

---

[18] Murder carries a mandatory life sentence, however, only in the most serious cases will the offender be given a 'whole life order' preventing them ever being released from prison.

was her birthday yesterday. She's at the university, studying to be a doctor.'

Robert turned his head slowly to look at her and seemed to be attempting a smile. His wife returned to her seat, watching him anxiously all the time.

'She shares a house with three friends,' Bernie continued. 'One of them is a young cousin of mine. I'm from Liverpool too originally.'

'Not that anyone would ever guess!' Jonah commented, smiling broadly at the idea that anyone who heard Bernie's strong Liverpool accent could ever be in any doubt on that subject. Robert turned his head again to give Jonah what was definitely a smile. Then chest and shoulders began to shake in what must surely be laughter. Bernie and Jonah joined in, but Shelley remained serious, apparently not sharing the joke.

'Lucy – that's Bernie's daughter – used to come to see me when I was in rehab after I was shot,' Jonah told Robert. 'She was the one that got me eating again. There was a time when it didn't seem worth the effort of going on, but it's hard to keep that up when you've got a nine-year-old pestering to eat up your greens!'

Robert smiled again and seemed to be trying to say something. His wife spoke for him. 'Robbie needs help with eating. His left arm and leg were crushed in the impact and the nerves to the hand were damaged, so he can't cut up his food for himself.'

'You ought to play on that,' Jonah replied, still addressing Robbie. 'There must be plenty of attractive young nurses and care assistants in a place like this all eager to help a police hero to his meals!'

'At the moment, I've got time on my hands,' Shelley responded, apparently missing the teasing tone in Jonah's voice. 'So I can always be here at mealtimes.'

'The first six months were the worst,' Jonah told Robbie, speaking seriously, but with a twinkle in his eye, 'and then the next six months – they were the worst too. After that, I went into a bit of a decline …'

'And then he got this chair of his and all its attachments and he discovered that he could still be just as provoking and difficult to live with as ever he had been!' Bernie finished.

'The best thing is this computer screen,' Jonah continued, making it rotate so that Robert could see the display. 'It enables me to surf the web to keep up with what's going on in the world, and to email anyone I like, and when I was still a working police officer, I could connect to the police computer system. I can't use a regular keyboard, but this special keypad is amazingly versatile and modern predictive text works surprisingly well to make typing quicker and easier.'

He demonstrated how he could produce words amazingly quickly on the screen. Robert watched, his mouth dropping open in concentration. Then he put out his right arm and took hold of Jonah's left hand. Jonah curled back his index and middle fingers to leave room on the key pad for Robert to press the letters.

'T-h-a-n-k you f-or c-o-ming,' appeared on the screen. Robert looked round at Jonah and then turned and nodded towards his wife. Jonah touched the joystick and made the screen rotate so that it was facing Shelley.

'Hasn't anyone offered you a voice machine?' Bernie asked suddenly. 'There must be lots of devices out there that you could use to change typing into speech.'

'He has speech and language therapy once a week,' Shelley cut in quickly, 'to help him get his voice back.'

'That's good,' Jonah agreed diplomatically, glancing up at Shelley briefly and then turning back to Robert, 'but meanwhile, Bernie's right, some sort of speech generation software might enable you to communicate a lot easier.'

'I've got an idea!' Bernie went behind Jonah's chair and pulled out a tablet computer from the storage space at the back. She switched it on and then knelt down beside Robert, holding it on his lap. He first grasped it in his right hand.

Then, he carefully brought up his damage left hand and attempted to grip it with that. A few frustrating minutes of trial and error resulted in the tablet being safely wedged between his left hand and the arm of the chair, leaving his right hand free to type on the touch screen.

'G-i-v-e me my g-l-a-ss-es,' he keyed in slowly.

'He's asking for his glasses,' Bernie said, looking enquiringly towards his wife.

'I'll get them,' Shelley said, getting up, crossing the room and picking up a pair of spectacles from a shelf. She came back and fitted them carefully on Robert's face. 'There you are, love!'

Bernie noticed that the left-hand lens was blacked out.

'The nerve to his left eye was damaged,' Shelley explained. 'He can't control it properly, so he gets double vision if he doesn't have his glasses on.'

She sat back in her seat and Robert began typing again.

'If you just let me change the settings,' Bernie said, putting out her hand towards the screen, 'I'll fix it so that everything you type here will come up on Jonah's screen too.'

Robert nodded vigorously and grunted his approval. Soon he and Jonah were conducting a real, albeit rather slow and stilted conversation. Bernie came round behind Jonah and leaned on the back of his chair, so that she could read the screen over his shoulder.

'One of Lucy's friends was involved in that acid attack last week,' Jonah said conversationally. 'Luckily, she wasn't the most badly hurt, but the doctors say she'll have the scars for the rest of her life.'

'Acid attack?' Robert typed slowly.

'Yes. Didn't you hear about it on the news?' Bernie replied, watching a puzzled expression spreading across Robert's face as he looked up from the screen. 'Four students were waiting on the corner of Mount Pleasant and Brownlow Hill when a man on a motorbike – or I suppose it could've been a woman – came past and sprayed them with acid. Lucy's friend was burned on the back of her head, but one of the others got it in her face, poor girl!'

'That's awful!' Shelley burst in. 'Do they know why it happened? Have they caught – no, I suppose they can't have.'

'Nobody knows for sure,' Jonah told her, 'but at the moment it looks as if it was probably an anti-Muslim attack. Three of the women were wearing headscarves, which made them recognisably Muslim.'

'Oh.' Shelley seemed taken aback by this statement, but she soon recovered herself. 'I didn't realise you were talking about that incident. I heard they were extremists who'd been trying to convert English girls. Wasn't one of them a white girl from St Helens?'

'Yes,' Jonah replied coolly, 'One of them was a convert. She was luckier than Lucy's friend, and only got very minor burns on her shoulder.'

'Acid attacks are awful,' Shelley conceded, 'but right now I find it hard to be very bothered about what happens to Muslims – after what one of them did to Robbie. And there was that poor girl too! Only thirteen! She didn't deserve to die, just 'cos that Shaladi slimeball thinks he's going to go to paradise if he kills as many white people as he can! If those girls aren't terrorists, why didn't they put their energy into stopping the likes of him, instead of going out brainwashing ordinary English girls?'

'You're right, Robbie,' Jonah said. 'It is a lot more complicated than that.' He turned his screen round so that Shelley could see her husband's words, which he had been slowly typing while she was speaking.

'It's complicated. I met some nice Muslims in my job.'

'Where are they now, though?' Shelley demanded contemptuously. 'They haven't lifted a finger to help you, have they?'

Bernie opened her mouth to respond, then closed it again as she saw that Robert was typing. Jonah also remained silent, waiting for him to finish. Shelley was more impatient.

'If Islam is this religion of peace, like they're always saying, why don't they put a stop to this sort of thing? Someone must've know what he was up to. They could've stopped him if they wanted.'

'T-h-ey s-e-nt me c-a-r-ds,' Robert typed slowly. 'T-h-ey n-e-v-er m-et S-h-a-l-a-d-i.'

'You shouldn't judge a whole religion by a single rogue individual,' Bernie began, but Shelley interrupted.

'It isn't just one, though, is it? It keeps happening. Nine-eleven, seven-seven, Lee Rigby, Westminster Bridge, the Manchester Arena, London Bridge, Parson's Green … it just goes on and on!'

'But compared with the number of Muslims living here,' Bernie argued, 'it's only a tiny, tiny minority, and most Muslims are as horrified about those attacks as we are.'

'Maybe they are,' Shelley conceded, her voice lacking conviction, 'but I still think Shaladi ought to have got a whole life tariff. And, if those girls didn't want people to think they're terrorists, they shouldn't wear those burka things on their heads. *I* wouldn't hang around the red light district in a mini skirt and a scoop neck shirt! It's the same thing. If you act provocative, you can expect trouble.'

'Actually,' Bernie retorted, knowing that showing anger would be counter-productive, but unable to stop herself, 'none of them were wearing burkas and Lucy's friend, Mariam, didn't even have a headscarf on. And in any case, why shouldn't they wear what they like – especially if it's part of their religion? Would you tell monks and nuns they shouldn't wear their habits in case it provokes the atheists? My mam was in the Salvation Army – surely their uniforms must be far more provocative than a headscarf! What about vicars in their dog collars or bishops in their mitres?'

'But none of them look like terrorists!' Shelley protested. 'I'm talking about scaring everybody by dressing up like a suicide bomber.'

'By wearing a headscarf?' Bernie exclaimed in disbelief.

'You can't be serious! How does that make them look like bombers?'

'I've seen the pictures,' Shelley insisted. 'Two of them had rucksacks on their backs.'

'To hold their text books!' Bernie said despairingly. 'They're students. They have to carry books round with them.'

'Do you think we could just cool it for a bit?' Jonah said quietly in the pause while both women caught their breath. 'Shelley's made a good point. Some people are frightened when they see Muslims, because they associate them with terrorism. The question is: who was frightened – or angry – enough to plan a vicious acid attack like that? It wasn't just someone panicking and lashing out in the heat of the moment.'

'Personally, *I* think the question is: why are the police so keen to protect Muslim extremists when they can't be bothered to look after their own officers? They've done nothing – literally nothing – to help Robbie, since he was injured! And then they complain at me for clamping down on Muslims hanging around the streets making a nuisance of themselves. The world's gone mad! All you have to do these days is to claim you're part of some minority religion and you can get away with murder – literally!'

Jonah listened patiently to this diatribe, while watching his screen where words were appearing slowly: 'Don't blame Shelley. She has a lot to put up with.'

Jonah made a small movement of his fingers and a "thumbs-up" sign appeared on the screen below Robert's words. Robert smiled back.

'I think it's time we went now,' Jonah said, turning to Shelley. 'It's been nice meeting you both.' He looked back at Robert. 'Have a word with the staff about getting you a voice machine, and meanwhile, maybe someone could lend you a tablet – or even just make an alphabet board.'

Shelley got up. 'I'll walk you to the foyer.'

They went out into the corridor, closing the door behind

them.

'Thanks for coming,' Shelley said as they made their way back to Reception. 'I've never seen Robbie so alert before – and – and I never realised …,' she hesitated. 'I didn't know he could still … I thought he wasn't taking things in – you know? I thought his brain was damaged, but it looks like he's just … well, he's just been locked inside himself, if you know what I mean.'

'It must be awful, knowing what you want to say and not being able to say it,' Bernie said, with feeling. 'We had a friend who lost his speech for a while after a head injury. He's much better now, but it's still a struggle for him.'

'I really think you ought to look into a speech synthesiser of some sort,' Jonah added earnestly. 'It will make such a difference to his morale if he can start communicating properly again. The speech and language therapist may be able to advise you on that.'

'Yes, I'll speak to someone about that,' Shelley said eagerly, briefly appearing much happier than they had seen her before. Then her face clouded over again. 'But he'll still be incontinent and wheelchair-bound and only able to see properly out of one eye.'

'Using a wheelchair isn't as bad as it seems,' Jonah told her gently. 'Like I said to your husband, it takes a while to get used to, but it's amazing how much I can still do.'

'And your Robbie's still got one good leg, hasn't he?' Bernie added. 'Have you talked to the OTs and the physios about getting him up out of his chair sometimes?'

'When he was on the rehab ward, one of the physios used to try to bully him into trying to walk,' Shelley admitted, 'but after he fell a couple of times, I got frightened he was going to hurt himself. Do you think I was wrong asking them to stop?'

'It was understandable for you to worry,' Jonah assured her gently, 'but now he's a bit further down the line, maybe it's time to re-visit the walking idea, don't you think? If Robbie wants to,' he added firmly. 'Don't forget, it's all up to him to decide.'

They came to the entrance and Bernie went over to the reception desk to sign themselves out of the building. Jonah looked up at Shelley, who had turned to go back.

'I gather you already knew about the acid attack,' he said casually. 'When did you hear about it?'

'It came on the radio while I was on my way over here to visit Robbie. Breaking news, they said. It must've been just after it happened. There were no details, just some students injured outside the Students' Union. To be honest, I expected it to be just some stupid fight or something – the sort of thing students get up to all the time.'

***

'Yes, I know Alex,' Mark Lansdale said, taking a grimy rag out of the pocket of his overalls and wiping his hands. 'I've serviced his bike – I do most of the bikes for the club. Why d'you want to know?'

Sandra hesitated, debating in her mind how much to reveal. She decided that a degree of openness was most likely to elicit useful information.

'Alex Knowsley's bike was used in an attack on a group of students last week. You may have heard about it. Three women were sprayed with acid outside the Guild of Students on Mount Pleasant.'

'Yeah. I saw about it on the news – Muslim girls, weren't they? Are you saying Alex did it?'

'He says the bike was stolen,' Oliver Ransom told him, trying not to indicate by his voice whether or not the police accepted Knowsley's version of events. 'So we're interested in who else might have known about the bike and where to find it.'

'You mentioned a bikers' club,' Sandra added. 'What club is this?'

'I think they call themselves the MerseyRiders,' Lansdale told them. 'They invited me to join, but I don't have the time. They meet in the evenings to swap tall stories and go off together at weekends. I negotiated a discount with them for servicing in exchange for them recommending me to new members – but that's just business. I don't know many of them personally.'

'Could you give us the names and addresses of any of the other members?' Oliver asked eagerly.

'I could,' Lansdale said cautiously, 'but I don't know I ought to. My customers' details are confidential. Why d'you want to know them?'

'Assuming Alex Knowsley's telling the truth when he says his bike was stolen, whoever took it knew exactly where to look for the bike and for the key to the shed where it was kept,' Oliver explained, 'which makes it highly likely that it was someone who knew Alex and had been to his house before.'

'Yeah, well,' Lansdale continued to hesitate. 'I suppose – tell you what! I'll give you the name of the club president and you can ask him for the list of members. How's that?'

'Thank you, Mr Lansdale,' Sandra smiled. 'That will do very nicely.'

'OK. Wait here a minute.'

Lansdale disappeared through a door at the back of his workshop, leaving the two police officers gazing round at an array of motorcycles in varying stages of dismantlement, racks of tools attached to the wall, and shelves containing cans of oil, bottles of brake fluid and other substances. Oliver walked over and started reading the labels.

'Here you are!' Lansdale was back. He held out a grubby piece of paper towards Sandra. 'Andy Beale's your man,' he told her. 'He'll be able to give you all the names you want. Mind you,' he added, 'personally, I wouldn't take a lot of notice of that story of Alex's about his bike being stolen. If you was to ask me, out of the lot of them, who was the most likely to go round spraying acid on a group of Muslims, I'd say Alex every time.'

'Really?' Oliver said excitedly. 'He didn't try to hide his anti-Muslim views then?'

'Hardly!' Lansdale laughed. 'Flaunted them, more like! To be honest, that was one of the things that put me off the club. He wasn't the only one who was a racist. I don't know the details, but I gather there was a bit of an incident last year with a black lad who tried to join. They gave him a bit of a hard time, by all accounts – don't quote me on that,' he added hastily. 'It was just a story that was making the rounds – probably just something and nothing.'

'OK. Thanks.' Sandra pocketed the piece of paper. 'And now, Mr Lansdale, just for the record, can you tell us where you were on the evening of Wednesday last week?'

'That's easy,' Lansdale smiled back unperturbed. 'We always go round to my mother-in-law's on a Wednesday. I shut up shop here at about five thirty and went home, had a shower and then we went over there. We must've got there about six thirty or seven at the latest, and we stayed until gone ten. Does that cover the time you're interested in?'

'Yes, thank you, Mr Lansdale. That will do nicely,' Sandra assured him. 'And thank you for this name and address. We'll leave you to get on with your work now.

Abercromby Square

14. INCONCLUSIVE EVIDENCE

'I think we ought to look into this MerseyRiders club a bit more,' Oliver said the next morning, after Sandra had summarised the outcome of their interview with Lansdale to the rest of the team. 'The way Lansdale spoke about them, it could be a front for another right-wing activist group.'

'Or that could just be a ploy to direct our attention away from him,' Jonah observed drily. 'I agree we need to check out the club, but we mustn't rule Lansdale himself out too quickly. The way you described him, he seems to have it in for Knowsley. Could he have deliberately framed him?'

'I'm not sure you're quite accurate in saying he's got it in for Knowsley,' Sandra objected. 'He made it clear he disliked him, but it was mainly that he disliked his racist views. He didn't have any *personal* grudge against him.'

'And he still services his motorbike for him,' Oliver pointed out, 'at a discount too!'

'OK,' Jonah conceded. 'Let's put Lansdale on the back burner for now; and I think we can do the same for Shelley Conway. She's got no love for Muslims, but my impression of her is that she's much more concerned about Shaladi himself not having got the sentence that she thinks he deserves.'

'And she's got an alibi of sorts,' Bernie added. 'She claims she arrived at the Care Home in Ormskirk just as the news was breaking on the radio. We didn't get a chance to confirm that, but if it's true, I can't see how she'd have had time to get changed out of her motorbike leathers, into her car and all the way over there.'

'They log the times when visitors enter and leave the

building,' Jonah added. 'So it'll be easy to find out when she did actually arrive that day.'

'OK.' Sandra nodded. 'Ollie – you check with the Care Home. It'll be quite a relief if we can rule Shelley out once and for all. She's got enough on her plate without being under suspicion for something like this. How's Robbie doing, by the way?'

'He'd be doing a lot better if people would start treating him like an intelligent adult instead of a helpless child,' Bernie declared forthrightly. 'I could hardly believe that nobody had thought of offering him some sort of speech synthesiser so he can communicate!'

'And Shelley needs to stop trying to do everything for him and start encouraging him to do things for himself,' Jonah agreed.

There was a stunned silence. Nobody knew what to say to this outburst.

'I – I was told he was like a vegetable,' a young constable ventured nervously from near the back of the room. 'They said the bang on his head messed up his brain so much that he could hardly move and couldn't even speak. I was going to go and see him in hospital, but when I heard that, I didn't see the point.'

'If Robbie Conway's a vegetable then I must be dead!' Jonah declared. 'He just needs people to stop dismissing him just because he grunts and drools.'

'He can't speak,' Bernie explained with as much patience as she could muster, 'but that doesn't mean he can't understand what other people are saying. As soon as we gave him a keyboard to type what he wanted to say, he got on fine. I don't know how he slipped through the net like this. It beggars belief that nobody thought of it before!'

'They've been concentrating on trying to get his speech back,' Jonah went on, 'and they've forgotten that speaking isn't the only way of communicating. And all the time he was only able to respond with grunts, they assumed that he didn't understand what they were saying.'

'And his wife makes things worse,' Bernie added, 'always answering for him.'

'OK,' Sandra said firmly. 'Let's put Shelley Conway on the back burner too and turn our attention to our main suspect – Alex Knowsley. He gave his mate Craig as an alibi, and Craig backs him up.'

'Not exactly convincingly, though,' Charlotte put in, 'and in any case, they could've been in it together.'

'Yes,' agreed Sandra. 'My money would be on Alex and Liam being the guilty ones, and Craig being brought in to provide Alex with an alibi. Did you notice the discrepancy between his story and what Alex's wife said about where she was that evening?'

'No?' Charlotte looked puzzled. 'Didn't they both say she was out with her friends?'

'That's what Craig said,' Sandra told her, 'but Alex's wife told Oliver that she was at her parents' house that night.'

'That's right,' Oliver confirmed. 'Alex tried to tell us he was working late that night, and his missus said, no that was the Thursday, because she went round to see her mum on Wednesday and he had to stay in to look after the kids.'

'Craig's mum wasn't very convincing either,' Sandra added. 'At first, she said he was at home all evening; then she said he might have gone out. Was she lying when she said he was at home, thinking that would put him in the clear, and then changed her mind when we told her that he said he was round at Alex's? Or does she genuinely not know whether he was in or out?'

'Either way, her evidence isn't going to be any use either for establishing or discrediting Knowsley's alibi,' Jonah observed drily. 'So it's pretty clear that Knowsley *could*'ve done it and he probably had the right mind-set to have *wanted* to do it. The question is: can we prove that he actually *did* it?'

'And for that, we need more forensic evidence,' Sandra said briskly, 'which brings me on to the various lab reports that have come through. I'm afraid they're not particularly encouraging.'

She shuffled a sheaf of papers in her hands, looking down at them to select the salient points.

'They picked up a few smudged fingerprints on the motorbike,' she announced. 'They aren't very clear, and they look likely to belong to Alex Knowsley. Since no one disputes that it's his bike, that doesn't tell us anything. There *was* one clear fingerprint on the sprayer, but it doesn't match any of our suspects or anyone on the database, so that's not a lot of use either. They haven't managed to find any DNA on either the bike or the sprayer and the sprayer is a very ordinary kind that you can pick up at any hardware shop or garden centre.'

She turned to look at Bryony.

'Would you like to tell us about Knowsley and his cronies' mobile phone and internet activity?'

'That's a bit inconclusive too,' Bryony said, getting to her feet. 'They all seem to spend quite a lot of time trolling people on social media. And they're fairly indiscriminate about who they pick on – immigrants, ethnic minorities, Muslims, LGBT – you name it! There is a bit of a tendency for them to target women in particular, especially women who stand up against gender-based violence or who have the temerity to suggest that there still isn't a level playing field in the workplace.'

'Are you suggesting that they could have targeted this *Feminist Sisterhood* more because of their feminism than their Muslim identity?' asked Charlotte.

'I don't know about that,' Bryony answered doubtfully. 'I mean – so many men go in for that sort of trolling and usually it's in response to something a woman has posted on social media. We haven't found any examples so far of any of them responding to a post from any of our *Feminist Sisterhood* – though Tahira in particular does put quite a lot up on Twitter and Facebook – and she's got a blog too, all about feminism in Islam. That attracts quite a lot of hostility from men, but usually Muslim men, telling her she's got things wrong.'

'To be honest,' Oliver added, 'I doubt if any of them even know the *Sisterhood* exists. The Muslims they target are mainly high-profile people, like Sadiq Khan[19] and Sajid Javid[20] and Sayeeda Warsi[21].'

'Baroness Warsi is a particular favourite of theirs,' Bryony agreed. 'She's a woman, a Conservative, a Muslim and her family was from Pakistan, so she presses almost all their buttons. Craig and Liam have made some really loathsome threats to her on Twitter.'

'Bad enough for them to be charged with hate crime?' asked Sandra quickly.

'Yes, quite probably,' Bryony answered. Then she hesitated. 'At least … I'm sure it would be if it was someone they knew personally, but with Baroness Warsi being a public figure … well the impact on her would be less, wouldn't it? Because there's no realistic chance of them actually carrying out their threats.'

'OK.' Sandra considered the matter. 'Carry on digging,' she instructed, and we'll keep the option of charging them with racially motivated harassment open for the time being.'

'Knowsley, O'Neill and Williams, all communicate with each other frequently via text messages and social media,' Bryony continued. 'Shaun Marsden is sometimes included, but not nearly as much as the others. I'd say that Knowsley and O'Neill are the active members of the group; Williams mainly sticks to online stuff; and Marsden just gets dragged in because he's in partnership with Knowsley.'

'So, your best guess would be that Knowsley was the masked motorcyclist and O'Neill helped him to get away

---

[19] Sadiq Khan is a Labour Party politician, who became Mayor of London in 2016.

[20] Sajid Javid is a Conservative Party politician who became Home Secretary in 2018.

[21] Sayeeda Warsi is a Conservative Party politician in the House of Lords.

afterwards – is that right?' asked Jonah.

'Yes. That's about it,' Bryony nodded. 'And Craig Williams may well have masterminded the whole thing from the comfort of his bedroom.'

'I agree that looks a likely scenario,' Sandra concurred. 'But it's going to be a heck of a job proving that's what happened.'

'And meanwhile, we mustn't lose sight of the alternative possibility that it was actually a lot more personal,' Jonah warned.

'Which is why I've brought PC Mohammed Anwar on to the team,' Sandra said, picking up his cue. 'Come up to the front, Anwar, and let me introduce you.'

A very young-looking uniformed officer got up from his seat at the back of the room and came forward to stand next to Sandra.

'PC Anwar finished his initial training two months ago,' Sandra announced. 'He's a Muslim himself and his grandparents all come from Bangladesh. He's based over the water in Wallasey, but I've got permission to take him away from his normal duties to help us with building bridges with the Muslim student community. I'm hoping that a fellow-Muslim of a similar age to themselves will find it easier to gain their trust and find out if there were any stresses and strains within the community that could have led to this incident.'

'Hi everyone,' Anwar said, looking nervously round the room.

'He's also going to try to find out if any of the students saw Knowsley or his mates hanging around the university,' Sandra went on. 'This attack must have been pre-planned, so you'd think they must've done a reccy before launching into it. OK, Anwar, you can sit down.'

The young man returned to his seat looking relieved that he had not been called upon to say anything more. Sandra turned to Charlotte.

'How have you been getting on looking into Jack

Hampton's background?'

'Nothing much so far,' Charlotte answered regretfully. 'I've been talking to his parents and his friends from home. He doesn't make any attempt to hide his resentment over Emily leaving him, but everyone seems to agree that he'd never do anything to hurt her. As far as I can tell, he's never had any girlfriends apart from Emily, which makes it not that surprising that it hit him hard when she dumped him. He was a model student at school and raised a lot of money for charity.'

'OK. Just keep digging,' Sandra told her. 'Find out where he was when the incident took place. If he's got an alibi, we can rule him out and cut down our suspect list a bit.'

She looked down at her notes and then round the room until she caught Oliver Ransom's eye.

'Ollie, I want you to check out Mark Lansdale's alibi. He says he was at his mother-in-law's house when the attack happened. Go round and call on her and see if he's telling the truth. And while you're there, see if you can get her to talk about how he's taken his wife and daughter's death. He seemed very keen to distance himself from the MerseyRiders and their racist views. It did strike me that maybe he was protesting a bit too much.' She turned to address the room in general. 'OK. That's it. You all know what to do – get on with it.'

University of Liverpool, School of Health Sciences

15. MOUNTING ANGER

The next day was Friday. Bernie insisted that they ought to spend the morning of their last day in Liverpool visiting Aunty Dot. Her conscience smote her at the thought that, over the years, she had sadly neglected her aging aunt, who surely deserved more in her declining years than to be cooped up in a Care Home all day with no physical contact with the outside world. Jonah at first put up resistance, claiming that they were there to assist Sandra in her investigation and should make the most of the time they had left. However, eventually the prospect of an enjoyable few hours of conversation, with Dot hanging on his every word as he described his involvement in the case and outlined the progress – or lack thereof – thus far, persuaded him to give way, and he agreed to leave any further police work until the afternoon.

Lucy had arranged to go to the mosque with Mariam. Knowing that there would be no lunch provided on this occasion, because it was Ramadan, she insisted that they ate together before setting off.

'Will it be OK for me to pray with you all?' Lucy asked anxiously as they sat together in the living room, with their revision books around them and a plate of home-made samosas (part of a large consignment that Mariam's mother had left for them at her last visit) on the coffee table in front of them. 'Or will anyone be offended at a non-Muslim joining in?'

'No, of course not!' Mariam assured her. 'After all, we're all praying to the same God. And *our* mosque makes a particular point of welcoming everyone, whatever their beliefs. Maybe you'd have to be careful at some others, but no one will bat an eyelid here.'

'And they won't think I'm taking the micky, wearing a hijab?'

'Don't be ridiculous!' Mariam was scornful. 'Stop worrying. Everyone knows who you are and why you're wearing it.'

'Do they? I suppose Tahira will have told everyone.' Lucy was still hesitant. 'You're sure I won't offend anyone?'

'No,' her friend told her firmly. 'And you need to stop expecting us to get offended at every little thing. That's just the sort of Muslim stereotype we're trying to get rid of. We don't get offended about things any more than you or anyone else does – OK?'

'OK,' Lucy grinned. 'I hadn't thought of it like that. I suppose it's a bit patronising always checking with people that they aren't going to get offended before you do anything, instead of trusting them to be sensible about it and just tell you if you've made a boob.'

***

'Have you heard the news about Salma?' Olivia greeted them as they entered the mosque. 'She's got a wound infection. They've had to cancel the surgery they'd planned to do until it's cleared up.'

'Is that serious?' Lucy asked anxiously. 'I mean – she is going to be OK, isn't she?'

'They're treating her with antibiotics,' Olivia told her, 'so it should just be a matter of time, but …'

'What *I'd* like to know is what the police are doing to find the guy who did it,' broke in a young man, who had evidently been listening to their conversation. 'The news reports just keep saying that they're *following several lines of enquiry*! Doing sod all more like!'

'That's not fair, Yousef,' Mariam cut in, quietly but decisively. 'They've been working hard interviewing people and collecting evidence. Lucy knows some of them. They've got a big team working just on that one case.'

'That may be what they're telling you,' Yousef retorted, unconvinced, 'but where are the results? It can't be that hard to track down a maniac on a motorbike!'

'They've found the bike,' Mariam told him, 'and they've found the owner too – even though the number plate had been changed.'

'They told us last night that they've been over it for fingerprints and DNA,' Lucy added, 'and forensics have already got the results back – which is quite quick, when you remember all the cuts they've had. Jonah – he used to be a DCI in Thames Valley Police – used to be always complaining that it sometimes takes weeks for results to come through.'

'Tell it your own way.' Yousef was angry and did not want to be convinced. 'All I'm saying is it would've been a different story if it was a Muslim on the bike attacking a group of white girls.'

Lucy opened her mouth to protest, but thought better of it and closed it again. Her indignation at the suggestion that Sandra Latham and her team – or worse still her friend Jonah and her beloved stepfather, Peter – would even think of treating cases differently based on the race of either the victims or the perpetrators was modified by a consciousness that she represented the oppressor and Yousef the underdog in this argument. It was undeniable that there had been occasions in the past when police officers had allowed racial prejudice to influence their behaviour and it was very likely that Yousef had personal experience of Islamophobic abuse at the hands of the white majority.

'They had two men in custody.' At the sound of a new voice, Lucy turned to see another young man standing behind her. He was darker skinned than Yousef and had a long black beard. 'But they let them go.'

'They're out on police bail,' Lucy told them, hoping to convince everyone present that the police were taking action and the case was progressing. 'They can't keep them for more than twenty-four hours without charging them, and they don't have enough evidence yet.'

'That's bollocks!' Yousef said scornfully. 'My brother was held for nearly two weeks last year, when they thought he might've had something to do with the Manchester Arena bombing. And they hardly even apologised afterwards when they realised it was mistaken identity.'

'Well, the rules are different if it's terrorism,' Lucy began.

'And isn't *this* terrorism?' demanded the other young man.

'It would be if they'd been white girls,' Yousef agreed forcefully.

'Yousef! Nazir! Cool it!' Imran, hearing the raised voices, came over and put his arms round the shoulders of the two young men. 'We're all upset about what happened to our sisters, but getting angry won't help the situation.'

He turned to Mariam. 'It's good to see you, Mariam. 'How're you doing?'

'I'm fine,' she smiled. 'The burns are a bit painful sometimes, but not as much as before. They've been starting to itch, which I think is a sign that they're healing.'

'That's good,' the imam nodded, 'and Emily seems to be quite well too. She said she might be here today, but I don't know if she'll make it. I told her not to come if it was going to be difficult. It's quite a journey for her on the bus.'

As if on cue, the doors opened and Emily came in. To everyone's surprise, she was no longer wearing her niqab. For the first time, Lucy was able to see her pale face, red cheeks and thin pink lips. Even more surprisingly, she was accompanied by her mother. Fiona Armstrong slipped silently through the door and stood behind her daughter, looking round nervously at the unfamiliar surroundings.

'Emily!' Imran immediately went to greet them. 'How good to see you! And you must be Emily's mother,' he added, smiling warmly towards Fiona. 'She looks very like you. Thank you for coming with her. Would you like a cup of tea?'

'I – I,' Fiona stammered. Then she pulled herself

together enough to say, 'thank you. That would be very nice.'

While Imran took her mother over to the table at the side of the room to get the tea, Emily greeted Olivia and Mariam with a hug.

'Mum didn't want me to come,' she explained. 'We argued and argued, and in the end we compromised, and she said I could, so long as I let her bring me in the car and I didn't cover my face. She's really scared that someone will attack me in the street.'

'Of course she is!' declared Hibaaq, who had seen Emily's entrance from across the room and hastened over to greet her. 'Any mother would be.'

'Has she come to terms with you reverting to Islam at last?' asked Tahira appearing from behind her taller friend.

'I don't know about that,' Emily answered with a wry smile. 'I think she's decided to enter into negotiations about it. Like today – I could come to the mosque, so long as I didn't wear a niqab.'

'Don't you think she's just struggling to understand?' suggested Mariam quietly. 'It must be confusing for her to see you in a niqab when there are people like Tahira and me who don't even feel the need to cover our heads.'

'I hope so,' Emily sighed. 'But I can't help suspecting that she's hoping to gradually wear me down one little thing at a time. But I'm not going to let her,' she added defiantly. 'I'm going to carry on wearing a hijab, whatever Mum and Dad say, because I'm not ashamed of being a Muslim and I'm not afraid of people knowing about it.'

Mariam looked up at the clock on the wall over the sink at the side of the room. 'It's nearly time for the sermon,' she told Lucy. 'Come with me and I'll show you how we perform wudu before we pray.'

She led the way up the steps to the empty area between the main hall and the prayer room. Following her lead, Lucy took off her shoes and left them on the floor there. Then Mariam turned to the right and headed off down a short corridor lined with tiles on the wall and the floor. She pushed open a door marked "Sisters" and Lucy followed her into a brightly lit room.

This too was tiled on walls and floor. Along the left-hand side there was a row of three taps sticking out from the wall at a height a little lower than Lucy's waist. Beneath the taps, there ran a narrow trough with a grid at one end, presumably to take the water away. In front of each tap stood a cube of concrete covered in tiles, forming a squat stool.

Mariam showed Lucy how to sit on the stool and perform the ritual washing of hands, face and feet. Emily came in and sat down next to her. She murmured soft prayers as she washed her hands beneath the running water three times. Then she cupped water in her hands three times to wash her face. By that time, Mariam and Lucy were holding their feet under the taps, washing them up to the ankles and carefully cleaning between the toes.

When they were finished, Mariam stood up ready to go. Lucy followed suit. Then they hesitated and waited for Emily to finish, so that they could all go into the prayer room together. Sensing that they were waiting for her, Emily hurried to finish her ritual ablutions. Then she turned to look at Lucy, her eyes shining.

'Are you reverting too?' she asked.

'No,' Lucy shook her head, smiling back. 'I'm already mixed-up enough belonging to two different churches. I just wanted to share with you all – especially after what happened. I don't think Allah wants us all to be the same. I think we each need to find the way that works for us.'

'Oh!' Emily looked disappointed. 'Well, maybe when you find out more about it …?'

'No, Emily,' Mariam was quiet but firm, 'Lucy's right. We all have different paths for our lives. There's a verse in the Qur'an about it. You'd better ask Imran to tell you properly, but it's something about God making different nations and tribes so that we could all learn from each other, or get to know each other or something like that. And it says we ought to listen to what Jews and Christians have to say about God, too. You ask Imran. I'm sure he'll agree that Lucy doesn't need to revert.'

'Oh!' Emily said again, looking puzzled now. 'I thought … Oh well! We'd better hurry or we'll miss the beginning of the Khutbah.'

Barefoot, they padded back down the corridor and entered the prayer room. The men's side was already crowded with boys and men jostling for space on the prayer mats. There was more room on the side reserved for women. True to form, Tahira was sitting cross-legged next to the aisle between the two sections. Hibaaq, who was sitting next to her, moved up to make room for Mariam, Lucy and Emily between them. They sat down and turned their heads to look expectantly towards the reading desk where Imran was already seated. Lucy noticed that he was now wearing a white turban-like hat, which he had not had on when they arrived at the mosque. Almost as soon as they were seated, he got to his feet and began reciting in Arabic.

Lucy listened patiently to the musical chanting. The words sounded strange and guttural, unlike any language that she knew. As her ears became more attuned, she thought she recognised a few phrases from having heard Ibrahim and Mariam praying at home. This must be what it used to be like in Roman Catholic churches back in the days when all the services were in Latin.

Glancing surreptitiously round, she detected varying degrees of attention among the congregation. Some appeared to be enraptured by the recitation; others fidgeted as if impatient for it to be over; two small boys were engaged in some sort of silent game together passing small objects from one to another and making hand signals.

The words stopped abruptly and there was silence for a few moments. Imran looked up and down the rows of people. Everyone looked back at him. Even the two boys stopped their game and paid attention as he addressed them.

'My dear respected sisters and brothers,' he began, 'I am

sure that you all rejoice, as I do, and thank Allah (Subhanahu Wa Ta'ala) that two of our sisters who were injured in the acid attack last week are out of hospital and, indeed, are recovered enough to be here with us today.'

All eyes turned as he looked towards Emily and Mariam. Emily went very red in the face as she realised that everyone was staring at her. Imran immediately shifted his gaze and appeared to address his next remarks towards the male end of the room.

'Sadly, I have to report to you that our third sister remains very sick. In fact, she has contracted an infection, which has set back her recovery.'

A soft gasp went round the room as members of the congregation who had not yet heard this news took in its implications.

'I have also had confirmation from her parents that her prognosis is not good. She will require extensive skin grafts, which will have to be done over a protracted period, and her eyes have been severely damaged,' the imam continued. 'Her family have requested that we do not visit her at the moment, but she will need all the help that we can give her to adjust to a very different life, once she is discharged from hospital. I ask you all to continue to make dua for all of our injured sisters and especially for Salma and for her family and all the staff in the hospital who are treating her.'

He paused to allow his words to sink in, before resuming in a sterner tone, pausing briefly between each sentence to emphasise his message.

'I have heard some of you talking about justice. I have heard some of you expressing impatience that justice is a long time coming. I have also heard some of you expressing anger. I can understand that. When I think about our beloved sister suffering in the hospital, I feel angry too.' He looked slowly up and down the rows of people, lingering for a few seconds on Yousef and Nazir. 'But that it not the way of Islam. That is not our deen. If you study the holy Qur'an and the Sunnah, you will see that over and over again, the prophet Muhammad (Salla Allahu alayhi wa sallam) tells us that, while justice is good – within proper boundaries – to forgive is better. Moreover, it is better to wait and to be patient than to rush to exact retribution. Therefore, my dear brothers and sisters, I implore you to be patient and to trust the police to complete their investigations, and above all, not to attempt to exact revenge on those whom you may believe to be responsible for this wicked act.'

Lucy looked along the line, craning her neck in an attempt to see Yousef and Nazir. Had they expressed an intention to take the law into their own hands? Was the imam warning them off a plan to exact revenge from Alex Knowsley or other members of *Britain for the British*? It would be disastrous for the reputation of the mosque if they were to attack them – even if they turned out to be guilty of assaulting Salma and her friends.

Imran's voice continued. Now he was relating a hadith in which Muhammad showed forgiveness to his enemies. Lucy found her mind wandering as unfamiliar names and quotations in Arabic rolled off his tongue. Then at last he paused and looked slowly round the room, before ending the sermon with a short quotation from the Qur'an, first in Arabic and then in English.

'Never forget the words of Allah (Subhanahu Wa Ta'ala) to the Prophet (Salla Allahu alayhi wa sallam) in Surah forty-five, "Tell the believers to forgive those who do not fear God's days of punishment. He will requite people for what they have done." May Allah (Subhanahu Wa Ta'ala) grant us taqwa and hidayah and help us to put into practice what we have learned today. What is good came from Allah (Subhanahu Wa Ta'ala). What I lack came from my own short-comings, and I seek forgiveness from Allah (Subhanahu Wa Ta'ala).'

He paused and looked slowly round the room once more, before picking up his notes from the reading desk and sitting down. Lucy waited to see what would happen next. Almost immediately, Imran was on his feet again, chanting in musical Arabic. Then he paused again and walked over to join the men in their half of the room. Mariam and Emily on either side of her got to their feet. Lucy hurried to do the same. There was a shuffling of feet, as everyone took up their positions ready for the prayers. Lucy looked sideways at Mariam and followed her example, raising her hands to her shoulders as Imran chanted, 'Allahu Akbar!'

***

Meanwhile, Bernie and Jonah were sitting in a meeting of Sandra's team, listening to PC Anwar reporting on what he had found out from his attempts at getting alongside Muslim students at the university.

'Most of them seem to treat the *Feminist Sisterhood* as a bit of a joke,' he told them. 'There were a few of the women – especially the overseas students from Arab countries – who were a bit anxious that they were drawing unnecessary attention by their outspokenness, but that's about all.'

'So, no suggestion that they were depraved or subversive or un-Islamic?' asked Jonah.

'None at all,' Anwar shook his head vigorously. 'They're just viewed as odd, that's all – harmless eccentrics, I'd say.'

'And what about the wider Muslim community?' queried Sandra. 'What do they think?'

'Tahira Siddiqui came in for some criticism from some of the elders,' Anwar admitted. 'They aren't used to a young woman speaking up without being asked; and some of them disapprove of some of the female scholars that she's fond of quoting. Mostly, though, they seem to put it all down to the arrogance of youth and they assume that they'll change when they get older and wiser.'

'What about Salma's sporting activities?' Bernie asked, 'and her habit of hob-nobbing with non-Muslim men? Her brother didn't seem to like that. Did anyone else suggest that she was behaving inappropriately?'

'I'm sorry – I didn't ask,' Anwar admitted. 'Nobody mentioned it, but …'

'That's fine,' Sandra assured him. 'If they didn't feel strongly enough to mention it without you asking explicitly, it's unlikely they felt strongly enough to want to spray her with acid over it.'

'I did interview Waseem Rahman,' Anwar continued. 'You're right when you say that he disapproves of his sister's behaviour, but he's also very angry indeed with whoever attacked her. I really don't think he would do anything to harm her.'

'What about her friends?' Charlotte asked sharply. 'Did he blame them for leading her astray?'

'He may have done,' Anwar answered slowly, 'but I don't really think so – not enough to have wanted to attack them, anyhow. Besides – it was Salma who got the worst of it, and he could hardly have failed to recognise her, could he?'

'Yes,' agree Sandra. 'You're right. Whatever he thought of his sister's behaviour, it beggars belief that he would attack her like that.'

'What if he thought she'd been having it off with that white boyfriend of hers?' asked DC Fisher from his usual place on the back row. 'I think it's a mistake to rule out the possibility that this was an honour-based crime.'

'Salma's brother was in Preston the day of the attack,' Anwar told him. He's studying at UCLan[22]. He was in a lecture until five p.m. He'd have had his work cut out to get to Liverpool in time to attack the girls.'

'And where did he keep the motorbike?' Jonah asked. 'It was stolen the afternoon before. Whoever took it must have had somewhere to keep it until it was time to launch the attack.'

'That's a good point,' Sandra agreed. 'And they'd need somewhere to go to switch the number plate.'

'Householders like Alex Knowsley and his cronies seem more likely than students like Waseem Rahman and Jack Hampton,' Bernie suggested.

---

[22] The University of Central Lancashire

'I was going to tell you about Jack Hampton,' Charlotte piped up. 'I think he *could* be our attacker. I've been talking to his mates. He isn't quite the butter-wouldn't-melt-in-his-mouth Mr Nice-Guy that Emily's parents painted him. Apparently, he has a reputation for getting drunk and then becoming violent; and his language against Muslims matches anything that the *Britain for the British* lot use.'

'But is this all since Emily reverted, or was he like that before?' Sandra wanted to know.

'I think the drinking was going on before, and the anti-Muslim stuff started as a reaction to her dumping him,' Charlotte told her. 'One of his mates, who knew both him and Emily, suggested that one reason that she was attracted to Islam was because of its rule about not drinking alcohol. I don't know how true that is, though. He may just have been putting two and two together. He did seem very definite that Emily didn't like the way Jack drank, though.'

'Did you manage to verify his alibi?' Jonah asked. 'There's no point bothering too much about him if it's not possible that he was our attacker.'

'He claims to have been in the bar in the Guild of Students,' Charlotte answered promptly. 'It seems pretty clear that he *was* there from about seven fifteen, but it's not so certain that he was still there when things kicked off outside. You'd have thought he'd have been one of the students who were hanging around there when the emergency services arrived, but he wasn't.'

'So, are you suggesting that he could've left the bike round the corner somewhere and slipped out of the bar and picked it up?' asked Sandra.

'Yes,' nodded Charlotte. 'A couple of his mates said they thought he was there right up until after the incident, but they were a bit vague and anyway they may have been stretching the truth in order to protect him.'

'No,' Jonah said firmly. 'That won't wash. It's all very well saying he could've parked the bike somewhere handy, but what about the leathers and helmet and the sprayer full of acid? Where were they? And how come he wasn't seen putting on the leathers?'

'The bike had aluminium panniers at the back,' Charlotte argued. 'He could've put all the stuff in there.'

'There's still the question of how he got himself dressed up in the street without anyone noticing him doing it,' Jonah persisted.

'That's a good point,' Sandra agreed, 'but it doesn't necessarily rule Hampton out. 'Let's put out an appeal for people to report if they saw anyone dressing up in motorbike leathers anywhere in Liverpool during the hour or two before the incident took place. Whoever it was, they must have put the leathers on somewhere, and they might well not want to have been seen leaving their own house wearing them. Now, let's see … who else have we got?'

'I checked with Mark Lansdale's mother-in-law, like you asked me to,' Oliver Ransom called out from halfway down the room. 'She backs up his story that he was round at her house all evening.'

'Thanks Ollie.' Sandra pursed her lips and stared at the list of suspects on the screen behind her. 'You know, I really think it *must* have been Alex Knowsley, but I don't know how we're going to prove it.'

Hope Street

16. DEVELOPING SITUATION

'Do you agree with Sandra's assessment that Alex Knowsley must be guilty?' Bernie asked Jonah as they drove home the following day.

'Well, he certainly fits the bill,' Jonah replied cautiously. 'There's no doubt he has an irrational hatred for Muslims – and for quite a number of other minority groups too.'

'But?'

'I'm wondering if he's just a bit too convenient,' Jonah murmured thoughtfully. 'It would suit everyone for it to be him – much less uncomfortable than if it was revenge from one of the victims of the Shaladi attack – a grieving husband and father or, worse still from Sandra's point of view, a police officer.'

'The worst thing would be if it turned out to be Salma's brother or someone else from the Muslim community,' Bernie suggested. 'I don't want to believe that's possible any more than PC Anwar does, but would he necessarily have picked up any antagonism that there might have been towards the *Sisterhood*? He may have dismissed any criticism that there was of them as just what you'd expect, and not noticed that it had a more sinister undercurrent to it. In my experience, men – and I'm not talking just about Muslim men – can feel very threatened by strong women, and sometimes behave quite irrationally as a result.'

'The other problem with Alex Knowsley,' Jonah continued as if he had not heard, 'is that I don't think he's bright enough to have thought out such an elaborate plan. He seemed to me more like the type who acts first and thinks – insofar as he's capable of thinking at all – afterwards. This was planned meticulously right down to the smallest detail.'

'But maybe it was one of the others who did the planning,' Bernie argued. 'Craig maybe? Shut away by himself with just his computers for company?'

'Yes, you're right,' Jonah agreed, 'I reckon Craig would have had the intelligence and the single-mindedness to plan the operation. And that business about him not remembering that he was with Alex that evening could've been a clever double-bluff to convince us that he was telling the truth.'

'You mean, he thought it might look suspicious if he had the alibi off pat, as if he was expecting to need it?' asked Bernie. 'Or could he be hoping that, even if you nailed Knowsley, he'd get away with *perverting the course of justice* rather than being convicted of being part of the plot?'

'Something like that,' Jonah agreed. 'If he played his cards right, he might even manage to convince a jury that he was naïve enough to have been just helping out a mate with a little white lie, thinking that Knowsley was innocent.' He sighed. 'When it comes down to it, the question really is: whose alibi is the weakest? For example, can Mark Lansdale's mother-in-law be relied on? She lost her daughter and granddaughter in the Shaladi attack. If he attacked the girls as an act of revenge, might she be prepared to shield him? And Jack Hampton's mates who were drinking with him in the bar when it happened – did they misremember when he left, because they can't believe that he could be guilty?'

'And was Waseem Rahman really in that last lecture of his that afternoon?' added Bernie. 'He could have turned up at the beginning, signed the register and then slipped out again. But I think you're wrong. It isn't a matter of breaking the alibi of someone we've identified as a suspect. The crucial thing is finding out who had Alex Knowsley's motorbike that evening. Either he did or it all comes down to a question of who stole it – and that could be someone we haven't even heard of yet!'

***

'I've arranged to go up to Stockport to visit Jane over the Bank Holiday weekend,' Peter announced that evening as they were sitting round the kitchen table eating sausages and mashed potato. 'She's always asking me to go.'

'And you're usually keen to come up with excuses why you can't,' Bernie commented. 'What's brought about this change of heart?'

'I've been looking into that Shaladi boy,' Peter admitted, rather shame-faced because he knew that this was just the sort of interference in police enquiries that he frequently criticised Jonah for indulging in. 'He's got an interesting background – rather sad, really. I'd like to know a bit more about him and why he launched that attack in Liverpool. It seems to have come right out of the blue.'

'Stockport's a big place,' Bernie warned him. 'What are the chances of you finding anyone who knew the lad?'

'Jane and her husband are teachers, don't forget,' Peter responded. 'He's head of a school in an area with a very mixed population, and he knows other heads in the town. If he didn't teach Shaladi himself, he'll almost certainly know someone who did.'

'My word!' Jonah exclaimed, smiling broadly. 'You've got it all worked out, haven't you? Nobody would think you disapproved of members of the public making their own investigations instead of leaving it to the police!'

'What is it about Shaladi that makes you so interested?' Bernie asked.

'He's a Libyan refugee,' Peter told them. 'He and his family fled Libya nearly eight years ago, when he was only thirteen. They must've been part of the élite back there, I should think. His father – Ahmed Shaladi – is an Oxford graduate. He's a geologist, who worked with various oil companies. That's probably why they felt threatened by the upheaval during the Arab Spring. He had contacts in Britain who helped him to get a job over here.'

'So he wasn't a home-grown terrorist,' Jonah

commented. 'That must've been a relief to a lot of people.'

'It doesn't do much for the cause of current refugees seeking asylum here,' Bernie pointed out drily. 'It's just the sort of narrative people like Knowsley and his cronies in *Britain for the British* want, to make their point that foreigners can't be trusted.'

'Mohammed was diagnosed with Post-Traumatic Stress Disorder soon after they arrived in Stockport,' Peter continued. 'Apparently he'd witnessed his grandparents being beaten to death in the uprising.'

'So, maybe not so surprising that he was vulnerable to radicalisation,' Jonah suggested.

'Olivia said he used to go home most weekends while he was at university,' Bernie recollected. 'That could be a sign that he still felt insecure. Was anyone keeping an eye on his mental state by that time?'

'I don't know,' Peter sighed. 'I've only got what was in the papers to go on. You'd have thought he'd have been receiving ongoing treatment, wouldn't you? But maybe he was considered cured and had been discharged.'

'He'd have been discharged from the Child and Adolescent service when he hit eighteen,' Bernie mused. 'Maybe he never got transferred to adult mental health services.'

'Or maybe he fell through the net when he went off to uni,' Peter agreed. 'Anyway, despite all the vitriol in the press, I can't help feeling that in some ways, he was a victim in all this as well.'

'Which is the sort of thing Tahira and Olivia were saying,' Bernie nodded. 'They said he was nice, didn't they? Olivia clearly liked him and didn't understand why he changed so suddenly.'

'So, is your idea that there must have been something – or someone – in Liverpool, which caused him to change?' asked Jonah excitedly, 'and that *that* could be what made someone want to attack a group of Muslim students in retaliation?'

'I don't know about that,' Peter shook his head. 'I don't think I've got anything as definite in mind as a direct link to the attack on Mariam and her friends. I just … I just think there must be more to it than just a young man suddenly going berserk for no reason.'

***

'Mam?' Lucy's voice sounded unusually tentative when Bernie answered her phone on the Sunday evening following her return to Oxford. 'I thought you ought to know – Salma's very ill.'

'I'm sorry to hear that,' Bernie tried to keep her voice calm and steady, not wanting to increase her daughter's evident anxiety. 'What's the problem?'

'She's developed sepsis,' Lucy told her in a shaky voice. 'They – the doctors say she could even die.'

'Well, at least they've diagnosed it,' Bernie replied, struggling to think of anything reassuring to say. 'And she's in the right place to get the treatment she needs.'

'I know, but … it's just so awful not being able to do anything.'

'You're doing a grand job looking after Mariam,' Peter cut in, coming up behind Bernie and speaking over her shoulder. 'Concentrate on that and leave worrying about Salma to her family and friends.'

'Peter's right, love,' his wife agreed, giving him a grateful squeeze on the arm. 'You've got plenty to do supporting Mariam through the exams. How is she? I suppose this latest news will have knocked her back rather.'

'Yes,' Lucy agreed, still sounding very subdued. 'She knows it's stupid, but I think she can't help feeling a bit of "survivor guilt" – you know, wondering why she got off so much lighter than Salma. We've all been trying to keep her mind off it but …'

'I'm sure you're all doing magnificently,' Bernie told her firmly, 'but if you'd like me to come up for a couple of weeks – to see you through the exams – it wouldn't be a problem.'

'I can cope on my own,' Peter backed her up quickly, 'if you'd like your Mam with you.'

'No, don't be silly!' Lucy laughed in spite of her anxiety. 'We've got plenty of people clucking round trying to help already. Ibrahim's taken two weeks off work so that he can escort us to and from the exams and makes sure that Mariam rests enough and eats properly, and Dom has insisted on doing all the housework because Mariam and I have exams and Ibrahim's fasting, and Mariam's mum keeps coming over with supplies. We even had DCI Latham round offering us police protection when we're going to and from to the exams!'

'Does she think you need it?' Peter asked anxiously.'

'I don't think so,' Lucy assured him, sounding much less low-spirited now. 'I think she was just wanting to make sure Mariam wouldn't be scared that it might happen again. We told her that we didn't need it. I can't see why Mariam would be a target any more than anyone else. It's not as if she could identify the man who did it.'

'I suppose Sandra Latham's just covering her back, because whoever it was is still out there, and we don't know for certain why they did it,' Bernie suggested. 'I understand you not wanting a fuss, but you might as well have accepted her offer. What harm would there be in letting them chauffeur you to and from your exams in a police car?'

'It would be like giving in,' Lucy told her. 'We don't want whoever did it to get the satisfaction of making us change how we behave. It's bad enough that Ibrahim's insisting on going with us. We told him we didn't need a male escort, but then Dom backed him up and said he'd come and meet us after the afternoon exams, so that Ibrahim could have our tea ready for us when we got home. Like I said, they're both clucking round us like mother hens!'

'It's only because they're worried about you both,' Bernie told her, suppressing a chuckle. 'You should be flattered – or think of it like this: they must be just as frustrated as you at not being able to do anything for Salma, and this is their way of coping.'

'I suppose so,' Lucy thought for a moment and then gave a little giggle. 'It just gets a bit oppressive sometimes, being treated as if I can't take care of myself, but I expect I'll manage.'

'That's the spirit,' Bernie said warmly, 'and good luck with the exams!'

She ended the call and was immediately conscious of Jonah speaking on the mobile phone attached to his wheelchair.

'Sandra?' she heard him say. 'We've just had Lucy on the phone telling us about Salma. What's the latest from the hospital?'

'They're treating her for sepsis, but so far she hasn't been responding,' Sandra Latham told him, 'not that I ought to be discussing it with you. However, her family have agreed the wording of a press statement, so I can tell you that much.'

'And Lucy also told us that you'd offered police protection to her and Mariam while they take their exams,' Jonah went on, 'but she turned it down. Do you really think they're at risk?'

'Your guess is as good as mine,' Sandra sighed. 'In all probability the perpetrator has done what he set out to do and will be lying low hoping we won't find him, but you never know with these fanatics. He may feel empowered by the fact that we haven't found him yet to do it again, or someone else may try a copycat attack, or if it was personal against Mariam or Emily, they might think they've failed and want to have another go.'

'Should we have a word with Lucy and persuade her to take up your offer?' asked Peter anxiously.

'Don't worry,' Sandra reassured him, 'I've got a couple of officers keeping a discrete eye on them. And Mariam's brother is going to be giving them a taxi service to and from the exams. Their parents have bought them a car.'

'Lucy has just been complaining about Ibrahim insisting

on escorting them,' Jonah told her, 'but she didn't mention the car. What about Emily? She must have exams coming up too.'

'Emily's still living at home and her mother's going to drive her to the exams,' Sandra explained. 'So there should be minimal chance of anyone getting close enough to any of them to make another attack. I'll be glad when term ends and they all go home, to be honest. At least then we'll be able to concentrate on nailing Knowsley, and not have to worry that he might strike again.'

'You're sure he's guilty then?' asked Jonah sharply.

'As sure as I can be. He's openly Islamophobic. It was his bike. His burglary story doesn't stack up. His alibi depends on the word of a man who hates Muslims even more than he does. We're working on trying to find some evidence of him obtaining acid or buying a garden sprayer.'

'And what about finding where the bike was kept overnight between the so-called burglary and the acid-throwing incident?' Jonah asked. 'And the motorbike helmet and leathers – where did the attacker keep them beforehand and where are they now?'

***

Three days later, Sandra spoke on the phone to Jonah again.

'I thought you'd all want to know,' she said sombrely, 'Salma Rahman died early this morning. This investigation is now a murder enquiry.'

'Does Lucy know?' Peter called anxiously from across the room.

'And Mariam?' added Bernie, looking up from the floor, where she was helping Peter's grandson, Ricky, to put together a jigsaw puzzle featuring a fearsome looking red dragon.

'I've spoken to Mariam's brother,' Sandra told them. 'The girls are both in an exam this afternoon, so I've arranged to go with him to meet them out of it so that I can tell them personally, rather than allowing them to hear it through the media.'

'What happened exactly?' asked Jonah.

'She was treated for sepsis, but she didn't respond. Then yesterday she developed septic shock and was taken to the ICU. She was pronounced dead this morning. We've got a press conference booked for an hour from now, which is why I rang you.'

'Has there been any progress in the investigation?' Bernie asked.

'No. We've had reports back on the fingerprints from O'Neill's taxi and they don't match Knowsley or any of the others – or anyone on the database either. But of course, he was wearing gauntlets when he was on the motorbike, so he wouldn't have left any prints on the car. There's no sign of acid in the car either, though, which is a bit of a blow. The only tiny bit of progress we've had is finding a witness who can confirm a racist incident among the MerseyRiders back in November. A black student by the name of Bradley Carver joined the club, and then left it again in a bit of a hurry after Knowsley attacked him verbally and physically in a transport caff, when they were off out together.'

'Have you interviewed him?' asked Jonah, with interest. 'What does he say about it?'

'The witness or the student?' asked Sandra. 'Yes, we've spoken to the owner of the café and to the secretary of the club, who keeps the membership list. The student's already gone home. He's at John Moores[23], which finished earlier than Liverpool uni. He lives down in Buckinghamshire, so it didn't seem worth sending someone to question him about an incident that probably has no connection with the acid-spraying at all.'

'I've been keeping an eye on their social media activity,' Jonah told her, 'as I imagine your team has too. They don't

---

[23] Liverpool John Moores University, formerly Liverpool Polytechnic, is one of the group of English Higher Education institutions that gained university status in 1992.

seem to have moderated their behaviour much, since you let them know they're under suspicion.'

'I know,' Sandra groaned. 'They're laughing at us. They know we don't have enough evidence to prosecute and they're enjoying watching us scramble around looking for it. And meanwhile, we've got an understandable upsurge of anger from the student population that we haven't nailed anyone yet.'

'Lucy told me there was a rally last Saturday, organised by the Student Union,' Bernie said, 'and an interfaith vigil. It looks as if they're all sticking together and seeing it as an attack on all of them, not just Muslims.'

'Yes,' agreed Sandra, 'which is all very fine and dandy, but it still makes more work for us, policing the demonstrations. And it's not as if all the other criminals have taken a holiday from their activities while we sort this one out!' She sighed, 'I'll be glad when term's over. If we can just keep a lid on things until the students go home ...'

Liverpool Philharmonic Hall

17. PORTRAIT OF A TERRORIST?

'Thank you for coming up,' Jude Kimbugwe greeted Peter, as he exited the barrier at Stockport railway station. 'Jane really does appreciate your friendship – we both do.'

'I ought to be thanking you for putting me up,' Peter responded, embarrassed by his host's enthusiastic welcome. He had only met Jude once before. That had been at his marriage to Peter's half-sister the previous year, when Peter had reluctantly agreed to take on the role of father-to-the-bride. 'Especially since I have an ulterior motive.'

'Ah yes!' Jude smiled. 'You're hoping to find out more about our most notorious resident. What makes you so interested in the Shaladi boy?'

'You know Lucy's studying at Liverpool University?' Peter began, as they made their way to the car. 'And I suppose you've heard about the acid attack there a few weeks ago? Well, she's friends with one of the students who had acid sprayed over her. Luckily, she got away with just some nasty burns to the back of her head and neck, but one of their other friends died from it.'

'Yes,' Jude confirmed. 'I've been following the story. I hadn't realised your family was so close to it though.'

'Mariam – the girl I was telling you about – shares a house with Lucy, and with Lucy's cousin Dominic and Mariam's brother Ibrahim,' Peter explained. 'We met Ibrahim a few years back when we were on holiday. Anyway, the thing is: one possible motive for this attack is revenge for what Mohammed Shaladi did last October. That made me start looking into that incident, and I'm intrigued to know why he did it. Everyone who knew him – including a couple of Mariam's friends – seems to think he wasn't the sort. So what prompted him?'

'And does it have any bearing on who sprayed your Lucy's friends with acid?' suggested Jude with a smile. 'Yes. I think I'm starting to see where you're coming from. I've been doing some thinking on my own account after we got your email. The imam from the mosque that his family attend is a good friend of mine. He comes into school once or twice a term to help with assemblies and RE lessons. I could introduce you, if you like.'

'Would you?' Peter's eyes lit up. All the way up in the train he had been regretting his decision to come and wondering how he was going to explain why he wanted to find out more about this convicted terrorist. 'I know it must all sound very tenuous, but I can't help having a feeling that if we could only understand what made Shaladi do what he did, we'd have a better chance of discovering who attacked Mariam and her friends. They said he was nice. So why did he suddenly run amok with a van?'

'If they were friends of his,' Jude suggested cautiously, 'could that have been why they were targeted?'

'According to them, they weren't exactly friends,' Peter told him, 'more just acquaintances. And nobody from outside their circle would have known about even that ... although ...,' he added slowly, 'of course, we never got the chance to talk to Salma – that's the one who died – so maybe she could have known him better, and have been known to associate with him. Yes! Why on earth didn't we think of that possibility before? All along we've been assuming that *either* it was a personal attack *or* it was revenge for what Shaladi did, but it could've been both!'

They drove on in silence. Peter was pondering on the possibility that Salma could have been in some way associated in someone's mind with Mohammed Shaladi and his bizarre attack outside the nightclub, while Jude was considering how best to approach his friend the imam to introduce Peter to him. After only a few minutes, they turned into a cul-de-sac in a residential area and pulled up outside an unpretentious semi-detached house.

'Jane's back,' Jude observed, pointing towards a small red hatchback parked on the drive. 'She sent me to fetch you while she stocked up on fresh vegetables from the market.'

'She didn't need to bother,' Peter protested. 'I won't be criticising her cooking.'

'I know,' Jude smiled, turning off the engine and getting out of the car. 'I told her that, but she knows you do most of the cooking at home, so she's paranoid that she won't be able to live up to your standards! And ... and she's desperate to make up for her mother's behaviour towards you.'

'Oh dear!' Peter sighed, thinking that this was going to be a very difficult visit and starting once again to wish that he had not come. 'She doesn't need to.' Then, in a lower voice, 'however much I'd like it not to be so, the woman *was* my mother too, and I behaved much worse towards her, considering she was dying of cancer when I met her. Can't you explain to Jane that she doesn't need to keep apologising?'

'Peter! How lovely to see you!' The front door opened and Jane appeared, hurrying down the drive to greet them. She held her arms wide as if intending to embrace him and then hastily changed her mind and shook him by the hand instead. 'How was your journey?'

'OK,' Peter mumbled. 'Of course, you never expect much when you're travelling cross-country.'

'And how are Bernie and Lucy?' Jane asked, 'and your friend, Jonah?'

'They're all well,' Peter answered. 'How about you?'

'We're all fine, aren't we Jude?' Jane looked towards her husband, who smiled his confirmation. 'Have you told Peter about Dorcas's news?' Jude shook his head. 'Jude's going to be a grandad,' Jane announced excitedly. 'She rang us last night.'

'Congratulations!' Peter felt relief that he was now on safe ground with a well-defined ritual of responses that he could follow. 'And when is the happy event expected?'

'December,' Jane answered happily. 'They've only just had it confirmed themselves. But don't let's stay standing here. Come in! Where's your bag? Jude will show you up to your room while I put the kettle on. I'm sorry about the clutter. It's Keziah's old room and she still hasn't taken all her stuff away yet. You know how it is when kids leave home. Is tea alright? Or would you prefer coffee?'

'Tea will be lovely,' Peter assured her, going round to the back of the car, where Jude had the boot open, and pulling out his suitcase. 'And I'm used to clutter. We brought up two kids in a two-up two-down in Cowley, remember!'

***

'Jude tells me you're interested in Mohammed Shaladi and why he went off the rails,' Jane said when Peter came downstairs, having unpacked his bag and freshened up after the journey.

'That's right,' Peter admitted. 'I'm intrigued to know what happened to change him from a likeable young man into a reckless killer.'

'I read he was a refugee,' Jane commented. 'That could be your answer. We've got some Syrian kids in our school, who've seen things that *nobody* ought to have to watch, never mind seven and eight-year-olds. He probably had mental health issues, and then something happened to trigger a response that went way over the top.'

'Yes,' agreed Jude. 'That would be my guess too. My oldest sister took her own life when I was seven. My mother always said it was because of seeing our father killed. I was too young to remember, but poor Grace was twelve and absolutely adored our dad.'

'He was killed by Idi Amin,' Jane explained. 'Jude's mother managed to escape to Britain with Jude and his four sisters after her husband was executed by his troops.'

'I was only three when we left,' Jude went on, 'so I've never known any home except here. My first wife was a

Ugandan refugee too, so I can't help feeling some sympathy for Mohammed Shaladi, whatever he may have done. I've arranged for Hassan Majid, the imam I told you about, to come round tomorrow afternoon. He knows the whole family, so he may be able to tell you what you want to know.'

***

'This is my brother-in-law, Peter Johns,' Jude said as he led the imam into the small front room. Peter immediately got to his feet and stepped forward to shake hands.

'Thank you for coming,' he said apologetically. 'You must think this is all very odd. To be honest, I'm not sure myself what I'm hoping to get out of this.'

'Jude tells me you know some of Mohammed's friends from Liverpool,' Hassan answered, smiling at Peter. 'I was quite surprised. He always found it difficult to make friends.'

'I think *friends* may be a bit of an exaggeration,' Peter smiled back. 'A woman student told me how he'd defended her against some girls who were bullying her on a bus; and another said that she's spoken to him a few times and he never seemed like a violent sort of person. They both said he was nice. That's why I can't understand what he did.'

'Neither can I, to be perfectly honest with you,' admitted Hassan. 'He was always very quiet and withdrawn and, as you say, never violent. The only thing that made any sort of sense of the whole business was what happened to his sister.'

There was a long silence, before Peter ventured to ask, 'and what was that?'

'She was raped by a group of boys from her school,' Hassan told them baldly. 'The defence team wanted to bring it up at his trial, but Mohammed didn't want her exposed to any more publicity and the boys' parents brought pressure to bear and got an injunction to stop the press being told anything about it. So ... nothing was ever said.'

For a few seconds there was a stunned silence. Then Peter asked, 'so what exactly happened?'

'It was over two years ago, now' Hassan told them. 'Fatima was cornered by two boys from her school, who pulled her down an alley and raped her. She was only fourteen and they were a year older. Because of their age, they were dealt with in the Youth Court. Their parents were very respectable and highly thought-of.'

'And white, presumably,' Jane added, pointedly.

'Yes,' Hassan confirmed. 'They hired good lawyers and promised to make sure the boys mended their ways. They made such a good case that they avoided them being sent to prison.'

'It's surprising that they didn't get a custodial sentence, even at that age,' Peter observed, 'but I suppose the judge didn't want to disrupt their education.'

'They got three-year Youth Rehabilitation Orders,' Hassan went on, 'with what they call "Intensive Supervision and Surveillance".'

'ISS,' repeated Peter thoughtfully. 'Yes. I can believe that. It ought to mean that Social Services are keeping a close eye on them and they should be receiving an intensive course of rehabilitation measures. In theory, it's a lot better than putting them in a Youth Offenders Institution, but in practice, I doubt if there are ever the staff available to do it properly.'

'I think everyone assumed that the parents would keep a sufficiently close watch on them, now they knew what they'd been up to,' Jude opined. 'I know the head teacher of the school. She said they are all pillars of the community and they were totally shocked to discover that their boys had been regularly watching porn movies together. If they promised to keep tabs on their TV viewing and internet access, most likely the magistrate just breathed a sigh of relief that a custodial sentence didn't seem necessary.'

'They probably made out the boys were victims too – or even that she led them on,' Jane added darkly, 'with them being so young themselves.'

'And what exactly were you suggesting the link is

between this attack on Shaladi's sister and him driving a van into a group of pedestrians in Liverpool?' asked Peter, turning back to Hassan. 'I don't really see the connection – apart from perhaps reawakening the trauma of his time in Libya.'

'He thought the sentence was derisory,' Hassan explained. 'And he thought British society must be depraved to have allowed the boys to get hold of so much pornographic material. Some of it was shown at the trial. It was part of the defence case that they had been influenced by it into thinking that such behaviour was acceptable and the norm. That's what he said at his trial – he was trying to stamp out the sorts of places that encourage those attitudes.'

'So you're saying he wasn't aiming to kill pedestrians, he was attacking the lap dancing club for corrupting its punters?' asked Peter.

'That's right,' Hassan nodded. 'That show of defiance when he was sentenced – shouting out at the judge and calling down the wrath of God on everyone – that was all put on, to cover up how frightened he was. I've been to see him in prison. He's really very subdued and scared. He wasn't part of a jihadist plot to destroy western society – he just wanted to stop the sex industry corrupting young men and putting young women at risk.'

'But, of course, the press took hold of it and made a big story out of it,' Jane said cynically. 'He gave them what their readers wanted to see – a violent jihadi shouting defiance while he was led away to jail.'

There was a long silence. Eventually Peter thought of another question that he wanted to ask.

'A group of women were attacked in Liverpool a few weeks ago. Someone sprayed them with acid. They were part of a feminist movement,' he told Hassan. 'Would Mohammed Shaladi have disapproved of that?'

'No, of course not,' Hassan answered at once. 'At least ... I don't know,' he added, looking thoughtfully at Peter. 'He was – or he became – rather conservative regarding things like women's dress. He thought that the way western women expose so much flesh to the gaze of men was encouraging the general state of depravity that he blamed for what happened to his sister; but I think he was still in favour of women getting an education and being allowed to work outside the home. I really can't emphasise enough – he was *not* a radical or a fundamentalist.'

'And he didn't make any friends, after he went to Liverpool, who *were*?' queried Peter. 'People who might take exception to a woman who, for example, expressed a desire to become an imam? Or who openly criticised those mosques who don't allow women to pray there?'

'I don't imagine he would have approved of either of those things,' Hassan admitted, 'and I know a lot of people from my own congregation who would have agreed with him about that. I can't say they are things that I would exactly encourage myself. Men and women are equal in Islam, but their roles are different. *But*,' he added with emphasis, 'that's a long way from condoning a physical attack on someone who expressed those views. I'm quite convinced that *nothing* would have induced Mohammed Shaladi to attack a group of women, and I've got no reason to think that he had any friends who would have done either.'

'Good,' Peter said apologetically. 'I'm sorry if that was offensive. I just had to ask, in case … well, the last thing we want is to find that the girls were attacked by a fellow-Muslim, but if there was any possibility, it would have only made things worse if the police hadn't considered it.'

'Are you with the police then?' Hassan asked sharply. 'I thought Jude said this was purely personal? You daughter knew Mohammed Shaladi or something?'

'Peter used to be in the police,' Jane explained. 'He's retired now.'

'And I know the officer in charge of the enquiry,' Peter added, 'but yes, this is just personal – trying to make sense of things. My stepdaughter, Lucy, is friends with the women who were attacked, and some of them knew Shaladi and liked him. The police are assuming that they were targeted as some sort of revenge for what he did. I'm sorry. I shouldn't have come. This is none of my business.'

'No, no,' Hassan leaned forward and put his hand on Peter's shoulder. 'It's important to ask these questions, and I'm grateful that you aren't just assuming that Mohammed is nothing more than a ruthless terrorist. There's so much fear and suspicion about nowadays. I've sometimes sat on a bus and felt that everyone was watching me in case I was wearing a suicide vest.'

'Jude gets that sort of thing too, don't you, Jude?' Jane said. 'Only I think they're more expecting him to knife them or pick their pockets.'

'Oh it's not so bad,' Jude protested with a smile. 'Now my hair is starting to go grey, not so many people seem to see me as a threat. It doesn't bother me. It's natural for people to be afraid of the unfamiliar. I can understand that. I just hope that we can bring up the next generation with all different races and cultures living and learning together so they won't need to feel afraid.'

'I hope so,' Jane sounded unconvinced, 'but I don't want you to have to wait that long. And even if the kids are all together in the same class, there's not much you can do about the parents. I've had seven and eight-year-olds using racist language that we certainly never taught them at school.'

'You're right,' Peter agreed. 'If education was the answer, racism would have died out by now. My first wife used to talk the same way as you, Jude, about people just being afraid of the unfamiliar and not letting it bother her. I didn't see it that way, but I managed to stop myself punching too many white supremacists on the nose, because I knew she wouldn't like it! I don't know what the answer is, except that it's white people who're the problem, not black or brown people or Polish immigrants or refugees.'

'I can't agree with you there,' Jude said quietly. 'You're

right that it's the racists who have to change, but racism isn't *just* a white prerogative. My father was killed because he stood up to Idi Amin's regime when he expelled the Asians from Uganda.'

'He did it in the name of Allah too,' Hassan agreed, 'which is what saddens me most.

'But it was the British who had helped to put him there,' Peter argued, 'and it was the British who had brought the Asians to Africa in the first place. I looked into it,' he added, looking rather shamefaced towards Jude, as he realised that it was rather arrogant to lecture his brother-in-law on his own nation's history, 'after Jane told me your family were refugees.'

'You're right,' Jude admitted, smiling towards Peter, 'but my point is that it's not that one race has a monopoly on xenophobia. It's all to do with power, and in particular power imbalances. And when the powerless get power, they often want to redress the balance by getting their own back on the ones who used to have power over them.'

'Exactly!' Peter agreed. 'It is all about power, but, the thing is – in most places in the world it's the white Europeans who have had the power and who don't want to give it up. That's what this *Britain for the British* nonsense is all about – people who expect everything to be handed to them on a plate, who feel threatened by anyone who gets on better in life than they do, whether it's "bleeding heart liberals" or hard working Polish plumbers! They think they've got a right to an easy ride just because they "belong" here. It's all so-'

He broke off suddenly and looked sheepishly round at the others.

'I'm sorry,' he mumbled. 'I didn't mean to rant at you. I just get angry when I see how hard people like you,' (he looked towards Jude and then Hassan), 'and Ibrahim and Mariam, and my two kids have to work just to be treated as equals to the likes of the four wasters who're under suspicion of that acid attack.'

Lime Street Station

18. SUMMERTIME

'I've never been to a funeral before,' Lucy told her mother as they headed south down the M6, 'or at least, not that I can remember; so I didn't have anything to compare it with. It was very interesting. The mosque that Salma's family go to is quite different from the one in Liverpool. Women had to come in through a different door and we weren't allowed inside the prayer room, so they had the funeral prayers outside. Everyone was dressed up in white robes and all the women were wearing hijabs – even Mariam's mum, and she never wears one. In fact, even Tahira had one on!'

Bernie had driven up to Liverpool to fetch her daughter home from her first eventful year at university. At Jonah's request – perhaps *demand* would have been a more appropriate word – she had invited Sandra to lunch at the shared house and pumped her for information on the progress of the police investigation. However, the inspector had little to report. Knowsley and his cronies were still denying involvement in the acid attack and no convincing evidence had been found to prove that they were lying.

Now they were alone in the car and Lucy was relating everything that had happened in the few weeks since they had last been together.

'Everyone was saying what a pity it was the funeral couldn't happen sooner,' she prattled on. 'You're supposed to bury the body within two days, but the hospital did a post mortem and then it was the weekend and then there was the Bank Holiday so it was nearly a week, which lots of them thought was far too long.'

'It must be difficult if the coroner doesn't release the body right away,' Bernie observed thoughtfully. 'They were lucky not to have to wait for the post mortem to be done too. Often there's a queue.'

'I think it was fast-tracked,' Lucy told her, 'because the family didn't really want one at all. It was lucky Mariam and I didn't have any exams that day, and Dom was on half-term, so Ibrahim drove us all over there. Salma's family invited everyone back to their house afterwards, but of course, they couldn't give people anything to eat or drink because of Ramadan, so it was a bit awkward, just standing around with nothing to do.'

'Yes,' agreed Bernie, 'It must be odd having guests round and not being able to make a brew for them.'

'We couldn't even understand what a lot of the older people were saying,' Lucy continued. 'Salma's grandparents and great-aunts and uncles and their friends were all speaking some Indian language – Urdu, I think – apart from when they were reciting pieces from the Qur'an or praying in Arabic. In the end, we went out in the back garden with Waseem. He seemed rather out of it as well.'

'How's he taken it?' Bernie asked. 'I gather he didn't approve of …,' she hesitated and then started again. 'I got the impression he was worried about Salma.'

'He was really cut up about her,' Lucy said emphatically. 'He kept asking us who could have done it, and why. He seemed sort of lost, as if he didn't know what to think anymore.'

There was a long silence. Bernie could not think what to say to this. It was quite unlike what she had heard of Waseem Rahman so far.

'I know you all have him down as a suspect,' Lucy went on, 'but I'm sure he's not like that at all. He saw himself as Salma's protector – and now he thinks he's failed her!'

'You don't think he might … do anything rash?' Bernie suggested cautiously. 'To avenge her, I mean?'

'No!' Lucy was adamant. 'I keep telling you – he's not like that. He – he – he's confused and upset – and angry too, but he's not violent. And he's blaming himself. She was his little sister and he was supposed to protect her. That's why he kept trying to stop her mixing with non-Muslims – especially men. He was afraid they'd take advantage of her. And he genuinely believed that playing sport was exposing her to danger because she couldn't keep herself covered when she was doing it. She always used to complain about him and laugh at him, but I think he really thought he was doing the right thing.'

'How did he get on with Tahira?' Bernie asked, trying to imagine what that forthright young woman would have had to say to a brother who felt obliged to police his sister's activities and wardrobe.

'Well ...,' Lucy grinned, 'to be fair to Tahira, she was very restrained – for her! She hardly lectured him at all. I think she was trying very hard not to offend anyone; but she couldn't resist giving him a few quotes from her favourite feminist writers on how misguided it is to think that the Qur'an puts men in authority over women. I think maybe she thought she was helping, by telling him not to feel responsible, because it was none of his business what Salma chose to do, but ... I'm not sure he appreciated her kind gesture!'

***

As the long summer vacation wore on, Lucy settled back into the routine of life in Oxford, helping Bernie and Peter to care for Jonah, playing with Peter's grandchildren and tending the large garden of their home in Headington. Now that she was no longer among her Muslim friends, she put the hijabs that Salma had shared with her away with other items that she would need when she returned to Liverpool in September. The events of the previous term faded in her memory – revived every so often by messages from Mariam documenting her continuing recovery. The expectation that the perpetrators of the atrocity would be apprehended diminished.

Jonah continued to scour the internet for anything that could provide a new lead to offer to Sandra, whom he pestered regularly for updates on the investigation. However, the inspector now had other cases to deal with and her reports were depressingly similar each week: no hard evidence to link Knowsley or his associates with the crime, no new witnesses coming forward, and no sign of the missing motorbike helmet or leathers.

'We've interviewed every single member of the MerseyRiders club,' she sighed one evening in answer to Jonah's questions, 'but none of them had anything particularly useful to say. Well, I suppose there was one thing. Several of them were able to tell me where Alex Knowsley kept the key to his bike shed. Apparently, there was an occasion when he was sounding off about how one of his kids had left the door open, with the key in the lock. He'd said something along the lines of, "I told them – lock the door and put the key back under the stairs!" So, I suppose any of them could've stolen the bike – assuming he was telling the truth about the burglary.'

'That's interesting,' Jonah said thoughtfully. 'You don't happen to know whether that happened before or after Mark Lansdale left the club? I mean, could he have been there and heard where Knowsley kept the key?'

'The way he spoke, I don't think he ever was a member,' Sandra answered, 'but he could've been lying – or maybe playing it down. I'll see if I can find out.'

'And I've been looking at press reports about that incident with the MerseyRiders and the black student, Bradley Carver,' Jonah told her. 'It turns out he lives in Bourne End in Buckinghamshire. It's not all that far from Oxford. Would you like us to go over there and have a word with him?'

'I'm not sure what the point would be,' Sandra answered cautiously. 'I mean – what could he tell us that we don't know already?'

'I was thinking he might be able to point us in the direction of which members of the club were most likely to want to attack a group of Muslim women and to frame Alex

Knowsley for doing it.'

'It's a bit tenuous,' Sandra said dubiously.

'I know. That's why I'm not suggesting you ought to send someone down to interview him. I was just thinking, since we're practically on the spot …'

***

'Dom seems to be having a good time, staying with Mariam,' Lucy said a few days later, as they all sat in the garden enjoying the sunshine and watching Peter's grandchildren playing in the sandpit. 'Here's a photo he's posted on Facebook of them both on top of Pendle Hill yesterday.'

Bernie leaned over to look at Lucy's phone.

'Yes,' she agreed, 'and Mariam looks well. If I didn't know that she's only wearing that headscarf to hide her scars, I'd never have guessed there was anything wrong.'

'She must be doing OK if she's up to climbing up Pendle Hill,' Jonah commented. 'I remember taking the boys up there when they were young. It was quite a pull up!'

'It looks as if it's blowing a gale,' Peter observed, coming up behind Lucy and looking over her shoulder. 'That headscarf looks as if it's about to come off.'

'It's always windy up there,' Bernie told him. 'Pendle Hill is isolated from the rest of the Pennines, so there's nothing to break the force of the wind. I ought to take you up there sometime. There's nothing like it down here.'

'And Jane says I ought to stay with her for long enough for her to show me the Peak District,' Peter murmured. 'But I'm getting a bit old for gadding about all the time like that. Oxford suits me fine – and I've got the grandkids to think about. They're more important than learning to appreciate *The North*!'

'You've got grandkids *Oop North* too,' Bernie pointed out with a laugh. 'Don't they count?'

'Of course they do, but Hannah doesn't need the childcare. She and Laurence both have good, stable jobs and don't have to worry about visas. It'll be easier for Eddie and

Crystal once Crystal's been here for long enough to get British Citizenship. As it is, she's got to work or she could be sent back to Jamaica.'

'I know. It's monstrous-,' Bernie began, but she broke off as her phone began to ring. She fished it out of her pocket and looked down at the screen. 'It's Joey! I wonder what he can want.'

'Hi Bernie,' her cousin's voice sounded anxious. 'Have you got a minute?'

'Yes. What is it?'

'It's Dom – at least, it's Ruth really ... or rather, it's Ruth and Dom.'

'Sorry, Joey, you're not making a lot of sense.'

'I just had to ring you, to find out what you know about all this,' Joey continued enigmatically. 'I thought maybe you would have seen it coming.'

'Seen what coming?' Bernie asked, trying to keep the irritation out of her voice. 'What're you talking about? Has something happened to Dominic? The last I heard of him he was having a whale of a time up in Blackburn with Mariam and her parents.'

'That's just it! He went over there for a week. We only heard about it from her brother. Ruth went round to the house for some reason, and he told her Dom had gone to see Mariam to keep her company because her Mum and Dad were out all day at work. We thought he was just being kind because of what happened to her.'

'And?' Bernie prompted, as he broke off and seemed to be waiting for a response. 'What's the problem?'

'I haven't got long,' Joey muttered with apparent irrelevance. 'I'm in the van. I told them I had to check I'd got enough copper pipe for the job I'm starting on Monday. I just wanted to find out what you know.'

'What I know about *what?*' Bernie looked round at the others and shook her head slowly to indicate her exasperation

'Dom and Mariam. They arrived here a couple of hours

ago and announced that they're engaged!'

'And?' Bernie asked, a smile spreading across her face. She switched her phone to loudspeaker and laid it down on her knee so that the others could hear both sides of the conversation.

'Well you can imagine what Ruth thinks about it! Don't get me wrong, we both like Mariam. She's a nice girl and no one can help admiring the way she's coped with this acid attack business. It's just ... well ... you know how keen Ruth is for all the kids to be good Catholics. She's been trying to be polite, but then she dragged me in the kitchen and it was all, "what will Father Nat say?" and, "Do you think she'll become a Catholic?" and, "I suppose they won't be able to marry in church." I was just wondering how much you knew about what was going on.'

'Well, the short answer is that I didn't know anything and it's none of my business,' Bernie told him, still smiling. 'I've got Lucy here. Shall I ask her if she had any inkling?'

'That's another thing,' Joey jumped in at the mention of his young cousin. 'We both thought Dom had his eye on Lucy. Ruth's afraid she's going to be disappointed when she finds out.'

'No I'm not!' Lucy broke in cheerfully. 'Dom's ever so sweet, but ...,' she hesitated, trying to think of a polite way of explaining why Joey's son did not match up to her exacting standards when it came to a potential life partner. 'But I've always thought of him more as a friend than ... well, we are cousins, after all,' she finished lamely.

'Only second cousins,' Joey objected. 'I'm sure there wouldn't have been any problems with you-'

'That's not the point,' Bernie interrupted sharply. 'The point is that Dom has chosen Mariam, and I personally can't see a problem with that. You've said yourself she's a nice girl. She's also very level-headed and intelligent and she's going to be a doctor, so there won't be any problem with her keeping your son in the manner to which he is accustomed!'

'It's not funny!' Joey complained. 'Stop laughing at us. Can't you see the difficulties there are going to be?'

'I'm sorry,' Bernie tried to sound serious, but her face was still smiling with amusement. 'I do realise it won't be plain sailing for them, but I also think you ought to trust them to work things out for themselves. Dom's twenty-three and Mariam's very mature for her age. Besides, presumably they're not planning to actually get married until she's finished her degree, so there's plenty of time for them to sort things out.'

'So what do you think I ought to say to Ruth?' Joey asked resignedly.

'Tell her these things happen and it's not the end of the world,' Bernie advised. 'And maybe get her to invite Father Nat round to meet Mariam. I bet he won't be nearly as worried about it as she is.'

'And if he is,' Lucy chipped in, 'tell him to talk to Father Damien. He'll put him straight.'

'And why not ask Mariam to tell Ruth about when she visited us and went with us to Midnight Mass on Christmas Eve?' Bernie suggested.

'You don't think this is just a flash in the pan?' Joey asked hopefully. 'I thought maybe it was just Dom feeling sorry for her and wanting to show her she was still attractive even with those acid burns on her head.'

'Sorry, Joey,' Bernie said, shaking her head. 'To be honest, now I look back, I reckon this has been brewing ever since they all moved in together back in September. Now just stop worrying, can't you?'

***

'I've been having a look at the list of gardens that are opening this summer for the National Gardens Scheme[24],'

---

[24] The National Gardens Scheme is an organisation through which thousands of people open their gardens to the public on one or more days in the year to support a range of health-related

Jonah said innocently, a few weeks later. 'I thought we might go round some of them. Now that I'm retired, we've got more time for that sort of thing.'

'That's a good idea!' Peter agreed enthusiastically, wondering if his friend had – at last – come to terms with retirement.

'Yes,' Bernie concurred, remembering that Jonah had been a keen gardener before his debilitating injury. 'It might give us some ideas for things to do here. Did you have anywhere in particular in mind?'

'There's this place in Buckinghamshire,' Jonah answered, rotating his computer screen to display a picture of wide beds of delphiniums, antirrhinums and phlox surrounding a perfect lawn. 'It's open next Sunday. We could go over in the afternoon. Google maps reckons it'll only take just over half an hour.'

'Bourne End,' Bernie read out. 'Where have I heard that name before?'

'You're right,' Peter agreed. 'It does sound familiar, but I can't think why.'

'Does someone famous live there?' Bernie wondered aloud. 'Or – hang on! What's the name of the family that owns this garden?'

'They're Nigel and Lucinda Carver,' Jonah told her promptly. 'It says here that he's a garden designer and she runs an interior design company. I looked them up. She's very much out of the top drawer – educated at Cheltenham Ladies College and the Slade – and specialises in designs for the aristocracy.'

'And her husband?' Bernie asked suspiciously. 'Does he have blue blood too?'

'No. He's the son of Trinidadian immigrants. He started out as a gardener for Camden Council and then worked for a company that was re-doing the grounds of a stately home up in Derbyshire, which is where he met Lucinda. She was

charities.

renovating the interior of the house.'

'And do they have any children?' Bernie persisted in her interrogation. 'A son who's doing a degree at Liverpool John Moores, for example?'

'Well, yes,' Jonah admitted. 'Bradley Carver is their younger son.'

'And you're proposing to go over there in the hope of just happening to bump into him?' Bernie said accusingly.

'Hang on!' Peter interjected. 'You've lost me here. *Who* is Bradley Carver?'

'He's the young black lad that Alex Knowsley made racist remarks about in a transport caff last autumn sometime,' Bernie explained. 'Sandra Latham told us about him. Jonah wanted to interview him at the time, but she thought it would be a waste of time – which it would be!' she added, giving Jonah a hard stare.

'But you're going to go ahead and do it anyway,' Peter said resignedly.

'You're forgetting, I can't even get there if you two don't take me,' Jonah pointed out.

'Which is precisely why it's so impossible for us to stop you,' Peter countered. 'We can't refuse to pander to your whim, because you don't have the option of going ahead without us.'

'Peter's right,' Bernie sighed. 'You've got us over a barrel. Still, we all agreed it was a good idea to go and look round that garden. We can only hope young Bradley keeps well out of the way while we do it!'

Liverpool Festival Gardens: Chinese Garden

19. DISCORD

'Dom?' Mariam sounded uncharacteristically fragile and unsure of herself when he answered her call. What could be wrong? 'We've been talking to the imam at our mosque. He says it's not allowed for a Muslim woman to marry a non-Muslim man.'

'I thought you said the Qur'an specifically said it was OK, so long as they are "people of the book",' Dominic objected. 'You read it out to me. You said Jews and Christians were OK.'

'I know! But he says that only applies to Muslim men marrying Christian or Jewish women. He said it's because the man is the head of the household, so a Muslim woman would come under too much pressure to convert.'

'But that's rubbish!' Dominic protested. 'I don't want you to convert! I want you to stay just as you are! Can't I just … I don't know, sign some sort of undertaking or something?'

'No. He says there's nothing anyone can do. That's just how it is.'

'But why? I thought it was going to be *my* religion that was going to cause the problems! Catholics aren't really supposed to marry out of the faith – not even non-Catholic Christians – but lots of them do.'

'He said if we had children, you'd want them to be raised as Catholics.'

'Well, strictly speaking, I would be supposed to promise to do all in my power to see that they were,' Dominic admitted, 'but I don't really believe in the idea of forcing kids into any particular religion. I sort of imagined that they'd go to church with me on Sunday and go to the mosque with you on Friday, and they'd obviously see you praying every day, and I could teach them the rosary and stuff. But anyway, that's all hypothetical. We don't even know if we'll have any children.'

'I know,' Mariam agreed miserably. 'I told him all that, and I explained how broadminded you are and how we'd all been sharing a house together and getting along just fine, but I think he thought that was rather shocking, and he wanted to know why I wasn't in a women's hostel or else just sharing with Ibrahim.'

'How dare he!' Dominic burst out, without thinking. 'I mean … I'm sorry, I didn't mean that. I just meant, surely he doesn't think you've done anything to be ashamed of? Did you tell him we'd all got separate rooms, and you and Lucy are up on the top floor with your own bathroom and everything?'

'In our little female enclave?' Mariam giggled, suddenly relaxing and feeling more confident. 'You're right, he's imagining things! Mum told him it was all perfectly proper and you weren't the sort to try anything on, but I think by that time he'd already decided that I must be completely debauched! What are we going to do?'

'Would you like me to go and have a word with Imran?' Dominic suggested. 'Maybe things aren't as black-and-white as your imam makes out.'

'Would you? Yes! I hadn't thought of that. I bet he'll be able to find a way. I was forgetting that there are nearly as many different versions of Islam as there are Muslims!'

'Yes,' agreed Dominic, brightening up. 'I remember when I studied Islam, there seemed to be so many schools of thought it made my head spin. That's sorted then. I'll go and see Imran and ask him what we can do.'

Before Dominic had the chance to visit the mosque in Stanley to consult the imam, he had other problems to worry about. His mother, finally plucking up the courage to tell her priest about her son's marital plans, had poured out the whole story to Father Nathaniel after Sunday morning

Mass. That afternoon, she arrived at Dominic's house, with Joey reluctantly following, to give him the official Catholic line on mixed-faith marriages.

'He said he'll ask the bishop,' she told him, as they sat drinking tea in the small front room, 'but he was sure that, even if you got permission to marry in church, it couldn't be within the Mass and it wouldn't be a sacrament, because Mariam isn't baptised.'

'Oh mum!' Dominic groaned and hid his head in his hands. After a few second, he looked up again and sighed. 'Why couldn't you just leave things alone? It isn't going to be for ages yet. Mariam's only just finished her first year at uni! I wish I'd never told you now. I thought you'd be pleased that we were going to get married. You make enough fuss about Chloë and Chris living together without tying the knot!'

Chloë was Dominic's older sister, who lived with her boyfriend in a flat in the West Derby suburb of Liverpool. Ruth had repeatedly complained about the arrangement, expressing her embarrassment at having to cover for them whenever their priest made friendly enquiries about her daughter's welfare.

'Well, that's the same as what you're doing, isn't it?' his mother retorted, her distress at the prospect of her younger son marrying in a registry office and provoking the wrath of the Catholic Church, making her unable to think rationally. 'When you all moved in here, I never thought you were going to-'

'How dare you!' Dominic exploded. 'Honestly, I don't know why I bother! I might just as well do what ninety-nine percent of people my age are doing and having it off with anyone I like – a different person every night – if you won't even trust me to be behaving responsibly with a girl when her own brother is living here as her chaperone.'

'I only meant …,' Ruth began, but her words petered out as she realised that she did not know what she had meant.

'Your mum's upset,' Joey told Dominic, trying to calm

the situation. 'She wasn't implying anything. She's just concerned about what people may think.'

'But nothing's changed,' Dominic insisted. 'That's what's so unfair! If you thought we couldn't be trusted, why didn't you say so when we first got the house?'

'We thought it would be nice for Lucy to have you to look after her,' Ruth began.

'And didn't you worry that I might not be able to keep my grubby hands off *her*?' Dominic demanded. 'Or did you think she'd have more self-control than a-'

'That's enough, Dom,' Joey intervened again. 'I told you, Mum isn't suggesting anything about Mariam. We both like her, don't we Ruth?'

'Yes. Of course we do! We're just worried that ...'

'We're worried that you may not have thought all this through properly,' Joey said firmly, putting his hand on his wife's arm to signal to her not to say any more. 'Marriage is a big step in any circumstances, and when someone's from such a different background ... it would be easy to bite off more than you can chew.'

'We know it won't be easy,' Dominic conceded reluctantly, 'which is why we told you both now, instead of waiting until we're ready to actually get married. We've agreed that we'll wait until Mariam's finished her degree, which is a whole four years off! Can't you just leave us alone until then, while we get things sorted?'

***

Meanwhile, Bernie, Jonah and Peter were strolling round the garden of the Carvers' family home in Bourne End, admiring the herbaceous borders and comparing the impressive rockery with their own in Headington.

'Cream tea, four pounds,' read out Peter as they followed the path that wound behind the rockery and on to the long terrace, paved with Cotswold stone, which ran across the back of the house. 'Shall we treat ourselves?'

'Yes, lets!' answered Jonah at once. He had spotted a

dark-skinned young man disappearing inside the house carrying a tray of used crockery.

'I think we should,' smiled Bernie, 'seeing as it's for charity.'

She rearranged the chairs around one of the small tables that were dotted about the terrace to make room for Jonah's wheelchair. As soon as they had sat down, an elegant woman wearing a frilled apron over a black dress came over to take their order.

'Three cream teas, please,' Bernie said, looking up at her smiling face.

'And a few minutes of your time, if you can spare it,' Jonah added. He had recognised the woman from a picture that he had found of her on the internet. 'I was hoping to pick your brains over some of the marginal plants you've got round your pond. There were a few I didn't recognise.'

'My husband will be able to tell you more about that,' Lucinda Carver smiled back at him. 'I'll let him know you're asking about them. He'll be only too pleased to come and have a chat with you. There's nothing he likes better than talking plants with another gardening enthusiast.'

She disappeared into the house. They could hear a murmured conversation through the open patio doors and then the young man whom they had seen a few minutes earlier came out and headed off down the stone steps that led to the lawn. They waited, basking in the warm sunshine and watching colourful blue tits and goldfinches fluttering around a cluster of hanging bird feeders attached to an ornate wrought iron stand set into the grass.

'Here you are!' Lucinda Carver arrived with a loaded tray, which she set down on the table in front of them. Bernie helped her to unload a pot of tea, a plate of scones, two small jars of jam and a bowl of clotted cream.

'We only need two cups,' she told their host, pointing at the plastic beaker that she had got out from the storage space at the back of Jonah's chair. 'Jonah has his own. It's easier for him, and less likely to end up with us smashing your best china.'

'I'll take the spare cup and saucer away then,' Lucinda smiled back, picking up the tray and stepping back from the table. 'Is there anything else I can get you?'

'Leave the cup,' Jonah said at once, treating her to one of his endearing lop-sided smiles. He had seen the young man returning across the grass, followed by his father. 'And perhaps you could bring another one and some more tea and scones. I think your husband and son deserve some reward for all their work, making this such a wonderful day out for us. We'd really like to treat them; and are you sure you can't spare the time to join us too? There don't seem to be any more customers queuing just at the moment.'

'Very well,' Lucinda Carver smiled. It was difficult to refuse Jonah any request when he exercised his special charm. 'I'll fetch another pot of tea.'

Peter got to his feet and started rearranging chairs to make room for the Carvers to join them at their table, while Bernie stepped forward and greeted father and son. Before long they were all sitting together enjoying tea and scones. Jonah chatted easily with Nigel Carver, a tall muscular man with skin even darker than his son's, and showed him pictures of their garden in Headington. Nigel appeared to be genuinely interested in the pictures and made several suggestions for innovations and improvements. His son, too, leaned forward to see the screen and commented on one or two of the photographs.

'Of course,' this garden is really Bernie's,' Jonah told them. 'I've just been helping to develop it a bit and keep it in trim. Before my wife died, we had our own place in South Oxfordshire. It was just a wilderness when we moved in, so I had a blank canvas that I could plan out from scratch.'

With a flick of a finger, he brought up on the screen a view of the family home where he and his wife Margaret had brought up their two sons.

'Back then, I was able to do my own share of the heavy lifting,' he went on, taking them through a sequence of slides showing beds of flowers, a large rockery and a productive vegetable plot, 'instead of my current supervisory role.'

Bernie watched with interest as he continued to talk inconsequentially on the subject of plant choice, propagation methods and garden design. She knew that he had spent a long time the previous evening collecting together this sequence of pictures and wondered how he was planning to use it to forward his enquiries.

She did not have to wait long. Unexpectedly – or so it seemed to the Carvers – the sequence of gardening pictures was interrupted by a photograph of a woman in a long divided skirt and cowboy boots siting astride a powerful-looking motorbike.

'Whoops!' Jonah exclaimed, just as if he had not deliberately arranged for it to appear. 'I wonder how that got there! Sorry about that. That's my late wife – she always was a difficult person to keep down! That motorbike of hers was her pride and joy. Well, each of them was until she swapped it for the next. That Honda was her last.'

'Bradley rides a motorbike,' Lucinda commented. 'Yours is a Honda too, isn't it?'

'Yes,' her son admitted, sounding rather reluctant to be drawn into the conversation.

However, he had given Jonah the opening that he needed. Bernie smiled to herself as he skilfully guided the conversation on to the subject of motorcycles and motorcycle clubs. He had got his fish hooked; now he was gingerly reeling in the line. Someone – she was not sure who – mentioned the MerseyRiders, and then it was not long before Bradley was recounting the incident in which Alex Knowsley had verbally abused and physically assaulted him. A few more casual questions from Jonah revealed that he also remembered the occasion when Knowsley had spoken about keeping the key to his shed in the under-stairs cupboard.

When the conversation appeared to be flagging, Bernie

racked her brains to think of a way of helping it along.

'My daughter Lucy's studying in Liverpool,' she told Bradley. 'She's hoping to be a doctor. She's sharing a house with another girl who's doing medicine too.'

'Bradley's in a hall of residence,' Lucinda put in, when her son did not reply to Bernie's remark.

'That must make it tricky to keep a motorbike,' Jonah commented. 'Does the hall have anywhere to keep it safe?'

'Bradley's rented a lock-up garage,' Lucinda answered. 'It's useful for storing his things out of term-time too. They won't let students leave anything in their rooms.'

'That's a good idea,' Jonah agreed, smiling encouragingly towards Bradley in the hope of persuading him to say something on his own account.

'Yes,' the young man agreed, apparently feeling obliged to respond. 'It's very handy.'

'Did you hear about the acid attack outside the Guild of Students?' asked Bernie, impatient to move on to the main line of investigation. 'One of the victims was a friend of our Lucy's.'

'You mean those Muslim girls?' Bradley asked, his voice unexpectedly hostile.

'That's right,' Bernie agreed. 'We heard one of the men from the MerseyRiders was arrested for doing it, but he was released again.'

'Maybe it was the same guy who made all those racist remarks about you,' suggested Lucinda. 'I said you ought to have reported him.'

'Maybe,' Bradley shrugged. 'I wouldn't put it past him.'

'One theory is that it was in revenge for another attack, back in the autumn of last year,' Jonah said casually. 'Do you remember that one? A Libyan refugee drove a van into a group of people outside a lap-dancing club. Do you know if any of the MerseyRiders had friends injured in that?'

Bradley shook his head. 'Not that I'd blame them wanting to get him,' he growled menacingly. 'Calling himself a refugee! They're all the same, that lot, coming over here, pretending to be refugees, when all they really want is to impose sharia law on us all and destroy our democracy!'

'Actually,' Peter interjected quietly, 'I've met Shaladi's family and they are genuine refugees. He was only thirteen when he was forced to watch his grandfather being tortured to death. He's suffering from PTSD. And then, after they were all supposed to be safe here in Britain, some boys from school set on his sister and raped her. That's why he attacked the nightclub – it represented everything bad about western society.'

'You can make whatever excuses you like for him,' Bradley retorted, suddenly becoming angry, 'but it won't make any difference. There's no place for his sort here! All these Muslim migrants – they're not real refugees! And stupid ignorant people like Alex Knowsley can't tell the difference between people like me, who've been here all our lives, and those immigrants who're all just terrorists who want to destroy our way of life! People like him think all black people are the same, but I was born here and so was my dad! Why do we have to put up with those Muslims coming here and stirring up trouble?'

'Bradley!' his father said sternly. 'Just calm down and show some courtesy to our guests.'

However, it was too late, his son had already got to his feet and stormed off into the house. Lucinda looked apologetically towards Peter. 'I'm sorry about that. Bradley finds it hard to keep a sense of proportion sometimes.'

'Don't worry,' Peter assured her. 'I've got two mixed-race kids of my own. I know it isn't easy for them sometimes.'

'Really?' Lucinda looked enquiringly in Bernie's direction, 'but I thought …?'

'I'm Peter's second wife,' Bernie explained. 'His children's mother was a Jamaican immigrant. She came over here to be a nurse.'

'Like my mum,' Nigel commented, 'only she and my dad were from Trinidad. He drove a London Transport bus for thirty years. I started my career with Camden Council, working in their parks and gardens. Dad would have been amazed if he'd lived to see me set up my own business and even more amazed to see this house we live in here!'

'And how many times a week do you get people asking you to let them speak to the boss?' challenged Peter. 'A fair few, I bet!'

'It doesn't happen so much since we managed to get a spot on TV,' Nigel grinned back at him, 'but you're right – people do tend to assume that I'm the monkey and not the organ grinder!'

'My daughter Hannah's kids are both white,' Peter smiled back. 'People keep assuming that she must be their nanny.'

'I got something similar when Bradley was a baby,' Lucinda chipped in, evidently relieved that her guests had not taken offence at her son's outburst. 'Only they tended to assume that he was adopted.'

'It was the same with me,' Peter agreed. 'It used to drive me mad when perfect strangers came up to me in the street and congratulated me on taking them in – as if my kids were somehow undesirable because of the colour of their skin!'

After that, the little tea party soon broke up. Lucinda had new customers to serve and Nigel went back to tending his garden and showing guests his prized flowers. Peter, Bernie and Jonah spent a few more minutes wandering around the extensive grounds admiring the blooms, and then headed for the way out. As Bernie stood holding the gate open for Jonah to go through, she heard a voice calling out to them. Looking up, she saw a young man with neatly cut dark brown hair and deep brown eyes hastening over to them with a paper carrier bag in his hand.

'Dad asked me to give you these,' he said, coming up to them and holding out the bag. Peter took it, looking enquiringly back. 'My name's Jake,' the young man explained. 'Jake Carver. I'm Bradley's brother. I know we don't look very alike. I take more after our mum. Anyway –

these are some of the plants you told Dad you liked. He said he wanted you to have them.'

'That's very kind of him,' Jonah said, peering down into the bag, which Peter held open in front of him. 'You must let us pay for them.'

'No, honestly!' Jake protested. 'Dad wouldn't hear of it. He loves sharing cuttings and things. He's written instructions for what to do with them and put them in the bag with the plants. Go on! You must take them!'

'Of course we'll take them,' Jonah assured him heartily, 'and you must tell him we're very pleased to have them, and I'll see that my staff follow his instructions to the letter,' he added looking round at Bernie and Peter, 'but, if we can't pay, we must at least make a donation to the charity.'

'Here! Put this in the pot,' Peter added, holding out a note towards Jake, 'and tell both of your parents that we've had a wonderful time this afternoon.'

'Thanks. I will.' Jake pocketed the money and seemed about to go. Then he turned back and said hesitatingly, 'You mustn't blame Bradley. He has a tough time sometimes and it makes him sore.'

'It's OK,' Peter was quick to assure him, 'we understand completely.'

'It's been difficult for him the last couple of years.' Having started, Jake seemed intent on laying out his brother's case comprehensively. 'He always expected to follow me into the army, but he failed the medical because of his asthma. So uni was always second best for him. Since he was a little kid, he's always wanted to do things the same as me – and he kept getting knocked back. I remember at Primary School, I got picked to be Joseph in the nativity play; but when Bradley's turn came, they said he had to be a sheep. He knew he was a better speaker than the boy they chose for Joseph, but I think the parents wouldn't have liked the idea of a black Joseph.'

'We had a similar tussle over my daughter, Hannah, being chosen to be Mary in her nativity play,' Peter told him grimly. 'Lucky for us, the teacher took her side.'

'That's just an example,' Jake continued. 'I was just trying to explain why he's a bit touchy sometimes. It seems so unfair that we've had exactly the same background and upbringing, but I don't get any of the stick, because I can pass for white. Sometimes, in the mess, I don't know where to look. There's a lot of banter goes on, which makes me feel uncomfortable, but I don't call it out because I'm the only non-white officer there – expect that nobody realises it – and it would take too long to explain how offensive it is.' He sighed. 'Sorry! I'd better let you go. I just didn't want you to think badly of him, that's all.'

View from Liverpool Festival Gardens

20. QUICKENING PACE

'Sandra?' Jonah asked excitedly when his call was answered the following morning. 'I think I may have made a bit of a breakthrough in your acid attack case.'

'Oh?' Sandra answered doubtfully. A dozen or more investigations had intervened to prevent her keeping her attention fixed on this attack and she had mentally filed it away in the depressingly large stash of crimes whose perpetrators were known, but where sufficient evidence was lacking for a prosecution.

'It's just a hunch at the moment,' Jonah went on, fulfilling Sandra's expectation that "breakthrough" had been an exaggeration, 'but I've found one angry young man with a motive both for attacking Muslims *and* for framing Alex Knowsley.'

'Oh?' Sandra repeated sceptically, 'and who might that be?'

'Bradley Carver.'

'And he is?'

'You know!' Jonah replied impatiently. 'That lad who tried to join the MerseyRiders and got drummed out by Knowsley because he was black. You were the one who found out his name. We went over to his family home yesterday and met him and his parents and older brother. He's got a chip on his shoulder a mile wide about Muslim immigrants queering the pitch for black British folk. He rides a motorbike *and* ...,' he paused dramatically, '... he has a lock-up garage in Liverpool where he keeps the bike during term time and stores his things when he goes home for the vacations.'

'You mean ...?' Sandra murmured slowly.

'I *mean* that it would be a good idea for you to check out his university room – not that there's likely to be anything there, because students have to clear them when they go home so they can be let out for conferences – and, more importantly, the garage that he rents,' Jonah answered promptly. 'It would be the perfect place to store acid-making equipment.'

'But surely, if he's been on the receiving end of racism, he'll be sympathetic to Salma and the others,' Sandra argued. 'I think you're letting your imagination run away with you.'

'No,' Jonah insisted. 'I just told you – he blames Muslims for fanning the flames of anti-immigrant sentiment and creating a hostile environment for everyone whose face doesn't fit. His father's a British-born West Indian and his mother has a pedigree that probably goes back to the Norman Conquest. He and his brother both went to posh boarding schools and brother Jake flew through Sandhurst[25], after being sponsored to a first class degree at Bristol University, and is now a Lieutenant in the Royal Engineers. Jake is fair-skinned and everything he touches turns to gold. Meanwhile, Bradley's been turned down by the army and gets stopped and searched by police every time he walks down the street; and he thinks it's all down to Muslims committing terrorist atrocities.'

'OK. I'll send someone round to have a look,' Sandra agreed 'You don't happen to have an address for that lock-up, by any chance?'

'No,' Jonah admitted. 'I thought it would look suspicious to ask, but I've done a bit of research online. I've identified a few places that would be convenient for someone studying at Liverpool John Moores and living in the hall of residence that Bradley was in last year. I'll email you the list. That'll get you started, and then presumably you can gradually widen the net if it isn't one of them.'

---

[25]Royal Military Academy Sandhurst trains officers for the British Army.

'OK,' Sandra repeated, wishing that she could find a good excuse not to send one of her already overstretched team on what would most likely prove to be a wild goose chase, but knowing that he would be expecting regular updates on progress and might take things into his own hands if she refused. Besides, Jonah had an uncanny knack for solving crimes through what, in anyone else would appear to be flights of fancy, and she would look very foolish if she ignored his suggestion and his hunch later turned out to be correct. 'Send me the list and I'll see what I can do.'

***

'OK, you win!' Sandra said cheerfully the moment Jonah answered her call, two days later. 'We tracked down Bradley Carver's lock-up and it turned out to be a regular treasure trove of evidence! Here's the inventory: two empty car batteries, a camp stove, conical flask, wire gauze, safety goggles, facemask, gloves … of course, he was studying chemistry, wasn't he? No wonder he knew how to make concentrated acid from old car batteries!'

'Of course, that doesn't absolutely *prove* that he's guilty of the attack,' Peter pointed out, keen not to allow Jonah to bask in glory prematurely.

'It is strong circumstantial evidence though, isn't it?' smiled Jonah complacently.

'I applied the thumbscrews to forensics,' Sandra continued, 'and they've already got results from some of their tests. Most significantly, they've found traces of concentrated sulphuric acid not only in the lock-up but also in Carver's university room. I've been on to Thames Valley and they're going to arrest him and bring him up to Liverpool tomorrow. They're also going to get a search warrant for his house in Bourne End.'

'Which is where his biking leathers and helmet will be,' Jonah interrupted triumphantly. 'He didn't need a clever hiding place for them because, unlike Knowsley, there was nothing obvious to link him to the crime.'

'Exactly,' Sandra agreed. 'I still don't know how you did it, Jonah. It would never have crossed my mind to consider someone from an ethnic minority.'

***

Sandra's was not the only call to come through from Liverpool that day. A few hours later, Bernie's phone rang. It was Aunty Dot. As soon as she recognised her aunt's commanding tones, she switched on the loudspeaker so that the others could listen in.

'We need you up here, Bernadette,' Dot said imperiously. 'Someone has to sort young Ruth out. I've talked myself blue in the face, but she won't listen! Perhaps you'll be able to convince her that the world isn't going to come to an end just because her kids haven't found a couple of nice Catholics to hitch up with.'

'What exactly do you want me to do, Aunty?' Bernie asked, smiling round at the others and rolling her eyes to the ceiling.

'Come up and tell her to stop worrying about what Father Nat thinks and what the bishop will say and get her to patch things up with Dominic and his young lady.'

'I hardly think she'll listen to me,' Bernie argued. 'I mean, she knows I'm only half Catholic myself.'

'At least you know Mariam and her brother,' Dot insisted. 'And Dominic likes you. Maybe if you can persuade Ruth to meet him half way, he'll apologise for some of the things he's said to her; and if you were to have a sensible conversation with Father Nat …,' she continued, her voice taking on a wheedling quality.

'Oh alright!' Bernie gave in, realising that her aunt was not going to accept "no" for an answer. 'I'll come up if you like, but I can't promise to make things any better. They'll probably both just resent me butting in.'

'Good. That's settled then,' Dot's tone of complacent satisfaction almost prompted Bernie to change her mind, 'and now, tell me how the police are getting on with that acid attack business. There's been nothing on the news for months!'

'Keep your ear to the ground for the next few days,' Jonah advised her cheerily. 'I think that's all about to change.'

'Really?' Dot exclaimed with great excitement. 'Do tell!'

'An arrest, as they say, is imminent,' Jonah replied mysteriously, 'and it isn't any of the people we've told you about before.'

'Really?' Dot repeated. 'Well, go on then – spit it out! Who is this new suspect?'

'I'm not at liberty to reveal his name,' Jonah answered, clearly enjoying himself, 'but we'll probably be able to fill you in on everything while we're up in Liverpool.'

'What do you mean?' Bernie leapt in at once, '*while we're up in Liverpool?* Who said anything about *us* going to Liverpool? This is just a private visit for me to speak to Ruth and Dom to try to help them make up their differences.'

'But you'll get on a whole lot better if old Peter's there to back you up,' Jonah argued. 'You know how taken Ruth was with him becoming a Catholic. And you can't expect Lucy to take care of me all on her own, can you?'

'I want to come too, anyway,' Lucy interjected. 'Mariam's my friend!'

'And I may be able to help Sandra with interviewing Bradley Carver,' Jonah added hopefully. 'After all, I've met him – and his family – so I know better than she does what makes him tick.'

'Quite apart from you being better at it than anyone else on God's earth,' Peter commented drily.

'Well, I'm not one to brag about my abilities,' Jonah smiled up at him complacently, 'but since you mention it …'

The Port of Liverpool Building

21. RESOLUTION

It took the whole of the next day to organise their trip to Liverpool. Jonah rang round hotels searching for a suitably accessible room to accommodate his needs, while Bernie sorted out all the clothes and equipment that they would need to take with them and Peter arranged with their old friends Stan and Sylvia to take care of his grandchildren for a day so that he would be free to go.

Once their accommodation was booked, Jonah turned his attention to monitoring the police investigation through news websites and by making calls to Sandra asking for updates. Bradley Carver was arrested during the morning and taken to Liverpool to be questioned. His computer and phone were seized and his bedroom searched. Jonah was delighted to hear that motorbike leathers and a black crash helmet had also been taken away for forensic examination. At last, all the pieces of the jigsaw puzzle seemed to be coming together.

They had an early night, with a view to starting off as soon as breakfast was over. Bernie smiled as she brushed Jonah's teeth that morning.

'It looks as if we'll be on the road by eight. Why can't you always be as co-operative as you were this morning? We'd get things done in half the time!'

'I am *always* co-operative!' her friend protested as soon as she had removed the brush from his mouth. 'It's just that usually there are so many other distractions. And there aren't always the staff,' he added with a grin, seeing Lucy coming into the room carrying various small items of equipment that she stowed in the space at the back of his chair. 'This morning, I've had three carers getting me ready

– sometimes it's only you.'

'Peter says he's ready when you are,' Lucy told him, returning his grin. 'And he says you're not to ring Sandra from the car, because she's bound to be busy, and he'll turn right round and come back home if you try!'

***

In this, Peter was right. Sandra and Charlotte had Bradley Carver in custody and were engaged in a second unproductive interview-under-caution with him. His mother and brother were also at the police station, sitting restlessly in the reception area. Jake Carver occasionally got up and paced the floor under the watchful eye of the desk sergeant, and then returned to his seat to continue muttered conversations with Lucinda.

'They'll have to release him soon,' he told her. 'There are rules about how long a suspect can be held before being charged.'

Sandra was also very conscious of this deadline. The circumstantial evidence was strong and there was a good chance that the result of forensic tests currently being carried out would add to it, but what she really needed was for Bradley to admit to his involvement in the incident. She looked across the table and tried to catch his eye, but he hastily looked down to avoid her gaze. His solicitor – an expensive one from a prestigious London practice – cleared his throat and stared stonily at Sandra without speaking. Sandra gave a quick glance down at her notes and then resumed the interview.

'Yesterday, you told us that you didn't know how the empty car batteries and chemical equipment got into your lock-up, but our experts have found your fingerprints on them. How do you explain that?'

'I – I ...,' Bradley looked round at his solicitor who raised his eyebrows and gave a slight nod. 'I'm sorry. I said that because I was scared. I was afraid you'd think ... They *are* mine. I admit it. It's all part of a project I'm doing for my degree.'

Sandra had the impression that he was making a great effort to hold himself in and to be polite. He had presumably been advised by his lawyers to co-operate with the police and not to allow himself to display his anger.

'I see,' she said calmly, matching her demeanour to his. 'That's very interesting. Perhaps you could tell me a bit more about this project. What exactly does it involve?'

'Sulphuric acid has a range of industrial uses,' Bradley said, sounding as if he was quoting from his lecture notes. 'I was investigating its role in the manufacture of dyes.'

'That's interesting,' Sandra said coolly. 'I'll get someone to speak to your tutor about it. Can you tell me their name?'

'Oh, they don't know anything about it!' Bradley said quickly, his voice rising a little and his eyes widening. 'I hadn't started the project officially yet. I was just trying to get ahead – doing a few experiments on my own before everyone else. That's why I did it in the garage, instead of using the labs,' he gabbled on. 'We aren't supposed to start our projects until next term, but I had a few ideas I wanted to try out before I committed to what my project was about. In fact, I probably won't do that one after all.'

'I see,' Sandra said calmly. She felt that she had him on the run now. 'Well, I'd still like the name of the tutor who will be supervising your project – just in case they can tell us anything about what sort of thing they expect students to do.'

Bradley said nothing. Sandra gave him a full minute before repeating her demand.

'I'm waiting. Who is supervising your project?'

'It hasn't been decided yet,' Bradley muttered. 'We all submit our project titles and then they allocate supervisors depending on what we've chosen.'

'OK. Tell me the name of the person in charge of the course – or maybe better,' Sandra added, thinking back to her own time at university, 'don't you have a personal tutor who looks after your welfare? We ought to let them know you're here and ask them to come in to see you. You'd better give us their name and contact details.'

'It's Dr Aisha Hussein,' Bradley mumbled, his eyes fixed on the table in front of him. Then he looked up and made eye contact with Sandra for the first time. 'You won't tell her I've been messing about with chemicals outside of the labs, will you? I've probably broken all sorts of university rules.'

'Not just university rules,' Sandra replied coldly. 'The sale of acid is regulated to prevent people from injuring themselves or using it as a weapon. With your knowledge of chemistry, you must have known how dangerous it was to be heating up battery acid over a camp stove in a garage. What made you do it?'

'I told you – I was trying to get ahead with my project,' Bradley sounded flustered again. 'I was doing a few experiments to decide whether that was a good topic to choose. I know I ought to have waited, but I just didn't think. I was just messing about with chemicals, like I've always done. Ask my mum! She'll tell you how I used to do experiments in the kitchen when I was a kid.'

'OK.' Sandra looked down at her notes. 'Let's leave your little acid factory for the moment and talk about your internet activity. Our IT experts have been having a look at your browsing history. You seem to have been very interested in violent crime. In particular, you've been researching bomb making and then, more recently, acid attacks. Why's that?'

Bradley looked towards his solicitor, who looked back expressionlessly.

'Well?' Sandra prompted.

'I was interested in the chemistry involved,' Bradley told her. 'It was purely theoretical. I never intended to do anything with it.'

'Except producing concentrated sulphuric acid in your garage following one of the recipes that you researched on the web,' Charlotte suggested menacingly.

'No!' Bradley's voice rose and there was fear in his eyes. 'I – I was just finding out how easy it would be for a terrorist to make a bomb or mount an acid attack. I – I – I was afraid *I* might be attacked. I've been threatened, you know!' he continued, sounding more aggressive than frightened now. 'People call me names all the time – and sometimes it isn't just names!'

'Which is why I can't make out some of your social media activity,' Sandra replied drily. 'Why would you want to belong to so many far-right groups? Aren't they just the very people who are making life difficult for you?'

***

Bernie and the others arrived in Liverpool in time for lunch, which Dominic provided for them in the house in Kensington. Ibrahim was out at work, which gave Bernie an opportunity to ask her young cousin about the rift with his mother.

'She just won't listen!' he complained. 'And she doesn't seem to be able to think beyond "what will Father Nat say?" and "what will the neighbours think?" I don't care what anyone else thinks!'

'I know exactly how you feel,' Peter said, diplomatically, 'but I think you're being a bit unfair on your mother. You may not care what other people think, but that won't stop them making life uncomfortable for you and Mariam. It's not surprising if your mum's worried.'

'But she-,' Dominic began, but Bernie cut him off.

'Peter's got a point, Dom. I'm sure you and Mariam can work things out together, but if you don't start out recognising that things won't be just plain sailing, you're going to make it all the harder for yourselves.'

'I know all that!' Dominic protested. 'We both realise there'll be people who make things difficult. The thing is – that's not what Mum's bothered about. She just wants us all to get married in church and settle down with nice Catholic partners and have a string of kids who will all come along to Mass every week and-'

'I know that's how it comes across,' Bernie interrupted again, 'but I'm sure you're wrong. I'm sure your parents both just want you to be happy – and you may not be if you aren't properly prepared for all the antagonism and misunderstanding that people are going to have about you.'

'We've got four years to get ready, for God's sake!' Dominic retorted. 'We're not exactly rushing into anything, are we?'

'How about just trying to cool it a bit?' suggested Jonah quietly in the silence that followed this outburst. He looked up at Dominic with a twinkle in his eye. 'Remember, Dom, you've got Aunty Dot on your side. There aren't many people who can stand up to her for long!'

They left Lucy with Dominic while Peter and Bernie went over to Cousin Joey's house in Toxteth to see Ruth, dropping Jonah off at CID headquarters on the way.

'We'll pick you up again on the way back,' Bernie told him firmly. 'That'll most likely give you a couple of hours.'

'And it will certainly be as much as Sandra wants to put up with you for,' Peter added. 'Do try to remember that she's in charge, and you're just a civilian now!'

***

'It's lovely to see you both!' Ruth greeted them, opening the door wide and ushering Bernie and Peter inside. 'Go on in and sit down while I make a brew.'

Obediently, they entered the cluttered front room where Joey and his elderly mother, Rose, were waiting for them. He greeted them by giving Bernie a slap on the back, shook hands with Peter and then motioned to them to sit down on a settee under the window. Rose smiled at them both and raised a blue-veined hand in a gesture of welcome.

'What brings you back to Liverpool so soon?' asked Joey, slumping down in one of the two easy chairs that stood on either side of the settee. 'We hardly see you for thirty years and then all of a sudden you can't keep away from the place!'

'We were summoned,' Bernie told him solemnly.

'Aunty Dot issued a royal decree,' Peter added, with a grin.

'Ah!' Joey grinned back. 'And this would be because ...?'

'She's worried that Dominic isn't getting as much parental support for his matrimonial plans as he deserves,' Bernie told him.

'Yes. I thought that might be it.' Joey became more serious and lowered his voice a little. 'Personally, I don't see it's such a big deal. So long as they love each other ... and Mariam seems a nice enough girl.'

'Oh she is!' Bernie assured him.

'But mixed marriages of all kinds do come with complications,' Peter added. 'I'd be the last person to suggest they don't work, but Dom and Mariam are going to need all the support they can get.'

'Which is why we agreed to come up and talk with Ruth about it,' Bernie added.

'I know why you've come!' Ruth declared, coming in and putting a tray of crockery down on the dining table at the other end of the room. She continued talking as she poured tea from a large brown pot. 'I know our Dom's put you up to it. He thinks I'm being unreasonable when I say that marrying a Muslim girl won't work. He doesn't realise ... He thinks I'm just upset because they won't be able to get married in church, but it's not that at all! I just don't want to see him getting hurt, that's all.'

'Of course,' Peter said quietly. 'You're bound to worry, but believe me – mixed marriages aren't always disastrous.'

'Think of my mum and dad for a start,' Bernie added more forcefully. 'By all accounts, Grandpa Fazakerley was dead against one of his boys taking up with a Sally Army girl, but it worked out, didn't it?'

'But that's not the same, is it?' Ruth argued, handing round cups of tea. 'With Mariam, there are all the cultural differences too.'

'Such as?' challenged Bernie.

'That hijab thing she wears, for example.'

'It's only a headscarf!' Bernie protested, 'and Mariam doesn't wear one for cultural or religious reasons. She's only started since her head was injured. It's to cover up where her hair's gone and the skin needs protection. She'll probably stop again if it grows back.'

'Well, there are bound to be lots of other things,' Ruth floundered. 'Food, for example. And her family will expect different things from what a British family would. Won't she have to look after lots of distant relatives?'

'Like the way Aunty Dot stepped in to look after me when my mum was ill?' asked Bernie. 'I'm only guessing, but I reckon Catholic Families are very much the same as Muslim ones! Honestly, Ruth, I do think you're worrying unnecessarily. Nobody's disputing that there will be difficulties to work through, but they *are* allowing four years to do it in. Don't you think it would be better to work with them to do that, instead of making it so clear that you'd rather they split up?'

'Alright then, Bernie,' Ruth said, rounding on her cousin-by-marriage, 'tell me honestly: how would you feel if Lucy said she was marrying a Muslim? Wouldn't you be worried for her?'

'Not at all,' Bernie answered at once. 'Well, not unless he was some extreme jihadist wanting to whisk her away to fight in Syria or somewhere. And I trust Lucy enough not to be so stupid as to choose someone like that. But, someone like Ibrahim, for example – why on earth not? There's no language barrier, no difference in education, nothing except religion that's any different. Where's the problem?'

'My mum always used to say, "the family that prays together, stays together",' Ruth said dogmatically.

'Who says Dom and Mariam won't pray together?' asked Bernie pugnaciously. 'Mariam prays five times a day, and there's nothing to stop Dom joining in!'

'But I don't want him to turn Muslim!' Ruth sounded dismayed.

'Bernie isn't suggesting that for a minute,' Peter intervened gently. 'She's just saying ...,' he paused and looked up at a picture that hung on the chimney-breast above the blocked-off fireplace. 'See that icon of Our Lady, Queen of Heaven?'

Ruth nodded, following his gaze. 'It was Joey's grandmother's – Rose's mum's.'

'We used to all sit round it on a Sunday evening and pray the rosary,' Rose said, joining in the conversation for the first time, her voice sounding weak and cracked.

'That's right,' Peter smiled towards her. 'The glorious mysteries: the resurrection, the ascension, the coming of the Holy Spirit, the Assumption of Mary and her coronation as Queen of Heaven.' He turned back to address Ruth. 'Did you know that Mariam is just the Arabic way of saying Mary? Or that Muslims revere Mary almost as much as Catholics do?'

'Are you sure?' Ruth asked, uncertainly.

Peter and Bernie both nodded.

'I think we ought to invite them all round,' Rose said, speaking slowly and pausing between words to get her breath. 'Mariam and her parents and ... Ibrahim, did you say her brother's name was? I'd like to meet them.'

***

'You!'

Jonah looked across the reception area as he entered the police station and recognised Jake Carver and his mother still sitting together waiting for news of Bradley.

'You!' Jake repeated, getting to his feet and advancing towards Jonah. 'You're responsible for this, aren't you?'

I'm sorry,' Jonah answered quietly, steering his chair past Jake and stopping it in front of Lucinda's seat. Their eyes met. 'I promise you, I didn't come to your home with the intention of tricking your son into giving himself away, although I admit I did have an ulterior motive. I was hoping that he might be able to tell me something about Alex Knowsley and his mates that would help us to convict them. I honestly believed that Bradley was a victim too. In fact, I still do.'

'What do you mean?' demanded Jake, returning to his seat and taking his mother's hand in his. 'If he's the victim, how come he's being interrogated by the police under suspicion of murder?'

'I think he was put up to it by others,' Jonah explained. 'I think he was groomed by nationalist extremists. He was just what they needed to justify their claims that they aren't racists, just patriots who are trying to save the country from being overrun by migrants. They filled his head with false ideas about Muslims taking over the country and immigrants being responsible for all the bad things that happened to him.'

'But you still think he did it, don't you?' Lucinda said coldly, staring blankly back at Jonah. 'And you're wrong. I'm his mother. I know him. He just couldn't do something like that – attacking innocent people in such an awful way!'

'That's what Mohammed Shaladi's mother thought too,' Jonah pointed out gently. 'Ask the parents of any of the young people who commit violent crimes. Nine times out of ten they didn't see it coming and they can't believe they did it; and very often the young people are acting out of character because they've been brainwashed by people who don't have the courage to do their own dirty work, or who don't realise that anyone is going to actually act on their hate-filled rhetoric.'

'But you don't understand,' Jake cut in. 'Bradley's not like that. He's not a stupid, impressionable kid. He's bright and educated and …'

'And despite all that, he's been thwarted in his ambition to become a military officer,' Jonah continued for him. 'And people like Knowsley and his cronies treat him like dirt. He was being made to feel he didn't belong. My guess is that this was his contorted way of showing that he was just as British as you or me or … Tommy Robinson.'

'There's no comparison!' Jake stormed indignantly. 'Bradley's never had anything to do with-'

'Inspector Porter?' the desk sergeant called out, cutting him off. 'DCI Latham says would you join her in Interview Room Two?'

Jonah looked up and smiled acknowledgement that he had heard the summons. Then he turned back to Lucinda and Jake.

'Think about it,' he said earnestly. 'You said yourself Bradley had a hard time with people who wouldn't accept that he wasn't an immigrant. He was desperate to belong, and some of the people he was mixing with gave him the impression that he could prove it by persecuting Muslims.'

He turned his chair and steered it towards a door next to the reception desk. The sergeant pressed a button and it opened automatically to allow him through to where PC John O'Connor was waiting for him. He led Jonah down long corridors to the interview room, where he knocked on the door and waited until Sandra came out before excusing himself and going off to resume his duties elsewhere.

'I've got Bradley Carver and his solicitor in there,' Sandra told Jonah in a low voice. 'He's still denying everything and claiming that the batteries and chemical equipment in his garage are all to do with his degree. The university says that's against all their regulations, but that doesn't *prove* it's not true. If a prosecution goes ahead without either more evidence or a confession, a good defence counsel will get him off.'

'OK,' Jonah smiled. 'I like a challenge. Let's see if we can't persuade him to be a bit more forthcoming.'

Sandra opened the door again and they both went in. Charlotte was there, sitting opposite Bradley and his lawyer.

'DCI Sandra Latham and DCI Jonah Porter have entered the room,' she said formally, for the benefit of anyone listening to the recording of the interview.

'Hello Bradley,' Jonah said in a friendly voice. 'We meet again.'

Bradley stared back in silence.

'I've just been talking to your mum and brother. They're out there, waiting to see what happens to you. I told them I don't think you're entirely to blame for what you did.'

'I haven't done anything,' Bradley responded in a low voice. 'All this is just a figment of your imagination.'

'Oh come off it Bradley!' Charlotte said scathingly. 'Your story about doing chemical experiments for your degree doesn't stack up and you know it! Why don't you just come clean and admit you sprayed those girls?'

'Because I didn't do it,' Bradley repeated doggedly.

'I'm sorry Bradley,' Jonah said quietly, 'but I think you did. I think you were put up to it by people in those social media groups you belong to. I've seen some of their conversations – people vying to say the vilest things about immigrants, and Muslim immigrants especially; and people making threats against them. I think you thought they all meant what they said – that they all intended to carry out the horrendous acts that they described. And I think you thought you'd gain credibility by doing the same.'

'I must protest most strongly,' the lawyer intervened. 'This is all speculation and conjecture. If you don't have any more questions for my client, you should release him and allow him to return to his home and family.'

There was a knock on the door and a uniformed officer came in and handed a sheet of paper to Sandra. She read it and then looked up at Bradley.

'I have a question for you,' she said coldly. 'I have here a report on an analysis that has been done on the motorbike leathers and crash helmet that you had in your room at your home in Bourne End. There are clear signs that they have both been exposed to concentrated sulphuric acid. How do you explain that?'

'I – I – I suppose it got on them while they were in the garage,' Bradley stammered, clearly shaken by this news.

'That's where I kept them – with my bike. My room isn't very big, so it made more sense, seeing as that's where I kept the bike. I suppose some of the acid must've got spilt – or maybe some droplets went up in the air when I was pouring it. That's all it is – it must be!'

'The report says that the results of the lab tests are consistent with the items having been exposed to a fine spray of acid, such as would have come from the garden sprayer that was used for the attack,' Sandra persisted. 'Are you sure you wouldn't like to change your statement and admit that you were the motorcyclist who sprayed Salma Rahman and her friends outside the Guild of Students building?'

'No,' Bradley said firmly, apparently having regained his self-assurance. 'I've explained how the acid got on the leathers and helmet. I don't have anything more to say about it.'

'That's a pity,' commented Jonah, 'because I'm confident that a judge would look sympathetically on your predicament, if you were to plead guilty and to display the remorse that I'm sure you feel towards the women whom you injured.'

Bradley looked uncertainly towards his solicitor.

'You have a right to remain silent,' the lawyer said impassively, then addressing Jonah, 'and that might well be construed as intimidation.'

'I'm merely offering your client a little advice,' Jonah smiled back. 'It's up to him whether he decides to take it.'

'I – I'd like to speak with my lawyer alone,' Bradley said suddenly.

'Certainly,' Sandra replied at once, 'we'll take a break now. I'll get an officer to escort you back to the cells and you can have a confidential talk with your solicitor there.'

'And would you like us to arrange for you to see your mother and brother after that?' added Jonah. 'They're outside waiting for you.'

'Yes – yes please!' Bradley looked round with a rather

bemused expression on his face. 'That would be good.'

***

'I think we may have him on the run now,' Sandra murmured a few minutes later, over coffee in her private office. 'I just hope that solicitor of his doesn't persuade him to try and tough it out on the assumption that a good barrister will be able to convince the jury that there's *reasonable doubt.*'

'That's why I suggested allowing him to speak to his mother,' Jonah agreed. 'She doesn't want to believe that he's guilty, but if she once accepts that he did it, she'll be keen to minimise his sentence and to find some justification for what he did.'

'And that's why I've applied for more time to question him,' Sandra smiled grimly. 'Another twenty-four hours may be enough to impress upon him that this isn't going to just go away.'

***

The next day was Saturday. Peter and Bernie were determined to return to Oxford that afternoon, so their final attempt at reconciliation between Dominic and his mother was scheduled for the morning. Mariam and her parents arrived from Blackburn shortly after breakfast, and they all set out for Toxteth in time for morning coffee with Joey and Ruth.

It was Joey who opened the door to them and led them into the front room, where Dominic's older brother, James and their grandmother were waiting for the guests to arrive.

'Go on in and sit down,' he urged. 'I'm sorry it's a bit of a squeeze. I'll let Ruth know you're here. She's just getting some cakes out of the oven.'

Dominic, Mariam and Lucy joined James in upright chairs around the dining table, leaving the three-piece suite for the older generation.

'This is my gran,' Dominic told the Ali family, waving

towards Rose. 'Gran – meet Mariam and her mum and dad: Tahmina and Abdul Ali.'

'I'm very pleased to meet you,' Rose said warmly. 'Forgive me for not getting up, but these days once I'm sat down it's a major operation to get me on my feet again. Old age is a very trying thing!'

'Oh please – don't mention it!' Abdul said quickly.

'Peter here has been telling us that your daughter is named after Our Lady,' Rose continued breathlessly. 'A very wise choice, if you don't mind me saying. I'm Mary Rose myself actually, but everyone always calls me Rose. There must've been a dozen Marys in my class at school.'

'There are more verses about Mary in the Qur'an than in the Bible,' Dominic told her, picking up on this potential opening.

'And some scholars even include her as one of the prophets,' Mariam added, 'alongside Jesus and John the Baptist.'

At this point Ruth entered, followed by Joey carrying a tray, which he put down on the table in front of James and Dominic. Ruth looked round nervously at everyone. Then she went over and shook hands with Abdul and Tahmina.

'Thank you for coming over,' she said a little stiffly. 'I know you're very busy with your jobs. How are you both?'

'Very well, thank you,' Tahmina smiled back. 'And you?'

'We're all well too. Would you like some coffee – and cherry cake? It is alright for you to eat cake?'

'Yes,' Tahmina smiled again. 'We all enjoy cake and coffee. Did you make it yourself? It looks wonderful!'

'Yes,' Ruth nodded. 'It's a recipe my mother gave me. It's always been a favourite with the kids.' She turned to James. 'Can you cut the cake while I take round coffee to everyone?'

Passing round the refreshments within the cramped confines of the crowded room took several minutes, but eventually they were all settled with plates of cake and cups of coffee on their laps. For a few moments nobody spoke.

'We wanted to tell you how grateful we are to your son Dominic,' Abdul said to Ruth and Joey, breaking the silence. 'He's been such a great support to Mariam these last few months.'

'I – I – well, thank you,' Ruth mumbled incoherently.

'He always was a helpful boy,' Rose added.

'Especially where a pretty girl's involved,' Joey grinned, seeing Dominic's red face and trying to cover his embarrassment at the praise with a joke.

There was another long silence.

'Dom and I have been talking to Imran – that's the imam at the mosque we go to,' Ibrahim said at last. 'He says he doesn't have a problem about a Muslim woman marrying a non-Muslim man.'

'Although, he did say that the vast majority of Muslim opinion is against that interpretation,' Dom pointed out dejectedly.

'Imran thinks that the verses in the Qur'an that say it's OK for Muslims to marry *People of the Book* can be applied to both men *and* women, now that society has moved on and women have a more equal role in choosing marriage partners,' Ibrahim continued. 'And he also says that there isn't any explicit prohibition of women marrying Jews or Christians – only that they mustn't marry polytheists.'

'Which is the same as for men,' Mariam put in eagerly.

'But won't you face all sorts of problems?' asked Ruth, looking towards Mariam. 'From your own people, I mean – if they don't think you ought to …?'

'Things haven't been exactly trouble-free for me so far, have they,' replied Mariam drily. 'In for a penny, in for a pound!'

'I don't know if this helps at all,' Peter said tentatively, 'but I had a word with Father Damien, and he said he'd marry you in church, if that's what you both wanted.'

'Did he really?' Ruth asked, turning to look at Peter. 'Are you sure? What about the bishop?'

'He reckons there wouldn't be a problem,' Peter told her.

'And he said he'd be much more comfortable marrying Dom and Mariam than some of the baptised atheists he's had through his hands over the years.'

'But it's up to Dom and Mariam to choose where they want to get married,' Bernie added hastily. 'It might be simpler to have a registry office wedding and then just a blessing in church – and in the mosque if that's something that could be done.'

'And the most important thing to remember is that we're talking four years down the line,' Jonah said firmly. 'Isn't it time we oldies all took a step back and let the youngsters sort things out for themselves?'

'I think that's a very good idea,' Abdul began. 'As I said-'

He broke off as Jonah's mobile phone began ringing. It was Sandra.

'I thought you'd like to know,' she said, sounding more cheerful than on previous occasions when she had rung him. 'We're charging Bradley Carver. Forensics have reported back on a rucksack that we found in his bedroom in the house in Bourne End. There's acid damage on the *inside* of it. It looks as if it must have been used for carrying the sprayer – or maybe more likely, for the leathers and helmet after the incident. It's big enough to take them, and we'd been wondering how the attacker got away without being noticed. I bet he took them off in Abercromby Square and stuffed them in the bag.'

'That sounds pretty definitive,' Bernie observed.

'And it gets better,' Sandra continued, with a note of triumph in her voice. 'D'you remember there was a fingerprint on the sprayer that we found in Abercromby Square? Well, it turns out it's a match for Bradley Carver's!'

'What does Bradley say to that?' asked Jonah.

'So far, he's still denying everything,' Sandra admitted, 'but I don't think it'll be long before he cracks. 'I showed the reports to his mum and she's as good as admitted that they prove he must be guilty. I reckon, between her and the brother – oh! And his dad's come up too, now that our people are out of their house – they'll convince him that the best thing is to come clean and throw himself on the mercy of the court.'

'And what about Knowsley and he rest of his gang?' asked Peter. 'Is there anything you can charge them with?'

'I've handed them over to Counter Terrorism and Cybercrime. I hope between them they'll be able to make something stick, but … Anyway, thank you for your help. I'd better go and sort out the paperwork now. I just thought you ought to know.'

The phone clicked off and they all looked round at one another.

'I suppose it's good that it's all over now,' Mariam ventured after a few moments.

'But it's not, is it?' Dominic objected, 'not for you or Emily or Salma's family.'

'Or for Bradley Carver and his,' Peter pointed out. 'It'll be a mandatory life sentence for him, even if he pleads guilty.'

'I just don't get it,' Lucy said, perplexed. 'You say he's black and he's been subjected to racist abuse. So why wasn't he sympathetic to other minorities?'

For a long time nobody said anything. Lucy had voiced something that they had all been feeling.

'I think maybe, when the whole world seems to be against you, logic goes out of the window,' Bernie suggested tentatively.

'Or maybe the girls were just collateral damage,' Ibrahim said grimly. 'Maybe all he was thinking about was framing that Knowsley fellow. He did go to a lot of trouble to make him look guilty – stealing his bike and everything.'

There was another long silence. Then everyone started talking at once, trying to sound natural and to start up normal conversation. Joey handed round more cake. James declared that he had an appointment elsewhere. Ruth offered to give Tahmina the recipe for her cherry cake.

Dominic and Mariam slipped out to the kitchen together, ostensibly in search of more coffee.

'I think she's coming round,' Dom whispered as soon as they were alone together. 'She doesn't give that recipe to just anyone!'

Hillsborough Memorial, Liverpool

THANK YOU

Thank you for taking the time to read Lethal Mixture. If you enjoyed it, please consider telling your friends or posting a short review. Word of mouth is an author's best friend and much appreciated. Thank you,

Judy

ACKNOWLEDGEMENTS

I would like to thank Ibrahim Syed, Imam Mushtaq Haque and everyone at the Wirral Deen Centre mosque, who made me welcome at their Friday prayers and answered my questions about life as a Muslim in Merseyside. For information about the Qur'an and Muslim beliefs more generally, I am indebted to Shaykh Mohammed Nizami, who patiently answered my questions about Islam and its holy scriptures. These people provided me with valuable insight, which I have tried to interpret accurately; any mistakes that I have made in the portrayal of Muslim life, worship or belief are entirely my own.

I am grateful to Gillian Gilbert for reading the manuscript, giving helpful comments and pointing out typographical errors.

I am indebted to the authors of a wide range of internet resources, which have been invaluable for researching the background to this book. These include (among others):

- Wikipedia (https://en.wikipedia.org/)

- Google Maps (www.google.co.uk/maps)

- The Disabled Police Association (www.disabledpolice.info)

- Amaliah (www.amaliah.com)

- Muslim Women's Network UK: (www.mwnuk.co.uk)

- Maslaha (www.islamandfeminism.org)

- Tweets from the many police officers (human and canine) with Twitter accounts

- Muslims in Britain (http://guide.muslimsinbritain.org)

- Understanding Islam and Christian-Muslim Relations (www.chrishewer.org)

I used many sources to research Islamophobia and the lived experience of Muslim women in Britain. The most important of these are:

- *Report on the inquiry into a working definition of Islamophobia / anti-Muslim hatred*, The All Party Parliamentary Group on British Muslims, 2018. Available from appgbritishmuslims.org.

- *Discrimination and Hate Crime*, Muslim Women's Network UK www.mwnuk.co.uk.

- *Women's rights in Islam,* Shaista Gohir OBE, Muslim Women's Network UK www.mwnuk.co.uk.

- *Experiences of Islamophobia*, James Carr, Routledge, New York, 2017. ISBN: 978-1-138-48487-0

- *The Things I Would Tell You: British Muslim Women Write*, Sabrina Mahfouz (Editor), Saqi Books, 2017. ISBN: 978-0-863-56146-7

- *The Qur'an and Hermeneutics: Reading the Qur'an's Opposition to Patriarchy*, Asma Barlas, Journal of Qur'anic Studies Vol. 3, No. 2 (2001), pp. 15-38

- *Beyond the Incident: Outcomes for Victims of Anti-Muslim Prejudice*, Tell Mama annual report 2017, Copyright © 2018 Faith Matters, https://tellmamauk.org/

- *How to be a Muslim Woman*, BBC Radio 4, broadcast November-December 2018, available through BBC Sounds:

www.bbc.co.uk/programmes/p06rvdbh/episodes/pla
yer.

- *How do I Pray?* Imam Mohamed Baianonie, December
  2005, raleighmasjid.org/how-to-pray/index.htm.

- *Finding Jesus among Muslims,* Jordan Denari Duffner,
  Liturgical Press, Minnesota, 2017. ISBN:
  978081465925

Verses quoted from the Qur'an are from the Oxford World
Classics translation by M.A.S. Abdel Haleem, © 2004, 2005,
2010, ISBN 978-0-19-953595-8

I am grateful to Notre Dame and Harvard universities for
their interesting and informative online courses
"Introduction to the Quran: The Scripture of Islam" and
"Islam through its Scriptures".

Every effort has been made to trace copyright holders. The
publishers will be glad to rectify in future editions any errors
or omissions brought to their attention.

Wirral Deen Centre

DISCLAIMER

This book is a work of fiction. Any references to real people, events, establishments, organisations or locales are intended only to provide a sense of authenticity and are used fictitiously. All of the characters and events are entirely invented by the author. Any resemblances to persons living or dead are purely coincidental.

Most of the locations and institutions that feature in this book are real. Their inhabitants and employees, however, are purely fictional. In particular:

- The mosque in Stanley that Marian and her friends attend does not exist;

- While there is an active Islamic Society at Liverpool University, the Feminist Sisterhood of Islam is an invention of my own;

- While most of the far-right organisations mentioned are real, the extremist group *Britain for the British* is fictional and not based on any real organisation of that or any other name;

- The MerseyRiders club is entirely imaginary and not based on any motorcycle club in Liverpool or elsewhere.

MORE ABOUT BERNIE AND HER FRIENDS

There are now twelve **Bernie Fazakerley Mysteries**. The other eleven (in chronological order of the action) are:

1. **Two Little Dickie Birds**: a murder mystery for DI Peter Johns and his Sergeant, Paul Godwin.
2. **Murder of a Martian**: Peter and Jonah solve a double murder and Peter meets Martin Reiss for the first time.
3. **Grave Offence**: Peter investigates an assault and a suspicious death, while Jonah is in rehab in the spinal injuries centre.
4. **Awayday**: a traditional detective story set among the dons of Lichfield College.
5. **Death on the Algarve:** a mystery for Bernie and her friends to tackle while on holiday in Portugal.
6. **Mystery over the Mersey**: a murder mystery set in Liverpool.
7. **Sorrowful Mystery**: Jonah investigates a child abduction and Peter embarks on a new journey of faith.
8. **In my Liverpool Home**: Bernie and her friends return to Liverpool to investigate a suspicious death in Aunty Dot's Care Home.
9. **Organ Failure**: a body is discovered under the organ in St Cyprian's Church and Jonah is called in to investigate.
10. **Rainbow Warrior**: One of their friends is injured in a hit-and-run incident and Jonah is convinced that this is attempted murder.

11. **Admission of Innocence**: Father Damien calls Peter and Jonah out of retirement to solve a murder case and prevent a miscarriage of justice.

Bernie also appears in two other novels:

- **Changing Scenes of Life**: Jonah Porter's life story, told through the medium of his favourite hymns.

- **Despise not your Mother**: the story of Bernie's quest to learn about her dead husband's past.

There is also a book of short stories, in which Peter narrates his side of the story:

- **My Life of Crime**: the collected memoirs of DI Peter Johns. This includes some episodes that appear in other books, but told from a new perspective, as well as some completely new stories.

You can find them all on Judy Ford's Amazon Author page: https://www.amazon.co.uk/-/e/B019315B1M

Read more about Bernie Fazakerley and her friends and family at https://sites.google.com/site/llanwrdafamily/

Visit the Bernie Fazakerley Publications Facebook page here: www.facebook.com/Bernie.Fazakerley.Publications.

Follow Bernie on Twitter: https://twitter.com/BernieFaz.

GLOSSARY OF UK POLICE RANKS

Uniformed police

Chief Constable (CC) – Has overall charge of a regional police force, such as Thames Valley Police, which covers Oxford and a large surrounding area.

Deputy Chief Constable (DCC) – The senior discipline authority for each force. 2nd in command to the CC.

Assistant Chief Constable (ACC) – 4 in the Thames Valley Police Service, each responsible for a policy area.

Chief Superintendent ('Chief Super') – Head of a policing area or department.

Police Superintendent – Responsible for a local area within a police force.

Chief Inspector (CI) – Responsible for overseeing a team in a local area.

Police Inspector – Senior operational officer overseeing officers on duty 24/7.

Police Sergeant – Supervises a team of officers.

Police Constable (PC) – 'Bobby on the beat'. Likely to be the first to arrive in response to an emergency call.

Police Community Support Officer (PCSO) – A uniformed civilian member of the police service.

Crime Investigation Department (CID) – Plain clothes officers

Detective Superintendent (DS) – Responsible for crime investigation in a local area.

Detective Chief Inspector (DCI) – Responsible for overseeing a crime investigation team in a local area. May be the Senior Investigating Officer heading up a criminal investigation.

Detective Inspector (DI) – Oversees crime investigation 24/7. May be the Senior Investigating Officer heading up a criminal investigation.

Detective Sergeant (DS) – Supervises a team of CID officers.

Detective Constable (DC) – One of a team of officers investigating crimes.

These descriptions are based on information from the following sources:
[1] Mental Health Cop blog, by Inspector Michael Brown, Mental Health co-ordinator, College of Policing.
https://mentalhealthcop.wordpress.com/, accessed 31st March 2017.
[2] Thames Valley Police website,
https://www.thamesvalley.police.uk , accessed 31st March 2017.

GLOSSARY OF LIVERPUDLIAN PHRASES

For those unfamiliar with the dialect spoken in Liverpool, some of the local language may be difficult to understand. Here are just a few frequently-used words and phrases.

Ace – Excellent (e.g. 'He's dead ace, he is!') It may also be used to congratulate someone: 'Ace!' means, 'Well done!'

Across the water – On the Wirral side of the Mersey (e.g. in Birkenhead or Wallasey).

Boss! – Good! Marvellous! Wonderful!

Chocka – Full, busy

Cracking the flags – Very hot (literally, hot enough to make paving stones crack)

Dead – Very (e.g. 'dead good', 'dead awful', 'dead handy')

Footy – Football (i.e. soccer)

Flags – Flagstones (i.e. paving stones)

Givin' it bifters – Doing your best, making an effort, working enthusiastically.

Gorra – Got a

Gorra cob on – Fed up, in a bad mood.

Lavvy – Toilet

Me 'ead's chocka – Literally, 'my head's full'. This indicates mental overload or disquiet.

Offy – off-licence, a shop licensed to sell alcoholic

beverages to be consumed off the premises.

Our – Used to indicate that a person is a member of the family or a close friend. E.g. 'Our Bernie', 'Our kid', 'Our Dad'. May be used when speaking of someone or when speaking to them.

Our kid – Brother, often, but not always, the youngest of the family.

Over the water – On the Wirral side of the Mersey (e.g. in Birkenhead or Wallasey).

Ozzy – Hospital

Phil – the Phil is short for the Liverpool Philharmonic Hall, a large concert hall situated on Hope Street.

Proddy – Protestant

Scouse – Used as a noun, this means either a type of stew, usually eaten with hunks of bread, or the dialect spoken in Liverpool. Blind Scouse, is scouse without any meat in it. Used as an adjective, it indicates that a person or object comes from Liverpool or is associated with Liverpool.

Scouser – Someone originating from Liverpool – a Liverpudlian.

Woolly back (or Woolly) – A derogatory expression for someone from Lancashire or Cheshire, sometimes used to describe any non-Scouser.

FAZAKERLEY FAMILY TREE

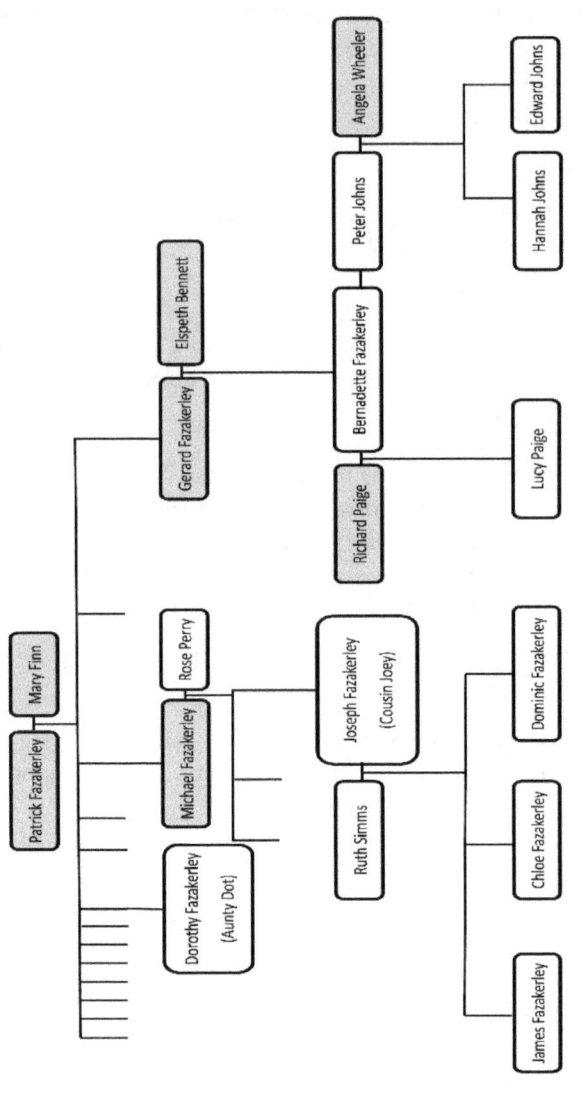

ABOUT THE AUTHOR

Like her main character, Bernie Fazakerley, Judy Ford is an Oxford graduate and a mathematician. Unlike Bernie, Judy grew up in a middle-class family in the South London stockbroker belt. After moving to the North West and working in Liverpool, Judy fell in love with the Scouse people and created Bernie to reflect their unique qualities. She has worked in academia and in the NHS.

As a Methodist Local Preacher, Judy often tells her congregation, "I see my role as asking the questions and leaving you to think out your own answers." She carries this philosophy forward into her writing and she hopes that readers will find themselves challenged to think as well as being entertained.

www.ingramcontent.com/pod-product-compliance
Lightning Source LLC
Chambersburg PA
CBHW060538180626
46817CB00002B/620